Nikhil

∞ ∞ ∞ ∞ ∞

M.K. Eidem

D1527396

M.K. EIDEM

The Imperial Series

Cassandra's Challenge

Victoria's Challenge

Jacinda's Challenge

Tornians

Grim

A Grim Holiday

Wray

Oryon

Ynyr

Published by M.K. Eidem

Copyright © 2016 by Michelle K. Eidem

Cover Design by Judy Bullard

Edited by: www.A-Z_Media@outlook.com

∞ ∞ ∞ ∞ ∞

I would like to thank my family for all their support. I would also like to thank all those that have been there to answer questions and help guide me; Julie, Sally Fern, Beth, Narelle and my sister Annie, thanks Ladies!

I also want to send out a special thanks to Michelle Howard who made me realize Nikhil and Mackenzie's story needed to be told first.

∞ ∞ ∞ ∞ ∞

Chapter One

Warrior Nikhil Kozar didn't hesitate to fire his blaster, killing the Zaludian that was attempting to stop him from gaining entrance to the cave. He had never cared for the Zaludians. They were a race of scavengers that traveled the Known Universes looking for discarded resources that they could use and sell. And it seemed they had decided to mine the weak energy crystals that remained on Pontus while the Kaliszians' attention was focused on the other side of their Empire, repelling the Ratak threat there.

He might have been able to forgive them as they were an opportunistic species, but he couldn't forgive their brutality. Six weeks ago, Emperor Wray Vasteri of the Tornian Empire was returning home from a meeting with the Kaliszian Emperor when his ship encountered Ganglians crossing between the Empires. Ganglians were banned from the Tornian Empire, so Emperor Vasteri fired on them, and then detained the Ganglian ship.

It should have ended there, but as the Emperor was traveling back from inspecting the Ganglian's ship, with the abused female he'd discovered on it, a Zaludian ship attacked and caused the Emperor's shuttle to crash on Pontus. It took nearly a week for the combined forces of the Tornian and Kaliszian Empires to locate the Emperor due to a Pontus ground storm. Once the storm ended, the Tornian Emperor and the female he'd placed under his protection left Pontus. It was then that Nikhil's Emperor, Emperor Liron Kalinin, had ordered General Treyvon Rayner, the Supreme Commander of Kaliszian Defenses, and his Elite Warriors to investigate why the Zaludians had attacked. Nikhil was one of those Elite Warriors.

What they discovered had been shocking even to seasoned warriors. The Zaludians had reopened the old power crystal mines on Pontus, and were using illegal slave labor in them. This was the sixth site they had found, and with each one they were finding more and more bodies, telling them that this had been going on far longer than anyone had imagined.

Ducking into the next opening, he fired again killing another Zaludian. This one wore the red beads of command around his neck. Nikhil would have preferred to use the sword strapped to his back. He wanted the Zaludian to suffer just a portion of what their victims had at their hands, but in the close confines of the mine, he couldn't do that. His gaze traveled over the room, making sure he had eliminated all threats. He was about to move on, when he noticed a still form lying on a stone platform.

Moving closer, he felt his breath catch. Lying there so still was a restrained and severely beaten female whose coverings were barely held together. What in the name of the Goddess were the Zaludians doing with a female, especially one like this?

Zaludians resembled Kaliszians in that they walked on two legs and had two arms, but that was where any resemblance ended. They had no hair on their head, had no honor, and more importantly, could not join with any female that wasn't from their own species because their reproductive organs were in an entirely different location. They would have had only one use for a female such as this. To sell her to a pleasure house.

Reaching for his comm, Nikhil called for assistance.

∞ ∞ ∞ ∞ ∞

"What have you got, Nikhil?" Commander Gryf Solaun entered the room to find Warrior Kozar, a Squad Leader, standing completely still as he looked down at what appeared to be a small creature on the stone table.

"A female," Nikhil told him.

"What?!!" Gryf hustled to Nikhil's side, looking down at the creature in disbelief. "Why in the name of the Goddess would they have a female? Are you sure it's female?" Gryf wasn't sure Nikhil had been around many females, no matter the species, for Nikhil's appearance put many off. Nikhil was a massive male by anyone's standards. Not so much in height, as both Gryf and the General were taller, but neither had Nikhil's girth which was all muscle. Because of his looks many avoided him, especially females. It didn't help that he rarely spoke, preferring to let his sword do it for him.

"Yes! Give me the covering!" Nikhil demanded, impatiently.

Frowning, Gryf handed what he'd brought to Nikhil and watched as Nikhil covered the female then carefully scooped her up, so her head rested over the heart in his mountainous chest.

"I need to get her to Luol."

Gryf knew he'd have a fight on his hands if he tried to stop Nikhil. He also knew he'd lose that fight. "Take Treyvon's transport. I will inform the General." Gryf turned to leave then stopped when his foot kicked something. Looking down, he saw a mangled metal restraint. He was about to ask Nikhil about it, but Nikhil was already gone.

∞ ∞ ∞ ∞ ∞

Mac wasn't sure where she was. She knew someone was carrying her, but she didn't know who. All she knew was that for the first time in what felt like forever, she felt safe. Why was that?

The deep rumble beneath her ear had her forcing her eyes open to find glowing, pine-green eyes staring down at her. She saw his lips move, felt the vibration of it in his chest, but she couldn't understand what he was saying.

"What?" she whispered back finding that one word a struggle, then cringed at the massive frown that filled her vision.

Nikhil couldn't believe what he was hearing. The little female in his arms was speaking Zaludian, and stranger yet, she didn't seem to understand Kaliszian.

"Do you understand me now?" he asked switching to Zaludian.

"Yes." Mac couldn't describe how it felt to know he understood her.

"What have you got there, Nikhil?" Onp asked.

Mac's eyes followed where the glowing green ones went, then cowered in his arms when she discovered several large beings staring down at her intently.

"Move on,! You are frightening her."

"Her?" The other warrior leaned in for a closer look and Mac began to tremble. "Are you sure that's female?"

"Move on or I will make sure all your training will be done solely with me for the next week." That threat had both males quickly moving on.

"Do not fear, Little One," Nikhil found himself pulling her close, cooing in her ear. "I vow you are safe." He pulled back slightly and found her staring up at him intently. "What is your name, Little One?"

Mac found herself lost in those glowing eyes, and for a moment, it was like she'd come home. "Mackenzie, Mackenzie

Wharton," she whispered weakly, and then exhaustion took over and she passed out.

∞ ∞ ∞ ∞ ∞

"What is that you are bringing me, Nikhil?" Healer Luol teased the massive warrior storming into his medical unit.

"A female. Harmed by the Zaludians."

"A female!" Luol lost his teasing demeanor and quickly move to a bed. "Lay her down here. Carefully!" The last word was unnecessary as Luol watched the lumbering warrior lay the female down as if she were the most fragile thing in the universe.

"Let's see what we are dealing with here." Opening the cape that had been wrapped securely around her, Luol sucked in a harsh breath at what he found. "Goddess!"

Blindly reaching for his hand-held scanner, he began running the machine as he visually took in the damage done to this small female. While her face was heavily bruised, Luol knew those wounds would be easily repaired. It was the rest of her that had him concerned.

He had never seen a body so thin. While her face was swollen and bruised from the beating she had taken, the rest of her body was the opposite. He could count every rib, and the way her skin was pulled tightly over her hip bones... He'd never seen anything like it.

"How long was she held?" Luol demanded.

"I don't know."

"Where is she from?"

"I don't know."

"Well, what in the name of the Goddess do you know, Warrior Kozar?" Luol demanded in frustration. He'd never encountered a female like this before.

"I know her name is Mackenzie Wharton, and that she is not Kaliszian."

"And how do you know that?"

"Because her eyes are a beautiful, golden brown, but they do not glow."

"Really?" Luol picked up a piece of her dirty, matted hair. "Then explain to me how she can wear *this*!"

Nikhil's eyes widened, and he reached back grabbing the braid that held his two most important Suja beads; one meant for his Ashe, and if the Goddess blessed him, the other for his True Mate. His True Mate bead was gone.

"I take it you didn't know."

"No," came Nikhil's hoarse whisper. "Help her, Luol." His green eyes begged.

"I will do all I can for your True Mate, Nikhil, but I have never treated one like her before. We can only pray to the Goddess that the deep repair unit can help her."

Luol pressed the button activating the machine, and as the domed cover closed, Luol was astonished to see Nikhil drop to his knees and begin to pray.

∞ ∞ ∞ ∞ ∞

As the Supreme Commander of Kaliszian Defenses, General Treyvon Rayner was a seasoned warrior. He had been in hundreds of battles, had seen and been the deliverer of more than his share of death. But as he stood on the narrow ledge outside the mine, looking at the carnage in the crevasse below, revulsion filled him.

"General." The call of his second in command and longtime friend, Gryf, had Treyvon turning to face him.

"What is it, Commander?"

"We discovered another pocket of survivors."

"Jerboaians?"

"No. I... I have never encountered a species like them before. They are similar to us only much smaller, but not as small as Jerboaians. Their eyes do not glow, and their hair covers all their head like the Tornians but in different colors. They also have hair on their faces like the Ganglians, and some even have it on their bodies."

"What?" Treyvon frowned at his second. He'd never heard of a species that was a mix of the three most powerful ones in the Known Universes.

"I know, it is very confusing. Until we can get them to use an educator with the Kaliszian language, we can only speak to them in either Ganglian or Zaludian."

"What are you talking about?" Treyvon demanded.

"Ganglian and Zaludian seem to be the only languages they understand. I spoke with the one that seems to be their leader, and he says the Ganglians captured them on their home world. A place they call Earth. Those were the only languages they were taught. I don't recognize the language they speak among themselves."

"That's impossible. Our educators are programmed with every known language. For it to not recognize theirs can only mean..."

"That they are a previously undiscovered species," Gryf finished for him.

"Take me to them."

"Yes, General." Gryf nodded then turned and led the way to the cave. "There's one more thing, General."

11

"What?" Treyvon demanded.

"There was an injured female that Warrior Kozar discovered in one of the outer caves. I ordered him to take her back to base for treatment. In your transport."

"In mine?"

"Yes, it is the fastest, and she seemed in bad shape."

"Alright, so what is the problem?"

"It seems the female is one of the unknown species, and they have been demanding to know where she is."

"What did you tell them?"

"That she was being treated for her injuries. It's this one." Gryf gestured to the cave opening to his left.

Ducking down, Treyvon stepped into the cave Gryf had indicated and was grateful he was able to stand to his full six-foot, eight-inch height once inside the room. The Kaliszians created these caves as they mined the powerful and abundant energy crystals that Pontus once contained. The crystals began to disappear five hundred years ago until only very weak crystals remained. They stopped all mining on Pontus hundreds of years ago as there was no market for the weaker crystals. It seemed the Zaludians had found one.

Before him, huddled together in a corner, stood the males Gryf had mentioned. They were just as Gryf described, only he left out how filthy they were or that the coverings they were wearing would be considered rags on the best of days. There was no way they could evacuate them with what they were wearing. The Pontus sun was setting, taking with it the heat of the day, and he didn't know if these creatures' bodies could compensate for the temperature change as the Kaliszians could.

"Have capes brought," Treyvon ordered over his shoulder.

"Yes, General." Gryf pulled his comm from his belt relaying the order.

"I am General Treyvon Rayner, Supreme Commander of Kaliszian Defenses," Treyvon spoke in Zaludian, his gaze moving over the sorry-looking group. "Who speaks for you? Who is your leader?"

A thin male with dirty, matted hair on his head and face separated himself from the group. "I am."

"What do you call yourself?"

"Craig. My name is Craig Collins."

"And your species?"

"Human."

"How long have you been here, Craig Collins?" Treyvon knew it couldn't have been long, not with how small and weak they appeared. The amount of work the Zaludians would have demanded of them would have killed them within days.

"We have no idea." Treyvon saw the others nod their heads in agreement. "Where is Mac? What have you done with her?"

"You speak of the injured female we found?" Treyvon asked.

"Yes."

"She is currently being transported to our base so our Healer can better treat her injuries."

"Why should we believe you?" another male demanded.

Gryf's deep growl had all the males moving fearfully deeper into the cave. As it should. The insult the small male had just delivered to his General brought into question the honor of a Kaliszian Warrior. No one did that and lived. Treyvon put a restraining hand on Gryf's arm as he went to draw his sword, and then Treyvon turned his head toward Gryf.

"It seems you were right, Commander, they know nothing of us. Just as we know nothing of them." Treyvon's gaze returned to the group. "They do not understand that insulting a Kaliszian Warrior's honor in such a way is tantamount to challenging him to a death bout." He watched as the males sank even deeper into the cave.

"We shall be generous to them, this *one* time," he stressed the word 'one.' "That it was the male's ignorance that had him speaking and not that he was issuing a challenge." When no one spoke, he continued. "Good. Now as I said, your female is being transported to our base. Is there one among you that is her mate?"

Silence reigned for several moments before Craig stepped forward again and answered. "No."

"Then after our Healer has cleared her, if she wishes to rejoin you, it will be allowed. Now," Craig's mouth snapped shut at the General's glare, "outer coverings are being brought for you. They will protect you from the conditions here on Pontus. Once you put them on, you will be escorted to the loading area where the other survivors are waiting. You will be taken to our base," Treyvon paused, letting his gaze travel over them. "Unless you wish to remain here."

"We don't," they immediately responded.

With a nod, Treyvon spun on his heel and left the cave.

∞ ∞ ∞ ∞ ∞

"What do you think, Jen?" Craig asked quietly.

Jen carefully stepped out from where she'd been hiding since they'd heard the unmistakable sounds of battle. She hadn't been able to see who had come in, but she had been able to hear them.

"I don't think there is much we can do, but what the General says. He seems to be the one in charge here."

"But..."

"We can't stay here, Craig. You know what Mac and I discovered outside this mine. We'll never survive such harsh conditions, and besides that, we can't just abandon Mac."

"What about you? What if they discover you're female too?"

"We'll deal with that if or when it happens. Right now we need to get to Mac." The sounds of someone coming closer had the men turning as Jen ducked down so as not to be seen, but she could still peek out between the bodies.

"Humans," the male seemed to sneer. "I am Warrior Parlan. General Rayner has put me in charge of making sure you get to the transport. These," he lifted his arm before tossing what he held on the floor, "are coverings. Put them on." He crossed his arms over his chest and stared at them.

Slowly Craig moved forward, keeping an eye on Parlan as he picked up the coverings, then stepped back to hand them out. What they discovered was the 'covering' was actually a cape with a large hood. It would be perfect for disguising Jen.

"Hurry up!" Parlan ordered angrily. "Everyone is waiting!"

Jen pulled the heavy cape on as quickly as she could. It was obviously made for a Kaliszian, as its sleeves hung a good distance past her fingertips and there was, at least, an extra foot of it pooling on the floor. But it had a hood and she quickly raised it, letting it fall forward covering her face. Lifting as much of the excess length as she could, she nodded to Craig that she was ready.

Craig and Paul flanked Jen as they followed Parlan through the tunnels, each gripping one of her elbows helping her keep up even though she knew the fast pace was hard on them too. They finally slowed as they passed through the mine's entrance and into a rapidly darkening landscape.

"Parlan!"

15

"Yes, Commander." Parlan turned to Gryf who was standing a few feet away.

"Get them on the transport! There's a ground storm coming in!" he ordered then turned to speak with another warrior.

"Yes, Commander!" Parlan turned back and began shoving them along. "Move!"

Jen sat as far back in her seat on the transport as she could, with Paul and Craig's thin shoulders doing their best to block others from seeing her. Looking across the room, she saw several Jerboaians huddled together against the opposite wall. She wasn't sure if they were the same ones that had arrived with them because large patches of their fur were missing. When Kaliszian warriors began to file in, she pulled her hood down even lower, hoping to go unnoticed.

"Is everyone accounted for, Commander?" Treyvon demanded.

"Yes, General," the Commander answered.

"Then get us out of here."

"Yes, General."

∞ ∞ ∞ ∞ ∞

"How is she, Luol?" Nikhil asked, still on his knees beside his True Mate.

"Better than I expected. The good news is that the repair unit was able to scan her and diagnose what she needs to recover."

"So what is not good?"

"What's not good is that she is severely underweight. While her overall health seems good, her body has been severely stressed and depleted of some very vital nutrients. It will take time for the unit to replace what she has lost."

"What about her other injuries?"

16

"Don't worry, Nikhil. The deep repair unit will easily fix those. How long did the Zaludians have her?"

"I do not know."

"Are there more like her?"

"I do not know that either. I left as soon as I discovered her."

"It probably saved her life. She wouldn't have survived much more abuse."

"Abuse? She was abused? By who? The Zaludians can't..."

"No, Nikhil! Not that kind of abuse! I'm sorry that my words caused you to believe your True Mate had been sexually abused. The deep repair unit found no evidence of that."

"Then what did you mean?" Nikhil sucked in a harsh breath trying to calm his pounding heart.

"I meant she would not have survived another beating. Her small body had reached its limit in being able to repair itself."

"She is small, isn't she?"

"Yes."

"She's... She is full grown, isn't she, Luol?" Nikhil's stomach sank at the thought that he might have found his True Mate while she was still young. He had heard tales of Suja beads doing this, and while he would willingly wait for her to come of age for claiming, he knew it would be torture.

"All my findings show that for her species, she is fully grown," Luol reassured him.

"Thank the Goddess."

"That doesn't mean you can immediately claim her, Nikhil. You will need to handle her with great care. For not only is she a great deal smaller than our females, but her body has been stressed beyond any I have ever seen. If she survives..."

"If? What do you mean if?!!" Nikhil rose to his full height, his anger easily heard.

17

"Warrior Kozar..." Both men froze when the female between them suddenly cried out.

"What's wrong?" Nikhil desperately looked to Luol. "Is she in pain?"

Luol checked the read out of the machine and shook his head. "No, I don't believe so. It seems your True Mate is reacting to your anger, Warrior Kozar."

"What?"

"It is well documented that over time True Mates will pick up on the other's emotions. It is part of the bond, but I have never heard of it happening so soon or being so strong, but that also may not be what we are witnessing."

"Why not? Do you think I'm not worthy enough to deserve a True Mate?!!"

"No, Nikhil, I don't think that at all," Luol quickly reassured him. "I know you are more than worthy of a True Mate. All I was trying to say was that we know nothing about her and her kind. Her reactions might not mean what we think."

"But you have heard of the bond being this strong before?"

"Yes, but as I said only with True Mates." He gave Nikhil a considering look. "Let's test it. Are you calm right now?"

Nikhil frowned. "Yes."

They both looked to Mackenzie and saw she was resting comfortably.

"Good. Then I order you to leave this female and never return."

"What?!!" Nikhil roared out, and as he did Mackenzie began to thrash violently in the repair unit, crying out.

"Calm, Warrior Kozar, or your True Mate will harm herself."

"But..."

"That was the test, Nikhil. To see if you could have bonded so quickly. I never expected such a violent reaction from her. I'm sorry... and I congratulate you, Warrior Kozar. You have found your True Mate."

"But..." He fingered the bead that remained in his braids, the one that he must offer and she must accept.

"Give it time, Nikhil. You are a worthy male, a noble warrior. She will need time to adjust, time to get to know you, but I have no doubt you will win her over. I have never heard of a True Mate not accepting her mate's Ashe bead. Congratulations again, Nikhil. The Goddess has blessed you with a True Mate."

"I..." Nikhil paled slightly. The greatest gift the Goddess could give a male was to have a True Mate. He felt his world shift.

"She is going to need a great deal of understanding and care," Luol warned.

"I can give her that."

"I hope you can, Warrior Nikhil. Because if you can't, I fear more will be lost than just your True Mate."

Chapter Two

Mac knew she was dreaming, but she couldn't bring herself to care as she watched her life play out. She was just too tired. It was all there, right from her first memory of her mom smiling down at her giving her kisses. Of her being handed to a man that was smiling just as broadly, her dad. Love and safety surrounded her.

Then it was gone.

Mac was six, and grief ravaged her mother's face. Her mother's eyes were red-rimmed from tears, with deep, dark pits of anguish filling them. She didn't acknowledge the confused little girl tugging on her arm her eyes remaining fixed on the casket being lowered into the ground.

They had told her that Daddy was in that box, but they wouldn't let her see him, and she didn't understand why. She didn't understand why he was going away, didn't understand why they couldn't go with him, and her mother wouldn't tell her. All her mom would do was cry.

Then Mac was crying, watching her mother walk away without a word, without a kiss, without a single look back. Mac tried to run after her, screaming for her, telling her she'd be a good girl, that she wouldn't cry anymore if her mom would just stay. But, two hands gripped her shoulders, keeping her in place. Then those hands lifted her up into strong arms and carried her away.

Her grandpa, her father's dad, had come for her after her father's death and taken her home with him when her mother had been unable to care for her. He'd taken her to the place he had raised her dad. A place she had only visited before on summer breaks.

Her mother never returned.

Mac knew it had been hard on her grandpa, raising a girl. He was still grieving over the loss of his only son, but he did the best he could. He taught her about what he knew and loved, his mountain. She loved that mountain. Loved knowing she was walking where her dad had once walked. It made her feel close to him as if he hadn't willingly abandoned her, not like her mother had.

Her father had been a firefighter, part of a search and rescue team that specialized in swift water rescue. He'd gone into a flooded river when he saw a child being swept away. The child had lived; he hadn't.

She knew she should be proud of him, knew she should hold no animosity for the child or his parents, but she did. She didn't want her father to be a hero; she wanted him to hug her and tuck her into her little bed at night. But he never would because of those people.

It had taken her years to get over it, to finally forgive not just the strangers that had destroyed her family, but her father for putting others before her. The one person she'd never been able to forgive was her mother. Her dad hadn't chosen to leave her; her mother had. It was something Mac knew she would never do. She would never abandon someone she loved.

The mountain had become her refuge. She had found peace there and a sense of belonging that she'd never found anywhere else. It's one of the reasons she'd gone to college and studied forestry. She wanted to be able to care for the mountain her grandpa so loved, making sure the impact from her grandpa's guide business didn't adversely affect the plants and wildlife.

Her grandpa had been a large, somewhat gruff man. At least that's the way others saw him, some were even afraid of him. Not Mac, because she'd seen his heart. He was a kind and gentle man with those he loved and what he protected. He only ever used his size and power against those who threatened that.

His last request was to be cremated, and for his ashes to be released from the highest point on his mountain. Mac had scaled that shear rock wall alone and done as her grandpa had requested. Then she'd sat there and watched the wind carry him away so he would forever be a part of his mountain.

She watched as time seemed to fast forward and saw how she always seemed to be alone. Even when she was in a relationship, even when the people, mostly men, she was guiding surrounded her. Maybe that's why she'd stayed with the group she'd led up the mountain because there was a woman with them. A woman that didn't want to be there. She was obviously out of her element and uncomfortable being in the great outdoors, at least until she started to cook.

Mac had been camping, hiking, and living in the outdoors most of her life. She was used to making meals from nothing, from using what she could find in the forest. But she had never had one of her meals taste as amazing as the one Jen had produced that night.

Mac loved her mountain. Loved and understood every creature on it. It was her home, and she felt safe there. Until that day when a creature had appeared she'd never seen before, pointing a strange device at her, and had taken away everything.

She'd woken up in a cage like she was an animal, when the real animals were outside the cage. They were large, hair-covered creatures, like bears, but they walked on two legs, like humans. They spoke with hisses and clicks, like insects, and stunk like rotten eggs. What the fuck were they?!! And what were those things in the other cage?

They reminded her of small kangaroos, but they obviously weren't, not with the way they were chattering to one another and looking around the room. She wasn't sure what had them so worried but quickly discovered it when one of the large, smelly creatures wearing a white collar walked into the room. He'd unlocked the other creatures' cage, and walking in swatted away any that got in his way. He grabbed one of them and dragged it out.

It was then that they all realized the other creature was female, and what was about to happen to her. It hadn't been long before her high-pitched squeals could be heard, and those left behind huddled together trying to comfort one another.

Mac had wondered how long it would be before they dragged her away, but then something unexpected happened. The men that she had led up the mountain, the ones she was supposed to be taking care of, pulled her deeper into their group placing her next to Jen.

That protection had continued even after the Ganglians had sold them to the Zaludians. They'd learned who the creatures were, and how to speak both their languages when the Ganglians had forced a device on Craig that they called an educator. They wanted them to be able to follow orders because they were now slaves, slaves to the Zaludians, and if they didn't do the work demanded of them, they would be killed.

If they became injured, they would be killed.

If they just didn't move fast enough, they would be killed.

Apparently, the Zaludians thought the Ganglians could obtain an unending supply of slave labor. Mac didn't know how long they'd been on the Ganglian ship. She normally judged time by the position of the sun. There was no sun on that ship. There was no sun in the caves, but it became readily apparent that she and Jen were not going to be able to do the work the Zaludians demanded.

Mac had inspected the cave they'd been led to, hoping to find a way out. Instead, in the deepest part of the cave she found a narrow opening, hidden behind a large rock. Working her way into it, she found it opened up into another smaller cave. Returning, she told them what she had found.

She and Jen had hidden there, remaining relatively safe, as one of the guys worked a double shift to cover for them. Mac had never felt more useless in her life as she watched the men come back shift after shift exhausted and with small injuries. She did what she could for them while Jen attempted to make the food they were given go farther.

That's how the Zaludians had discovered her. She'd been in the larger cave, treating a cut on one of the guys when a Zaludian suddenly appeared. He took one look at her and knew from the condition of her clothes that she was female. She could have made it back to the smaller cave, but that would have led the Zaludians to Jen, who had been badly injured. If they found her, the Zaludians would kill her. She'd told the guys not to fight, to let them take her. There was no reason for all of them to die for her.

She'd waited until they were away from the cave before she started to run. She wasn't going to let them rape her like the Ganglians had done to the Jerboaian females. She got away for a moment but ran straight into another Zaludian, and with one hit her world went black.

∞ ∞ ∞ ∞ ∞

Nikhil stood as still and as silent as the mountain he was often compared to. His glowing, green eyes kept close watch on

24

the deep-repair unit as it continued to work on his True Mate. How had this happened? What could he have ever done in his life for the Goddess to bless him with a True Mate? Especially such a small and fragile one.

He knew what others saw when they looked at him. A monstrously, large male that they only wanted around when there was a threat. When the threat was gone, they wanted him gone too for they worried he would demand more than his share of their food stores because of his size. It had been that way since he was a very young male.

He'd been lucky. He knew that. While his father wasn't a Warrior, he had worked for Minister Descarga on the planet Dzhalil. Minister Descarga was one of the few ministers that shared the excess food stores he and his family didn't need with his people instead of selling them for extra credits. It made him very popular with the citizens he served.

When Nikhil started growing astoundingly large, Descarga had been one of the few that hadn't believed it was because he was receiving extra rations. He sat Nikhil down and told him he was this way because it was the will of the Goddess, that she must have something very important for him to do, and she needed his size to achieve it. It was only then that Descarga made sure Nikhil received what he needed to accomplish it; education, training, and yes, extra food rations. But Descarga made Nikhil understand that he expected Nikhil to make sure extras would go to others when Nikhil was in the position to receive more than he needed.

Nikhil had vowed that he would, and he worked hard to keep that promise. He was only twenty-one when he'd achieved Elite Warrior status, and then became the youngest Warrior to ever become a Squad Leader.

Thanks to his father's continued position with Minister Descarga, Nikhil didn't have to help supplement his family's food stores, as so many other Elite Warriors did. So to keep his vow to Minister Descarga, he began distributing his extra rations to individuals wherever he was stationed. If he couldn't do that, then he would distribute credits, so the citizens were able to purchase what they needed.

That couldn't be enough to be gifted with a True Mate, could it?

Seeing his True Mate twitch slightly as if she remembered something painful, he took a step closer and cursed the closed dome of the repair unit that kept him from reaching out to comfort her. Knowing she couldn't feel it, he still put his hand on the dome as close to hers as he could.

"She knows you are near." Luol walked up to stand beside him.

"Truth?"

"Yes. I came to see why her heart rate had increased, but as soon as you moved closer and put your hand on the dome, it returned to normal."

"It did?"

"Yes."

"What am I to do, Luol?" Nikhil finally pulled his gaze from Mackenzie, and Luol saw the anguish in them.

"What do you mean?"

"How can someone as large and clumsy as me," he said, looking at his massive hands and thick fingers, "be responsible for a being as small and fragile as my Mackenzie?"

"First of all, yes, you are large, Nikhil. That is undeniable. But clumsy? I have seen you train, and you are always very precise and are always in control. You are not clumsy."

"I am around females... our females and they are so much bigger than my True Mate."

"Then you and she will have to find a way to make it work because the Goddess would never bless you with a True Mate that was not perfect for you. Have faith, Nikhil."

"I scare many females, Luol."

"For some reason, I don't think you will scare this one. Here." Luol slid a chair up to him. "Sit. Talk to her."

"Talk to her?" Nikhil gave the Healer a confused look.

"We've already established that she can hear you and that she reacts to what you are saying and feeling. She needs to know she's safe and not alone, and I believe you are the only one that makes her feel that way."

Slowly, Nikhil sat, the chair creaking from his weight and asked. "What am I supposed to talk to her about?"

"I don't know. Anything, everything. Tell her about yourself, about what matters to you, what's important to you. It will come to you." Dimming the lights slightly, Luol left them alone.

∞ ∞ ∞ ∞ ∞

Nikhil looked down at the tiny figure lying so still and wondered what he was to say. He rarely spoke to females, except his mother and sisters, because they all took one look at him and hurried the other way. He'd even had males step between him and a female as if they thought he would harm her by just walking by. The few times a female had offered him her friendship there hadn't been much talking. Where to start?

"Hello, Little One. It seems I have forgotten all the manners my mother worked so hard to instill in me. I asked your name but never told you mine. I am Elite Warrior Nikhil Kozar of the

Kaliszian Empire." He shook his head when he found himself pausing, waiting for her response.

"I am the Warrior who found you. In the mine. Do you remember the mine?" Nikhil could have kicked himself for saying that when she jerked and cried out softly. Of course, she remembered the mine.

"Calm, Little One. You are safe. My vow." He consciously forced his hand to relax when the dome creaked slightly from his hand pressing against it, trying to soothe her.

"I am sorry. I did not mean to upset you. I am not used to talking to females, especially one as beautiful as you." Nikhil knew if anyone heard him right then they would have thought him crazy, for the little female lying still once again was currently anything but beautiful. Her hair was a dirty tangled mess, with dried blood and who knew what else in it. And while the swelling had gone down on her face, it was still filthy and bruised. Her coverings were nearly non-existent, revealing the harsh conditions she'd survived. Layers of the dark, gritty dust the mines produced covered her body. There was only one thin trail that revealed her true skin tone, and it ran from the corner of her eye and disappeared into her hair. His heart stopped for a moment, then tried to pound out of his chest as he realized what had created that line. A tear. Her tear. He would make sure she never cried one again.

No, no one looking at her now would think she was beautiful, but she was to Nikhil. She was here, and she was his.

His True Mate.

∞ ∞ ∞ ∞ ∞

Gryf walked into the medical wing, surprised to find Healer Luol treating one of his Warriors.

"What happened to you, Warrior Onp?" he demanded.

"Just a cut, Commander. Part of the ceiling gave way from a Zaludian blaster shot. The portable repair unit pretty much took care of it. Healer Luol is just making sure."

"Luol?"

"He'll be fine, Commander."

"Good." Gryf's gaze traveled around the medical unit. "Where's the female?"

"Still in the deep-repair unit," Luol told him, his gaze still on Onp.

"Still? It's been hours." Gryf didn't try to hide his shock. "We have other survivors that need the unit."

"They will have to wait. She was in terrible shape, and as I have never treated one like her before, I refuse to overwhelm her system with everything she needs at once. How she has survived this long, only the Goddess knows." Luol looked to Onp. "Rest that overnight, and by tomorrow, it will be fine." Nodding his understanding, Onp rose and left the room.

"Did she say anything?" Gryf asked once they were alone again.

"No, she's been unconscious the whole time. There is something you should know though, Commander."

"What?"

"She wears Nikhil's True Mate bead."

"What?!! Impossible!" Luol just raised an eyebrow at him. "Show me!" Gryf ordered.

Luol led the Commander into the darkened room that contained the deep-repair unit. He understood Gryf's disbelief, and if he hadn't witnessed it himself, Luol knew he would be just as disbelieving. Ashe's were precious enough to a Kaliszian. Finding one meant the male could have healthy offspring with her. Something that wasn't possible with *every* female a male

29

gave his seed to. But if one of them were to die, the survivor could still carry on, might even find another Ashe or Dasho.

A True Mate was something entirely different. True Mates were the greatest gift the Goddess could give a Kaliszian. The bond would bind them together for life. If one died, the other would soon follow.

It was whispered that with just a look, True Mates could know what the other was thinking. With just a touch, could feel what the other was feeling. It was whispered because, since the start of the Great Infection, there hadn't been a single pair of True Mates.

"Why is the room darkened?" Gryf demanded.

Luol just shrugged, and turned the lights up slightly, "It seemed appropriate."

Gryf slowly walked across the room, his gaze moving from the tiny body in the repair unit to the enormous one sitting next to it, a giant hand seemingly touching the still one. "Squad Leader."

Slowly, Nikhil looked away from his True Mate to Gryf. "Commander," he said, not rising in respect to Gryf's higher position, and Gryf's eyes widened slightly. Nikhil was always respectful.

"What is going on here, Squad Leader? I gave you permission to bring the female to the Healer, not to remain. Why have you not returned to your duties?"

"I couldn't leave her. She needs me," the quiet words shocked Gryf as did the look in the much larger male's eyes. Nikhil rarely showed much emotion. He was the strongest and most silent of the Elite Warriors. He never gave away what he truly thought, but right now his eyes screamed for Gryf's understanding.

"She has Healer Luol," Gryf told him harshly. "You are not required here. You will return to your duties."

"No! I won't leave her! She is my True Mate and she is injured!" Nikhil's voice rose as he did, his fist clenching as he tried to control his rage.

"You will do as I ordered..."

A gut-wrenching scream had all the males freezing, and Luol running to the repair unit. Inside the unit, the female was violently thrashing her arms, hitting the dome while her feet kicked.

"Luol! What is going on?" Nikhil questioned.

"She's scared out of her mind," Luol told him looking at the readings. "You are angry, and speaking a language she doesn't understand? Talk to her before she injures herself."

"Little One. Calm. Please calm."

"In *Zaludian*, Nikhil!" Luol ordered, and Nikhil immediately complied, but it didn't seem to help.

"Luol. Help her!" Nikhil begged.

"I can't give her halcyon. I don't know what affect it will have on one so small. It could kill her. She needs *you*, Nikhil. Get ready."

"Get ready? Ready for what?"

"I'm ending the treatment, and I am going to open the dome. It will be up to you to subdue her."

"Subdue?"

"Calm her! Hold her! She needs your touch. You are the only one she knows." Pressing the release, the dome opened, and Nikhil was there, caging the thrashing bundle in with his massive arms and chest, grunting slightly at the strength of the blows she was landing. His True Mate might be small, but even in this condition, she was a fighter.

31

"Calm, Little One," he whispered in Zaludian, his lips grazing the delicate shell of her ear. "I'm here, Mackenzie. I've got you. All is fine. There is nothing to fear. My vow."

With each statement, the bundle beneath him struggled a little less until she finally stilled. Nikhil lifted his head to find confused, dark brown eyes gazing up at him.

"It is alright, Mackenzie. I am sorry I frightened you. It was not my intent. It will never be my intent."

"Ni... Nikhil?" came the broken whisper.

"Yes, Little One." Nikhil's voice broke slightly, realizing she had heard him speaking to her. "I am Nikhil. You are Mackenzie, and you are safe."

"The Zaludians?"

"Will never harm you again." He watched her lick her dry lips.

"How long have I been here?" she asked.

"You arrived over six hours ago."

"What about the others? What about J..." she trailed off, and Nikhil turned his head to look at Gryf.

"The other ten human males are here."

"Ten..." she whispered.

"Should there be more?"

"No." Her quick response had all three males frowning, but before Gryf could ask anything else, a cough racked her small body.

"Water!" Nikhil ordered, then carefully helped her sit up and placed the glass, Luol had brought, to her lips.

The first sip tasted like ambrosia to Mac, and she quickly covered the large hand holding the glass with both of hers, trying to tip it higher. Some of it ran down her chin as she greedily gulped it down.

"Easy, Little One, there is plenty."

"How long has it been since you've had water?" Luol asked quietly.

"I don't know. Since the Zaludians discovered me."

"How long ago was that? How long have you been on Pontus? Where did the Zaludians find you?" Gryf's rapid-fire questions had the glass slipping from Mac's hands as she sank deeper into Nikhil's embrace, trembling.

"Enough, Commander!" Nikhil ordered, catching the glass. "You're scaring her."

"I must agree with Squad Leader Kozar, Commander. She has only just regained consciousness and is not yet ready to answer questions. Maybe tomorrow, after she's eaten, rested, and cleansed."

Gryf opened his mouth to argue, when one of the energy crystals flared slightly, reflecting off Nikhil's True Mate bead in her hair. Snapping his mouth shut, he turned on his heel and stormed out.

Mac exhaled the breath, she hadn't known she'd been holding, when the one Nikhil called Commander had started firing questions at her. His eyes seemed to burn as he looked at her. Why? What had she ever done to him?

"Ignore Commander Gryf, Ashe Mackenzie," Luol reassured her gently. "His anger is not because of you."

"Then why? He seemed so angry at me."

"It is a story for another time. Now, Nikhil, if you will lay her back down, I would like to make sure she hasn't harmed herself."

"No!" Mac clenched at the black vest that attempted to cover Nikhil's chest.

"Ashe Mackenzie, I will not harm you."

"No! I'm not going to be restrained again! I'm not going to be poked and prodded again!"

"No, Mackenzie, no! My vow! Luol would never harm you that way!" Nikhil told her.

"Your Dasho is correct, Ashe Mackenzie. I would never harm you," Luol tried to reassure her, taking a step back to show he was no threat.

"I... I don't understand. I thought your name was Nikhil, not Dasho. And I know my name is Mackenzie Wharton. Not Ashe Mackenzie."

"It is a sign of respect for a Kaliszian," Luol quickly said, when he saw Nikhil didn't know what to say, deciding not to tell her it was a respect only given to a female wearing a male's Ashe bead or True Mate bead. "I do not know what it translates into your native language."

"Oh."

"May I use this to examine you?" Luol held up the handheld unit. It couldn't treat her as well as the deep-repair unit, but it would be better than doing nothing, and it would, at least, tell him if she had severely damaged herself.

"What are you going to do with it?" she asked.

"Just run it over you like this." He demonstrated by turning on the unit and holding it several inches above his arm and ran it along it. "It causes no pain."

She looked like she was about to refuse when Nikhil spoke.

"Please, Mackenzie. You can stay in my arms. I need to know that I have not harmed you."

Mac found she had to tip her face up, and up, and up to look into Nikhil's worried face, his eyes glowing with concern. "Why would you think you had hurt me?"

"Be... because I caged you under me, just to make sure you didn't harm yourself," he quickly added. "I am very large and..."

"You didn't hurt me, Nikhil," she frowned remembering how panicked she'd been. "If I remember it correctly, *I* was hitting *you*! Did I hurt you?"

The question stunned Nikhil. No one had ever worried about hurting *him* before. With that one question, he started to fall in love with his True Mate.

"I am fine, Little One." Carefully he reached up, touching her cheek, and was amazed when she tipped her head silently accepting his touch.

Luol clearing his throat had them both looking toward him. "May I?" he asked, lifting the handheld unit.

Nikhil looked down at the female that was quickly becoming his whole world. He needed her to know that he would always protect her, always put her needs first. "It is up to you, Mackenzie. I know you have been through a great deal and are still unsure of all that has occurred. But I need you to know that I would never allow anything to be done to you that would cause harm."

"If I didn't want..." she gestured to Luol, her eyes returning to Nikhil.

"Scanned," he filled in the word she was searching for, "then no, I wouldn't force you to have it done."

"But you would like me to."

"I would very much like to know that you are unharmed."

"And it won't hurt?"

"No, Mackenzie, it won't."

Mac silently stared up at Nikhil. She really didn't know him, but for some reason she trusted him, and that was saying something after all that had happened to her. He was telling her what he preferred while still giving her a choice.

"Alright," she finally said. "He can scan me."

"Thank you, Little One." Nikhil found his head lowering. He wanted to kiss her so badly, to give her what he had given no other female, but he knew it was too soon. He settled for resting his forehead against hers. "It means a great deal to me that you would trust me in this."

"If you would lean back slightly, Nikhil, I will begin my scan."

Mac stiffened slightly as the machine began to hum. Feeling it, Nikhil tried to distract her. "Will you tell me where you are from?" he asked quietly.

"Earth."

"Earth?" he raised his eyes to Luol and saw his head move ever so slightly, indicating the Healer had never heard of the planet.

"Yes. You've heard of it?"

"No, Little One, I'm sorry, but I haven't."

"Really? But..." Mac didn't know why those simple words hit her so hard, but suddenly she felt her breath catch, and her eyes began to well up. It all became too much. Whatever had been holding her together, keeping her strong, was suddenly gone, and she broke down in his arms.

Nikhil looked to Luol desperately. "Luol..."

"It is to be expected, Nikhil." He turned off the scanner. "She has endured more than any being should and handled it extremely well. But now she doesn't have to. She has you to help her."

"I would do anything for her."

"Then comfort her. You will know what she needs. What she is ready for. You are her Dasho. She is your Ashe."

"The scan?"

"She has caused herself no further harm. She needs food, rest, to cleanse, but mostly she needs time to heal."

"How do I give her all that?"

Luol looked from the largest, strongest male he had ever met to the smallest, most fragile looking female he'd ever seen and somehow it just seemed right.

"Take her to your quarters, Nikhil."

"What?" Nikhil looked at the Healer in shock. "How can I do that? She needs..."

"She needs *you*. I have done all I can do for her right now. Her body needs time to absorb the treatment." He switched to Kaliszian. "She is your True Mate, Nikhil. You will always know what she needs. Trust that the Goddess wouldn't have given her to you if you didn't. Take her to your quarters and care for her. Bring her back tomorrow, and I will finish treating her. You know where I am if you need me."

Chapter Three

"How many, Gryf?" Treyvon asked his second as they walked into his Command Center.

"Eight Tafaians, six Nekeokians, three Jerboaians, and ten of the ones that call themselves Humans."

"What about the human female? The one Nikhil found. Is she going to survive?"

"Yes," Gryf told him shortly.

Treyvon sat in his chair. He and Gryf had been serving together since they were young warriors. He knew Gryf's moods, and right now he was struggling.

"What has you so unsettled, Gryf?"

"What?" That Gryf didn't understand the question revealed just how rattled he was.

"What has happened?"

"It's Nikhil," Gryf started.

"Nikhil? What's happened to him?"

"He has found his True Mate."

"What?!!" Treyvon sat straight up disbelievingly.

"The human female. She wears Nikhil's True Mate bead."

"That's not possible! She's not Kaliszian! We don't even know what she is."

"I know, but I saw her react to Nikhil's emotions myself, even though she was unconscious. I saw how he was able to calm her, even in that state." Treyvon silently listened as Gryf continued. "She woke, and seemed to recognize him. *I* frightened her."

Treyvon understood what Gryf meant. While his Commander was a large male, Squad Leader Nikhil was twice his size. For a female to be afraid of Gryf, and not Nikhil, could only mean one thing. She *was* Nikhil's True Mate.

"I would like to meet this female." Treyvon rose and headed for the medical wing.

∞ ∞ ∞ ∞ ∞

Mac knew she needed to pull herself together. She knew she should be protesting as Nikhil stood up, tucked her safely into his arms, and carried her out of the medical unit. They'd switched back to the language she didn't understand, and she should be demanding to know what was going on. But she couldn't find the strength or desire to. It felt good to not have to be strong, to not have to hide her fear, to let someone else be in charge for a while.

The guys had done so much for her when they didn't have to. She was their guide. She was the one that should have been stepping up and leading them, finding a way to get them home. After all, that's what she'd promised them she'd do. Take them up the mountain so they could have a 'Warrior's Weekend', and then make sure they got back down. They hadn't seen it that way. Especially after they realized what the species that took them, the Ganglians, did to females. They'd all rallied around her and Jen, protecting them, never letting the Ganglians know they were females.

In return, Mac tried to stay strong for them, tried to help whenever she could. She had the skills to survive outside in harsh conditions, and she'd needed all those skills to help them survive. They had relied on her for that.

Now there was someone *she* could rely on, and he was carrying her somewhere.

Nikhil glared at every warrior that looked his way. They were all trying to see what was wrapped up in the blanket he was carrying, but he refused to let them. Luol had wrapped a blanket securely around his True Mate since her coverings were nearly non-existent. He would have to see what he could find for her to wear.

"Squad Leader," a warrior approached.

"Not now!" he growled, his arms tightening around Mackenzie, and the male quickly moved away.

"Where are we going?" Mac asked quietly.

"To my quarters. So you can rest without being disturbed."

"Oh."

Rounding one more corner, Nikhil stopped in front of his door, and shifting her slightly, pressed his palm against the access panel. The door silently opened, and he took his True Mate inside.

Mac pulled down the edge of the blanket that had been partially covering her face, and tried to look around, but the room was too dark.

"Is it always like this?"

"Like what?"

"So dark?"

"No, let me increase the energy crystals."

Still carrying her, Nikhil stepped deeper into the room and waved his hand over a bowl of crystals, and the room began to brighten.

"Better?" he asked.

"Yes, thank you."

For several minutes Nikhil just stood there, holding her as he gazed down at her.

"Umm, Nikhil?"

"Yes, Little One."

"Are you ever going to put me down?"

"Only if that is what you wish."

"I think you should. I have to be getting heavy."

"You could never get too heavy for me to hold," he snorted at the thought, but slowly lowered her feet to the floor. Yet he couldn't bring himself to release her completely. "Luol said you should eat, rest, and cleanse. Which would you like to do first?"

Mac's first thought was to say eat; it had been a long time since she had. The Zaludians hadn't given her anything since they'd discovered her. Punishment, they'd said. But then he said 'cleanse.'

"Cleanse... you mean as in bathe? A shower? Getting clean?"

"Yes."

"Cleanse." God, how long had it been, she thought, since she'd actually bathed? The morning before she'd led them up the mountain? The Ganglians had kept them in that cage giving them very little water, and even if they had given them more, she wouldn't have risked washing in front of them. Wouldn't have risked them discovering she was female. And in the mine... there'd only been a small stream that trickled down the back wall of the cave. It had been because of that stream that she'd found the narrow crack that led to the smaller cave where her and Jen were able to hide. And while the stream was big enough for them to get some extra water to drink and cook with, it wasn't enough to cleanse.

Just the thought of getting clean, of getting rid of all the grime and stink that clung to her body, had her trembling with need. She'd grown used to the smell. They all had. But now that she was free it suddenly overwhelmed her.

"Where is it?" she demanded.

"It is this way." Nikhil guided her out of the living area, through his resting area, and into his private cleansing area. Only those of the highest rank received quarters such as these, and Nikhil had almost declined the room, knowing he would rarely use it. Now he was glad he hadn't, for if he had, he would

41

have had to take his True Mate to the large shared shower where males cleansed together. And that would never do.

Mac barely noticed the rooms Nikhil led her through. She could investigate them later. Right now she was totally focused on finding out if this cleansing room was anything like a bathroom on Earth. A little cry of joy escaped her when she saw it was.

"This is the cleansing room," Nikhil said stepping into the room. "And this is the cleansing unit." Mac's little cry had him spinning around. "What is wrong?"

"Nothing's wrong!" she immediately told him, "It's a shower! How does it work?" She let the blanket around her shoulders fall away, and walked straight into the stall.

"You press here to turn it on," he barely touched a crystal just inside the entrance of the stall, "and here to adjust the temperature." His finger moved to the next crystal. "There is cleanser on the shelf, and I will get you a cloth." He turned, retrieving a cloth from a cabinet behind him, then stilled when he turned back around.

Mackenzie had already turned the water on and was just standing there, her upturned face letting the steady stream run over her, soaking what little covering she wore. Goddess, she took his breath away, even in this condition. He wanted to be near her, found he needed to be near her.

"Mackenzie..." His voice was lower and rougher than he had intended.

"Hmmm?" she asked, her face still worshiping the flow of water.

"I cannot leave you alone... leave you to cleanse... alone. What if you were to fall?"

Mac realized she had forgotten Nikhil was even in the room because of the incredible feel of the water flowing over her.

There had been no room for modesty or privacy in that mine even though she and Jen had some in the smaller cave. Her hands quickly covered her breasts that used to be D's but were now barely there, and the wild thatch between her legs that she used to trim, even though remnants of her clothes still covered them.

"I'm sorry. I wasn't thinking. I just wanted to get clean so bad. I'll just..." she turned away from him.

"No, I didn't mean for you to..." Nikhil ran a frustrated hand through his hair, causing his Suja beads to hit together angrily. "I am not explaining myself well. I am not used to this."

"To what?" she asked over her shoulder.

"Speaking to a female," he admitted. "To a beautiful female."

"I'm not beautiful," she denied. "I'm filthy and dirty, and I stink. I've lost so much weight. I mean I know I needed to lose weight, but I never wanted to be a size zero. A size ten maybe, but still that's stretching it the way I like food."

"You are beautiful to me... You used to be larger?" Nikhil asked hopefully. Kaliszian women were larger than Mackenzie, and taller. Not as tall as him, but a good six to eight inches taller than her, and they carried their size proudly. It was seen as an honor to carry some extra weight. It meant the female's male was able to provide for her, to see to her needs.

"Yes." Mac frowned at how happy that seemed to make Nikhil.

"Then we will make sure you are that way again?"

"You want me larger?" Mac couldn't believe it. It wasn't what gorgeous hunks on Earth wanted, at least not the ones she ever met. They'd always wanted those super-thin or super-toned women, and she had struggled with her weight all her life. She wasn't weak or lazy. After all, she spent most of her time outside hiking, biking, or being a guide on her mountain. She was active, but she just always seemed to carry this extra weight in her breasts, ass, and thighs. No matter how many diets she went on, it never went away. Her grandpa called her a full-figured girl. He would tell her that this was the way God made her, the way he wanted her, that he had a reason for her being the way she was. Maybe he was right because that extra weight had been what had helped her survive on the little food she and Jen allowed themselves. They had agreed that the guys needed larger portions than them as they were the ones working in the mine. Mac had even snuck more into Jen's bowl when she could since Jen weighed so much less than her.

"I want you to be as the Goddess created you to be," he told her, his gaze still running over her. "What I was trying to say is that, while you have been strong enough to survive, you are now weakened. I understand why you wish to cleanse, but it will take some time, and you could tire and slip. There will also be areas you will be unable to reach. I would be honored to assist you in cleansing if you would allow it."

Mac just looked at him for a moment then said, "You want to get naked with me?"

"No!" he immediately denied. "I would not expect you to allow that." He barely stopped himself from saying yet. "I will leave my pants on. I only wish to be there for you, Mackenzie, to assist you. Will you allow it?"

Mac didn't realize she'd turned to face Nikhil as he spoke, her thin wet coverings clinging to her like a second skin. The thought of sharing a shower with him, of him touching her. It had her breath catching for some reason. Well not for some reason. She knew the reason. He was gorgeous. Different than anyone she'd ever met. Yes, he was large, extremely large, but she wasn't intimidated by his size. Maybe if she had met him before being taken she would be, but now his size made her feel safe, and she hadn't felt that way in a very long time.

"I would allow it." She reached out to grip his hand. "And the honor is mine, Nikhil. Thank you."

Nikhil closed his eyes at her touch, then after handing her the cleaning cloth, stepped back and started removing his uniform.

Mac knew she should be using the cloth to start cleaning herself. It was why she went into the cleansing unit fully clothed in the first place because she wanted to get all the Ganglian and Zaludian grime off her. But she found she couldn't pull her gaze away from the prime specimen of man stripping before her.

Nikhil started at his feet, undoing the straps on the snug, over-the-calf boots he was wearing. Toeing them off, he pulled out weapons she hadn't even known were there, setting them behind him on the counter, before kicking the boots aside. His hands then went to the buckle that crossed the front of his tight black pants hanging low on his hips. She held her breath. She wasn't going to remind him that he planned to leave those on. When the buckle released, it was the blaster on his right thigh that released, and he set it behind him. Next came the array of blades strapped to both his massive arms and they joined the other weapons on the counter. Finally, he removed his vest, revealing what little of his massive chest it had been able to cover, and it fell unheeded to the floor.

"Is there something wrong, Mackenzie?" he asked stepping into the shower.

"I... what... no," she stuttered. "Why would you think that?"

"Because you are not cleansing. Are you feeling ill? Weak?" He took the cloth from her hand. "Here, rest against me."

Mac offered no resistance as Nikhil's large, calloused hands lightly cupped her shoulder blades, pulling her near so she could rest her head on his chest.

"Will you allow me to cleanse your hair?" he asked quietly.

"My hair?" Mac looked up at him, her chin resting on his chest.

"I know it is asking much when we have just met."

"Are you sure you want to?" she questioned. "It's a tangled mess. It might just be easier to cut it off."

"No!" Nikhil's instant denial boomed off the walls of the cleansing room causing her to jump. "I am sorry, Little One," he was instantly contrite. "I did not mean to cause you fear."

"You didn't. You just startled me. Why does the thought of me cutting my hair upset you so?"

"Because it is not done."

"Kaliszians don't have short hair?" she asked, her gaze traveled over his hair that only covered the center of his head before it flowed down his back in long thin braids with beads attached.

"No. One's hair is cut only if they have committed the most heinous of crimes."

"Oh."

"So would you allow me the honor of cleansing your hair?" he asked again. "I would never do so without your permission."

Mac frowned at his words. Why would he consider it an honor to wash her hair? But she could see he wouldn't do it if it made her uncomfortable.

"I would allow it, Nikhil. I just hope you don't regret doing it. It hasn't been brushed since the Ganglians took us from Earth."

Nikhil had filled his hand with cleansing liquid, eager to perform such an intimate act for his True Mate, when her last words had him stilling.

"Ganglians..." he growled. "The *Ganglians* took you from your home world?"

"Yes. Didn't you know that?"

"No. The Ganglians..."

"I know what Ganglians do to females, Nikhil," she whispered.

"Luol said you weren't abused that way," he growled back, his need to protect her surging through him.

"I wasn't." She put a calming hand on his suddenly heaving chest. "The guys protected me. They made sure the Ganglians didn't know that I and... that I was female," she stuttered over her words.

"You were not..."

"No! No, Nikhil, I wasn't raped."

"Thank the Goddess," he whispered shakily, finding he didn't know what he would have done if she had been. Forcing his hands to unclench, he began caring for his True Mate. "Lean against me, Mackenzie. I will care for you, and vow to make sure you never have to fear again."

Mac was about to tell him he couldn't promise something like that, but then his fingers sunk into her dirty, matted hair to massage her scalp, and all she could do was moan in pleasure.

"Oh, Nikhil, that feels so good."

"Then I will continue to do so, Little One. You just close your eyes and enjoy."

Mac did just that. Her chin remained on his chest as her hands drifted down his sides until they came to rest on his pant-encased hips.

Nikhil couldn't believe the honor his True Mate was giving him. For a Kaliszian, one's hair was almost a sacred thing, for it is where their Suja beads lived. Where their place in society was revealed, along with their lineage, and their personal achievements. The beads alone decided where they settled, their height displaying the worth of those that wore them. Only the closest or most intimate to a Kaliszian was ever allowed to wash another's hair. The only one Nikhil had ever allowed to do this was his mother, and that had been years ago. For Mackenzie to allow him this honor humbled him.

"Tip your head back, Little One," he murmured, and his heart beat faster when she didn't hesitate to obey him, and he rinsed part of the filth away.

"Have you gotten it clean already?"

"No. I am sorry. I did not mean to fail you.'"

"What?" Her head whipped up, her eyes flying open. "Why would you say that?!! Why would you even think that?!!"

"You wished your hair to be clean in one cleansing, and I did not do that."

"Nikhil," her hands reached up, gripping his cheeks, forcing him to look into her eyes. "It was a question, not a criticism. If anyone could have gotten my hair clean in one washing, I know it would be you."

"You truly believe this?" His dimly glowing eyes searched hers.

"I do."

"Would you allow me to cleanse your hair again?"

"I would allow you to cleanse my hair and every other part of my body until there's not a speck of that grime left on me."

"I will not fail you, this time, Little One."

"Nikhil," she stilled his hand from getting more cleansing gel. "You could never fail me." Releasing his hand, she let her chin return to his chest and closed her eyes.

Nikhil looked down at the little female in his arms. When had he ever been trusted so completely? Believed in so completely? It was then he realized he already loved this little female... completely.

It took three more cleansings for Nikhil to finally remove the last speck of dirt from his True Mate's hair, and once it was done, he was stunned. "It's beautiful," he whispered in awe, never having felt such thick, silky hair before, or seen so much of it. Not only did it cover the top of her head and run down her back, as a Kaliszians did, but it also covered the sides of her head.

"Hmmm?" Mac hummed, having been lulled nearly to sleep by Nikhil's attentions.

"Your hair, it is beautiful."

"I think you're overusing that word." Opening her eyes, she gave him a teasing smile. "It's just brown hair."

"I do not overuse the word, and if your hair is just brown, then it is just every shade of brown known in the universes from darkest to lightest, all mixed up together. And that, my Mackenzie, is beautiful."

Mac stared up at Nikhil in shock. She'd never heard her hair described in such a way. Yes, she knew her hair had different shades of brown in it, but that was because she was out in the sun so much and parts of it had faded. At least, that was how she saw it. Nikhil obviously saw it in an entirely different way.

"I... Thank you, Nikhil."

"I just speak truth. Now let me tend to the rest of you." Reaching for the cloth he had set aside to cleanse her hair, he gently began to remove the dirt from her face that the water hadn't already taken care of.

"How bad is it?" Mac asked, keeping her face tipped up to his.

"It is beautiful."

M.K. EIDEM

This time, when he used that word, Mac pinched one of the prevalent muscles at his waist, hard, causing him to jerk slightly.

"Why did you do that?!!" he demanded.

"Because you used that word again and you are *lying*," she told him angrily. She didn't need him to keep trying to placate her with pretty words. She wasn't beautiful, had never been beautiful, and after the blows the Zaludians had landed on her face, knew she never would be.

"You think I would not speak truth to you?" Nikhil stiffened in outrage.

"I *think* you are a nice guy. I *think* you are trying to keep me calm. But I *know* there is no way you can see me as beautiful," her voice broke slightly. "Not with all the damage the Zaludians did to my face!"

"You think..." he carefully framed her face with his hands, gently forcing her to look up at him even as he leaned in closer. "I don't *think* you are beautiful, Mackenzie. I *know* you are. Yes, you are still covered in dirt, but that can be washed away. Yes, there is still some bruising on your face, but those will fade. What you don't seem to understand is that while you were unconscious, the deep-repair unit removed the damage the Zaludians inflicted."

"What?" Her eyes widened at his words, and slowly she ran her tongue along her bottom lip. A lip she knew had been split open by a Zaludian fist. She knew it because she had tasted the blood, but now there was nothing there.

Nikhil's eyes followed the path that sexy little tongue took across his Mackenzie's full, lower lip. How could such a small movement captivate him so?

"It's gone," she whispered quietly.

"What is?" he replied just as quietly.

"The split where the Zaludian hit me when I wouldn't tell him my name."

"The one wearing the red beads?" Nikhil asked gruffly, then cursed in Kaliszian at her answer.

"Yes. What's wrong, Nikhil?" she asked not understanding what he was saying.

"I shouldn't have killed him so quickly. I should have made him suffer the way he made you suffer."

"What? You killed him?" Her eyes widened when she realized he was serious. "He's dead?"

"Yes. He was in the cave where I found you. I killed him to get to you." Would she turn away from him now? Become afraid of him? How would he survive it?

"Thank you." Bracing her hands on his washboard abs, she rose on her toes, and pressed her healed lips to the corner of his mouth.

Nikhil felt his entire being still as her lips grazed his. A completeness he'd never felt before filled him, and it was all because of this one small female.

"For what?" he murmured, struggling to stop himself from crushing them under his, and was bereft when she pulled them away to respond to his stupid question.

"For making sure I'll never have to face him again. That I will never have to worry about him suddenly showing up and attacking me again."

"You never will." While he spoke softly, his words held an unmistakable power behind them. "He will never harm you again, Mackenzie."

"I believe you." Lowering her heels back to the floor, she just looked at him and waited. Slowly, he lifted the cloth again and with an intensity that should have frightened her, began to carefully and methodically cleanse her.

Cleanse. What a perfect word, she thought, for that was exactly what it felt like he was doing. Cleansing her body and soul, removing every remnant of her time spent with the Ganglians and Zaludians.

He started at her forehead then moved down, making sure he was extremely gentle around her eyes and lips. Once he was satisfied with the results, he started on her neck and shoulders, moving her cleansed hair from side to side.

"Mackenzie."

"Yes?" she asked when he paused.

"These coverings..."

Mac felt her eyes start to well. She knew the clothes needed to go, wanted them to go, there was nothing left of them, and they only reminded her of everything bad that had happened. But still... they were all she had left from home.

"Things don't make a home, Mac." Her grandpa's words echoed in her head. *"The people do."*

"Don't matter," she told him, then frowned when Nikhil stilled her hand as she went to remove them. With a tug on each piece, the offending garments were gone. "Okay, I guess that's one way to take them off." Nikhil just grunted, but she could feel the satisfaction he felt in how he removed them.

Nikhil couldn't express how it made him feel to be able to remove those offending coverings from his Mackenzie. She should never have to wear anything that a Ganglian or a Zaludian had touched. He would make sure she had only the finest of coverings from now on. His mother would know where to find them. He would... his thoughts of coverings disappeared as he realized he was touching one of her breasts.

Carefully he cleansed the small globe, trying not to be distracted as it seemed to swell slightly at his touch; its dusty, pink nipple tightening. He was tempted to sample the small treat just to see what it tasted like, but knew now wasn't the time for that. Hopefully later, after his True Mate had fully recovered, she would allow him to claim her and offer her his Ashe bead.

Mac couldn't believe how gentle Nikhil was being. She knew if she were cleansing herself, she probably would have removed a layer of skin trying to rid herself of all the grime that covered her. Not Nikhil, he used care as he firmly cleaned first one spot then another with the cloth, rinsing it out in the stream of hot water flowing down her back.

When had anyone ever been so intent on caring for *her*? Not her parents, although she knew they loved her, but it was a secondary love. Looking back with new eyes, she realized the majority of her father's attention had been focused on the career that had killed him, and her mother's had been focused on her father.

Not her grandpa. While he had done his best, his mountain had always drawn most of his attention.

Not the guys, even though they had tried. But she wasn't one of their group. They didn't know her, she was just their guide.

No, no one had ever cared for her the way Nikhil was. As if her needs were all that mattered. She felt him tense for a moment while cleaning her breasts. They'd responded to his touch, and she knew if he had wanted to try something, she wouldn't be able to stop him. But he hadn't taken advantage of the situation, just quickly moved on to clean her stomach and hips. This extremely, large male, who barely knew her, was caring for her more than anyone else ever had.

She was about to thank him, to tell him how much she appreciated what he was doing when he shocked her by dropping to his knees.

"Nikhil..." her hands gripped his shoulders.

"I know you are getting tired, Little One." He looked up at her with concerned eyes. "It won't be much longer. Lift your foot." He gently gripped her ankle and lifted it onto his thigh. "You are doing so well," he told her as he began cleansing her leg.

"I don't feel like I am. You're doing it all."

"There is nothing wrong with letting someone else help you when you need it." He carefully moved the cloth between her thighs, cleansing an area he wanted to know more intimately, but refused to let himself linger there. Now was not the time.

He had never actually given any thought to how beautiful and sexy a female's leg could be. How the larger thigh connected to the thinner calf. How that continued on to become a delicate ankle and foot. He'd never considered a foot delicate before, having only ever looked at his huge ones. But Mackenzie's were.

Reaching the end of those delicate bones, he gently massaged each toe, his thumb working its way between them making sure not a single speck of grime remained. Setting her foot back down, he touched her other ankle, and she willingly placed it on his thigh. Carefully, he reversed his actions and worked his way up her other leg.

Mac looked down at Nikhil's lowered head, awed at the attention he was giving each leg. Her breath caught as he cleansed between her legs, brushing her sex, but as before, he paused for only a moment then quickly continued.

She found her hand rising to touch the wide strip of hair that covered the top of his head. It was softer and thicker than it looked, pulled back as tightly as it was. For some reason, she'd thought it would feel slick or oily, but it wasn't.

At the nape of his neck was some kind of clip that controlled all those strands. But what was curious was that when the strands came out of the clip, they were thin braids with a variety of colored beads affixed to them at different levels.

"These are beautiful," she whispered lifting several braids, letting them slip through her fingers, caressing them. It was the strangest sensation because it felt like the beads were caressing her back.

Nikhil's hands stilled, his head snapping up when she touched his beads, his gaze capturing hers. "You find my Suja beads... beautiful?"

Mac gave him a slight smile since she just used the word she'd been giving him such a hard time about. "Yes, I do. Especially on you. Why do you wear them?"

"They signify my lineage, who my parents are, and what I have accomplished in my life," he told her, then carefully stood and moved behind her, blocking the water's spray. "Tip your head back," he encouraged softly, and when she trustingly did, he rinsed her long, gorgeous hair one more time. He made sure none of the grime from her back clung to it, then gathering it up, placed it over one of her cleaned shoulders.

"I will cleanse your back now; then you will be able to rest, Little One."

Mac just nodded her understanding and leaned forward slightly giving him better access to her back. It didn't take him long to cleanse it since the steady stream of water had already removed the majority of it. Only a few spots remained that needed his attention. But he still took his time, amazed at how soft her skin felt beneath his warrior's hands. He tried not to notice the two sexy indentations just above her rounded ass, or how perfect that ass felt in his hands. Mackenzie was already everything he wanted in a female. How amazing would she be when she regained her health and previous size?

Mac closed her eyes as Nikhil's hands ran along her back. She knew he was only cleansing her, caring for her, and while she didn't understand why he would do this, she wasn't going to deny that it felt incredible.

"Are you okay, Mackenzie?" he asked, his arms wrapping around her waist pulling her back against him as he finished.

"I am, with you holding me," she admitted. Slowly, she turned in his arms, tilting her face up to look at him. God, he was so amazing to watch with the spray of water bouncing off his back. Sinking deeper into the comfort of his arms, she felt her knees give out as the last of her strength left her.

"Mackenzie!" Nikhil swept her up into his arms, carrying her out of the unit. Ripping a drying cloth off the wall, he wrapped it around her. "I will take you to Luol."

"No!" She immediately rejected the idea even as she fought to keep her eyes open. "Just give me a minute and I will be fine."

"You are not fine!" he argued back. "You collapsed in my arms."

"I just need to rest for a minute."

"You will have all the minutes you need, my Little One." Carrying her to his bed, he ripped back the covers and gently laid her down.

"Nikhil," she protested, "I'm soaking wet."

"I don't care. You need rest." Pulling the towel from her body, he quickly covered her back up with the bed's coverings, making sure they were tucked in close. Then he began removing the excess moisture from her hair.

"Nikhil." She tried to free herself from the cocoon of covers that enveloped her, but his hand stilled her.

"No, Mackenzie, everything will be fine. Just rest."

Mac found she could only do as he asked. The heat of the shower had relaxed her. Combine that with the comfort of the bed, and the feeling of safety her eyes closed and she was fast asleep.

Chapter Four

Treyvon frowned when he entered the medical unit and found it empty.

"She is in the deep-repair area," Gryf told him, gesturing to the partially closed door on the other side of the room.

"She's still in the unit?" Treyvon couldn't believe it. The female's injuries must be truly grave for the unit to still be treating her.

"No, she's not," Luol told them, walking out of his office. "I had Squad Leader Nikhil take her to his quarters."

"What? Why?" Treyvon demanded.

"Because she is his True Mate and he is the only one that she trusts. Especially after the way the Commander treated her." Luol gave Gryf a disapproving look.

"What are you talking about?" Treyvon spun around to look at his second-in-command.

"Commander Gryf tried to order Squad Leader Nikhil away from his unconscious True Mate."

"He did what?" Treyvon's gaze remained locked on his commander.

"Yes, and that understandably upset Nikhil significantly. His emotions transferred to his True Mate causing her to become very agitated. Had Nikhil not been able to calm her, she could have severely damaged herself as she was still in the deep-repair unit."

"You attempted to force a Warrior, one of our largest, to desert his True Mate while *inside* the deep-repair unit?!!"

"At the time, I only had Healer Luol's opinion that she was Nikhil's True Mate. He could have been wrong."

"But he wasn't."

"No." Gryf had to break eye contact with his General and friend.

"Then once she finally calmed, Commander Gryf felt it would be a good time to interrogate her," Luol continued.

"Commander?"

"She spoke of her time with the Zaludians," Gryf said, defending his actions. "I was only attempting to find out how long she was with them."

"By barraging her with questions, and giving her no time to answer?" Luol fired back. "You frightened her!"

"That was not my intention!" Gryf took a threatening step toward the Healer.

"What is her condition, Luol?" Treyvon asked, interrupting the growing argument between his Commander and Healer.

"She is weak, which is to be expected after what she has survived." Luol pulled his gaze from Gryf, giving the General his full attention. "The deep-repair unit was able to treat the injuries caused by the Zaludians, and I have begun replenishing the nutrients she was deficient in."

Treyvon frowned at that. "Did you consider that perhaps her species does not require the same nutrients that we do?"

"I did, which is why I only gave her a portion of what the unit recommended. I did not want to overwhelm her system."

"And?"

"Her body seemed to readily absorb what I gave her with no side effects. After she has rested, I will complete the treatment. Then she should be ready to use the educator."

"It would have been better for her to remain here," Gryf said stiffly.

"No, it wouldn't have. Not only would I not separate Nikhil from his True Mate but from what I've heard, there are going to be other survivors that need the deep-repair unit. Having other males around his weakened True Mate would raise all Nikhil's protective instincts, which would in turn agitate his True Mate. She doesn't need that. She will rest better in Nikhil's quarters."

"You are sure she is his True Mate, Luol?" Treyvon asked quietly.

"She wears his True Mate bead, General. And while I don't think she realizes it or knows what it means, she responds to Nikhil's words, touch, and emotions as only a True Mate would."

"A True Mate hasn't been found in nearly five-hundred years, Luol."

"I know that, General, and had I not witnessed it myself, I wouldn't believe it. But I did. Her responses were true."

"I need to see this for myself. Gryf, with me."

Gryf silently walked beside his General, knowing some things still needed to be said. "I should not have approached her like that."

"No. You shouldn't have," Treyvon agreed, continuing to walk.

"I didn't believe she was his True Mate. I mean how could she be? She isn't even Kaliszian."

"You know there was a time when Kaliszians found their True Mate within other species, Gryf."

"Before the Great Infection, perhaps, but not since."

"True, but that only means we should thank the Goddess that she has blessed a male with one."

"Thank the Goddess..." Gryf shook his head in disgust. "She is the one that took away our True Mates along with our ability to provide for them. If not for her, Mica..." he cut himself off.

Treyvon stopped walking and turned to confront his friend. "Mica was never meant to be yours, Gryf. If you can't believe that by her actions alone, then believe your True Mate bead. It refused to accept her."

"I left her alone too many times. I didn't..."

"That doesn't matter! Your True Mate bead still would have accepted her. *It* refused to do so, so she was never meant to be your True Mate. You have to accept this."

"There was still a chance."

"Only if Mica had accepted your Ashe bead. She refused it, Gryf. She has moved on, and so must you. One of our finest Warriors has found his True Mate. We will celebrate his good fortune as if it were our own." Turning, Treyvon continued to Nikhil's quarters.

∞ ∞ ∞ ∞ ∞

Nikhil gathered up his weapons, worried Mackenzie might harm herself with one, and changed into a dry uniform. Now he just stared down at her sleeping so deeply in his bed, still finding it hard to believe she was there, that she was his. Carefully he reached down, lifting the section of her hair his True Mate bead had claimed. It responded to his touch by glowing slightly and giving off a sense of peace that told him she was well.

It was one of the carefully guarded secrets of the True Mate bead. The True Mate beads connected a couple. Just by touching it, one would know the condition of the other. If it were two Kaliszians that exchanged their beads, they needed only to touch the one in their hair to know if the other was okay.

Nikhil had to admit that he wished Mackenzie had a True Mate bead for him to wear. Then when he was away from her, he would know she was okay. But he was also grateful that she didn't. He didn't want her knowing if he was hurt during a mission, which was always a possibility. He didn't want her feeling what he felt as he killed, even if it were justified. None of that darkness that was a part of his life should ever touch this amazing creature the Goddess had entrusted to him. She didn't even realize how she had already lightened the load he carried. She looked at him and *saw* him, not some large, oversized male that others did. She didn't fear him. She trusted him when she was most vulnerable, and he would never betray that trust.

The sound of a fist meeting his outer door had him releasing the bead and quickly rising. Crossing the room, he closed the door to his resting chamber so she wouldn't be disturbed by the fist that was starting to pound harder on his outer door.

"What?!!" he growled, hitting the crystal that would open the door. The fierce look on his face would have deterred a normal male, but General Treyvon Rayner was no normal male, and Nikhil straightened to attention. "General."

"Warrior Nikhil. I was informed congratulations are in order. You have been blessed with a True Mate."

"Yes, General," Nikhil took a step back allowing Treyvon to enter his living area. When Gryf followed, he found his fist clenching. He had always respected Commander Gryf, had always considered him an honorable male, but he had tried to come between him and his Mackenzie, and that Nikhil would never allow.

"I regret that I upset your True Mate, Squad Leader Nikhil," Gryf spoke first, knowing he was the one at fault.

Nikhil silently stared at the other male for several moments then stiffly nodded, knowing that was as far as the Commander would go.

"Why are you here, General?" Nikhil addressed Treyvon.

"I hoped to speak with your True Mate," Treyvon told him. "We still do not know exactly what the Zaludians were doing and why. We don't know why the Ganglians are assisting them. She might know something as they held her separately."

"She is resting, and I will not disturb her. Not when there are others you can gather that information from."

"True, but she was held separately. She might have overheard something. Has she said anything to you?" Treyvon asked.

"Only that her home world is a place called 'Earth', and that the Ganglians took them from there and brought them here."

"That's all she said?!!" Gryf's roar of disbelief bounced off the walls, and he took a step toward Nikhil. "You've been with her for hours. She had to have told you more than that!"

"She's been unconscious nearly the entire time, and unlike *you*, Commander," while Nikhil's anger rose his voice didn't. "I care more about her well-being than gathering information on the Zaludians."

"There could be more sites!" Gryf argued back. "More like her being held!"

"And how would she know that?"

"Enough! Both of you," Treyvon ordered. "This is getting us nowhere. Squad Leader Nikhil is right. The health of his True Mate is more important than any information she might be able to provide right now. We know from the survivors at other locations that they never traveled from one site to another. There's no reason to think it was any different at this site."

"But it could be with the number of bodies found..."

"Nikhil?" The faint voice had all three males turning to look at the closed door.

∞ ∞ ∞ ∞ ∞

Mac tried to block out the raised voices filtering in from the outer cave into the small one where she and Jen were sleeping. It didn't often happen, since the guys were always too exhausted when they returned from the mine to argue. But it did happen.

As their voices grew louder, she frowned. They never got that loud. To do so would draw the attention of the Zaludians, which was never good. Maybe one of them was hurt. She needed to get up and find out what was going on. If she didn't, Jen would, and Jen was struggling enough as it was.

Forcing her eyes open, Mac stilled when there wasn't the rock ceiling she was used to seeing above her. Where was she? Turning her head to the side, she realized it rested on a pillow, and that her body was lying on a soft bed. There were blankets tucked securely around her. Where the hell was she?

The careful breath she took teased her senses. It was clean and fresh without the dust that was always prevalent from the mining. There was something in it familiar, though. Listening closer to the voices, she couldn't understand what they were saying, but she could recognize one of them no matter what language he was speaking... Nikhil. Suddenly it all came back to her.

Nikhil had rescued her from the Zaludians. He said they had all been rescued and even though she hadn't seen anyone yet, she believed him. He hadn't said anything about Jen, about there being another female, only that there were ten *males*. The guys must still be protecting Jen. She needed to find out if Jen was safe.

She knew she felt safe with Nikhil, but she didn't understand why. After all, he was huge by anyone's standards, but he had been so gentle with her. Especially when that other guy, what

64

had Nikhil called him... Commander had been firing questions at her.

Nikhil had brought her back here to his quarters, and carefully cleansed her. He could have taken advantage of her then, but he didn't. Instead, he cared for her making sure there wasn't one speck of dirt left anywhere on her body. Then he'd tucked her carefully into his bed.

Reaching up, she touched her hair and for the first time in... she didn't know how long... she could run her fingers through it. It was silky and smooth without a single snarl. Reaching the end of one strand, she frowned feeling something. Lifting the offending strand, she saw there was a bead attached to the end of it. Twirling it between her fingers, she was surprised at how warm it was, how it seemed to glitter at her. But why was it there?

Holding the bead, a feeling of anxiety filled her. She didn't understand where it was coming from, but she knew something was wrong, and she needed to get to Nikhil. Sitting straight up, she fought her way out of the covers meaning to find him. When the cool air hit, it reminded her she was naked. Looking around the room, she didn't see anything that resembled a closet or dresser, so she pulled one of the blankets off the bed. Wrapping it securely under her arms, she went to find Nikhil.

"Nikhil?" she called out, moving to where she knew the door had been when she entered the room, but now there was just a solid panel. Running her hands over it, she couldn't find a handle and panicking, she began to pound on the door. Why was she locked in? Was she a prisoner? Had it all been a trick? "Nikhil!"

One moment she was pounding on a solid, cold door, and the next on a solid, warm chest.

"Mackenzie." Nikhil wrapped his arms around her not liking the fear he heard in her voice. "What is wrong? Why aren't you resting?"

"I heard yelling. What's going on? Why was I locked in?"

Nikhil wanted to pound Gryf into the floor for waking and scaring his True Mate again. He couldn't do it now, but the next time they met on the training field, Gryf would feel his displeasure.

"I am sorry we woke you, Little One." His large hands rubbed her bare shoulders trying to reassure her that everything was fine, then frowned when he realized she was wrapped in only a blanket. There were two other males in the room. He pulled her deeper into his embrace.

"Why was I locked in?" she asked.

"You weren't. I only closed the door so you could rest undisturbed. I should have realized you might not know how to open it." Pulling her forward slightly, he took her hand and touched it to the crystal on the wall. "This is what you press to open or close the door."

As she pressed it the crystal, the door closed. Pressing it again, it opened.

"There is one next to the door in the resting area," he told her.

"Oh," Mac was starting to feel foolish. "I'm sorry. I guess I over-reacted."

"You woke up alone in a strange place, and heard angry voices." His voice was quiet as he spoke. "After all you have been through, it is only natural that you reacted the way you did."

"Why was there yelling?" she asked rubbing her cheek against the bare skin of his chest feeling herself settle.

"That would be my fault." Hearing the Commander's voice, she immediately stiffened in Nikhil's arms.

"It is alright, Little One," Nikhil reassured her, his arms tightening.

"Nikhil, may I be allowed to speak to your Ashe?" Treyvon asked, remembering to speak in Zaludian so she would understand.

"Mackenzie?" Nikhil looked down at her questioningly.

"Who is he?" she asked, trying to peek around Nikhil to see who spoke.

"General Treyvon Rayner, the Supreme Commander of Kaliszian Defenses," Nikhil told her quietly. "He is the male the Emperor put in charge of discovering why the Zaludians were on Pontus."

"He's your superior?" she returned just as quietly. Mac wasn't all that familiar with military hierarchy, especially with alien hierarchy, but 'Supreme Commander' and 'put in charge by the Emperor' seemed to indicate that this General was up pretty high.

"Yes, but that does not matter if you are not ready to speak to him." He saw the unease in her eyes. "Let me take you back to the resting area. It's too soon."

"No," Mac resisted when he tried to lead her away. "I'll talk to him, but I don't know what I can tell him, tell any of you."

Nikhil turned, and Mac got her first real look at the General and felt her breath catch. While she still thought Nikhil was the most gorgeous man she'd ever met, the General ran a close second. He wasn't as broad as Nikhil, but he was taller. And while Nikhil's power was undeniable, the General's was more subtle, but just as powerful.

"Ashe Mackenzie," the General bowed slightly to her, "it is an honor to meet you."

"Honor?" Mac sat on the couch where Nikhil indicated. "Why is it an honor?"

"Because you are Nikhil's Ashe." Treyvon frowned at Nikhil, who shook his head ever so slightly.

"Nikhil's Ashe?" she looked up at Nikhil questioningly. "I thought Ashe was just a sign of respect."

"It is," Treyvon quickly informed her, wondering what to say.

"There is more to it, Mackenzie," Nikhil admitted, reaching for the edge of the blanket that had shifted exposing a pale calf. Then he put an arm around her shoulders, pulling her close. "But I would prefer to explain it to you later, in private."

Mac was silent for a moment, her gaze searching Nikhil's. There was something there, something he was uneasy about, but he wasn't trying to hide it from her, just asking her to wait so he could explain. "Alright," she told him then looked to the General and waited.

"Ashe Mackenzie," the General sat down in a chair across from her. "It is our understanding that the Ganglians took you from your home world, a place you call Earth."

"Yes."

"Can you tell us where that planet is?"

"No." Her short, blunt answer seemed to surprise the General.

"Why not?"

"Because I don't know where it is." Her tone implied that should be obvious.

"How is that possible?!!" Gryf demanded, glaring at her as if she were an idiot. "Every species knows where they are from!"

Mac had worked with men all her life; it was the majority of her guide business. There had been plenty of them that thought they were better and smarter than her just because they were male. She didn't know why she thought it would be different with these males just because they could travel in space, especially after meeting the Ganglians and Zaludians. Well, she

68

didn't back down on Earth, and she wasn't going to back down here.

"I do know where I'm from. It's a planet called Earth! That *you've* never heard of it isn't *my* fault!"

Treyvon's eyes widened slightly at how she challenged his Commander, and Nikhil looked down at her with pride. His True Mate had been through a great deal, but she hadn't let it break her as it had so many of the other survivors. She was strong and had fire. She was the perfect True Mate for him.

"Ashe Mackenzie," Treyvon's words broke the stare down Gryf and Mackenzie were having. "You are currently on the planet Pontus. Does that mean anything to you?"

"No. Should it?" she asked.

"It is a small planet in the Kaliszian Empire near the Tornian Empire," Treyvon told her.

"Okay."

"That means nothing to you?" Treyvon questioned.

"No."

"What about the planets Crurn, Imroz, Dzhalil or Kuzbass?" Treyvon continued to question.

"Never heard of them."

"Luda or Tornian?" Treyvon tried again.

"No."

Treyvon leaned back in his chair, thinking. This female didn't appear unintelligent, or uneducated, even though she did not know how to open a door. But different species did things differently. "What planets do you know then? What ones do you travel to?"

"You mean physically or with satellites?"

"Physically."

"We've only ever traveled to our moon. We don't have any ships like the one the Ganglians took us in."

"You..." Treyvon looked at her in shock. "You do not travel to other worlds? Do not interact with other species?"

"No. While there are those that believe there is life on other planets, we've never had any direct contact with them. Not until the Ganglians took us. And now that we've 'interacted,' as you so nicely put it," she gave Treyvon a hard look, "with the Ganglians and Zaludians, I can honestly say we're not missing much!"

"I can understand that," Treyvon agreed. "You have unfortunately experienced two of the worst species in the Known Universes. Had I been able to prevent it, I would have. And if possible would like to make sure they are not the first the rest of your species encounter, but I need your help to do that."

"My help?"

"Yes, we have no idea where your home world is."

"What? How is that possible? I mean we were brought here on a ship."

"On a Ganglian ship," Treyvon said, "and none of them we have encountered contained any information on any previously unknown planets or species."

"How is that possible? Were we the only ones taken?"

"No. There was a ship six weeks ago now, a Ganglian ship. It is what brought our attention to what was happening here on Pontus." He gave her a regretful look. "They carried Jerboaian males in their haul that we believe they were going to sell to the Zaludians for the mines... and a female. But they deleted all their navigational history."

"A female?"

"Mackenzie," Nikhil turned to face her, not liking how pale she'd suddenly become.

"A Jerboaian female?" she asked, remembering the terrified squeals of the Jerboaian females as they'd been dragged away, one by one, until there were none left. Even worse, she could still hear the pain-filled cries that followed. But even more terrible was when they stopped and all you heard was the hum of the ship's engine. And you knew...

"No. She was similar to you, yet still very different, and the Ganglians severely abused her. It is why we need to understand why they abused her and not you." Treyvon flinched when Nikhil began to growl angrily at him. He understood Nikhil's anger and he hated pressing a female like this, especially one that had obviously survived a great deal, but they needed this information. The Ganglians would never have sold a female to the Zaludians. There was no point in it. They would have used her themselves then sold her if she managed to survive.

"They didn't know I was female," she whispered, putting a hand on Nikhil's chest and to Treyvon's surprise, the growling stopped.

"How could they not know?" Treyvon asked because looking at her now, there was no way he would mistake her for anything other than what she was, a beautiful female.

"We were all dressed the same. My hair was pulled up, and it wasn't this long." She touched the hair hanging down past her shoulders, absently fingering the bead in her hair. "The guys made sure they never did."

"You're saying the Ganglians never knew you were female?" Treyvon asked in disbelief.

"No. I mean yes, they never knew. They may be vicious, savage creatures," her eyes flashed at Treyvon, "but they aren't that smart. Neither were the Zaludians. They just believed what the Ganglians told them."

"Yes, they would," Treyvon agreed. "Can you tell us more?"

"M... more?" She was surprised when her voice broke on the word, but even more so when she began to tremble.

71

"Enough!" Nikhil swept her up into his arms and rose. "This is too much, too soon. She needs rest."

"Wait." That one soft word from Mac had Nikhil pausing. "The female..." Mac turned tear-filled eyes to Treyvon, who had risen when Nikhil had. "The one the Ganglians abused... What happened to her?"

"Emperor Wray Vasteri of the Tornian Empire was able to save and heal her. She is now his Empress."

With a nod, she laid her head against Nikhil's chest, and he carried her away.

∞ ∞ ∞ ∞ ∞

Nikhil carefully laid his Mackenzie down in the center of his bed, then pulled the other covers over her, and felt his heart clench at the tears that were streaming down her face. He didn't need to touch his True Mate bead to know she was in pain.

"What can I do, Mackenzie?"

"Hold me? Will you just hold me for a little bit?"

"I will hold you for as long as you wish." Reaching down, he quickly removed his boots then climbed onto the bed with her, and pulled her into his arms. "I am here, Little One, I am here."

∞ ∞ ∞ ∞ ∞

"We need to get more information from her, Treyvon," Gryf said.

Treyvon looked through the door that Nikhil had forgotten to close, and watched his most powerful warrior pull the crying female into his massive arms with more care than a mother cradling her newly presented offspring. "Not tonight, Gryf," he replied quietly.

"But..." then cut himself off when Treyvon turned his glowing blue eyes on him.

"If that was *your* True Mate," his head gestured to the couple on the bed, "would you put *anything* before what was best for her? After all that she has been through? Even us? We have been here six weeks, and unfortunately, I'm coming to believe she has been here a great deal longer than us."

"That can't be," Gryf denied. "She is too small and fragile to survive the mines. She couldn't have been there that long."

"She has because no Ganglian or Zaludian ship has landed on Pontus since we have arrived. Unless you believe they have been able to slip through our defenses."

"Impossible! We can identify every ship within a half a day of Pontus."

"So what does that tell you, Gryf? I know what it tells me."

"And what is that?"

"That we have underestimated these humans, just as the Ganglians and Zaludians did."

∞ ∞ ∞ ∞ ∞

Treyvon sat back in his chair, tapping his fingers against his lips thinking about everything that had happened and what he had learned. The female, Nikhil's True Mate, Mackenzie, while similar to the female he'd briefly met weeks ago, the one the Tornian Emperor had claimed. She was not the same. Her hair color was the major difference, he had never seen hair the color of flame before, and that's what the Emperor's Kim had. Mackenzie's was more a brown and that wasn't uncommon for a Kaliszian, although she had it covering all her head.

None of his warriors had met the other female as they'd been with a different group searching for the Emperor. Only he had seen her. Only he knew what Emperor Vasteri had threatened. Him and Liron, his Emperor. He needed to contact Liron. Leaning forward he entered the code that would connect him directly to his Emperor and friend.

"Treyvon, what are you doing up so late?" Liron asked, knowing that Treyvon was one of his few General's that drove himself relentlessly, trying to make amends for acts he was not responsible for.

"We discovered another site," Treyvon told him.

"Daco!" Liron cursed. "How bad?"

"Bad, the worse yet. Liron..."

Liron didn't like the way his General and trusted friend seemed to hesitate. "What is it Treyvon?"

"They had a female."

"What?!!" Liron exclaimed in shock. "Why? Zaludians can only join with females of their own species."

"She wasn't Zaludian."

"She was Kaliszian?"

"No. Liron... she says they are called 'humans'."

"Humans... I've never heard of them."

"Neither have I but while she is very different, she also resembles the female Emperor Vasteri discovered on the Ganglian ship."

"The one he has declared his Empress?"

"Yes."

"The one that Wray threatened to end all the food transports to us if we offered her sanctuary?"

"Yes, and there is more."

"Tell me."

"She wears Squad Leader Nikhil Kozar's True Mate bead," Treyvon informed him.

Liron's silence didn't surprise Treyvon. He knew his cousin. When surprised he took his time to consider all the new information.

"I informed you of the rumor that we are starting to hear whispers of," Liron finally said.

"That the reason Wray declared her his new Empress is because she is breeding compatible, yes."

"Which makes no sense as Wray refused to take another Empress after the death of Empress Adana, so other Tornians could have offspring."

"That was before the death of his second male," Treyvon said quietly.

"Truth," Liron agreed. "You have seen the bead yourself?"

Liron finally asked the question Treyvon knew was coming. "Yes. There can be no doubt that she is Nikhil's True Mate."

"It has been so long since a Kaliszian has found one," Liron whispered quietly. He had almost given up hope of a Kaliszian ever finding one again.

"Yes."

"It could also create a major problem."

"I know. If she is the same species as the female Wray has claimed," Treyvon started.

"And if she is breeding compatible with the Tornians," Liron continued the thought as he and Treyvon had done since they were young.

"And if the Tornians discover she is here..." Treyvon trailed off.

"They will demand we turn her over to them by threatening our food supply again," Liron finished on a hard note.

"She is the first True Mate for a Kaliszian since the dawn of the Great Infection," Treyvon knew he didn't have to remind Liron of that but he did need to tell him truth. "Nikhil will never allow her to be taken from him. Their bond is already strong even though she has no bead to offer him."

"I would never ask anyone to sacrifice their True Mate, Treyvon. Not even for the betterment of our people."

"So what are we to do?"

"Nothing. Not yet. Right now we don't even know if they are the same species. We also don't know if the new Empress is even with offspring. Until we do, we keep this information to ourselves, just as the Tornians would do if the situation was reversed."

"Alright but I must tell you truth that I do not feel right not informing Nikhil that there may be a threat to his True Mate."

"We do not know there is one, not yet. This is the way it must be, Treyvon, until we know more."

"Alright, but if there comes a time I feel Nikhil needs to be informed I want your permission to tell him." When Liron didn't immediately reply Treyvon pressed harder. "If she were yours, and at risk, you would demand to know."

"Alright but only if necessary. Once the Tornians find out about her there will be no going back.

Chapter Five

Nikhil lay on his side, his Mackenzie in his arms, and knew that if all the Known Universes were to end right then, that he would die a happy male. For all that mattered to him was in his arms. His manno had once tried to explain what it felt like to be so connected to an Ashe, but Nikhil had never truly believed him, even though he'd seen the devotion between his manno and mother.

Now he understood, for there was nothing he wouldn't do for his Mackenzie. Even ignore his General, if it meant she was cared for.

"I suppose you need to get back to your General," Mac said rubbing her cheek against his chest, trying to find the will to move away from him.

"The General and Commander left some time ago, Little One."

"They did?" She raised her head and looking through the open door, saw the room was empty. "Are you going to be in trouble?"

"Trouble?"

"Yes, because I didn't finish answering their questions."

"No, you did fine and answered what you could. The General may want to talk to you again later, but for now, it is fine."

"You're sure?"

"Yes. All you need to do right now is rest."

Mac laid her head back on Nikhil's chest with a tired sigh. She knew she needed to sleep and eat since she couldn't remember the last time she had, but there was still so much she didn't know.

"Nikhil?" she asked quickly.

"Yes?"

"Why couldn't I understand what you were saying earlier when you were talking to the General and Commander?"

"We were speaking Kaliszian, our native language."

"And what are we speaking now?"

"Zaludian."

"Zaludian. How is that possible?" Mac listened carefully, and for the first time realized she wasn't speaking English.

"Did either the Ganglians or Zaludians put a device over your eyes?"

"The Ganglians did. Two of them held down Craig and forced it on him. When they took it off him, Craig could understand them. They tossed the educator at him and left."

"They expected him to use the educator on you?" She didn't see the worried look he gave her.

"Yes. They told him that anyone who didn't agree would be killed. Once it was done, we could understand what the Ganglians were saying, and once we got here the Zaludians, but I never realized we were speaking it."

"You probably weren't amongst yourselves." When she tilted her face up frowning at him, he continued. "It is part of what the educator does. It allows you to understand a language spoken to you and for you to speak it back. If one of your males spoke to you in your language, that is the language you would respond in. You wouldn't even realize it."

"So if I wished to speak my language, you would understand it?" Mac carefully listened to herself and knew she was speaking English. She saw Nikhil frown.

"Is that your language?" he asked in Zaludian.

"Yes," she responded in Zaludian. "Did you understand what I said?"

"No, I'm sorry, Little One."

"But I thought you said..."

"You will only understand and speak the languages programmed into an educator, and it seems the Ganglians only gave you theirs and the Zaludians."

"Will I be able to learn your language?"

"Yes, Little One, and so much more." He gently caressed her cheek. "Tomorrow, if you are feeling up to it, Luol would like to place our educator on you. It will contain all the languages in the Known Universes, and also a history and background on each."

"I will be able to speak and understand you in your language?"

"Yes."

"And you will understand mine?"

"No, as it is not one of the known languages. But with time, if you and your males work with Luol, we should be able to learn and record it so it can eventually be programmed in." He saw her start to chew on her upper lip. "What is wrong, Little One?"

"It's just... I just..."

"What? You can tell me."

"I want to learn your language and know more about... well everything. It's just I hated having that thing on last time. It was uncomfortable, and I was scared."

"Uncomfortable? What do you mean?" Nikhil's entire body tensed. An educator should never cause discomfort. Had the Ganglian one harmed his Mackenzie?"

"It was hard and cold, and seemed to press so tightly against my temples." She didn't realize she reached up to touch the spot. "I didn't like it."

Nikhil rolled slightly so she was on her back, caged between his massive arms, surrounding her with his protection. "It will not be that way this time, Mackenzie, my vow. You will be safe.

"And I will understand things better, like how to open a door?"

"Yes, Little One."

"And what your beads mean?" She reached up touching the braided strands that had fallen over his shoulder.

"It will help you understand, yes. But I will tell you whatever you wish to know about my Suja beads."

"Suja beads... Why do you wear them?"

"All Kaliszians wear them." He shifted to his side, propping himself up on an elbow, then reached behind him to bring all his braids forward so she could see them. "These are my Bloodline beads, which I received during my naming ceremony shortly after my presentation."

"Presentation?"

"When I took my first breath?"

"You mean when you were born. Okay, I understand."

"This bead," he touched the red and amber one on the bottom of the braid, "represents my mother and her bloodline that now runs through me. And this one," he touched the green and amber bead above it, "represents my manno and his blood line."

"Manno... your father?"

Nikhil thought for a moment. "If father means the male whose bloodline you come from, then yes."

"So what does this one represent?" she asked, touching the large dark amber bead above it that was swirled with lighter amber.

"Me. If I am blessed with offspring, I will be able to take a portion of this bead and transfer it to him or her, claiming forever that the offspring is mine."

"And they will be able to carry that piece of you with them. Forever."

"Yes."

Mac thought about that for a moment and realized she wished she had something like that from her father. "So what ones did you get next?"

Nikhil went on to tell her about his beads, about how he earned them, how for certain achievements he received more. The majority of his beads were strung down his center braids and went nearly as high as his clip. These he refused to go into detail about how he had earned them, and only said that they were his Battle beads. Her grandpa had been that way with his medals. He would tell her what battle they were from, and the names of all the men that had been lost and how brave those men had been, but he wouldn't go further than that.

"What about this one?" she touched the single braid that hadn't been pulled over his shoulder. Instead, it brushed his massive bicep that was resting on the bed and held only one bead. A white bead with green swirling through it.

"That is my Ashe bead," he told her in a hushed tone.

"Ashe bead..."

"Yes. It is the only bead I have the power to offer to the female I wish to have my offspring. If she accepts it, she will become my Ashe, my Lady."

"But... then why is everyone addressing me as Ashe then? Why have you called me your Ashe? Why is this," she lifted the bead in her hair, a pine green bead with white swirling in it, "in my hair?"

When Nikhil didn't answer, instead looked uncomfortable, she frowned. "Nikhil?"

"That's my True Mate bead."

"True Mate?"

"Yes."

"Why did you put it on me?"

"I didn't."

"What do you mean you didn't?"

"I cannot give my True Mate bead to a female."

"What?"

"The bead makes that decision."

"The bead... it's alive?" She jerked slightly.

"Not in the way you mean," he quickly reassured her. "It is hard to explain. Suja beads are a reflection of the one wearing them. They absorb their energy and respond accordingly."

"What do you mean?"

Nikhil selected several of his braids and showed them to her. "Do you see how there is a bead at the end of each of these?"

"Yes."

"These are my Elemental beads. They always remain at the bottom of all my braids."

She carefully touched the dark beads, and while they were warm, they didn't seem to respond to her touch the way the one in her hair did. "Alright."

"The beads above them are called Attainment beads. They reflect my accomplishments or milestones that I have achieved in my life. The height of the bead on the braid indicates the worthiness of those accomplishments or milestones."

Mac reached out, taking more of his braids in her hand. Only in the center braid did the beads touch his Elemental beads, and yet there were more beads there and they extended higher than on any other braid.

"These braids are thinner." She caressed the center braids.

"I have been in many battles," he told her quietly. "If it is believed I have performed... well, then I may be awarded more beads. If that happens, the new beads are placed on one of my existing braids. The Elemental beads will then divide, and a new braid will form with the new beads migrating to that braid."

"That... that's amazing."

"It is not this way on your Earth?"

"No. Not even close."

"Then how can you know if you are dealing with someone who is worthy?"

"You have to trust what you see, and your instincts."

"What you see can be manipulated."

"Yes, it can." Mac thought back to one of her only two boyfriends. Derek, who had looked like a nice guy, but turned out to be a total jerk.

"Are you alright?" Nikhil asked.

"Yes. So these can't be manipulated, as you say, or removed?"

"They can, but only for a short period. No more than a day."

"What do you mean?"

"If I wish to thoroughly cleanse my hair, I release my Suja clip, and then I will be able to remove the beads. After I am done, they are replaced."

"How can you remember where they all go?"

"I don't, they do. While I cleanse my hair, the beads will combine. I separate my hair, into that many strands, then place an Elemental bead at the end of each one. They attach themselves, and then I replace my clip and the other beads. Within a day, they will divide and return to their proper position."

"That... that is amazing. Do you do it often?"

"No. Normal cleansing is usually enough as the beads can be moved slightly. It is only if I have been in an intense battle, or there is an important occasion I must attend that I will remove them."

Mac just lay there for several minutes, letting everything he'd said settle in, as her fingers lightly played with his beads. Some were warm, some seemed to glow, others sparkled. But there were a few, mostly the ones on the thinner braids, that were cold and made her think of violence and death. Nikhil's hand reached up and gently pulled her fingers away from them.

"You don't need to touch those," he told her quietly.

"Why do they feel that way when the others don't?"

"As I said those are my Battle beads, some... reflect moments of the battle."

"You have to carry that with you?"

"Every warrior does, whether he wears the Battle beads of it or not."

"I guess that would have to be true, but I hate to think of you carrying all that weight alone."

Nikhil lowered his forehead to hers, feeling his chest tighten at her words. She saw more than the glory the Battle beads represented; she saw what he had to do to wear them, and the burden he would carry for the rest of his existence. Yet he didn't want her to worry. Lifting his head, he reassured her. "I am strong."

"I can see that," she gently rubbed the muscle on his arm. "But some loads are too much for even the strongest to carry alone."

"That is why, if the Goddess finds a warrior worthy, he will find his Ashe." His finger ran along her cheek again.

"Ashe." Mac reached up and touched the bead still in his hair.

"Yes, but if the Goddess truly wishes to bless a male, she will grant him a True Mate." He reached down and touched his True Mate bead that was now in her hair.

"You still haven't told me how it got into my hair."

"I can't tell you because I don't know."

"What do you mean?"

"There was a time, long ago, when many found their True Mate. But since the Great Infection, there hasn't been a single one. Until you." His eyes glowed brighter as he gazed into her eyes, fingering the bead in her hair. "It is said when one meets their True Mate, their bead will transfer to them on its own. I believe... when I carried you on to the transport, my bead recognized you as mine and transferred to you."

"But... I'm not Kaliszian."

"That has never mattered. The Goddess considers us all her children, and, therefore, our True Mate can come from any species."

"I..." The sudden growling of her stomach cut her off and had her blushing.

"What was that?"

"Just my stomach. Ignore it. Tell me more about True Mates."

Nikhil's eyes widened when he realized what she was saying. Of course, she was hungry! He hadn't given her what Luol said she needed.

Food.

Rest.

Cleansing.

He'd done two of those things but had failed the most important one. Goddess, how stupid was he? How could the Goddess trust him with such a precious gift if he wasn't even smart enough to care for her? He was immediately out of the bed and rushing into the outer room.

"Nikhil?" she called out, sitting up in the bed. But the only reply she got was what sounded like cabinets opening then slamming shut. Before she could get up to find out what was going on, Nikhil was back, his arms filled with what appeared to be foil pouches that he dropped on the bed. "What are those?"

"Food packets. Warriors are given an allotment to maintain their daily needs."

"But..." She watched as he picked one up, pressed a white dot between his thumb and index finger, then grabbed the opposite end and ripped it open. She was about to say something else when she smelled the aroma of hot... something, and her stomach growled again. All she could do was stare at the steam rising from the pouch, her mouth watering.

"Open," Nikhil ordered, and looking up she saw he had a portion of the packet's contents in front of her mouth on what looked like a spoon. Obediently her mouth opened and she let him feed it to her. She closed her eyes as the most delicious thing she'd ever tasted hit her tongue. Well, the most delicious thing since she'd been taken, and she wasn't going to complain. Not after what they'd been forced to eat.

"Again," he ordered, lifting the utensil in his hand to her lips. The feeding continued until the packet was empty. Flinging it aside, he reached for another.

"No." Her hand on his stopped him from pressing the spot on another packet. "That's enough."

"It can't be. You need more. You..."

"Nikhil, I would love to eat more. I would love to gorge on everything in front of me until I burst. I never want to feel hunger like that again, but if I eat anymore, it will all just come back up."

"You don't know..."

"I do. The Ganglians... I don't know how long they had us, but they rarely fed us, and when they did, they were scraps. Except for the three meals they gave us right before they sold us to the Zaludians. The first meal we were all so hungry that we couldn't eat it fast enough and all got sick. The next two, we ate more slowly."

"They wanted you to appear strong for the Zaludians."

"Yeah, we figured that out. After that, it was only what the Zaludians gave us."

"How often was that?"

"They had the guys working in shifts, half on the first, half on the second. In between those shifts, they would bring food."

"That would be once a day."

"If you say so." She found her eyes growing heavy now that her stomach was full.

Nikhil noticed, and immediately cleared the extra packets off the bed. "Lie down, Mackenzie."

Mac wanted to protest, there were still so many questions she wanted to ask. But she found herself obeying, her eyes nearly closed.

"Later," he reassured her. "I will answer any question you have after you have rested."

"Lie with me?" she asked, her blurry gaze searching for his. "Hold me?"

"I will, Little One. Just let me dim the crystals, and I will hold you for as long as you want."

∞ ∞ ∞ ∞ ∞

"It's been a long day, Gryf. Get last meal and then get some rest. We'll deal with everything else tomorrow."

"And you? Will you be doing the same?"

"Eventually. I want to talk to Luol again." With that, Treyvon headed for medical.

Luol looked up from the tablet he was reading when the door to his office slid open, and then he leaned back in his chair. "I figured you'd be back."

Treyvon went to the chair, that was normally against the wall but was now in front of Luol's desk, and sat. "Tell me what you know, Luol."

Treyvon barely stopped the tablet, Luol pushed across the desk at him, from falling to the floor. Picking it up, he began to read.

"Is that possible?" Treyvon asked, raising his eyes to Luol.

"It's what the unit found."

"But she is so small, and I don't just mean in height. How can she be nearly identical to us?"

"The same way we are almost identical to the Tornians. You, better than anyone, know it is possible. You, yourself, translated the ancient text telling how once there was only one species, one people, one Emperor."

"It was nothing more than a fable, Luol, a story for offspring that one of our ancient ancestors wrote down for some reason. It was never meant to be taken seriously."

"I've never understood why you felt that way, Treyvon. You don't discount any of the other ancient texts, so why do you this one?"

"Because it isn't possible! We weren't able to travel between the stars that long ago!"

"But if we were, would you then believe?" Luol frowned at the expression on Treyvon's face. "Treyvon? What is wrong?"

"Don't you understand, Luol? If that text is true, if we were once one people and peace reigned, then that means something happened. Something catastrophic that separated us, something worse than the Great Infection, and it might still be out there affecting us."

Luol was silent for several minutes thinking about what his General and friend had said. He knew Treyvon carried the weight of what his ancestor, Chancellor Aadi, had done helping to cause the Great Infection that had quickly spread throughout all the Known Universes. It wasn't Treyvon's weight to carry, but he refused to believe that and worked his entire life to prove he had nothing in common with Aadi. That's why Luol understood why Treyvon would see the text as he did. He worried that maybe another one of his ancestors had done something.

"Or maybe what caused it is fading. We rediscovered the Tornians millenniums ago. We know both races are similar to the Ratakians, and now we've found these Humans. Perhaps what the ancient texts say once was, is trying to return."

"Perhaps." Treyvon looked at Luol, returning to the original subject. "I've just come from Nikhil's quarters and spoke with his Ashe. You said you would be giving her another treatment?"

"Yes, I told Nikhil to bring her back tomorrow. After, if she is up to it, I plan to place our educator on her so she will be able to understand and speak Kaliszian, and better understand what has happened to her and her people."

"Do you think it will help her understand where she is?"

"What do you mean? She doesn't know she's on Pontus?"

"She knows she is on a planet called Pontus, and that the Ganglians took her and the others from her planet. A planet called Earth. But she can't tell me where it is in relation to Pontus, and has never heard of any of the other planets I named. Could it just be because of the educator used on her that the names don't translate for her properly?"

"It could be. The Ganglians wouldn't have put much effort into the programming since they were selling them. They only needed to be able to understand the orders they were given. I will adjust the educator, and give her a more detailed location of the planets. That might help."

"She says the people of her world do not travel to other worlds, that they've never interacted with other intelligent species."

Luol's eyes widened. "They've never traveled in space?"

"She says they have only traveled physically to their moon. From the way she said it, I don't believe it could be that far from the planet."

"If that is the case, then no amount of detail I put in the educator is going to help her tell us where this Earth is."

"I was afraid of that. If she, or one of her males, can't tell us, then there is no way for us to get them home."

"What's bothering you, Treyvon?"

"Nikhil has found his True Mate with a species we didn't even know existed. The first True Mate since the Great Infection struck. What if there are more on this Earth, and we can't even find it?"

"Then we must find it. Because if the Ganglians can, we can. We are better than them."

"Truth," Treyvon agreed. "When will you begin treating the other humans?"

"I want to treat the others first, and have sent word to have the Jerboaians brought here."

"Why?" Treyvon demanded.

"Each human is going to require a great deal of time. Not only with the time they will need in the deep-repair unit, but also, because they will need the use of our educator. Ashe Mackenzie had nearly succumbed to the injuries inflicted on her. Had she not, I would have delayed placing her in the unit."

"Why?" Treyvon asked again.

"Because I believe she would have tolerated the treatments better had she been rested and fed."

"You said she tolerated it well."

"Her body did while she was unconscious. But she woke before the unit had finished and she panicked, not understanding what was going on. If Nikhil had not been there, and been able to calm her because of their bond, she might have severely harmed herself."

"But that wouldn't be the case with the males. You could explain..."

"I would still like them to have some rest and nourishment before that. It would also be helpful if Ashe Mackenzie were completely healed and has experienced our educator. These beings have been treated harshly by two of the worst species the Known Universes have to offer. They are not going to readily trust us. We wouldn't if the situation were reversed."

"Truth," Treyvon found he couldn't disagree.

"The Jerboaians, Tafaians, and Nekeokians are known species and are used to repair units. They will not fight or question what we are trying to do."

"Also, we will then be able to return them to their homes sooner." Treyvon nodded his head in agreement. "I can agree with this as long as there are no humans as injured as Nikhil's Ashe was."

"The report I received from Parlan stated they were all able to walk onto the transport with no assistance."

"Alright. I trust your judgment on how to proceed with this." Treyvon rose from the chair. "I expect you to keep me informed."

"Of course, General."

∞ ∞ ∞ ∞ ∞

Parlan couldn't believe he'd been assigned this task. He was Warrior Parlan Spada! He could trace his manno's bloodline back to the dawn of the Kaliszian Empire, and his mother's manno's brother was currently one of the most influential Ministers in all the Empire. It was beneath him to have to be dealing with 'survivors'. If they were stupid enough to be captured by the Ganglians, then they deserved what they got.

But Goddess they stunk, and they were dirty, and they were *ugly.* Especially the ones he'd been ordered to guide out of the mine. And now... *now* he'd been ordered to bring them nourishment! There were warriors that didn't have his status that should be doing this menial task. Warriors like Gulzar, who had yet to achieve Elite status, and if Parlan had any say in it he never would.

Gulzar came from an inferior bloodline, one that had never produced an Elite Warrior and Parlan intended to make sure that bloodline never did. Gulzar didn't know his place, thought he would be Parlan's equal if he became an Elite. He was wrong. Gulzar would never be his equal. Pushing the doors open to the area where the survivors were housed, he stepped inside.

"Put them over there," he ordered the two warriors following behind him. All but the humans quickly moved toward the boxes, knowing what was in them. Parlan turned to face them.

"I forgot, you *humans,*" he said the word as if it were distasteful on his tongue, "know nothing, and that I must speak Zaludian. I am Warrior Parlan. I am an Elite Kaliszian Warrior and General Rayner, the Supreme Commander, realizing I am the worthiest of his Warriors has tasked me with overseeing you. As you were with the Zaludians the shortest amount of time, you will be the last to see our Healer. Cots will be brought unless your species prefers sleeping on the floor." The look on the warrior's face said that is what he assumed.

"We would prefer cots." Craig stood facing the warrior. "Blankets would be appreciated too."

"I will order them brought," Parlan made it sound as if it were a hardship.

"And food."

Parlan growled at him. "That is what has been provided *there*." Parlan pointed angrily behind him. "General Rayner has ordered you to be treated as a Kaliszian."

"What does that mean?" Craig asked.

"It means you will receive three meals a day, just as a real Kaliszian would, even though you obviously aren't worthy of being one," he sneered. "It means a worthy Kaliszian on some other planet will have to do without because of it. It also means that new coverings will be supplied to you along with proper foot coverings. But before you place them on, you *must* cleanse. Wash that stink from your bodies," he expressed, as if they didn't know what that meant, and pointed. "The room is over there."

Once Craig nodded he understood, Parlan turned and walked away.

Chapter Six

Mac lay on her side, her head comfortably resting on Nikhil's impressive bicep while she stared at his sleeping form that was facing her. She couldn't remember the last time she'd slept so deeply or so peacefully, even back on Earth, and it was all because Nikhil had held her while she slept. He'd quickly dimmed the crystals, and then stripped before climbing into bed with her, pulling the remaining covers over them both. He slid an arm beneath her head, and the other around her blanket-covered waist and pulled her close making her feel safe and secure.

While the other covers had remained around her shoulders as they'd slept, they had fallen off Nikhil's giving her an incredible view of his massive chest, a chest that was slowly rising and falling. Her fingers slowly traveled over his large, pectoral muscle grazing its hard, flat nipple. She slowly circled it several times, watching it tighten at her touch, before her fingers moved up and along his side learning the bulge of each muscle, and the depths in between them. His skin was so warm and smooth without the marks and scars the Battle beads indicated he should have. How was that possible? Her fingers continued their sensual journey, slipping under the blanket that had settled just above his hips, when Nikhil's hand stopped her from exploring further.

"Mackenzie..." he growled, and her eyes shot up to find him awake, and watching her intently. Gently gripping her hand, he slowly pulled it back up his body until it reached his lips, and he kissed her palm.

Mac felt her heart melt at the sweetness of the action. No one had ever treated her with such care before as if she were the only thing that mattered to them.

"Did you rest well, Little One?" he asked, his eyes glowing softly, his voice husky with sleep.

"I did." Moving her hand slightly, she cupped his jaw, her thumb caressing his full lower lip. "Thanks to your arms around me."

Nikhil allowed his large, calloused hand to slide along her arm, unable to believe how smooth and silky her skin felt. The bruises that had been there the day before had faded away. While he knew the deep-repair unit had been responsible for that, it wouldn't have made her skin feel like this. Not if it wasn't the way it was naturally supposed to be. He had thought it was the cleanser that had made her skin feel this way when he'd cleansed her, but now he wanted to know if her skin was like this all over, and felt his shaft hardening at the thought of finding out.

Mac saw Nikhil's eyes flare, and felt the hardness growing between them. She knew it was his cock and felt her channel clench in response. Sliding her hand along his jaw, she gripped the back of his neck and pulled his lips down to hers.

Nikhil's entire body stiffened as Mackenzie pressed her lips fully against his for the first time. Goddess, they were softer than he ever imagined they could be. He'd woken to her fingers running over him, and it had felt amazing, but this, this was something more. He needed to stop her delicate fingers from exploring further because he wasn't sure she understood what she was doing to him.

"Mackenzie..." he whispered against her lips.

Mac pulled back slightly, gazing up at Nikhil. She wasn't sure what had made her kiss him like that. She'd never been the aggressor in her previous relationships, but after everything he'd said about them being True Mates, and kissing her palm, she hadn't been able to stop herself. Now she could see that was a mistake. She had totally misread the situation.

"I'm sorry." She immediately dropped her hand, then pulled the blanket tightly between her breasts keeping it from falling further, and slid out from under the other covers to stand.

"Mackenzie..." Nikhil frowned at her. What was she apologizing for? Why had she stopped touching him? Why was she getting out of their bed?

"The cleansing room... I assume there is something in there that I can use to... relieve myself."

"Yes, I will show you..." Nikhil moved to get out of the bed.

"No!" She held out her hand stopping him, then moved quickly around the foot of the bed. "I'm sure I can figure it out." With the blanket swishing behind her, she entered the cleansing chamber then quickly turned looking for the crystal to close the door. Seeing it, she pressed it then watched Nikhil rise from the bed, the blankets falling away revealing more and more of his naked glory. The door slid closed before she got a full frontal.

Nikhil rose not understanding why his Ashe didn't want him to help her. Hadn't he just proven he was worthy by not taking advantage of her in her weakened state? Why had she run from him? Why had she shut him out? Had his body's reactions to her closeness caused her to distrust him? He needed to correct that.

∞ ∞ ∞ ∞ ∞

Mac leaned her forehead against the door, her breath coming out in little gasps. Dear God, she'd nearly gotten a full frontal of Nikhil. If the blanket hadn't snagged on the bed she would have, and she wasn't sure if she was grateful for that or resentful.

Pushing away from the door, she took in the room that she'd spent so much time in yesterday. Well, she'd actually spent it all in the shower with Nikhil... No, she wouldn't think about that.

Along the far wall, she saw several crystals. Moving across the room to them, she pushed the top one and what looked like an alien urinal appeared. Quickly, she pushed the crystal again, and it disappeared.

Pressing the next crystal, what appeared to be a tankless toilet popped out of the wall, and she sighed in relief. She hadn't realized how badly she needed to use it until she saw it. Turning, she was about to remove the blanket that had been covering her when the cleansing room door slid open.

"What the fuck?" Her hands tightened on the blanket as Nikhil stormed in, grateful to see he had at least pulled on his pants. "I shut that door!"

"You did not seal it."

"Well, how the hell do I do that?"

"You hold the crystal down."

"Then get out and I will."

"Mackenzie... what is wrong? Why are you so angry?"

"Why? Oh, I don't know why? I mean, what do I have to be angry about? I was taken from my home against my will. Sold as a slave, then starved and beaten when it was discovered I was female! Then I get thrown into some God damn tube, and when I come out, I'm supposedly the True Mate to someone I've never met!" Mac found she was slapping her hands against his chest with each exclamation, and that he was backing up with each one. "Now all I want is some *privacy*! Some time to figure out what the hell is what, and you come storming in here acting like *I* owe *you* an explanation!"

"Mackenzie... I am only trying to help..."

97

Mac felt her eyes fill because she knew he was telling her the truth. He was only attempting to help. She was the one that seemed to be wanting more.

"I know," she said trying to calm down. "I just need a few minutes alone. Please. Let me take care of what I need to and then I'll be out. Maybe you could find me some clothes?"

"Clothes? You mean coverings?"

"Ummm, yeah, sure, coverings. As long as that's something that means I don't have to walk around naked."

"You will not do that!" Nikhil growled.

"I have no plans to if you can find me something adequate."

"I will do so."

"Then I will be out in a few minutes." With that, Nikhil was outside the room, and she pressed the crystal, and, this time, she held it and heard the silent 'snick' of the lock engaging.

Nikhil stared silently at the now sealed door of the cleansing room, unsure of what just happened. There had been tears in his Mackenzie's eyes, tears of hurt and confusion. Why? He had thought he had adequately explained what had happened, was happening between them. His True Mate had seemed willing to rest in his arms, implying it was why she had rested so well. Yet she had jerked out of his arms after pressing her lips to his.

It had been Nikhil's first kiss from a female, well a female not his mother or sister. He had wanted to take it further, the way his mother and manno did. He'd seen them kiss on the lips many times, and knew it was the way to show affection between a male and his Ashe, but that was never done in relationships that a bead had not been exchanged.

He had wanted to kiss his Mackenzie on the lips, had wished to share that special intimacy with her, but he hadn't been sure what practices her species followed. So he'd forced himself to settle for kissing her palm instead, hoping she would accept it and know how much she meant to him.

He hadn't been prepared for the feelings that had rushed through him as she touched his jaw, her thumb caressing his lip. Or for the suddenness of her pressing her lips to his. His entire body had just frozen, not sure what to do, and then she was gone.

He had caught the flash of hurt in her eyes before she'd fled his bed. Had he somehow insulted her? Hurt her with his response? Or lack of it? He just hadn't wanted to do anything wrong... but still he had.

Spinning away from the door, he went to the far wall and pressed a crystal revealing his closet. Looking at his coverings, he frowned. There was nothing here she could wear; there were only his uniforms. He'd never been like some males that would purchase pretty coverings to entice a female to share her friendship with him. He would on occasion find something special on the planet where he was stationed, and send it home to his mother or sisters, but Pontus had no such things.

He growled angrily at his stupidity for not planning for every possibility, something that as Squad Leader was his duty if he wanted to keep his warriors alive. He scanned the contents one last time and saw the sleeve of a covering pressed against the wall. Pulling it out, he let his gaze run over it.

It was a covering with long sleeves that was meant to be worn by a warrior if he were suddenly caught out in a Pontus ground storm. It was made from a very thin, but nearly impenetrable material that was easily stored in a Warrior's kit. If a storm suddenly appeared, all a warrior needed to do was pull it on over his head and he was protected.

It would have to do for now until he was able to provide his True Mate with proper coverings. The sound of the cleansing room door opening had him turning to find his Mackenzie slowly walking toward him.

"I'm sorry about coming unglued on you back there." She gestured to the cleansing room with her head.

"Unglued?" Nikhil frowned at the word.

"It's a figure of speech. I yelled at you for no good reason."

"You felt you had a reason."

"But not a good one."

"You have been through much, Mackenzie. I did not mean for my actions to make you feel uncomfortable."

"They didn't. You have been nothing but kind and understanding, Nikhil, going way beyond what was necessary. It's my own actions that have made me uncomfortable, and you too it seems."

"I do not understand."

"I realize that, after all, we've just met, are two entirely different species, and literally don't speak the same language. It makes 'misunderstandings' really easy. Especially on my part." She looked at what he was holding in his hand. "Is that for me?"

"What?" He looked to where she pointed and remembered the covering in his hand. "Yes. It is just a storm covering, it's all I have for now. But I will acquire something else for you. Something better, prettier, more..."

"Nikhil, stop!" she cut him off. "I'm sure whatever it is will be fine after wearing the same coverings for... I don't know how long. Anything would be better. You don't have to acquire anything else for me."

She reached out for the shirt but stopped short of touching him. She wasn't going to force herself on him again. She knew he said she was his True Mate because of the bead in her hair. She had assumed that it was something like Soul Mates back on Earth, that they would share a deep love and affection for each other. Something she found she was already feeling for the large male. But for her that included touching and kissing, but Nikhil had stopped her from touching him and not responded to her kiss. Was it something different for a Kaliszian? Until she found out, she would proceed with caution.

Nikhil braced himself for her touch, ordering his body not to respond and frighten her again. But it was all for nothing when she just held out her hand and waited. She'd willingly done so in the cleansing stall the night before, and again as she rested. She'd even willingly caressed his jaw with her tiny hand. Had his actions caused her to fear touching him? Carefully, making sure not to touch or startle her, he placed the covering in her hand.

"I'll... I'll just step back into the cleansing room and change." Turning, she hurried away.

Nikhil watched her go with troubled eyes, not liking how quickly she moved away from him. He needed to win back her trust, to show her he was worthy of being her Dasho and True Mate. He just needed to figure out how to do that.

Mac just stared at herself in the mirror for several minutes taking in her appearance. The shirt, no covering, Nikhil had given her had been loose when she'd first put it on, the ends of its long sleeves going way past her fingertips. The neckline hung like a cowl neck, and the bottom went past her knees. But after wearing it for several moments, she felt it begin to tighten, to conform to her body.

The sleeves were still long, reaching halfway down her fingers, but she found she liked it there. The cowl neck had receded to become more of a tight turtleneck but didn't feel restrictive in any way. The rest of the covering had changed too. It now hugged her body like a second skin, and the hem was now several inches above her knees.

She'd seen other woman wear dresses like this on Earth, but they had always had those perfect, amazingly toned bodies to show off. She didn't. Turning slightly, she looked at the way the material seemed to hug her ass. She had to admit it didn't look half bad, and there wasn't a line or seam to be seen since her underwear was one of the first things to succumb to the harsh conditions they'd endured. It's what she got for indulging herself in lacy bra and panty sets instead of practical ones. Facing forward again, she realized the material lifted and cupped her breasts better than any bra could. When she moved they didn't bounce around, but that was probably because of how small they were now.

Her brown hair, that Nikhil had taken so much time cleansing, fell around her face in soft waves that reached the upper curve of her breasts. She'd never had her hair this long before. It had to be at least three inches longer than when they'd been taken from Earth. Could that in any way tell them how long ago that was? She had no clue how fast a person's hair grew. Maybe Jen or one of the guys did.

"Shit!" she exclaimed quietly. Here she was looking at her hair, worrying about the way Nikhil's shirt fit, about him not liking her kissing him, and she hadn't given one thought to her friends! Where were they? How were they? Were they being treated well? Had they discovered Jen yet? Spinning around, she went to find Nikhil and get some answers.

She found him in the outer room, dressed in his full uniform with the complete accompaniment of weapons from the day before, minus the sword strapped to his back. But it lay just within reach. He had an array of silver packets sitting on the table in front of him.

Nikhil heard the door to the cleansing room open and turned to let her know where he was. But the words remained lodged in his throat. He'd never known a mere storm covering would look so sexy on a female. On *his* female. The material was made to conform to the wearer's body, preventing the elements of the storm from harming the wearer. But this... It accentuated every curve, every line of the beautiful body he had cleansed last night. Goddess! She was beautiful. The crackling of a packet being crushed in his hands brought him out of his daze.

"Which would you like?" he asked gruffly.

"I'm fine," she replied even though her stomach growled quietly in protest. "I need to know about the others."

"The others?"

"Yes. Where are they? Are they okay? Have they gotten anything to eat?"

"Mackenzie, I am sure they are fine."

"You're *sure*. That means you don't *know* they are. My God, they must be worried out of their minds about me. I need to get to them."

"I *know* that all the survivors are being kept in one area. I *know* that they have been fed, allowed to cleanse, and given places to rest. I *know* that if any were in dire condition, the warrior in charge of them would have brought them to Luol for treatment. None were while you were there."

"How can you know all that?"

"Because it has been the procedure for the survivors we found at the other sites."

"Other sites... you mean there were more places... more mines..."

"Yes," he told her quietly, wanting to hit himself for revealing that. Especially when he saw her pale.

"How many?"

"Yours was the sixth one we found."

"Six...?"

"We believe we have found them all."

"Why?"

"Because no more Zaludian ships have attempted to approach Pontus since our arrival six weeks ago. We have learned they arrived once a month to retrieve the mined crystals and restock the sites."

"Then why were they still having us mine?"

"That I do not know, but I'm sure the General will discover it from the Zaludian survivors."

"Some survived?"

"I would think so, although I do not know that for truth. There were some from other sites."

"And were there any other humans found?"

"No, Mackenzie. You were the first of your kind we found." He lifted the packet again. "Will you eat now?"

"I need to *know* they are okay." Her eyes pleaded with his, and Nikhil found he could refuse her nothing. But that didn't mean he wasn't going to get his way too.

"I can contact the warrior in charge and find out, but only if you eat while I do. You have been through a great deal."

"So have they."

"Yes, but *you* are the only one I'm concerned about." Nikhil refused to back down in this. She was his True Mate, and hopefully one day his Ashe, and while it seems he had done some things wrong in caring for her, this he would do right.

"Alright," she finally said. Sitting down, she chose a packet.

"Let me help..." He reached out to take it from her, but her look stopped him.

"I saw how you did it last night." She pinched the dot. "I'm not stupid, you know."

"I never thought you were. I was just trying to help."

"Help by finding out about my friends. You said you would if I ate." She ripped the top off the pouch, grabbed one of the utensils on the table, and began to eat.

Nikhil unclipped the comm he carried at his waist and contacted Warrior Parlan.

Parlan had just finished enjoying his first meal when his comm rang. "Parlan," he answered, his displeasure at being contacted before going on duty easily heard.

"Warrior Parlan, this is Squad Leader Kozar."

Parlan sat up straighter hearing who was contacting him. Squad Leader Kozar was someone you didn't want to be on the wrong side of; not even him. For not only was Nikhil the largest among them, but he was also one of the strongest. He never said more than needed saying, letting his skill with the sword, blaster, and blade speak for him. His manno was also in the employ of Minister Descarga, one of the most influential and respected ministers in the Empire. Not even Parlan's own connection with Minister Stepney would help him if he offended Descarga.

"Squad Leader! What can I do for you?"

"I want to know the condition of the humans."

"Humans... Oh, you mean those filthy, strange-looking creatures that were rescued yesterday."

Nikhil gritted his teeth, glad that Mackenzie still didn't understand Kaliszian so she couldn't understand Parlan.

"Their condition?" he demanded.

"I have not yet checked on them this morning, but they were fine when I went off duty last night. Food, cots, and clean coverings were provided as the General ordered, and I assume they knew how to cleanse themselves."

"Did you show them how to use the cleansing room?"

"Why would I do that? Every known species knows how to use a cleansing unit."

"But they are not a known species to us or us to them." Parlan remained silent. "Were any of them taken to Luol?"

"No. None of them mentioned the need."

"Because they would know they could, right? As they know nothing about us." Nikhil had never liked Parlan. Oh, he was a highly, efficient warrior and did his duty, but he never did more than that and felt he was always entitled to more because of his family's bloodline and connection to Minister Stepney.

"I want you to go and check on them, and then report their condition to me."

"With all due respect, Squad Leader, General Treyvon assigned me this duty. I follow his orders and report to him. When it is my assigned time to see to that duty, I will." With that, Parlan disconnected his comm.

Nikhil couldn't believe it! That self-important caca had disconnected from him. Him! Squad Leader! While Parlan was right that he didn't report to Nikhil, not in this, he had forgotten that he did report to him on the training fields. Nikhil would make him pay for this insult.

"What did he say?" Mackenzie's question pulled his thoughts away from his and Parlan's next encounter on the fields.

"That they received food, beds, and new coverings. That none requested to see the Healer."

"Did they know they could?" she immediately asked.

"Wouldn't they have if one of them was in dire straights? They were informed we were treating you."

"They were?"

"Yes." He saw she had finished the packet she had chosen. "Do you need more?"

"No."

"Then are you ready to return to medical?"

"I'd rather check on my friends." She frowned when he seemed to hesitate and stood to confront him. "Nikhil? What are you keeping from me? Why don't you want me to go there first?"

"I am not keeping anything from you!" Nikhil reached out, cupping her cheek before he could stop himself. "My vow. I only thought that you would be better able to assist your... friends, if you had a better understanding of the world you are all now in. You can't do that without first using our educator."

Mac stilled at his touch. It surprised her, especially after the way he reacted to her lips on his. Maybe he was right. If she couldn't understand what was going on between them, after the time she'd spent with Nikhil, how was she going to be able to explain it to everyone else. She needed to use their educator.

"Alright," she finally said. "Let's go see Luol. The sooner this is done, the sooner I can be with my friends."

Nikhil frowned at that. Did she really expect him to just let her leave him, to let other males surround her? It wasn't going to happen, but he knew he couldn't tell her that right now.

"Let us go to the Medical Wing, and Luol can finish treating you, and then he can apply the educator."

"Finish? What do you mean?"

"You became agitated while the deep-repair unit treated you. Luol wanted me to bring you back today so it could finish replenishing your system with what you have lost."

"Replenish..."

"It means to restore what your body has lost."

"I know what it means," she told him shortly. "You never said anything about needing more treatments, only that I needed to use the educator."

"I... I did not mean to mislead you, Little One. We discussed so many things yesterday that I didn't realize we had not discussed that."

Mac stared up into Nikhil's softly glowing eyes and knew he was telling her the truth. She wasn't sure how she knew, she'd never been that good at reading men before, her past relationships were proof of that. But somehow with Nikhil she just *knew*.

"Alright, but I'm tired of only being told what others think I need to know." She watched Nikhil stiffen before he sunk onto the couch, his hand running over the tightly restrained hair on the top of his head.

"That was never my intention, Mackenzie. I have only tried to care for you to the best of my abilities. I am greatly sorry that I have failed you."

Mac felt her mouth drop open. She hadn't meant for Nikhil to take her words so personally or for him to feel like he had failed her. Ever since she'd seen him in that mine, he'd been the only one she'd known she could completely trust. Why did she doubt that now? Because he was no longer essential to her survival? Wasn't that wrong? God, she was so messed up.

"Nikhil..." she slowly moved and sat down beside him. "You haven't failed me. How could you even think that? From the first moment I laid eyes on you, *you* have been my one constant, the only one I've totally trusted, the only one whose only concern was for me. *Me*." She started to reach out and touch him but pulled her hand back. "I know I'm not what you were looking for when you woke up yesterday. All you wanted to do was your duty, not get saddled with a mess like me."

"Saddled?"

"Burdened with..."

"Burdened?" Nikhil's eyes began to burn more than glow, and he gripped her upper arms lifting her off the couch, pulling her in front of him so they were eye to eye. "You think you are a *burden* to me?!! That I regret having you come into my life?"

She let out a little squeak when Nikhil pulled her onto his lap, her hands gripping the thick muscles of his arms, that were now vibrating with rage, for balance. She should have been terrified at being manhandled like this, especially after how the Zaludians had treated her, but she wasn't. This was Nikhil, and he'd never harm her.

"I think." She carefully licked her lips before continuing. "That I have complicated your life. I'm a mess, Nikhil. My emotions are all over the place. I'm happy I'm alive, and scared out of my mind at the same time. I want to be with my friends. They are the only ones that really understand what I've gone through, and yet..."

"And yet?"

"And yet I don't want to leave you," she whispered. "That's not fair to you, not when you are only doing what you feel you must because of this." She reached up and touched his True Mate bead in her hair.

"Mackenzie..." The anger that had filled him quickly faded, He had failed her because he hadn't adequately explained the connection between True Mates. She was feeling it, and it was confusing her. Especially after all that had happened to her. He would not fail her again. Taking a deep breath, he spoke to her from his heart.

"You truly don't understand what a gift... a blessing from the Goddess herself, it is to have a True Mate. You complete me in a way I cannot adequately express. I am no longer alone, there is now more to my life than just duty and battle. There is *you*." His gaze traveled over her, and he still couldn't believe she was here. "I know this is all new and confusing to you. Your people seem to practice different traditions and don't have True Mates, but..."

"We have something similar," she whispered. "We call them Soul Mates."

"Soul Mates," Nikhil tried the words on his lips.

"Yes. They are said to be a person's other half. The one that makes them whole."

"As you have made me." Nikhil's knuckle gently caressed her cheek.

"Have I?" she asked looking up at him uncertainly.

Nikhil frowned at the doubt he saw in her eyes. "Yes! What is making you question it? I already feel you, here." He thumped a fist against his chest. "You are a part of me. The most precious part."

"Then why..." she bit her bottom lip and looked away.

"Then why what?" Nikhil cupped her chin, tipping it up then waited for her to look at him. "Mackenzie... tell me."

"Why do you not want me to touch you or kiss you? Is it something Kaliszians don't do?"

"No! I mean, yes! Yes, we do touch and kiss."

"But you don't want to with me."

"Of course, I do!"

"Then why did you stop me from touching you. Why didn't you like it when I kissed you?"

"I *did*!" he instantly denied. He couldn't believe it; *this* was what was causing all her doubt and confusion. Him, trying to restrain himself so he wouldn't overwhelm her? Well if that were the case, he would show her exactly how much he wanted her. Sinking his fingers into her lush dark hair, he pulled her lips to his.

Chapter Seven

Mac was shocked when Nikhil's fingers suddenly sank into her hair and pulled her forward, capturing her lips in a hard kiss. She hadn't expected it, but before she could respond, he pulled away.

"You think that I do not want you?" he growled, ripping his lips away from hers. "That I wouldn't welcome your touch, your lips, *anywhere* on me?"

Before she could answer, he captured her lips again and gave her a longer, harder kiss that had her heart pounding, and her hands gripping his braids.

"You are my True Mate," he said breaking off the kiss again to glare down at her, "and I will never be able to live without you now that I have found you."

"Nikhil!" It was Mac's turn to growl, and she tugged on his braids. "Stop teasing and *kiss* me!"

Nikhil's eyes widened slightly at her demand, and then obeyed, covering her mouth with his, his tongue demanded entry and she gave it.

She let out a little cry of joy as her tongue touched Nikhil's and she tasted him for the first time. He tasted like that first crisp hint of winter on a cold mountain morning. Fresh, clean, and welcoming, at least to her.

Nikhil's hands moved, one cupping the back of her head, tilting it so he could attack her mouth from a different angle. It all felt amazing, and she let herself sink deeper into the kiss as her tongue curled around his returning the caress. She'd kissed a man before, had been kissed back by one, but it had never been like this. Nikhil was strength and gentleness, demand and retreat, his tongue first caressing then sparring with hers. All the while his other hand slid down along her back until he

111

reached bare skin where his shirt ended along her thigh and the calloused tips of his fingers began caressing her skin.

Mac broke off the kiss gasping for breath and gazed up into Nikhil's glowing eyes. "Damn, you're a good kisser," she whispered.

"So are you," Nikhil growled, pulling her lips back to his and she couldn't wait for the next assault on her senses. Instead, Nikhil stilled and pulled back to gaze down at her sharply, the glow in his eyes changing. "You've kissed a male on the lips before."

"Of course." She tried to close the distance between their lips, but was held firmly in place, and she looked up at him in confusion. "Nikhil?"

"Many males?" he questioned.

"A couple. I don't see what..."

"Only Pleasure Workers kiss males on the lips," he told her shortly.

"Pleasure workers?" Mac jerked her mouth away from his. She knew what a pleasure worker was. The Zaludians had meant to sell her to a Pleasure House. The one wearing the red beads had gone into great detail about how with her many 'openings', a wide variety of males would be able to find their relief with her. He'd been nearly giddy with the amount he planned on selling her for. "Pleasure worker! You think I'm a Pleasure Worker because I've kissed a few guys?!!" She jumped off his lap. "How *dare* you!"

"A female only kisses her Dasho on the lips."

"What?"

"A female..."

"I heard you. Are you telling me you've never kissed a female before? Never had sex with one?"

"I have kissed a female before," Nikhil jerked back at the thought she believed him inexperienced. "There have been several females that have sought out my friendship, and my lips have brought them great pleasure. But I have never kissed their lips, and they have never kissed mine!"

"Friendship is sex?" she asked frowning.

"I do not know this word," Nikhil told her.

"Sex. You sticking that," she pointed to the visible outline of his cock in his pants, "inside a female."

"Yes, that is friendship."

"So you have had sex with Pleasure Workers!" she accused.

"Never! I would never seek out a Pleasure Worker! I have only offered my friendship to worthy and honorable females! Ones I respect. We exchange friendship. We do not kiss on the lips!"

Mac paled at his words. "Worthy and honorable... so you and your females can fuck all you want, do whatever you want with your mouths, and as long as you don't kiss each other on the lips, you are considered worthy and honorable."

"Yes. The meeting of lips is the most intimate of acts and reserved for one's Ashe. This is readily known."

Mac took a stumbling step back. Nikhil thought she was some slut, a whore, a Pleasure Worker, all because she knew how to kiss. Because she had kissed other men on the lips.

"Mackenzie..." Nikhil frowned at her reaction to his words. "Is it not that way on your Earth?"

"No. Kissing is not the most intimate act."

"Then what is?"

"It doesn't matter. It's not going to happen." She forced herself to look at Nikhil, who was slowly rising from the couch, a determined look on his face. "You need to take me to Luol."

"We will finish discussing this first."

113

"No, we won't. I'm not feeling well, and I want to see Luol." She wasn't lying; the food she'd eaten didn't want to stay in her stomach. Spinning on her heel, she headed for the door.

∞ ∞ ∞ ∞ ∞

Luol looked up when he heard the door to the medical unit open, and was surprised to see Mackenzie entering, Nikhil following close behind. He knew Nikhil would be bringing her in so he could complete her treatment, but he hadn't thought it would be this early. He also hadn't expected the tension that seemed to surround them.

"Mackenzie isn't feeling well," Nikhil told him tensely getting straight to the point. He hadn't liked that she wouldn't let him carry her to Luol. Hadn't liked how she kept her distance from him, making sure they didn't touch. He especially hadn't liked other warriors looking at her as they passed.

Luol was immediately across the room. "What is wrong, Mackenzie? Are you in pain?"

"No. My stomach's just a little upset."

"I see." Luol scanned her with his palm unit. "That's to be expected with the difference and quantity of food you are now receiving. I find no signs of illness."

"Squad Leader told me you needed to complete treating me this morning." She used the title she'd heard Nikhil addressed as.

"I... yes," Luol's gaze shot to Nikhil and saw the warrior stiffen at her use of his title.

"After that it's the educator?" she continued.

"If you are up to it." Luol returned his attention to Mackenzie.

"I will be. So where? In there again?" She pointed to the room Nikhil had carried her out of the day before.

"Yes."

"Then let's get this show on the road." She started toward the room. "The sooner this is done, the sooner I can get back to where and with who I belong."

Luol just stared at her retreating back, shocked by her words. Didn't she understand that her place was now with Nikhil? Looking to the giant warrior, he saw that Nikhil was more than shocked, he was devastated, and Luol took a step toward him. "Nikhil..."

Nikhil just shook his head, his lips clamped tightly together, and followed his Mackenzie into the next room. Inside, he found her struggling to get onto the bed of the deep-repair unit that was set at the waist height of a Kaliszian. He immediately moved to lift her onto the bed, but she spun around, and her quiet words stopped him.

"Do not touch me," she hissed, then doing a deep knee bend gripped the bed frame and jumped, finally making it on the bed. Wiggling, she made sure her covering was pulled down as far as possible and swung her legs up onto the bed.

"I assume I need to be lying down?" she asked Luol, who had entered behind Nikhil.

"For the unit to close. Yes." Luol watched as she lay down, keeping her arms at her sides, her hands fisting the material of her covering as she stared directly up at the ceiling. What could possibly have happened between these two that had her acting this way? "Are you comfortable, Ashe Mackenzie? Warm enough?" His eyes went to her bare feet. It was still early and the floors of the base had to have been cold on her feet.

"I'm fine."

"It is surprising that your feet were not damaged by your time in the mine," Luol commented absently as he began pushing buttons on the control panel.

"That's because I was wearing boots."

"Boots?" Luol gave her a puzzled look.

"Foot coverings?" she finally turned her head to look at Luol. "Like you and N... like you are wearing." She barely stopped herself from using Nikhil's name.

"I don't remember you wearing any when you were brought in. Did you remove them for some reason, Nikhil?" Although Luol turned to Nikhil for answers, it was Mac who replied.

"No. The Zaludians removed them after they discovered me."

"Why would they do that?" Luol asked.

"So they could inspect me to see if I had any hidden orifices that would make me more valuable when they sold me as a Pleasure Worker." She ignored Luol's shocked expression, and looked back to the ceiling. "Can we just get this over with?"

After a moment, the curved cover of the repair unit began to slide up from her feet until she was fully enclosed in the tube. The bed began to hum, and a fine mist appeared.

"Just breathe normally, Ashe Mackenzie," Luol instructed. "This won't take long."

"Stop calling me that! My name is Mackenzie or Mac, if you want. I'm no one's Ashe." With that said, she closed her eyes.

Nikhil could only stare at his Mackenzie in disbelief, the pain flooding his system nearly driving him to his knees. He'd been in hundreds of battles, thousands it seemed. He'd watched warriors die, some as close to him as brothers. He had been injured himself, and yet none of that had ever caused him this much pain.

He knew his reaction to her honest answer about kissing had hurt her, especially his reference to Pleasure Workers. Was it really that different in her world? He had wanted to talk to her about it, but she refused, and when she said she wasn't feeling well... His only concern had been getting her to Luol so he could fix what was harming her.

He hadn't realized that what was harming her was him.

Somewhere between rescuing her and that amazing kiss, he had forgotten she wasn't just his Ashe, wasn't just his True Mate. She was a female who had survived a horrible experience and had no knowledge of the world she found herself in.

She wasn't Kaliszian. Yet he expected her to understand how his world functioned, to have the same traditions. Her reference to the Zaludians inspecting her for her worth as a Pleasure Worker shamed him. Did she really believe he thought of her in the same way? Was that why she refused to be his Ashe?

"Nikhil," Luol softly calling out his name in Kaliszian finally had him looking away from his Mackenzie. "What in the name of the Goddess is going on?!!"

"We..." Nikhil found he had to swallow hard to get his scratchy throat to work. "We had a misunderstanding."

"That's an understatement. I sent her with you because I believed you were the best one to care for her. That because of your connection, you would know what she needed. I see now that was a mistake."

"It wasn't! Everything was fine until..."

"You do realize talking in front of someone in a language you know they don't understand is rude. Right? Or is that a courtesy you only give to known species?"

Mac's muffled voice coming from the still closed repair unit had both males turning to find her glaring at them.

"My apologies... Mackenzie," Luol said in Zaludian, moving away from Nikhil and back to his patient. "I am so used to other species always understanding what is being said that I forgot you did not."

"Of course, you did." She gave him a disbelieving look, then turned her gaze back to the ceiling. "How much longer?"

"A few more minutes. Are you feeling any discomfort?"

"No."

"That is good. The General will be very pleased to hear that."

"The General?" Her gaze flew to Luol. "Why would you tell the General?"

"Well, because he is the General. He will want an update on your condition."

"But you are a Doctor... Healer," she corrected.

"I am." Luol gave her a confused look.

"You don't believe in doctor-patient confidentiality?"

"What? What is that?"

"It's when a doctor or in your case, Healer, isn't allowed to disclose anything about a person's medical condition without that person's express consent."

"It is that way on your Earth?"

"Yes, it ensures that a person can trust what they tell their doctor stays just between them."

"I see. I'm sorry, Mackenzie, but that is not the way it is here."

"So anything I tell you, you will report directly to the General."

"Yes," Luol admitted.

"And you do too?" She turned her gaze to Nikhil and saw the truth in his glowing eyes. He did. The General would know she had allowed him to cleanse her. He would know that as far as the Kaliszians were concerned she was a Pleasure Worker. What would happen to her now? What would happen to all of them?

Nikhil wasn't prepared for the look of utter betrayal that filled Mackenzie's eyes before she turned her gaze back to the ceiling. It made him feel as if he had let her down when all he had been doing was his duty. But wasn't his duty to her now? His True Mate? Never in his life had he been so conflicted.

Mac silently stared at the ceiling for several minutes listening to the repair unit hum. She didn't know why she hadn't realized Nikhil would tell his General everything. She had trusted him for some reason, had believed him and his True Mate crap. She should have known better. She had a lousy track record with men; it's why she spent so much time on the mountain.

The first time she ever kissed a boy on the lips had been Derek Emery, her senior year in high school. She'd had a crush on him for years and would secretly watch him as he worked at his dad's shop. One day, to her amazement, he asked her out. They'd gone to a movie and he'd put his arm around her. When he took her home, he kissed her goodnight. She'd floated into her grandpa's house thrilled out of her mind. It wasn't until the next day that she found out it had all been a joke. Derek and some of his friends were posting their dates to their social media accounts reporting everything that had been done and said, then ranking and grading the girl. She'd been ranked a three because she wouldn't let him do more with his hands. She'd been humiliated.

The second time had been in college. Chase had been a nice guy and a great kisser. They'd shared the same interests and had a lot of fun together, and he never pressured her for anything more than she was willing to give. She'd gone home for a long weekend to help her grandpa guide a hunting group and realized she was ready to take her and Chase's relationship to the next level. When she got back to school, she found him waiting at her apartment. It seems while she'd been off helping her grandpa, he'd met someone, a 'really, really, special someone' named Tina and he wanted her to find out from him. To say she'd been shocked was an understatement, but what really hurt was how he kept going on and on about how beautiful *Tina* was. About *Tina's* long, blonde hair and how tall and thin she was. That *Tina* was perfect; a total 10. That any guy would be proud to have someone like *Tina* on his arm. He was sorry and hoped they could still be friends, but he had to go, *Tina* was waiting in the car for him.

Mac never spoke to him again.

Yeah, her track record sucked, but at least, she'd never been considered a whore.

The sudden absence of sound followed by the click of the repair unit opening brought Mac's thoughts back to the present. She was on a planet called Pontus. She was lying in a deep-repair unit. Soon an 'educator' would be placed over her eyes. Nikhil had vowed it wouldn't be the same as with the Ganglians, but could she trust that? She knew she needed to do this, for everyone else. If she was going to help them, she needed information.

"Ash... Mackenzie." Luol moved to her side. "Are you all right?"

"Yes." She looked at Luol. "What exactly does this machine do?"

"It repairs whatever is wrong with you." He frowned at her question, then asked. "I take it you do not have machines like this on your Earth."

"No." She didn't expand further. "So it fixes everything?"

"The only thing it can't repair are severed limbs, fully-healed hard tissue injuries, and injuries caused by Tornian steel," Luol told her.

Mac understood severed limbs. She didn't care about whatever Tornian steel was. What she wanted clarification on was 'fully-healed hard tissue injuries'. It was important.

"So you're saying that it can't heal broken bones?"

"Of course, it can. It just can't repair what has already healed."

"But it can heal scars?" She looked to Nikhil's chest, suddenly realizing why there'd been no scars on it.

"As long as Tornian steel did not cause them, then yes. Soft tissue injuries are easily repaired."

"Why am I the only human you've treated so far?" she demanded.

"You were the only female we discovered, and you needed a great deal of time in the deep-repair unit. You will also need to use the educator, and that takes additional time. Because of that, it was decided that I should first treat those that were with the Zaludians the longest."

"And how was that decided?" she demanded.

"How was what decided?" Luol asked frowning.

"Who had been there the longest."

"We spoke to the others. They were able to tell us when they were captured."

"I see."

Luol's frown deepened. "Do you know something we do not?"

"Of course not," she instantly denied. "After all, I'm the 'species' that can't even tell you where her world is." She figured she had gathered all the information she could without putting her friends in jeopardy. "So where are we going to do this educator thing?"

"I thought you would be more comfortable on the couch in my office."

"Does my comfort really matter?"

"Of course, it does!" Luol looked from her to Nikhil in shock.

"The Ganglians forced their educator on one of their males," Nikhil told Luol quietly.

"On Craig," she told him.

"On Craig," Nikhil corrected, grateful that at least for a moment her gaze met his. "They then expected him to make sure the others used it or they threatened to kill them."

"It was *forced* on him?!!" Luol took a startled step back.

"Yes."

"And he suffered no ill effects?" Luol continued to question.

"Not that I noticed," she told him.

"Mackenzie experienced some discomfort when it was placed on her," Nikhil informed Luol, and his reward was the tightening of his Ashe's lips and her gaze leaving his.

"Discomfort?!!" Luol was immediately at Mac's side.

"It doesn't matter," she told Luol tensely.

"Of course it does!" Luol argued. "The educator should never cause any discomfort. I need to make sure no harm has been done to you."

"Shouldn't your repair unit have taken care of that?" she asked hitting her palm on the bed.

"Well... yes."

"Then there is no need for you to examine me *and* there was no reason to mention it," she glared at Nikhil.

"Luol needs to know what happened to you, Mackenzie," Nikhil told her quietly.

"Apparently, *everyone* needs to know what happened to me. And between you and Luol they will." Swinging her legs over the edge of the bed, she leveled herself up and jumped off. When her feet slipped on the cool floor, Nikhil was immediately there steadying her.

While she didn't jerk out of his arms, Mackenzie quickly stepped away, giving him a wary look then turned to Luol. "Where is this couch?"

∞ ∞ ∞ ∞ ∞

Luol showed her the educator, and she was surprised at how streamlined this one was. It was so different than the one the Ganglians had forced them to put on, but she couldn't stop the shudder of apprehension that ran through her at seeing it.

"Mackenzie?"

Nikhil's voice was so full of concern that she wanted to turn to him, wanted to let him wrap his massive arms around her and keep her safe, but she couldn't trust him. Not that she really came first, as he said an Ashe or True Mate would. Not when he thought her no better than a Pleasure Worker.

"Put it on," she said and closed her eyes as Luol lowered the educator.

Luol made sure the educator was sending out the deep, penetrating waves needed to put Mackenzie into a deep sleep and transfer its knowledge before rounding on Nikhil.

"What in the name of the Goddess happened?!!" he demanded.

"That is something between me and my Mackenzie, Luol."

"Not if it has her refusing to be your Ashe, Nikhil," Luol walked over and put a hand on a bulging muscle of Nikhil's arm. "I am your friend, I only wish to help."

∞ ∞ ∞ ∞ ∞

"It was a misunderstanding. I... over-reacted to something." Nikhil walked over to his Mackenzie, he didn't care what she said, she *was* his Ashe whether she accepted his bead or not, and ran a calloused finger over the back of the small, pale hand that was resting on her stomach. She'd willingly touched him with that hand, had caressed him with it. Would she ever again?

123

"Nikhil..." Luol watched as the Empire's largest and most deadly warrior carefully touch the hand of his newly discovered True Mate as if he feared she would disappear.

"I insulted her, Luol. Accused her of being something that I would never think to accuse one of our females of being."

"What did you accuse her of?"

"Acting like a Pleasure Worker." He pulled his hand away from Mackenzie as he said it, and took a step back.

"Nikhil! Why would you accuse her of that?"

"I woke this morning with my Mackenzie in my arms, and her running her hands over my body. It was the most incredible feeling, Luol."

"I'm sure it was."

"My body responded to her touch, especially when she pressed her lips against mine, but I worried it was too soon, and I withdrew. She misunderstood and took it as a rejection."

"How does that make her a Pleasure Worker?" Luol demanded.

"It doesn't." Nikhil ran a hand over his head causing his beads to hit together angrily. "It was later and we were... talking and it led us to more touching and kissing. It was then I realized she was experienced... in kissing on the lips. I questioned it and she admitted it. Apparently certain things aren't as sacred to them as they are to us," he said quietly. "I... didn't react well, and said only a Pleasure Worker would do such a thing."

"And she knew what a Pleasure Worker was because the Zaludians were going to make her one."

"Yes." Nikhil's gaze returned to Mackenzie. "I did not mean it, Luol. She is my True Mate, and I want her to be my Ashe."

"She *is* your True Mate, Nikhil. The bead proves that. Give her time to come to terms with all that has happened, to get to know you, and I'm sure she will come to realize you did not mean it the way it sounded and forgive you."

"Will she? Would *you* if you were insulted so? If another male were to insult her like that, I would kill him without a second thought. So why would I think I had the right to say it?"

"She isn't the only one that needs time to adjust to what has happened, Nikhil. *You* do too. Your life is now forever changed. You are the first to find your True Mate in nearly five hundred years. Others are going to want to know about her, see her, talk to her."

"She is *mine!*" Nikhil growled angrily at the thought of other males approaching her.

"I know this, Nikhil, and so will every other male when he sees her wearing your bead, but they are still going to be curious. You are going to have to be able to handle it along with helping her, handle it."

Chapter Eight

Mac could have sworn the educator had just gone on when Luol was removing it. "Is something wrong?"

"No. Why would you think that?" Luol replied.

"Because you just put the educator on."

"That was nearly two hours ago, Mackenzie."

"It was?" A movement behind Luol had her looking to see Nikhil standing there.

"What are you still doing here?" she asked.

"I would never leave you in such a vulnerable position," he said, his glowing green gaze never leaving hers. "I vowed to keep you safe. I keep my vows."

"Nikhil remained at your side the entire time, Mackenzie. Caring for you while I was treating the Jerboaians."

"How many?" she asked.

"Jerboaians?" Luol questioned.

"Yes, twenty of them arrived with us."

"Twenty arrived with you?" Luol gave Nikhil a sharp look. "There were only three left for me to treat."

"Why does that surprise you?" She caught the look Luol gave Nikhil.

"Jerboaians are perfectly suited for the harsh conditions of mining. It's what they do. For them to have arrived with you and so few to have survived... It means you and your people were there much longer than we believed."

"And that surprises you. That such a small, insignificant species, one that doesn't even travel in space, could survive longer than one you do know."

"I do not consider you or your species insignificant, Mackenzie. But yes, I am surprised that you were able to survive so long. Zaludians aren't known for treating those they enslave... kindly."

"Know that first hand."

"Yes, unfortunately you do," Luol agreed. "Now let us make sure you can access the information the educator gave you. Do you know how far Crurn is from here?"

Mac thought for a moment. "Yes, it's three days travel from here."

"Good. Now do you know who Chancellor Aadi Rayner was?"

Mac saw Nikhil jerk slightly at the question and frowned. "I take it that's not a standard question."

"Why would you ask that, Luol?" Nikhil took a closer step toward his Ashe.

"I need to make sure she understands the world she is now in, Nikhil. Everything about it. This is the quickest way to make sure she does."

"Why are you so concerned, Nikhil?" Mac nearly reached out to touch him, then remembered she was mad at him.

"I do not want you further upset..." Nikhil glared at Luol.

"But why would..." Suddenly she knew why he was so concerned, and rubbed her temple as the information came flooding in. "Chancellor Aadi... He's part of the reason the Great Infection struck. Why nothing edible grows in the Kaliszian Empire."

"Yes," Luol confirmed.

"Is General Rayner related to him?" she addressed her question to Nikhil, wondering if he'd tell her the truth.

"Distantly," Nikhil instantly admitted, not wanting her ever to doubt he would tell her truth, "but he is nothing like his ancestor."

"Are you sure of that?"

"Yes."

"Anything else you want to ask me?" She returned her gaze to Luol.

"Just one more question."

"Alright."

"Do you now understand what it means to a Kaliszian to find their True Mate?"

"I..." Mac felt her throat tighten as she finally realized what having a True Mate really meant. It was like Soul Mates on Earth, but so much more. The bead that she wore, Nikhil's bead, allowed him to feel what she felt, to know if she were safe, well, and *alive*. She looked at Nikhil in shock, and saw the truth in his gaze. The True Mate bond was so strong between couples that when one met the Goddess, the other almost always chose to join them. She rose from the couch and walked directly to him, slapping both her palms against his chest, causing him to lean back slightly. "You will *never* do that!"

Nikhil grunted slightly at the sting of her palms against his skin, but he would always welcome any touch she was willing to bless him with. "Mackenzie..."

"Your vow, Nikhil. I will have it!" she demanded, gripping his vest, pulling him forward.

"I will never give you a vow that I don't intend to keep, my Mackenzie. So I cannot vow that," he told her allowing her to pull him down.

"That's ridiculous! You barely know me! There's no reason for you to..."

"There is *every* reason!" he growled his arms pulling her close. "I would already willingly sacrifice my life to protect you, and I have only known you one day. I cannot imagine how devastated I would be if you were no longer in my life."

"But..." That was as far as she got before Nikhil lifted her off her feet and covered her mouth with his.

Mac found herself sinking into Nikhil's kiss, the emotions behind it pouring through her.

Regret.

Loneliness.

Doubt.

Desire.

Uncertainty.

But the strongest most undeniable emotion that ran through it all was the all-consuming love... for her. Ripping her mouth away from his, she stared up at him with confusion-filled eyes.

"That's not possible..." she whispered.

"It is, because I feel it. Nothing will ever change it. Not even death. You make me whole and give me a purpose I never knew I was missing. You are all that matters to me now, Mackenzie."

"You have your people, your Emperor, your duty."

"All that, I would willingly forsake if it meant keeping you safe."

"Nikhil..." she reached out, running trembling fingers over his lips.

"It is truth, Little One. One I know will take time for you to fully accept. But never doubt that you are my True Mate, and I hope that one day you will be able to forgive my thoughtless words and agree to be my Ashe." He gently kissed her fingertips. "I will now take you to be reunited with your people, as I vowed I would."

∞ ∞ ∞ ∞ ∞

Mac stood in the door of the survivors' area, her gaze taking it all in. It was one large, open room with drab-colored walls and several more doors on one end. The survivors had each claimed their own area. In the far corner, where the most cots were set up, were her friends all huddled together wearing gray capes. Letting out a little cry of relief, she hurried over to them.

Nikhil barely restrained himself from grabbing his Mackenzie and dragging her from the room, especially when male arms began to envelop her. He knew these were her people, and that they would all want to greet her, but it went against every instinct he had to allow them to touch her with such familiarity. He didn't like that he couldn't understand what was being said, as they were speaking their native language including Mackenzie. But what he couldn't tolerate most was losing sight of her golden, brown hair. Growling, he went to find her.

"I'm fine, Craig, really." Mac moved out of the arms of the man that had become their leader, all because the Ganglians had put the educator on him first. She remembered when she'd first met him. He'd been your typical cocky, good-looking guy, with blonde hair, sparkling blue eyes, and a big, unnaturally white smile. He'd flirted with her, but she instantly knew it was because he was a natural flirt, and she was the only available female. He'd quickly lost that smile. His eyes no longer sparkled, and the blonde hair he always fussed with was now dull and lifeless.

"We were so worried. I wish...”

"There was nothing you could have done." She let her gaze travel over the rest of the group. "Nothing any of you could do. Where's...” A deep, angry growl had her turning to find Nikhil shoving people aside on his way to her. "Nikhil...”

"Mac..." Craig went to step in front of her, but she put a restraining hand on his arm.

"It's alright, Craig. He's not going to harm me." She switched to Kaliszian. "Nikhil, what's wrong?"

"They are touching you," he growled back, the intense glow of his eyes causing several of the guys to take a step back.

"They are just hugging me. It's a common way for us to greet one another," she explained.

"I do not like it."

"Well, I'm sorry, but I'm not going to not hug my friends just because *you* don't like it. Now I need to talk to them, need to make sure they're all okay. You need to leave."

"You wish for me to leave you? Leave you alone with other males?"

"I'm not going to be with 'other males.' I'm going to be with males that are my friends. Males that have been keeping me safe for a long time."

"They let the Zaludians take you," he said between gritted teeth.

"That's not their fault." She turned and knew what Nikhil thought when he looked at the guys all huddled together. He believed they had been unwilling to protect her, but she knew better. "We're safe here, aren't we? No one's going to attack us, are they?

"Of course, no one will! You are all protected here!" Nikhil told her.

"Then there is no reason I can't be alone with my friends."

Nikhil didn't like his Ashe's logic. He especially didn't like that she was right. Logically, he knew he couldn't be constantly at her side, but he would prefer to know she was safely secured in his quarters when he wasn't with her.

"Please, Nikhil."

Nikhil hated that he couldn't deny her something she wanted. Especially, when there was no reason to, except for the fact that he didn't like it. "I will, but I will return for you later. You rest with me."

"Nikhil..."

"It is that, or I carry you out of here now, and your... friends can fend for themselves."

Nikhil's hard look told her he would do just that if she didn't agree. And really, did she want to sleep away from him? "Alright," she agreed softly.

Nikhil nodded stiffly, almost hating that she had agreed. He would have preferred to be forced to carry her back to their quarters. "Warriors Onp and Nroa are just outside the doors. If you need anything, let them know, and they will contact me."

"Alright, but everything will be fine," she reassured him. Nikhil didn't reply. Instead, he lowered his head, capturing her lips with a kiss that left no doubt who she belonged to, then giving the males behind her a hard glare, spun on his heel and forced himself to leave her.

∞ ∞ ∞ ∞ ∞

Nikhil's hands were fisted as he walked out the doors of the survivors' area. His heart was pounding, his jaw was clenched, and he found his breath was coming in short pants.

"Is something wrong, Squad Leader?" Onp asked carefully, earning himself Nikhil's harsh glare.

"The female I just escorted into the area," Nikhil began.

"She is the one found in the mines."

"Yes. You are to guard her with your life, or I will end yours! She is my True Mate."

"What?!!" Onp and Nroa exclaimed in unison.

"She. Is. My. True. Mate." Nikhil repeated through clenched lips. "She wears my bead." He lifted the braid that now only held his Ashe Bead. "If there are *any* problems, you are to notify me immediately!"

"Yes, Squad Leader!"

∞ ∞ ∞ ∞ ∞

Mac watched Nikhil until the doors closed behind him, then turned and discovered every eye staring at her curiously. Feeling her cheeks flush, she cleared her throat. "So how are you guys really?" she asked moving closer.

"What was that all about?" Craig demanded.

"What?"

"He kissed you! You talked to him in *his* language!"

"Yes and yes." She ran an agitated hand through her hair, tucking some of it behind her ear. "Look, there's a lot that we need to talk about. A lot you need to know, but right now you know who I want to see. Where?"

"I'm right here." The low, husky voice came from the back corner. Making her way between the guys, Mac finally found the cape-wrapped, hood-pulled-low person she was looking for sitting on one of the cots.

Mac felt her eyes fill as her gaze settled on her friend. God, had she looked that pitiful when Nikhil found her? No wonder he had rushed her out of that mine. Slowly, she sat down. "Are you okay?"

"I'm fine. The guys helped get me out of the mine."

"And no one noticed?"

"They were all too worried about some incoming storm."

"Oh." Mac hadn't known there had been a storm.

"What happened to you after the Zaludians took you?" Jen's eyes filled with tears and guilt. "Oh God, I'm so sorry about that, Mac."

"It wasn't your fault," Mac immediately tried to reassure her. "It wasn't anyone's fault."

"You could have gotten into the cave," Jen whispered.

"And then what? What were we going to do then? Let the Zaludians kill the guys one by one to force me out? Let them find *you*?" Mac took a deep breath and tried to calm her racing heart as she remembered how terrified she'd been, thinking she was going to be raped like the Jerboaian females had been. She hadn't been, and she forced her thoughts away from what might have happened and looked at the group around them. She needed to help them.

"I was told you received food," she looked up to Craig for confirmation.

"We did," he confirmed. "Packets. Last night and this morning."

"That's what I got too." She didn't tell them how Nikhil had fed her the meal the night before. "And I see they brought you cots and blankets."

"Yes," Craig continued to answer.

"New coverings?"

"Coverings?"

"Sorry. Clothes? They said you were shown the cleansing room and given new clothes."

"We did receive new clothes, but weren't 'shown' how to use the cleansing room. But we figured it out."

"Good."

"Mac..." A thin, pale hand, crisscrossed with scars reached out to grip hers. "Tell us what we need to know."

"I will, but first, let me get a look at you." Carefully she pulled back the hood that covered her friend's face, and felt her breath hitch. Somehow she'd forgotten how bad the damage to the left side of Jennifer's face was. Refusing to let Jen see how her injury affected her, Mac gave her a teary smile. "Hi. I've missed you."

"Oh God, Mac. I've missed you too."

The men closed ranks, even as they uncomfortably shuffled their feet and looked away as the two women hugged. Jen was the first to pull away, and pulled her hood back up. And although she didn't pull it as low, she turned so the damaged side of her face was away from the guys.

"Tell us, Mac," Jen said. "Tell us everything you've learned."

∞ ∞ ∞ ∞ ∞

Treyvon was surprised to see Nikhil enter the training field. He silently watched as Nikhil, stripped to the waist, and put Warrior Parlan through his drills with a single-minded intensity that had the smaller warrior struggling to defend himself. It was not how the Squad Leader normally sparred with those under his command unless he was making a point.

"Squad Leader!" Although Treyvon didn't raise his voice, it was easily heard across the training field, and Nikhil instantly ended his attack on Parlan.

"General." Nikhil turned to face Treyvon.

"A word." Nikhil nodded then looked back to Parlan.

"We will finish this another day, Warrior Parlan." With that, Nikhil walked over to his General.

Treyvon waited until Nikhil neared, then turned and walked to a quieter part of the training field. "I didn't expect to see you here today, Squad Leader. I expected you to stay with your True Mate while Luol completed treating her."

"I did."

"It has been completed?" Treyvon asked surprised.

"Yes. Mackenzie woke early and wished to have the treatment completed and the educator applied."

"Where is she now?"

"She wished to meet with her people, to explain what was happening. Alone."

"And you allowed this?" Treyvon frowned. If he were ever blessed with a True Mate, he'd never let her out of his sight.

"It was her wish and..."

"And?" Treyvon pressed.

"I found I couldn't deny her, not when it was something I would demand if I were in her place."

Treyvon said nothing, just stared at Nikhil until the larger warrior had to look away.

"Warrior Onp and Nroa were guarding the entrance, and I informed them they were to defend my True Mate with their lives, or I would end theirs."

"Justifiable." Treyvon nodded his support then pulled out the sword strapped to his back. "So she was able to understand the information the educator provided?"

"Yes, and Luol has guided her through the educator." Nikhil took a step away from his General and pulled his own sword out.

"She understood the information?" Treyvon asked, stretching slightly.

"Yes, very well. She was even able to associate that information with present day." Nikhil waited for the General to assume his fighting stance. Nikhil always enjoyed sparring with Treyvon. He was the only one that truly challenged him with the power of his sword, and while Nikhil was strong, the General was faster. It was always a good match.

"What do you mean?" When Nikhil just looked at him, Treyvon understood. "She knows my family helped cause the Great Infection."

"Not your *family*, General. An ancestor, but yes."

"I see."

Can she tell us where her Earth is now?" Treyvon asked.

"No."

"You know I will need to speak with her again."

"Yes."

Treyvon gave him the nod, assumed his stance, and the match began.

∞ ∞ ∞ ∞ ∞

Parlan ran the portable repair unit over his arm as he watched the General and Nikhil spar. Injuries happened during drills, which was why a unit was always available, but rarely were the injuries caused by Nikhil. The Squad Leader was renowned for always being in control of his blade, of always pulling back at the last minute.

Today, with him, Nikhil did neither; driving him to the ground again, and again while other warriors looked on. It was humiliating because that was the way Squad Leader intended it to be. All because Parlan had dared to speak up to him about the 'humans.'

"It seems you have displeased the Squad Leader," Warrior Gulzar commented as he walked by.

"Shut up, Gulzar!" Parlan spat back. "You will address me with the respect I've earned, or you will be in need of the deep-repair unit after this *Elite* Warrior is done with you."

Gulzar stared at Parlan for a moment. They both came from the same planet of Sustus, but that was the only thing they had in common. Parlan's bloodline held many Elite Warriors while Gulzar was attempting to become the first in his. Few Elites demanded to be addressed with the 'respect' Parlan was referring to. Especially not from one that was so close to joining their ranks, but Gulzar knew he couldn't refuse.

"Of course, Elite Warrior Parlan." Gulzar bowed slightly to him. "I meant no offense, just stating an observation as is part of my training."

"You were taught to *observe*, not *comment*," Parlan fired back.

"Of course, Elite Warrior Parlan."

"The Goddess has blessed you this day, Warrior Gulzar," Parlan told him, dropping the repair unit. "I do not have the time to show you why you will never become an Elite Warrior. I must oversee the survivors. A task the General personally assigned to me."

"An important task indeed," Gulzar agreed. "Especially now that the Squad Leader's True Mate has been found among them."

Parlan was about to spin away when Gulzar's words stopped him. "What are you talking about?!!"

"You have not heard?" Gulzar gave him a surprised look.

"Heard what?" Parlan demanded.

"Squad Leader discovered a severely injured female in the mine. It seems the Zaludians were going to sell her to a Pleasure House. She is his True Mate."

"The Zaludians had a Kaliszian female in that mine?" Parlan couldn't believe he hadn't heard this.

"No. She is one of the new species. The one that call themselves hu... humans."

"That's impossible! They aren't Kaliszian!"

"Yet she wears his True Mate bead. I saw it myself this morning when she was walking beside Squad Leader Nikhil in the corridor."

Parlan spun around and left without another word.

∞ ∞ ∞ ∞ ∞

"So what's going to happen to us?" It was Paul who asked the question after Mac finally stopped speaking. "If we can't tell them where Earth is?"

"I don't know," Mac told them honestly. "What I do know is that they are nothing like the Zaludians or the Ganglians."

"And this repair unit... it helps?" All eyes went from Mac to the three Jerboaians that had returned a short while ago. There were still large patches of fur missing, but what remained now seemed shiny and silky, healthy-looking.

"It does. I'm feeling much better, not so weak and tired. I was bruised and had a split lip yesterday. Today that's all gone. It can even heal scars." She looked at Jen and saw the shock on her face.

"It... it can take this all away?" She did a circular gesture in front of her face.

"Yes, it can repair all the scars, Jen. It can repair any internal damage. It just can't..."

"Can't what?"

"It can't repair your ankle."

"Why not!" Paul demanded.

"Because it's fully healed. If it weren't..."

"I see," Jen whispered.

"I'm sorry, Jen."

"It's not your fault. It's not anybody's fault." She looked up at her friends. "You all have to use this machine and their educator. Maybe then, between all of us, we can figure out where Earth is."

"You need to use it too, Jen," Mac told her.

"No. There's no reason to."

"No reason..."

"Mac, what good does it do to fix the outside if what's broken is on the inside?"

"Jen..."

"And I don't mean my leg. I mean my heart. They can't fix that, so what's the use. You guys have a chance though, a chance to fully recover from all this. To get back home and return to your lives. I don't."

"Don't say that, Jen!" Mac wrapped her arms around her friend trying not to cringe when all she felt was bone. "You still have Kimmy. You know she's looking for you. You got that text from her right before we left."

"That I ignored."

"So."

"Mac, you know Kimmy and I hadn't talked in nearly six months. For me to just ignore her when she finally reached out... she must hate me."

"I'm sure she doesn't. No one could hate you, Jen."

"Yeah, well you didn't know me before, Mac. I wasn't that nice of a person."

"That's a lie," Craig spoke up. "You've always been a nice person, Jen, a good one. Look at all of Todd's crap you put up with."

"Craig!"

"I know, and I'm sorry I shouldn't speak ill of the dead, but you did. I was on the receiving end of his phone calls and texts when you first took Kimmy in. He could have been more supportive."

"Maybe, but I wasn't that nice to Kimmy either, especially toward the end... now she'll never know how sorry I am."

"She will," Mac said, squeezing her hand. "You can tell her when we finally get back home, as long as you don't give up. You didn't in that mine, Jen. When we were all so hungry, you found a way to make the food stretch. We wouldn't be here if it wasn't for you."

"And I wouldn't be here if it wasn't for *you*." Jen squeezed Mac's hand in return.

"Then don't give up. Not yet. Not anyone." Mac looked at the nine men encircling them. "We've come this far together. Let's see if we can't make it home together too."

The men mumbled their agreement, and Mac turned to look at Jen.

"Alright," Jen reluctantly agreed. "No giving up."

"I think we need to continue to keep Jen's existence a secret," Craig announced.

"What?" Mac's eyes shot to his. "Why?"

"Because we don't know what these... Kaliszians will do to her. Look at you!"

"Me?" Mac gave him a shocked look. "What are you talking about?!!"

"You were *kissing* one!" he told her angrily. "Why? How do we know they didn't do something to make you do that?!! That their machine didn't...”

"It didn't! Look that kiss... Nikhil and I...”

"Nikhil? That's his name?" Jen asked quietly.

"Yes. He's the one that found me in the mine. He carried me directly to the Healer, Healer Luol, and Luol put me in the deep-repair unit."

"How long were you in it?" Jen asked.

"Six hours."

"How do you know it was that long?" Craig demanded.

"Because that's what Luol told me when I asked."

"And you believed him?"

"Yes. There was no reason for him to lie about it."

"What happened next?" Jen pulled Mac's gaze back to her.

"They asked me some questions, most I couldn't answer, and then Nikhil took me to his quarters."

"He..."

"Did nothing... at least not the way you mean. He helped me with the cleansing unit, fed me, and then I fell asleep. When I woke up, he made sure I ate again, then took me back to Luol to finish my treatment and then I used their educator. That's why I can speak and understand their language now along with every other known species. I also know a great deal about them and their history. The one the Ganglians forced on us only contained two languages."

"You *know* about them? These Kaliszians?"

"Them and every other species. It's amazing, Jen, the things I know now that I didn't before."

"And that's all because of their educator?"

"Yes."

"Do you know why we were taken?" Craig asked quietly.

"Not really. I mean," she held up her hand to stop everyone from talking at once. "I know we were taken for slave labor. The Zaludians were illegally mining on this planet, which is called Pontus by the way. The Kaliszians only just discovered what was going on because they were on the opposite side of their Empire, defending it from another species. The Kaliszians don't know why the Ganglians were assisting the Zaludians. Apparently, the two don't normally get along. There's more."

"What?"

"It seems the Kaliszians have intercepted several Ganglian ships; one had a female on it they claim was similar to us."

"So they do know where Earth is."

"No. The Ganglians had deleted their navigational information before they were boarded."

"Why would they do that?"

"My guess is they are trying to keep Earth's location a secret for some reason, but no one knows why."

"Do you think they would tell you if they did?" Jen asked quietly.

Mac thought about it for a moment, not because she didn't know the answer, but because they deserved her to take her time. "Nikhil would tell me."

"You trust him that much?" Craig asked doubtfully.

"Yes." Mac's eyes silently pleaded with Jen's for understanding.

"Jen," Craig pulled her gaze from Mac's. "We can't trust that."

"I trust Mac, but I understand your concern, Craig. I'll stay back until we know more."

"Jen, you need the repair unit if only to manage your pain."

"Pain?!!" Paul sat down next to Jen and cupped her jaw, making her gaze meet his. "What pain?"

"It's nothing, Paul." She gave Mac an angry look.

"Mac?" Paul looked at her.

"She's been in constant pain since the attack," Mac told them for the first time.

"Mac!" Jen exclaimed.

"Why didn't you tell us?" Paul asked quietly.

"What good would it have done to tell you, Paul?" Jen said. "When there was nothing you could have done."

"But there is now." Mac broke in. "You can be pain-free."

"You don't know that," Jen argued back. "If they can't even fix the problem, why do you think they can make the pain go away?"

Mac couldn't argue with that because she didn't know. "If I find out they can, will you, at least, let them do that?"

Jen was silent for so long that Mac didn't think she was going to answer. "I will," she finally said.

"That still doesn't explain why you were kissing that man!" Craig said.

"Male," Mac corrected.

"What?" Craig frowned at her.

"They don't use the term man; they say male. You'll learn that after you use their educator. And it's a much better experience than what we had with the Ganglians."

"You keep dodging the question," Craig snarled.

"I don't mean to, it's just hard to explain... you see Kaliszians wear these beads in their hair and..." The doors of the area slamming against the wall cut her off.

Chapter Nine

Parlan ignored Onp and Nroa as he shoved open the doors to the survivors' wing, uncaring that it sounded like a blaster shot as they slammed against the walls, causing all the traumatized beings inside to jump. His anger and disbelief had grown as he cleansed and every step it took him to get here. How could the Goddess have blessed one like Nikhil with a True Mate, even if she was one from another species? Nikhil was a large, blundering male with no connections to power except for the fact that his manno worked for a Minister.

He was an Elite Warrior.

He descended from a powerful bloodline.

He had access to more credits than any Squad Leader.

He was Parlan Spada.

If anyone deserved a True Mate, it was *him*.

His gaze scanned the area, searching for the humans, until he found them huddled in a corner like the insignificant beings they were. They didn't look any better to him cleansed than they had filthy. Could the Goddess really have chosen one of these creatures as a True Mate for a Kaliszian? Maybe she was punishing them, the way she had because of General Rayner's ancestor, with the Great Infection.

"I will speak with the female," he announced in Kaliszian, as he walked toward the group.

"What's he saying?" Jen asked, pulling her hood down lower.

"He wants to talk to me. Stay here." Rising, Mac weaved her way through the guys that were closing ranks around them, not knowing what was going on. "It's okay, guys," she spoke in English, knowing only they would understand. "He wants to talk to me and no, he can't understand anything you say in English."

"He's an asshole, Mac," Paul informed her from the back.

"I'll keep that in mind," she replied, then stepped out and faced the Kaliszian Warrior that had stopped in front of them.

Parlan didn't know what he expected, but it wasn't the beautiful creature that stepped out from behind the gray wall of capes. She was exquisite, if slightly strange looking. Waves of dark, multicolored hair flowed loosely around her face. He'd never seen a female's hair loose before, as Kaliszian females always restrained theirs with a clip and it was braided. She wore what appeared to be a storm covering, and it conformed to a body that while thinner than what he liked, still had his shaft stirring with interest.

"Who are you?" Mac demanded.

Her question had him pulling his gaze from where her covering ended, to find brown eyes staring at him defiantly. Good, he liked a female that fought. He enjoyed making her submit to his wishes. "I am Elite Warrior Parlan Spada. I am the warrior General Rayner felt most trustworthy to see to you and your people."

Mac just stared at the male speaking to her in an oily voice. She didn't like the way his gaze traveled over her. It made her feel like she needed another shower.

When she didn't immediately respond, he frowned. "You do understand Kaliszian, don't you?" Parlan demanded. "Aren't you able to speak it?"

"Yes," she answered.

"Then give me your name!" he demanded.

"Why?"

"What do you mean, why? Your species does have individual names, don't they?" he asked snidely.

"Yes."

"Then what is yours?" Parlan demanded again.

"Why do you want to know?" Mac continued to question.

"Because I have been put in charge of you," he told her smugly.

"You think you are in charge of me?" Mac raised an expressive eyebrow at him.

"Yes."

"That is an untruth, Parlan!" Nikhil roared, storming into the area followed by Onp and Nroa. He'd been enraged when Onp had contacted him to say Parlan was demanding to speak to the Earth female. He hadn't even taken the time to explain himself to Treyvon as he rushed to his Mackenzie's side. He did not trust why Parlan was demanding to see her. "How dare you try to deceive my True Mate!"

"Nikhil," Mac cried out, gratefully taking the hand he held out to her. She hadn't realized how truly uneasy Parlan had made her, not until she felt the security of Nikhil's embrace.

"You are safe, Little One, as I vowed you would be," Nikhil reassured her, pulling her close.

"True Mate?" Parlan, as far as Mac was concerned, gave a bad impersonation of confusion.

"You are saying you did not see this?" Nikhil lifted the strand of her hair that held his True Mate bead.

"Of course I didn't, Squad Leader," Parlan denied. "Had I seen it, I never would have approached her. As your... True Mate is not Kaliszian, perhaps you should instruct her on what is the proper conduct for one. Obviously she isn't intelligent enough to know."

"Why you..." Nikhil moved her behind him, stopping her from saying more, as did the sound of him pulling out the sword strapped to his back. Onp and Nroa moved in to flank her, silently letting Nikhil know that they would protect her.

147

"You dare to insult my True Mate, Warrior Parlan?!!" Nikhil growled lowly, pointing his sword at Parlan.

Parlan took a startled step back, unable to believe Nikhil had reacted so strongly to his words, and frantically reached behind him searching for the hilt of his sword. There was no way he could not respond to Nikhil's challenge, for Elite Warriors did not back down.

"*Squad Leader*! What in the name of the Goddess is going on?!!" Treyvon's question echoed in the room full of silent observers, having followed Nikhil from the training field.

"Warrior Parlan has not only insulted my True Mate but has tried to deceive her," Nikhil replied lowly, never taking his gaze off of Parlan.

"Warrior Parlan, is this truth?" Treyvon demanded.

"I merely stated that perhaps she should be instructed on the proper conduct of a True Mate."

"Sheath your sword, Squad Leader," Treyvon only addressed Nikhil as Parlan was never able to draw his, and waited until Nikhil did before turning his attention to Parlan. "Now tell me, Parlan, how would *you* know what the proper conduct is for a True Mate? Do you have one no one knows about?" Treyvon questioned.

"I... Well, no," Parlan reluctantly answered.

"Does your manno?"

"No."

"Do you know any other True Mates?"

"Of course not, General! There hasn't been one in nearly five-hundred years."

"Then perhaps Squad Leader Nikhil's True Mate is conducting herself properly."

"General! She never presented herself as his True Mate. If she truly were, she would wear his bead proudly for all to see, not hide it in all that... hair."

"How dare you!" Moving quicker than any of them could have anticipated, Mac was around Nikhil, slapping Parlan across the face before anyone could stop her. Her small hand left angry, red slashes across one cheek. "You know *nothing* about me or my feelings for my True Mate! I wear my hair the way *I* wish, and Nikhil's bead hangs where *it* wishes! You have no right to criticize something you know nothing about, and from what I've heard and witnessed, never will, as the Goddess would never bless a self absorbent prick such as *you* with a True Mate!"

Silence reigned in the room, as everyone including Mac's friends, were shocked at her bare-handed attack on the much larger Parlan. Few attacked an Elite Warrior and lived, especially not a female.

Nikhil was the first to react as Parlan's face swung back to his Mackenzie, pulling her away from the enraged male who this time managed to find the hilt of his sword.

"Parlan! You will stand down!" Treyvon ordered, drawing his own sword as he stepped between Parlan and the couple.

"She had no right!" Parlan sputtered.

"She had every right! You insulted not only her but her bond with her mate. Something you would never do with a male." Treyvon's gaze trailed over the group behind him, frowning when one figure ducked away fearfully. This would not do. "I placed you in charge here because I thought you would treat these survivors with respect. I see now that is untrue." He looked over his shoulder. "Warrior Onp."

"Yes, General." Onp immediately presented himself to his General.

"The care of the survivors is now your responsibility."

"Yes, General. I will not fail you." Onp gave him a slight bow.

"I know you won't, Onp." Treyvon's gaze returned to Parlan. "Parlan, you will now stand the wall."

"But, General..." Parlan started to argue.

"Silence!" Treyvon ordered. "You have dishonored not only your fellow Elite Warriors but also your people as a whole. A True Mate is always honored. I will make sure Minister Stepney knows of this."

"But..."

"Report to Warrior Marr. I will inform him you are coming and why."

Parlan glared at Mackenzie as he released the hilt of his sword, then giving Nikhil wide berth, walked out of the area.

Nikhil gazed down at his Mackenzie. He couldn't believe that she had attacked Parlan, couldn't believe her words or how she defended their bond. Not after what he'd said to her that morning. His Mackenzie might be tiny, but she was fierce.

"Mackenzie." His softly spoken word had her turning to gaze up at him, and he saw her beautiful, brown eyes were still filled with anger.

"He's an ass, Nikhil, and he's wrong. I am proud to be your True Mate." She turned to face him, and the hand that had slapped Parlan rose to rest over his heart. "I know we still have a lot to work out, but if you believe nothing else, believe that."

Nikhil found he could only cover her hand with his and nod, as his throat was too tight to allow words to pass.

"Mac?" The question from Craig had her looking back to her friends. She saw the confusion and worry in their gazes. "Are you alright? What's going on?"

Giving Nikhil's chest a soft caress, she turned and went to them. "Everything is fine. Have you met General Treyvon Rayner?" she asked gesturing to the General.

"Yes. Once. In the mines," Craig said, and Mac nodded.

"He has removed Parlan from being in charge. Now this warrior will be." She gestured to the other male. "Warrior Onp."

Nikhil listened as his Mackenzie spoke to the male that seemed to be the leader of their group, and while he didn't understand her words, he could tell she was explaining what had happened, and that Onp was in charge now from her gestures. He could also tell she was tiring. It was in the way she was starting to lock her knees to keep from swaying, it was in the slightest tremble in her hand as she pointed at Onp, and it was in the slight paling of her skin.

"Mackenzie." He stepped close, offering her his strength and support. ""Come, Little One."

"Just a minute," she said in Kaliszian, then switched back to English. "Jen, it might be best if you stay hidden for a while longer. I'll be back as soon as I can." With that, she smiled up at Nikhil and let him lead her away

∞ ∞ ∞ ∞ ∞

"I am taking you to Luol, Mackenzie. I want him to examine you before you rest. You have been through a great deal," Nikhil said leading her to medical.

"I'm fine, Nikhil."

"You have paled, and do not think I haven't notice how your hands are trembling. Luol will reexamine you."

"I can't believe you only have one deep-repair unit on this entire planet."

"That is because we did not think that we would need one when we first arrived," Treyvon told her, quietly moving up behind her. "When we began to discover survivors, I had the one from my ship sent down."

"You have them on your ships?"

"Several, yes."

"Then why not send down the another one?!!" Mac rounded on the General, forcing him to stop or knock her over.

"That would leave my warriors without one, should they need it."

"Aren't they all down here?"

"No. There are those that patrol the area around Pontus, intercepting any ship that might be Ganglian or Zaludian. Our intervention is not always... appreciated."

"Have any of them needed the unit?"

"I... no."

"Then it needs to be brought down," Mac told him. "My friends need treatment."

"They will receive..."

"No! We've been through more than you can imagine, and I won't allow others to be treated first just because you have never encountered us before."

"The others were there longer than you."

"You don't know that for sure! And even if that was true, how long did it take Luol to treat those three Jerboaians?"

"I..."

"Three hours. An hour for each one," Luol said, walking out of medical when he heard the argument going on in the corridor.

"And how long did it take you to treat me?" She turned to face Luol.

"Seven total," Luol admitted.

"So doesn't that tell you something?!!" Mac demanded, swinging back around to Treyvon. "I'm still not sure how long ago we were taken, but I'm starting to get an idea, because of this." She lifted the strand of her hair that held Nikhil's bead.

"What does my bead have to do with how long ago you were taken, Mackenzie?"

"It's not the bead." She turned toward Nikhil. "It's the length of hair it's on."

"I don't understand," Nikhil frowned down at her.

"It's longer."

"Your hair? It continues to grow?"

"Of course!" It was her turn to frown, and she reached out to touch his. "Doesn't yours?"

"No."

"But..."

"Perhaps this would be better *not* discussed in a corridor," Luol stated as warriors paused around them.

"Agreed," Treyvon said.

"Yes, then you can reexamine Mackenzie."

"Reexamine?" Luol's concerned gaze shot to Mackenzie and he took a step closer to her. "What is wrong, Mackenzie?"

"Nothing. Nikhil is over-reacting. I'm just a little tired."

"Come," Luol gestured to the still open door. "She can lay down on an exam bed, and I will use the portable unit as the deep-repair unit is currently in use."

"I want her in the deep-repair unit!" Nikhil growled, guiding Mackenzie into the room.

"Hard to do when there is only one, and after all... I wasn't held any longer than my friends, now was I?" Her question had all three males looking uncomfortable.

"Mackenzie..." Nikhil growled.

153

"What?" She turned to gaze up at Nikhil and was surprised to find tears were making him blurry. "I'm not supposed to speak the truth? If the Zaludians hadn't discovered and beaten me, I wouldn't even be here now, would I? You wouldn't even know about me. I wouldn't be your True Mate. I could have died before you thought me worthy of treatment."

Nikhil couldn't stand seeing his True Mate so upset, couldn't stand that he was unable to prevent it, and what he really couldn't stand was that her words were true. Again. Immediately at her side, he swept her up into his arms.

"I don't believe that! I will never believe that! The Goddess guided me to you, and while I will never agree with how she brought you into my life, I'll never regret that you are in it." His words had her sobbing, and he looked to Luol in a panic.

"I could give her a calmer, but her system is already trying to adjust to so much..."

"No..." Mac's voice was muffled against Nikhil's chest. "Just give me a minute."

"You can have all the minutes you need, my Mackenzie," Nikhil reassured her, his arms tightening around her, giving her what comfort he could.

"Nikhil, if you sit, I can scan her while she's still in your arms," Luol murmured.

Nikhil immediately scooped Mackenzie up in his arms and moved to sit on the exam bed. "Do it," he ordered.

Mac couldn't believe she was falling apart like this. Again. What was wrong with her? She'd never been like this before.

"It is understandable, Little One," Nikhil murmured in her hair, making her realize she'd spoken out loud. "You have been through a great deal, and handled it all with grace and strength. Let me be your strength now. I have more than enough."

Mac found herself chuckling as she rubbed her forehead against his chest before gazing up, giving him a wobbly smile. "You are rather strong, aren't you?"

"I am," he agreed.

"That's one of the things I like about you," she said and found herself sinking into her True Mate's warm, glowing gaze.

"Do you?" he quizzed quietly.

"Yes."

"Ahem," the sound of Luol clearing his throat had Mac pulling her gaze from Nikhil. "I believe you just need rest, Mackenzie. Your system just hasn't had the time to absorb everything it has been given."

"Then that is what she shall have." Nikhil rose with her still in his arms.

"Wait!" Treyvon's exclamation had everyone freezing. "I need to know why the length of your hair tells you how long ago you were taken."

"Does your hair really not grow at all?" Mac asked, reaching out to touch one of Nikhil's braids. "Is that why you were so upset when I suggested cutting mine?"

"You did what?!!" Both Luol and Treyvon exclaimed, drawing Mac's gaze.

"On Earth, hair comes in varying lengths. Some even prefer to have it all removed."

"What?!!" This had all three males exclaiming.

"I know for you that is a sign of disgrace, but it's not that way on Earth."

"Your hair continues to grow even after you mature?" Luol asked carefully.

"Yes. I take it yours doesn't."

"No. Our hair reaches its final length around our sixteenth year. From then on, it only grows enough to maintain that length."

"And if it is intentionally cut?" she asked.

"It will eventually grow back, but very slowly. How fast does yours grow?"

"I'm not exactly sure. I was hoping one of the guys knew, but didn't have time to ask."

"Why?"

"Because other questions were more important. What I do know is that I used to get my hair trimmed every four to six weeks, and had it done right before we were taken."

"And how long was it then?" Nikhil asked gently fingering the ends of her hair.

"Up to here." She put her hand even with her collarbone and watched Nikhil's eyes widen.

"That is a great deal longer, Mackenzie," he whispered.

"I know, I've never let it get this long before."

"So how fast does your hair grow?" Treyvon asked.

"My beautician would usually cut a quarter inch off ever four to six weeks."

"That means..." Treyvon frowned unable to believe what she was saying.

"That we were taken five to six months ago," she said and was greeted with a stunned silence.

"But that... that's impossible. No species could survive that long under such harsh conditions," Luol said, looking aghast.

"But you've never met *my* species before now, have you?" she challenged.

Luol looked to Treyvon. "General, if this is true, then I must insist that I begin treating the humans immediately, and for you to send for the other deep-repair unit. Mackenzie was highly deficient in many of the vital vitamins and minerals that are essential for every known species. I assumed it was because a human's requirement was different, but now that I am aware how long they may have been held, I realize it is because they were just that extremely depleted in the struggle to survive. They need immediate treatment."

"That's what I've been saying!" Mac exclaimed.

"Nikhil, take your Ashe to your quarters and make sure she rests," Treyvon ordered.

"But..."

"I will see to it that your fellow humans are treated, Ashe Mackenzie," Treyvon informed her, "but not unless you allow Nikhil to take you back to his quarters and rest. I can't have my Squad Leader distracted."

∞ ∞ ∞ ∞ ∞

"I could have walked, you know," Mac told Nikhil even as she settled deeper into his arms.

"I am strong, remember?" he said, shifting her slightly to press his palm against the access panel of his quarters.

"I remember."

"You need to rest, but first you will eat," he informed her, setting her down on the couch before moving into what looked like a small kitchen area to retrieve a packet.

"Why is there a kitchen in your quarters?" she asked. She'd learned from the educator that Kaliszians didn't cook, because only the wealthiest had fresh food stores that required might require it.

"It was here when we arrived. This base was here when Pontus was a live and viable planet. One full of edible plant life."

"So Kaliszians used to eat more than these premade packets?" she asked, taking the packet he handed her.

"When we are on missions, we consume three packets a day. But when we are stationed somewhere, we receive extra rations to prepare one fresh meal a day."

"And you prepare it here?"

"No. We combine our rations, and the task of preparing the meal is assigned to a warrior. We've only been receiving fresh meals here on Pontus for the last four weeks when we began discovering survivors and this base was reestablished."

"I see."

"I will take you to last meal once it's prepared after you have rested. Now eat."

"Aren't you going to eat too?"

"I will later."

"But..." she looked down at the pouch in her hand. "Oh my God, I'm eating your rations."

"Mackenzie..."

"Here!" She shoved it at him. "Take it!"

"No, stop!" he ordered, as she continued to try and press it into his fisted hands. "Mackenzie, I'm fine."

"No. You didn't eat breakfast either. You're giving me your food rations."

"Mackenzie!" Nikhil rose and pulled open a cabinet revealing it was full of packets. "Elite Warriors are always given three food packets a day, no matter where they are, even when stationed at a permanent base. It is one of the benefits of achieving Elite status."

"One of them?" she questioned.

"The other is that we receive extra credits to use any way we see fit."

"So why aren't you eating then?"

"Because I am more concerned about you than me right now. I will eat when I become hungry, my vow."

Mac bit her bottom lip to keep it from trembling. She was tired of her emotions being so out of control, especially around Nikhil. Maybe if she rested, like Luol suggested, she wouldn't feel so out of control.

"I think I'd like to rest now," she told him.

"Finish eating first," he argued.

"No. I'm not hungry. I'm not used to eating this much anymore, Nikhil." She held up her hand to stop him from arguing with her. "What you gave me for first meal is more than I'm used to for two meals in the mines, maybe three. My system isn't used to it. All I want right now is a pillow and blanket."

Nikhil took the packet from her and set it aside. "Then come," he held out his hand, "I will help you to the bed."

"No. I can sleep here."

"What?" He gave her a confused look. "Why?"

"Because there's no reason for me to be in your bed."

"It is where you belong!" Nikhil bit out, then took a deep breath trying to force himself to calm.

"I'm not sure it is, Nikhil," she told him sadly. "Not now."

"Why would you say that?!!" he questioned then realized why. It was because of what he had said. Never in his life had he felt like he had failed so badly the one person he should never fail. Slowly he moved across the room to settle heavily on the couch next to her. "This is because of what I said this morning... I thought..."

"Thought what?"

"That you had forgiven me for my hasty words."

"They weren't hasty, Nikhil," she told him quietly. "They were your truth. What you truly believe. What your culture believes. My culture believes something different, and I don't know how we can ever get past that."

"You said you were proud to have me as your True Mate," he told her.

"And I am, but I don't believe that *you* are." She gave him a dejected look. "How can you be, when you believe me to be no better than a whore or a slut."

"I do not know what those words mean," he told her.

"A slut is a female that will have sex with any male that she feels like. A whore is a female that does the same, except the male exchanges something of value with her for it, gives her credits for it. That's what your Pleasure Workers do, don't they? And those you give your 'friendship' to. I've never done that and never will. But I have kissed men on the lips and for you, that is no different."

Nikhil just stared at her at a loss for words. Did she really believe that? That he thought so little of her? All his life he had been judged harshly, been misunderstood because of his size by his own people. It was something he'd vowed he would never do to another being but it seemed he had... and to his True Mate.

"We are different, Nikhil, and I'm not talking about size. I'm talking about culturally. For you, this," she lifted the bead in her hair, "is irrefutable. You have no doubts. It's not that way for me. It takes actions and words and feelings. It takes trust and belief on both sides. You are asking me to just believe in something I've never heard of or experienced before. Before the Ganglians took me, I might have been able to do that... and because of *you*... I did, then you rejected me."

"I didn't!"

"You did, Nikhil. You judged me, and found me unworthy." She felt her eyes fill. "And that is more painful than anything the Zaludians did." Finding she could no longer look at him, could no longer take seeing the pain her words caused him, she curled up into a ball and laid her head down on the arm of the couch. It was more comfortable than the mine floor, and it only took seconds for her to fall asleep.

Nikhil stood in a corner of the room he'd darkened and watched his True Mate sleep. He was at a loss at what to do to fix this. He would rather be fighting hand-to-hand with the Radek, with the Ganglian, the Zaludian, or the Tornians than to be standing here not knowing what to do. Mackenzie wasn't wrong. He had judged her. Doing what he'd vowed he'd never do.

Moving to her, he reached down, rolling her True Mate bead between his fingers. It didn't radiate the warmth that it had when it had first been in her hair. Now it felt cold and dark like the pain he'd seen in her eyes. How did he fix this? Spinning on his heel, he went to contact the only male he'd been able to rely on his entire life.

Chapter Ten

"Nikhil!" Cirrus Kozar exclaimed, his pleasure easily heard. "Where are you? Can you tell me?"

"I am on Pontus, Manno," he told him, knowing that for once his location wasn't a secret.

"Pontus? What on Crurn for?"

"That I cannot tell you, Manno. What I can tell you is that I have found my True Mate."

"What?!!!" Cirrus didn't try to hide his shock. "Nikhil, that's..."

"I know, Manno. I was shocked too."

"Your mother is going to be beyond thrilled!"

"You can't tell her, Manno. Not yet."

"What? Why?"

"It's why I contacted you. I need your advice."

"My advice? Nikhil, what is going on?"

"My True Mate... she is not Kaliszian, Manno."

"Not... she's Tornian?"

"No."

"Kalbaughian?"

"No."

"Not Ganglian!"

"Goddess, no! She is human."

"Human? What is a human?"

"It is a new species that we have just discovered in the last few days... Manno..."

"What is it, Nikhil?"

"I need your vow that you will not repeat anything I am about to tell you. I am not even sure the Emperor knows everything yet."

"Nikhil... you have my vow. You know I would never betray you, but are you sure you should be telling me this?"

"I need advice, Manno, and you are the only one I completely trust."

"I am honored, Nikhil, for you are one of the most worthy male's I have ever known. And that is not because you are mine, but because you have earned it. Now tell me how I can help you."

"I have harmed my True Mate, Manno."

"What? That's impossible! You will never make me believe that you would physically harm your mate."

"I didn't, but I emotionally harmed her, Manno, with my words and I do not know that she can ever forgive me."

"What did you say to her, Nikhil?"

"It seems that for her... for her species... kissing a male on the lips is not considered sacred. When I discovered this, I did not react well."

"Nikhil, you have always known that different species can have very different customs."

"Yes, but she is my True Mate, and so similar to us that I just assumed..."

"Always a mistake. Especially concerning a female, for no two are the same. It is what makes each so special. So what does her species consider sacred?"

"I do not know. She was so angry at me for comparing her to a Pleasure Worker that she refused to tell me. And then later..."

"You compared your True Mate to a Pleasure Worker?!! Nikhil, how could you possibly..."

"She has kissed other males, Manno! On the *lips*! Would Mother do that? Would you be able to accept it if she did?"

"No. Never. But then your mother is Kaliszian and would respond as a *Kaliszian*. Your True Mate is not. What you need to do, my male, is find out what *she* considers sacred. Perhaps it is something we do not."

"But what?

"She's given you no clue?"

"Clue?"

"Son, females are always giving you clues. Clues to what they like. Clues to what they don't like. A male only has to actually to listen to know."

"She said something about how while she had kissed two men on the lips, that was all she had done. That she hadn't offered her friendship to any male."

"And that didn't tell you what she held sacred? What she wanted to offer only to her True Mate?"

"She said they don't have True Mates, but what they called Soul Mates. That they also have no outward sign of who that is, like we do with our bead. Only a belief in the person and a trust."

"A much harder way to know then."

"I... yes, I guess it would be."

"So has she never trusted you? Or was it lost by your words?"

"She trusted me to cleanse her, to feed her, and to sleep in my arms," Nikhil told him quietly. "It was only this morning that I broke that trust."

"I do not know this female, Nikhil. I do not know if she is worthy of you, but..."

"She is!" Nikhil instantly defended her. "She is the worthiest female I have ever known. She is strong and kind. She cares about others and defended me, even after I failed her."

"So you love her."

"I... Yes... I do... and not because she wears my bead."

"Of course not. What I was going to say is that for us the beads are never wrong. You have found *your* True Mate, Nikhil. So now it is up to you to show her that you are *hers*."

"I... how do I do that, Manno?"

"By always telling her truth, my male. By making sure she knows your true feelings and that they are all for her," Cirrus paused. "Your mother may not wear my True Mate bead, but I love her, and in my heart she is my True Mate.

∞ ∞ ∞ ∞ ∞

Mac hadn't meant to eavesdrop on Nikhil's conversation with his manno, but she hadn't known how to tell him she was awake. Then after a little while, she hadn't wanted to. She learned more about Nikhil and his real feelings for her in that short conversation than he had told her in the hours they had been together. Nikhil seemed to be a lot like her grandpa. A big, gruff male that had a hard time expressing his real feelings, but that would change. She would make sure it did.

"Nikhil?" she called out as he disconnected from his manno.

"Mackenzie?" He was immediately at her side. "I thought you were resting. Why aren't you resting? You need to rest."

"Would you mind if I rested in your bed?"

"I... no, I wouldn't."

"Would you help me get there?" she asked holding out her hands.

Taking them, Nikhil carefully pulled her to her feet. "Do you need Luol, Mackenzie?"

"No, I just need you to take me to bed."

Nikhil said nothing, just stared at her for a moment. There was no way she could have meant those words the way they sounded.

"Then that's where I will take you, Little One." Scooping her up into his arms, Nikhil carried her into his resting area. Once inside, he ripped back the covers and gently laid her down. "You are safe here, Mackenzie."

"I know." She moved over on the bed, then lying on her side, patted the spot next to her. "Lie with me, Nikhil."

"I thought..."

"Thought what?"

"That you didn't feel safe with me."

"You know better than that," she softly reprimanded. "I've never felt safer in my life than when I'm with you."

"Then why..."

"Get into bed, Nikhil, and maybe we can figure it out."

Nikhil quickly kicked off his boots, then lost his vest and weapons before joining her on the bed.

"I'm not sure where to touch you," she whispered.

"Touch me anywhere you want, Mackenzie, and I will respond."

"Maybe that's what I'm afraid of. How you will respond."

"Why?"

"You didn't respond well the last time."

"Mackenzie." Stretching out on his side, Nikhil braced himself up on an elbow, his head propped up on one hand while his other reached out to tuck a strand of hair behind her ear, remaining there to caress the soft skin of her neck. "You were right with what you said before. We are different, very different, and have a great deal to learn about each other. I had no right to react the way I did, to judge you by my people's customs without considering what yours might be. I would very much like to learn what those customs are, and then maybe between us we can find a way to create our own customs."

"Do you think that is possible?" she asked reaching out to touch his cheek.

"I think, that with you, anything is possible."

"What about the men I've kissed?" She felt him stiffen and started to pull her hand away, when the hand covering hers, stopped her.

"Kissing is different for your people," he said quietly.

"Yes, it is."

"Will you explain to me what it means to you?" he asked.

"Kissing?"

"Yes."

"Well, there are different kinds of kisses, and they mean different things depending on who is giving it and to whom."

"All on the lips?"

"No. You can kiss someone on the cheek, the forehead. Some males even kiss the back of a female's hand or palm. They all mean different things."

"The back of the hand..." Nikhil brought her hand to his lips. "Like this?"

"I... yes," she said, her breath catching at his gentle caress.

"What does it mean?" he asked, his eyes glowing softly into hers.

"It is normally a gesture of courtesy or respect between diplomats, people in government, or royalty."

"And the kissing of the palm," he asked, turning her hand over placing another soft kiss there.

"It's more intimate, caring, given only to someone you love or care a great deal about."

"You have done this before?" he questioned and tried not to be upset when he could see she had.

"Yes, with my grandpa."

"Grandpa." Nikhil frowned, hating that he did not understand the word.

"My manno's manno," she told him, realizing not all the words she was using translated into Kaliszian. "He was ill... dying. I sat beside him. Held his hand." She reversed their hands. "And did this." She tipped her head into his hand and lovingly kissed his palm.

"It is full of affection, of devotion. It even feels comforting," he said in a hushed tone.

"Yes, because that's what I felt for him. He raised me after my manno died and my mother abandoned me."

"Your mother did what?" It was then that Nikhil realized he knew very little about his Mackenzie. Oh, he knew what had happened to her but nothing about her life before that.

"She fell apart after my manno died and could barely function. I was only six, and she couldn't deal with it and me."

"When did she return?"

"She never did. It was just me and grandpa until he died. Then it was just me."

"You were forced to survive on your own?" That explained a great deal.

"I guess you could say that, but it wasn't like I was thrown out onto the street. I still had my mountain."

"Mountain... you mean..."

"Mountain," she told him firmly. "My grandpa's family has had the honor of caring for it for centuries."

"You cared for land? For the creatures and life it supported?"

"Yes. We ran a guide business on it."

"Guide business?"

"Earth has a very diverse society. Some live in large cities, some live in smaller towns, and some live in the country. Many like to go to places and spend time where no one lives. Grandpa and I would take them there on our mountain."

"You would... escort groups around your land?"

"Yes, it was what I was doing when the Ganglians found us."

Nikhil silently stared at her for a moment, realizing that his True Mate was a leader of people and a caretaker of the land. She was amazing, and he wanted to know more. "Tell me more."

"About kissing? I don't know what else to tell you. We kiss friends and family members on the cheek."

"We do this too... but only with females." He waited for her to continue.

"So I suppose now you want to know about kissing on the lips."

"I would," he said carefully. "The males you have kissed...”

"There were only two."

"Two.”

"Yes."

"They were... special to you?"

"One was. I thought... well it doesn't matter what I thought, and the other, it was just a first kiss."

"First kiss," he repeated.

"Yes. I liked him. We went out on a date, and when it ended, we kissed goodnight on the lips. It is a common way to end a date. It wasn't the same way I kissed you."

"In what way?"

"It was closed lips."

"Closed...” Nikhil thought back to how her tongue had caressed his and was relieved that it wasn't something she had shared with one not special to her. It made him think. "So what is it that you do share with a male that is special to you?"

"I... that...” Mac found herself blushing.

"Mackenzie," Nikhil frowned at her reaction. "What is wrong? Why won't you tell me?"

"It's not that I don't want to tell you, it's just something that isn't normally talked about on Earth. We just know, like you do with kissing."

"But I don't know."

"I know... You said you had received... friendship from females before."

"Yes." Nikhil frowned at her. What did that have to do with anything?

"How old were you the first time?"

"I was still in my training. She..."

"I don't want to hear about it!" she cut him off, jerking her hand from his.

"Mackenzie, why are you so upset with who I have joined with?"

"Why were you so upset with who I've kissed?!!" she fired back.

"But they aren't the same thing."

"No, they're not."

"I... are you saying that for you... a male and female joining is the most intimate act for your people."

"Not for all, but for me... yes."

"Oh, so how many males have you been..."

"None, alright? None." She rolled away from him, meaning to get out of bed only to find herself suddenly flat on her back, with Nikhil straddling her thighs and her wrists being pulled over her head.

"I would be your first?" he asked quietly, his eyes searching hers and saw it was true. The feeling it gave him knowing that not only would he be her first but her only, had him hardening with need and desire.

"Yes," she whispered, looking up at him. While he straddled her low on her thighs, he wasn't resting his weight on them or making her feel restricted. It was more like he was corralling them, allowing her to move but only so much. She also didn't feel overwhelmed by his massive size looming over her. He was so much larger than her that while her arms were stretched out, his were barely extended.

"This is what you were offering me earlier today, the one thing you had gifted to no other, and I was more concerned about kissing."

"You didn't know."

"I do now." His gaze traveled over her face, a face that was growing more beautiful to him every time he looked at it. "Do you still offer that to me, Mackenzie? That thing most sacred to you, that thing you can only give once, the one that would make you mine and only mine?" He watched as uncertainty filled her eyes and felt his heart clench. Did she no longer wish to give him her most sacred gift? "Mackenzie?"

"You don't see it that way. You..."

"You think I don't value what is sacred to you?" he asked quietly, bringing his face closer to hers. "What you have offered to no other male? I do, Mackenzie, because I offered the same thing to you with my first kiss."

"So we will be each other's first, in our own way, even if it's not our culture's way."

"Yes."

"Then kiss me, Nikhil. I want to experience that incredible feeling again."

"Oh, I plan on kissing you, my Mackenzie, all of you." His eyes searched hers. "Are you alright with that?"

"As long as I get the chance to do the same thing," she countered and saw his glowing eyes flare slightly. "Why are you holding my wrists?"

"Because you challenge my control when you touch me." Shifting his grip, so both of her delicate wrists were now in one hand, he allowed his other to trail down her arm. He hated the way the sleeve of his storm covering prevented him from reaching her smooth, silky skin, but he could still feel her warmth and the slightest of tremors. "Am I frightening you, Mackenzie?"

"No," she whispered, surprised to find it was true. She'd never expected that, not after the way the Zaludians had restrained her. But this was Nikhil, and this was different.

Nikhil nodded, then allowed his hand to continue its journey down along her collarbone and the edge of the covering where it met her neck. He wanted to grip the covering and rip it away, exposing her beautiful skin, but knew it was impossible even with his great strength, for the material was made to survive in the harshest of conditions. It was impenetrable to anything but the sharpest of blades.

Knowing there was only one way to remove it, he allowed his hand to continue exploring her form, cupping the small, firm breast the material so perfectly molded. He loved the way it seemed to welcome his touch and how the dusty rose nipple he'd seen in the shower was pebbling up through the material, begging for more.

Lowering his head, he gave it more, sucking the taut nipple deep into his mouth through the material and flicking it with his tongue. Slowly pulling away, he kept the nipple in his mouth for as long as he could, his tongue circling it until finally it popped out from between his lips.

The corner of his mouth jerked into a small, arrogant, self-satisfied smile hearing his Mackenzie moan and seeing the wet mark his mouth had left on her breast. He wanted it on her skin.

While his mouth was teasing her nipple, his hand moved down over her lower abdomen, his fingers spreading out to massage the firm flesh he found there. Knowing there was still more to discover, his hand moved along the outside of her thigh, and finally he reached warm, silky, bare skin. Lifting his gaze to hers, he watched her carefully as his hand slid up her thigh, his calloused thumb running along the softer inner skin, taking the fabric with it. Reaching the juncture between her thighs, he veered off, sliding the covering up and over one hip.

"Nikhil..."

"Patience, Little One. I told you I wanted to kiss all of you. Leave your hands over your head." His gaze was filled with promise as he waited for her nod of agreement. When she gave it, he slowly released her wrists and his second hand slid down her body until it reached the other side of her covering and pulled it up. Her hips instinctively lifted and the covering settled around her waist.

Shifting his weight, he slid first one of his legs and then the other between hers, forcing them apart. Lowering himself onto his elbows, he nudged a leg over each one of his wide shoulders as his hands slid under and around them, opening her fully to his gaze.

"Goddess, you are beautiful, Mackenzie," he whispered, gazing at her glistening, wet folds. She truly was a goddess, his goddess, and he was going to treat her like one. Using his thumbs, he parted her dark curls until he revealed her pleasure nub, then lowering his mouth worshiped at it.

Mac knew Nikhil wanted her to keep her hands over her head, but she just couldn't. She wanted to do more than just feel

Nikhil's touch. She wanted to see him touching her. Propping herself up on her elbows, she watched him settle between her legs and couldn't believe how arousing it was.

She'd never believed the stories other women had told about how excited and turned on they could get when their boyfriends touched them. It hadn't been that way for her and Chase. It had always seemed awkward and embarrassing to her. She'd had to consciously force herself to relax whenever he touched her, and normally closed her eyes. She had wondered what was wrong with her. Now she knew nothing was, it wasn't her, it was Chase... he wasn't Nikhil.

The simplest of Nikhil's touches turned her on. When he did it with intent like now, he left her breathless with anticipation. When his eyes started to glow brighter, her heart pounded heavily and her channel clenched with need. Watching him now, touching her so intimately, his eyes glowed brighter than she'd ever seen, and it had her core throbbing with an incredible ache that she knew only he could ease. Her eyes widened when she saw him lower his head, then gasped when he began licking and sucking on her clit.

"Nikhil!" she cried out, her fingers digging into the bed to stop herself from touching him since she'd agreed not to.

Nikhil growled as Mackenzie's taste exploded on his tongue. Goddess, nothing had ever tasted as sweet or as perfect or as *his* before. At her cry, he lifted his glowing gaze to hers, while his mouth continued to suck on the small bundle of nerves. She'd moved, even though he'd told her not to, and they would discuss that later, but at least, she wasn't touching him. He didn't think he could control himself if she did. His shaft was already painfully swollen in the confines of his pants, and only his warrior's control kept him from releasing. He wanted to make sure she never regretted giving him this gift, that her first experience in joining was memorable because of the amount of pleasure he gave her, and not because he thought only of his own.

Shifting his arms, he wrapped one around her hips keeping them from rising as he continued to lavish her nub with attention while the other moved to explore her slick folds. Slowly he slipped a finger into her channel. He knew she would be small, for everything about her was small compared to him, but Goddess, not this small or tight.

He could feel the walls of her channel clenching tightly around his finger as he slowly began to work it in and out. How amazing would that feel wrapped around his shaft? Carefully, he added a second finger and felt her body's instinctive resistance to the increase in size, but he continued to press, for as large as his two fingers were, his shaft was so much larger. Goddess, she was tight! Pressing as deeply as he could, he felt a barrier then froze when she gasped in pain.

"Mackenzie..." he lifted his mouth slightly, his gaze piercing hers. What was this? Why was it causing her pain?

"It's okay. It's my hymen. It's supposed to be painful the first time."

Nikhil frowned at that. He knew Kaliszian females had such a thing because he had sisters. He could still remember how his mother had cried and hugged each one the day they went in to be treated, stating that they were no longer just her female offspring but now truly female. It was done so they wouldn't experience pain when they first joined. Why hadn't Mackenzie's been treated? Was it not the way of her people? "Why?" he found himself asking.

"It's just the way it is. In our past, it was expected that a female would still have it when she married, found her Dasho or True Mate," she corrected. "It's not that way so much anymore because..."

"Because?"

"Because times have changed, and most males don't want to be a female's first. They find it an inconvenience, they want someone experienced, and..."

Nikhil growled at the thought that anyone would consider her innocence an *inconvenience*. It made him question why his parents had allowed his sisters to have theirs removed. While the thought of knowingly causing her pain was repulsive to him, the thought of knowing he was her first and her only, was indescribable.

"It is an honor to be your first, Mackenzie," he told her, then attacked her nub even more furiously knowing he had to bring her to release at least once, had to give her pleasure before breaking her barrier. Then he would give her even more pleasure, and she would be his forever.

She couldn't hold back her moan as Nikhil renewed his attack on her clit and began twisting his thick fingers inside her. God, it felt so good! No wonder people talked about sex so much. When he added a third finger, a tension began to build in her body that she had never experienced before. It grew stronger and stronger until every muscle in her body had tightened, and she found she couldn't breathe.

"Nikhil!" she cried out, and after feeling a slight pinch, her first orgasm rolled through her.

Nikhil knew her orgasm was nearly on her. He could feel it in the way her channel tightened around his fingers, the way her hips struggled against his hold, and how short her breath had become. When he felt it all converge, he broke through her barrier and prayed to the Goddess that he hadn't hurt her more than necessary.

Lifting his head from a place he never wanted to leave, he found her head had fallen back to rest on the bed, her arms having relaxed. Her entire body seemed to glow, making him want to soak it up. Her chest was still heaving, tempting him to capture one of the taut nipples, and the faintest of smiles turned up the corner of her mouth making him want to kiss them. As his gaze traveled over her, he found himself sinking into the bottomless depths of her satisfied, brown eyes.

"Nikhil..." She couldn't stop herself from reaching down to touch his cheek.

"You need to give me a moment to regain my control, my Mackenzie," he told her, the muscle in his jaw clenching beneath her hand.

"No, I don't. What I need is for you to kiss me. I need you to kiss me, Nikhil."

"Then I will." Using his upper body strength, he pushed himself up then slid his hands under her covering, pulling it up as he moved up her body, torturing himself by letting his bare chest graze hers. "For I will always give you what you need, my Mackenzie. You are all that matters to me now."

Mac felt something shift deep inside her. Suddenly, she knew she was where she was always supposed to be, with who she was always supposed to be with. It no longer mattered what had to occur to get her here. It no longer mattered that there was still so much she and Nikhil needed to learn about and tell each other. Was this what Nikhil had felt when he saw his True Mate bead on her? She found her thoughts scrambling as instead of attacking her lips as she expected, Nikhil treated her as if she were something to be relished.

Nikhil nipped and sucked his way along his Mackenzie's full, bottom lip. He hadn't done this the last time they'd kissed. He'd been too overwhelmed with discovering his True Mate and let blind need guide his actions. He'd lost control. She had given him something she had never given another male, and he was going to make sure she knew he would always cherish it. Cherish her. When he reached a delicate corner, he gave her upper lip the same attention, capturing the sweet gasp that escaped her mouth with his own.

Goddess, she was sweet and addictive, and he wanted more, more than just her lips. "You are so sweet, my Mackenzie," he murmured against her lips.

"I don't want to be sweet. I want to be yours. Kiss me, Nikhil. Really kiss me." His gentle kisses were driving her crazy. He had just given her her first orgasm, but she still burned, still wanted more, more of him, and he was treating her as if she were some fragile, delicate female.

Nikhil found himself growling, his control slipping with her words. Closing the minuscule distance between their lips, he crushed hers beneath his, his tongue plunging into her mouth.

Mac wrapped her arms around his neck, her fingers spearing through his braids as if he were the last solid thing in her world, and maybe he was.

Nikhil broke off the kiss, pulling back only far enough to glare down at her. "I told you not to touch me."

"I don't take orders very well," she whispered, "and I'd like to see you hold off from touching me as long as I did you."

"Mackenzie... I did it for your protection. You challenge my control."

"I don't fear your loss of control, Nikhil, because I know here," she touched her chest where her heart rested, "that you would never harm me. Your size has never scared me, Nikhil. Only the thought of you holding back, of you not trusting me, does."

"Mackenzie... you are so small... have been through so much."

"I am... and I have been... but both of those things will change. Hopefully."

"What do you mean?"

"Hopefully, I will return to my normal size... I'm not sure you will like it... but..."

"I will 'like' you no matter what size you are! Do you think your size matters to me?"

"But you think *yours* does to me?" she fired back. "You think because you are so much larger than me that I will fear you."

"Others have," he told her quietly.

"Just as others have disliked me because of my larger size."

"That is ridiculous! No one would ever consider you large."

"Maybe not in your universe, but in mine, there are those that think a female beautiful only if they are this size." She gestured to her current body size.

"For Goddess sake why? Is food so scarce on your planet?"

"No, for most it is plentiful, and those are the ones that view thin as beautiful."

"Your Earth is very strange, Mackenzie."

"No stranger than yours that judges you for being too big, Nikhil. You are perfect just the way you are. The way the Goddess intended you to be." Sliding back from him, she sat up and gave him a steamy look. "So, are you going to finish getting me out of this shirt? Or do I have to do it myself?"

Chapter Eleven

Parlan stood alone on the wall, his eyes angrily scanning the barren landscape on its other side. He couldn't believe he'd been assigned here.

To the wall!

Especially on Pontus.

There was no life on Pontus. No one that would attack. No one that needed defending. At least, no one that deserved to be. Those survivors surely didn't. If they were stupid enough, weak enough, to be caught by the Zaludians, then they deserved whatever they got.

Apparently, *General* Treyvon Rayner didn't feel the same way, and all because of that female. The one that Nikhil seemed to think was his True Mate. Which was impossible! She wasn't even Kaliszian! Reaching to his belt, he ripped off his comm and contacted the one person he knew would understand.

"Parlan..." the husky voice answered. "Where are you? Tell me you're on Crurn."

"Don't I wish. No, I'm stuck on Pontus. Walking a *wall!*"

"Walking a *wall?!!*" The disbelief he heard was satisfying. "Whatever for? You are Elite Warrior Parlan Spada!"

"*Exactly!* I knew you would understand."

"Rayner put you on the wall?"

"Yes," he hissed.

"Whatever for?"

"Because of a female."

"A female!" The female on the other end screeched.

"Calm down. She isn't Kaliszian. She's one of the Zaludian survivors we found in the mines."

"Zaludian... you..."

"She isn't Zaludian either. You haven't heard this yet?"

180

"Heard what?"

"In the last mine, we discovered a previously unknown species that calls themselves humans. There was a female among them. Nikhil discovered her and has claimed her as his True Mate."

"*What!*"

"I can't believe you haven't heard any of this."

"I've been... traveling. How long ago were they discovered?"

"Day before yesterday."

"But I thought...″

"Thought what?"

"Nothing. So you found them in a mine. Were there any Zaludian survivors?"

"No, they all died like the vermin they are."

"Why are you calling me, Parlan?" she demanded.

"I just wanted someone to vent to. That... human female... slapped me, for no reason, and when I would have retaliated, Rayner assigned me to the wall."

"Rayner never did have any loyalty to his own people, but I guess that's to be expected with who his ancestor is."

"Agreed."

"He needs to be reminded that he is not truly one of us, that he is not worthy of being one of us."

"He does," Parlan readily agreed.

"So does Nikhil. That he would think a female *not* Kaliszian could be his True Mate!" The rage in the other voice grew. "Impossible!"

"She wears his bead," he informed her.

"She does?" Now the voice quieted and turned speculative.

"Yes, I've seen it myself."

"How... committed are you to making everyone see Rayner and Nikhil the way we do?"

"As if that were possible. Rayner has Liron's ear, always has, and Nikhil..."

"Is now vulnerable."

"Nikhil?!! Vulnerable?!! Have you forgotten his size? He's never vulnerable."

"He is now. If another is wearing his True Mate bead."

"What..."

"Do I have to explain *everything* to you, Parlan?"

Parlan was silent for several moments, his mind racing. "But I thought that was a myth."

"Don't you think it would be worth finding out?"

"What do you need me to do?"

∞ ∞ ∞ ∞ ∞

Nikhil pushed himself up to his knees, his eyes glowing as he gripped the edge of Mackenzie's covering and ripped it over her head before tossing it aside. All he wanted was to claim his Mackenzie, but he couldn't stop his breath from catching at what his actions had revealed.

How could he have forgotten the severity of what she had recently survived and thought only of his own desires? While the bruises on her face and body had faded, the treatments she'd received had yet to restore her to full health. She had only had three meals and hadn't finished the last because her system still wasn't used to normal quantities.

He'd loved the way her small, pert breasts had felt in his hands and mouth, but seeing them this way he knew they used to be larger, much larger, because of the way her skin sagged. He'd seen it before, in the war-torn areas the Ratak had invaded where food supplies had been cut off. Not around a female's breasts, but in other areas.

"Nikhil, what's wrong?" She reached out to cup his cheek tipping his face up, her eyes searching his. What she found had her breath stalling, her eyes filling, and her ripping her hand away. He was disappointed. Covering her exposed chest with an arm, she tried to move away, but his gentle yet firm grip on her shoulders stopped her.

"Where do you think you are going?" he asked roughly.

"I... I need to get my covering, need to..."

"No. You need to tell me what is wrong? What we did before... has it harmed you?" Nikhil felt his gut clench at the thought.

"No."

"Then what?" When she just shook her head, his breath caught as his bead in her hair bumped against his arm, her utter devastation filling him. "Why do you feel this way? What have I done to you?"

"What? What are you talking about?" Mac stilled, her eyes searching his. "You haven't done anything to me, haven't harmed me."

"Then why are you feeling this way?" he demanded.

"Feeling..." She looked from the bead in her hair to him. "You... you can really..."

"Yes. It is part of the gift of having a True Mate. One will know what the other feels and needs. You become one and are never alone again."

"I..."

"Truth, Mackenzie. I need you to tell me truth. I have somehow upset you, made you feel as if you needed to hide your beauty from me." He reached up, and after a brief and fruitless struggle from her, pulled her arm back down. "Tell me."

"You are... disappointed when you look at me," she found herself admitting.

"*I am not!*" Nikhil all but roared.

"I saw it in your eyes, Nikhil," she argued back, but her voice was as quiet as his was loud. "You didn't like looking at my body."

"I didn't," he admitted because he would never give her an untruth, "but only because I know it is not your body's natural form. It hurt me to know you suffered so greatly, and I did not prevent it."

"You couldn't have prevented it. You didn't even know me when it was occurring."

"That does not matter. You are my True Mate. I should have known!"

"Nikhil..." She felt her eyes begin to fill again at the pain in his eyes.

"And now I put my needs, my desires before yours. You need rest and food and care."

"All I need is you, Nikhil. Don't you know that?" She dropped her head to catch the gaze he had lowered. "You give me life, make me strong. With you..."

"With me?"

"With you, I am who I was always meant to be. Because of you, I am now whole. Don't abandon me now," she begged.

"I never would. You are mine, Mackenzie," he said framing her thin, heart-shaped face with his large, calloused hands, his eyes glowing the soft pine green of the trees she so loved on Earth. "Mine. My Mackenzie. My True Mate. Mine."

"Then why are you pulling away from me? Why don't you want to love me... to join with me?"

"I do! Goddess, Mackenzie, I want you so much that I hurt for you, but I would never want to harm you. You need more time."

"No. What I need, is you, Nikhil. I need to connect with you in the most basic of ways. To give myself to you, and for you to do the same with me. Am I asking too much?"

"No. You could never ask too much of me."

"Don't be so sure of that," she said, giving him a small smile. "You don't know what I might ask."

"You can ask for all my credits. You can ask for my honor. You can even ask for my life's breath. And I would willingly give it, if it is what you need, my Mackenzie, for without you in my life, none of it matters."

"Nikhil... don't you know I feel the same way about you? If I had a True Mate bead you would wear it. I wish I could give that to you."

"You have already given me so much more, my Mackenzie."

"What? What could I have possibly given you?"

"You gave me your innocence. Did you not realize that?"

"You... it's gone?"

"Yes, I did not want you to feel any pain when we fully joined. I still don't, which is why we must wait."

"No, Nikhil, it is why we don't have to."

"I can't stand the thought of hurting you, Little One."

"Then let me do it."

"What? What do you mean?"

"Do you trust me, Nikhil?"

"With my life."

"Then roll over onto your back." She pushed against one of his massive shoulders knowing she was only able to move him onto his back because he allowed it, and moved between his thighs. "It's time to see how long *you* can go without touching *me* while I drive *you* crazy."

"You don't want to do this, Mackenzie."

185

"Oh, yes I do. And what I want to do first is get rid of these."
Her hands went to the waist of his pants that hung low on his
hips, slipping her fingers under and sliding them along until
they met at his back. Nikhil lifted his hips, and her hands got
their fill of his taut firm ass, that flexed as they moved over it,
leaving it bare.

Skimming her way along, baring his haunches as she went,
she brought her hands back to his front, getting her first chance
to look at and touch his male beauty. Goddess, the male really
was big all over. He was also hairless. She hadn't realized it
until just then that the only place he had hair was on his head.
Shimmying back, she pulled his pants down passed his knees,
letting him work them the rest of the way off, as she reached
between his massive thighs, and gently cupped his heavy balls.
As amazing as they were, it was his engorged shaft that held
her attention. It was as long and as thick as her wrist.
Tentatively, she circled its base and found her fingers didn't
touch.

Using both hands, she slowly began to stroke him from the
thick root of his shaft to its mushroom-shaped head and back
again. Her thumb captured the drop of pre-cum escaping from
it. Bringing her gaze to his, she found him watching her intently
as she lifted the thumb to her mouth, tasting his strong, spicy
flavor for the first time.

"Mackenzie..." Nikhil moaned, his hips instinctively pressing
into her hand as he fought for control.

"Goddess, you taste good," she whispered, then lowering her
mouth licked the next bead that quickly appeared before taking
him into her mouth. She'd never given head before, but from
Nikhil's reaction, she must be doing it right.

Nikhil couldn't believe his Mackenzie was doing this. The
females he had shared his friendship with before had never

done this... and he'd never heard other males talking about it either. It felt amazing, but it also challenged his control. He wanted to thrust his shaft deep into her mouth, wanted to feel her swallow him. The thought alone had his balls starting to draw up against his body, wanting to spill his seed, but he didn't want to do it in her mouth. Not this time. He wanted to be deep inside her when that happened.

"Mackenzie!" Using the strength of his abs so his hands could sink into her hair, he sat up and pulled her mouth from his shaft, replacing it with his, giving her a deep scorching kiss. His tongue speared her mouth the way his shaft wanted to her body.

Mackenzie ripped her mouth away from his, breathing heavily even as a devilish look filled her eyes. "You were supposed to see how long you could go without touching me. Remember?"

"I will never be able to go very long, Mackenzie. I need you too badly."

He covered her mouth again, and while she was on her knees between his thighs, he pulled her close enough that she could feel his stiff cock poking into her belly. Never breaking off the kiss, she gripped Nikhil's forearms and shifted so she was straddling his lap. The long length of his hard cock sliding along the hot slickness of her slit, causing both of them to moan.

"Mackenzie... I am not going to last long if you keep doing that."

"Neither am I," she told him breathlessly, continuing to coat his cock with her slickness. Realizing she couldn't rise high enough on her knees to set him at her entrance, she gave him a pleading look. "Help me, Nikhil."

Nikhil's large heart began to pound wildly at her request. He wanted to refuse so there was no chance of him harming her, and he wanted to comply. He wanted to spear her with his shaft, wanted to drive into her again and again until he released deep inside her.

"It will be okay, Nikhil. My vow."

Slowly, he gripped her waist and lifted her the last few inches needed to set the engorged head of his shaft at her sweet tiny opening. "Are you sure, my Mackenzie?"

"Yes," she said wiggling slightly in his arms. Her breath caught as Nikhil slowly lowered her onto the bulbous head of his cock, his massive arms trembling with the restraint he was exerting. She couldn't hold back the small moan that escaped her lips as her channel strained to accept him. It was nearly painful, but in the most wonderful of ways, and it only added to the tension building inside her.

Finally, her knees made contact with the bed, but Nikhil's arms didn't relax. If anything, they stiffen more knowing he was no longer in control. Reaching up, she grabbed the braids that were flowing over his chest, pulling on them until he lowered his head for her to capture his lips in a torrid kiss as she took another inch of him.

"Goddess, Mackenzie!" His fingers dug deeper into her flesh. He'd never experienced such an exquisite pain before.

He wanted it to end.

He wanted it to last forever.

"Oh my God, Nikhil!" She threw her head back as the tension in her body began to wind tighter and tighter. She'd never experienced anything like this before, but instinctively she knew if she just trusted her body it would be alright. Relaxing her thighs, she slid the rest of the way down Nikhil's massive cock, and couldn't stop the startled cry that escaped her mouth. God, she'd never felt so full before. She knew immediately what

Nikhil's reaction was going to be, and clamped her knees on his hips. "Don't you dare!" she warned.

"Mackenzie," the strain in his voice was easily heard. "I am harming you!"

"You aren't!" she choked out. "Just give me a minute. The Goddess wouldn't have made me your True Mate if we weren't compatible."

Nikhil's hands shifted to her ass, pulling her closer as he sat up higher. She knew his intent was to give her no room to move, but instead it had her clit rubbing against his washboard abs and this time when she cried out, it was in pleasure.

"God, Nikhil! Do that again!" she demanded.

Nikhil's eyes flashed a brilliant green at the pleasure he heard in her voice and didn't deny her. Slowly, he repeated the action and had to grit his teeth when her channel spasmed in response, nearly causing him to come as if it were his first time.

"Like that do you, Little One?" he asked huskily, watching the color bloom on her face. Her breath became short pants as her body reacted to the pleasure he was giving her.

"Yes! Again! Please! I'm so close!" And she was. The tension in her body was nearly unbearable and it wouldn't take much... then Nikhil twisted his hips ever so slightly and her world exploded.

Twisting Nikhil took Mackenzie to her back, and with one hard, deep thrust he released all his control and joined her in paradise.

Chapter Twelve

Nikhil lay on his back, where he had rolled after experiencing the most explosive release he'd ever had in his life. With his Mackenzie sleeping deeply in his arms, he reached down, touching the bead she wore and was immediately filled with a sense of well being that told him she rested peacefully. How did her species know their Soul Mates were well if they didn't have the bead?

She didn't wake as he pulled the covers up over them. It spoke to the amount of rest she truly needed before she would be fully recovered from her ordeal, and he would make sure she got it. He would also make sure that she ate, that she was never harmed again, and that she knew, every day for the rest of her life, that she was the most precious thing to him in the entire universe.

Making sure she was secure in his arms, he closed his eyes and slept.

∞ ∞ ∞ ∞ ∞

Jen leaned back against the wall, trying to nonchalantly stretch out the aching muscles of her injured leg. It had been a long day with a lot to take in. Mac had tried to explain the best she could about what had happened to her since she'd been taken from them. She told them how much better she felt since using something called the deep- repair unit and how she could now, thanks to another educator, understand not only Kaliszian, but also what everyone else in the room was saying.

Making sure the hood of the cape still covered her face, Jen let her head fall back to rest against the wall; she was so tired.

Tired of hurting.

Tired of putting on a brave front.

Just tired.

"You should lie down on your cot, Jen."

"Yeah, I probably should. Help me up?" She held out her hands and Paul took them pulling her carefully to her feet.

"How you holding up?" he asked leading her to her cot. When she sat and leaned back against the wall, he sat down next to her.

"I'm good, and you?"

"Not too bad. Glad to be out of that damn mine but..."

"But, at least, we knew what to expect there... right?"

"Yeah."

"How's Eric doing?" she asked. "You know you should have been with him; instead of helping me get out."

"Eric is fine," he reassured her. "He understood that we couldn't risk losing you too."

"You two are so good together." She let her head come to rest on his thin shoulder.

"We are. I just hope we're allowed to stay that way."

"Why wouldn't you be?"

"We have no idea who these guys are, Jen. What their real beliefs are. Or if they accept that a man can love another man."

"Well if they can't then I guess they aren't as advanced as we thought they were. Love is love, Paul."

"True. Except for them being able to travel in space and some of their weaponry, I haven't seen anything that makes them more advanced than us."

"True, but maybe these Kaliszians will be."

"Seriously? They carry *swords*, Jen, and it looks like they rely on brute strength. We haven't been like that since the middle ages."

"True, but I can't say automatic weapons and nuclear bombs are that much better. At least theirs seem to take some strength and skill to use. While all ours require is some idiot willing to either pull a trigger or push a button."

"That's true too." Paul looked up and smiled as Eric moved to sit on the other side of her.

"Hey, beautiful, how you holding up?" Eric asked.

"Eric..." Jen felt her eyes fill again. She knew she was no longer beautiful, especially not on the side where Eric was sitting.

"Shhh. You will always be beautiful to me. To us. Now," Eric put his arm around her thin shoulders, pulling her close and her head shifted to his shoulder. "Rest."

Knowing arguing would do no good, Jen settled deeper into Eric's embrace and felt Paul move in closer, putting his arm around her as he gripped Eric's waist. Knowing she was safe in their embrace, she let sleep claim her.

∞ ∞ ∞ ∞ ∞

Mac rolled onto her back, stretching her arms up over her head and yawned. God, she felt good. The sound of water shutting off had her eyes opening and her head turning to see Nikhil walking out of the cleansing room. A towel was wrapped low around his hips while he used another one to remove the moisture from his hair. His hands stilled seeing her watching him and he was immediately moving to the bed.

"You're awake," he said moving to sit down next to her.

"I am."

"How are you feeling?"

"I feel good. Really good." Reaching up, she cupped his cheek. "I suppose I should get up so we can go to last meal." She frowned at the strange look Nikhil gave her. "Nikhil? What's wrong?"

"Nothing is wrong, Mackenzie. It is just that it is morning."

"Morning? I slept through the night?"

"Yes. I thought to wake you for last meal, but Luol said if you were hungry you would wake on your own."

"You contacted Luol?"

"Yes. I was concerned. I..." He looked away.

"It's alright, Nikhil." She pulled his face back to her. "He's right. I've eaten so much in the last few days that all I needed was sleep. But what about you? Tell me you didn't skip last meal."

"You think I would leave you unprotected? That because of my size, food would be more important to me than you!??"

"Nikhil?" Mac flinched back, her eyes widening at the venom in his voice. "That's not what I was implying. I just... I don't want you to do without because of me."

Nikhil forced himself to relax the fists he hadn't realized he'd clenched. Where had that come from? It had been years since he'd let what someone else thought about his size bother him, but this wasn't someone else. This was his Mackenzie.

"I'm sorry, Mackenzie, I shouldn't have spoken to you like that." When he would have risen from the bed, her hand on his arm stopped him.

"I take it that's a sensitive subject for you." Sitting up, she caught the sheet, keeping it from falling and held it across her chest.

"Yes... growing up it was. I am sorry, Mackenzie, I should not have reacted like that."

"You were bullied." Mac couldn't believe anyone would be brave enough to do something like that to Nikhil. It just went to show that anyone could be bullied.

"I do not know this word, but when I was a great deal younger, others would comment that I must be receiving more than my fair share of the food stores to reach such a size." He felt his face flushing at the remembered taunts. "It was an untruth," he growled.

"Of course, it was an untruth," she immediately agreed.

Reaching out, he touched the bead she wore, and was humbled by the absolute belief she had in him, but he still found himself asking. "How can you be so sure?"

"Because I know you, Nikhil. I don't need you to wear my bead, to have to touch it, to know you would never do such a thing." Her fingers tightened on his arm. "It must have hurt to have others think something like that about you."

"It was long ago," he said quietly.

"But it still affects you, just like my mother's abandonment still affects me."

"How does it affect you, my Mackenzie?" He reached out to run a gentle finger along the curve of her breast that was pressing up because of the way she held the sheet. "When I see you, all I see is a strong, confident female."

"Who deep inside always fears that everyone she loves will leave her and never return."

Nikhil just stared at his Mackenzie. He wanted to vow to her that he would always return to her, but he knew he couldn't. He was an Elite Warrior. A Squad Leader. What he did was dangerous and he would never lie to her, so he gave her what he could.

"I can only vow that I will fight with my last breath to return to you, my Mackenzie. I will never abandon you."

Mac's gaze searched Nikhil's, and she knew he was telling her the truth. His truth. He wasn't going to give her a false promise, but he also wasn't going to abandon her willingly. "Alright, I can live with that."

Her stomach growled, stopping her from saying anything else.

"I will get you first meal," he said immediately getting up.

"I could eat, but first I need to use the cleansing room." She blushed as she told him that.

"Alright, I will help you." He held out a hand to her.

"I can handle it myself," she told him, but still took the hand he held out.

"You are sure?" he asked helping her up, frowning as she tried to keep the sheet wrapped around her.

"Yes, but first." Reaching up, she pulled his head down for a deep kiss. "Good morning."

Nikhil's response was instantaneous as he wrapped his arms around her, lifting her off her feet to capture her lips for another kiss. Goddess, he would never get enough of her. He felt his shaft rising as she wrapped her arms around his head pulling him even closer. He moved to lay her back down on the bed when her stomach made its desires known again. Reluctantly he broke off the kiss and put her back on her feet.

"Use the cleansing room," he told her gruffly. "I will have first meal ready for you when you return."

"Alright, but make sure you get some for yourself too," she said and lifting the sheet so she wouldn't trip on it, made her way to the cleansing room.

Nikhil watched her hurry away and waited until the cleansing room door closed before moving to dress. His shaft was still extremely hard and it wasn't happy at being confined inside his pants. If it had to be confined, it wanted to be inside her tight channel, not his uniform. Ignoring the discomfort closing his pants caused him, he went to get his Mackenzie's first meal, stopping only long enough to lean down and pick up her covering from the floor, placing it on the bed where she would see it.

Mac stared at her reflection in the mirror and couldn't believe what she was seeing. Her hair was flowing in waves around her face, and she knew she had Nikhil to thank for that, vaguely remembering him running his fingers through it during the night. Her lips were puffy and swollen, again thanks to Nikhil, this time from his kisses that had rocked her world.

Smiling, she touched the crystal revealing the tankless toilet and hurried to complete what she needed to do so she could get back to Nikhil. Wrapping the sheet tighter around her, she exited the cleansing room. Meaning to find Nikhil, she paused seeing the shirt she had been wearing lying on the bed. Quickly, she put it on and went to find him.

She found him frowning, putting his comm back on his belt as she walked into the room. She felt her breath catch and her heart beat a little faster at the stunning specimen of male. He was standing there in just his pants, and he was all hers. Smiling, she walked up to him.

"Is everything alright?" she asked.

"Yes, but I need to report to duty."

"Right now?"

"Not until after we have first meal. Come," he gestured to the couch where he had placed two meal packets.

"Are these always the same?" she asked after heating and opening hers.

"They can vary, it all depends on what the Tornians send," he told her.

"The Tornians?" she asked looking at him as she took a bite.

"Yes, the majority of our food comes from Vesta in the Tornian Empire," Nikhil frowned as he spoke. "Wasn't that in the educator?"

"It was. I mean I knew that's where you got the majority of your food, but not that there was so little variety."

"It is all taken to Crurn where it is processed before being distributed."

"I see."

"Is it not this way on Earth?"

"No. We have a large variety of food, and everyone chooses what they want and cooks their own."

"Truth?" Nikhil's eyes widened at the thought.

"Truth. Packets like these," she lifted what was in her hand, "are normally reserved for military, survivalists, or disaster areas."

"It is not something you eat every day?"

"No. These are the only ones I've ever had."

"I see." Nikhil silently ate his meal and wondered for the first time if what he would be able to provide for his Mackenzie would be enough to satisfy her. It seemed his world offered so little compared to what she was used to.

"Nikhil?"

"Yes?"

"Do you think you can get me one of those gray capes that the other survivors have?"

"What? Why?" he asked frowning at her. Those capes weren't meant for one such as his Mackenzie. They were made from an inexpensive, coarse fabric that could be rough on the skin. It was something that should never touch his Ashe's soft skin.

"Well... as much as I like wearing your shirt," she gave him a small smile, "it doesn't cover all that much. And since I don't have any underwear..."

"Underwear?"

"Small coverings worn under outer coverings. They make it so if this pulls up," she indicated the bottom of the cover, "no one sees anything they shouldn't."

"I see."

"Do your females wear coverings this short?" she asked.

"No, they typically reach the floor. What do you normally wear?"

"Pants mostly, like what you wear." She gestured to his.

"Your females like to wear pants?"

"I guess most do. It depends on what they are doing; where they are going. I normally only wear a dress on special occasions."

"I see."

"What's wrong, Nikhil."

"I... when I spoke to Luol about waking you, I also talked to him about your lack of coverings."

"You did? Why?"

"Luol's Ashe resides on Crurn and in four days our resupply ship will arrive from there. He is going to have her select proper coverings for you and have them sent along with it."

"I... you did this for me?" she asked, and felt her eyes start to fill.

"I wanted you to have something more, something better, than just my storm shirt," he admitted.

"I... thank you, Nikhil."

"They will be dresses, Mackenzie. Long dresses."

"That's okay," she reassured him.

"But..."

"Nikhil, I'm not on Earth anymore, and while I admit I am more comfortable in pants, I can adjust."

"I will arrange it so that there are pants included for you on the next supply ship. My vow. That way you will have a choice."

"Thank you." Reaching over, she put a hand on his leg.

"I want to give you everything you desire, Mackenzie. So you never regret having me as your True Mate."

"Nikhil." She set her food packet aside then rose to her knees, so she was eye to eye with him. "Don't you know all I desire is *you*? You don't have to give me things for that to happen, and I could never regret having you as my True Mate."

"You say that now..."

"I will always say it, Nikhil. I may be new to your world, to your universe, but I know I'm getting the best it has to offer."

∞ ∞ ∞ ∞ ∞

Nikhil wasn't happy as he led his Mackenzie into the area housing the survivors. A gray cape, that he had altered with his blade so it fit her better, was wrapped around her. He had wanted her to remain in his quarters while he attended to his duties, but she insisted on being brought here. She wanted to check on her friends and answer any more questions they might have. He knew he was being irrational, but the thought of her being around so many other males without him there raised every protective instinct inside him.

It didn't matter to him that she had already spent a great deal of time alone with these males. It didn't matter to him that none of them were her True Mate and that he was. They had failed to protect her from the Zaludians, and that was something he would never forget or forgive.

"I will be fine, Nikhil," she said, turning to face him as she sensed his growing tension.

"They allowed you to be harmed once, Mackenzie," he said through gritted teeth, his glowing green eyes hard and piercing as they traveled over the males standing behind her.

"That wasn't their fault, Nikhil. There was nothing they could have done."

"They could have fought for you," he growled.

Knowing there was no way she would ever change her mate's mind on this, she changed the subject. "Will I see you for midday meal?"

"I will be here," Nikhil promised.

Putting a hand behind her head, he tipped her face up to his and captured her lips for a deep, hard kiss that left no doubt in the minds of the males in the room that she was his female. Giving the males behind them one last look, he spun on his heel and forced himself to leave her.

"Onp," he growled, looking at the warrior standing by the door who was in charge of the survivors.

"With my life, Squad Leader," he vowed then watched Nikhil leave after giving his True Mate one last long look.

∞ ∞ ∞ ∞ ∞

Mac turned and immediately felt the weight of her friends' eyes on her, especially Craig who was glaring at her.

"What the hell is going on with you?!!" he demanded angrily in English, grabbing her arm. "Have they brainwashed you?"

While Mac knew only their group understood Craig's words, she realized the others in the room understood the tone behind them especially the Kaliszians by the sound of them drawing their swords.

"It's fine," she said in Kaliszian, looking over her shoulder to see she was right and ordered, "Sheath your swords."

"No male should be touching you," Onp growled angrily.

"Craig, let her go!" Jen's quiet but cutting order from the back of the group had him immediately dropping his hand.

"He's not touching me now, Warrior Onp, so sheath your sword." When he didn't immediately, she continued. "We are a species that touches. He wasn't attacking me. Were you, Craig?" she turned her gaze back to him and realized he didn't understand what she was saying. "Shake your head, Craig," she hissed, "unless you want a blade at your throat."

Craig vigorously began to shake his head from side to side and slowly Onp replaced his sword.

"To answer your questions Craig. I was kissing my True Mate goodbye, and no, I haven't been brainwashed. Now," she looked over the group. "We need to talk because I think I've come up with a way to figure out how long ago the Ganglians took us."

"What? How?" Craig demanded, and while he kept his voice down, his eyes shot to Onp who was still watching him closely.

"Where's Paul?" she asked.

"Here," Paul's voice came from the back of the group.

Mac was about to ask Paul her question when she saw Jen shifting her weight. "Come on, let's all sit down and I'll tell you what I'm thinking."

Jen gave Mac an irritated look. She knew what her friend was doing. She didn't need to be coddled.

"Come on, Jen," Mac put an arm around her shoulders pulling her back, her brown eyes pleading with blue. "I need to know what you think but I also need to know that you are okay."

With a heavy sigh, Jen nodded and let herself be led to a cot where she sat. "Okay, I'm sitting. Now tell me what you've learned from the Kaliszians."

"I haven't learned anything from them, at least not concerning where Earth is or how long ago we were taken."

"But you just said," Craig started angrily.

"I *said* that *I* thought of something," Mac emphasized her gaze traveling over the shaggy, dull hair and scruffy beards on the faces looking at her. They had all been a well-groomed group when she first met them, with only Eric sporting a very short well- trimmed beard. "And that I need Paul to tell me if I could be right."

"What can I possibly tell you, Mac?" Paul asked.

"How fast does hair grow?" she replied.

"What?" Paul frowned at the question.

"Hair. You're a barber. You know hair." She lifted some of hers that thanks to Luol's treatment and Nikhil cleansing it was silky and shiny. "Mine has to be at least three inches longer than it was when we were first taken."

"It... it varies from a quarter to a half an inch a month," Paul told her.

"So if mine is three inches that means six months."

"I... yes." Paul's hand reached up to touch his own hair. Why hadn't he thought of that? His wasn't three inches longer but then his hair had always grown slower. Looking at Eric's, whose hair he knew had always grown faster, he saw it was at least three and a half inches. "Dear God, I think you're right."

"Six months?" Jen whispered, her eyes filling with tears as she saw the shock and disbelief in everyone's eyes. "We've been gone six months..."

Mac was about to say something when she saw Luol enter the room and hearing what he was saying, she was up and across the room.

∞ ∞ ∞ ∞ ∞

Luol walked into the survivors' area greeting Onp as his gaze traveled around the room. "Warrior Onp."

"Healer Luol, you are ready to resume treating the Nekeok?" Onp knew only four of the Nekeok had been treated so far and that the eight Tafa and all the humans were still waiting, with the exception of Nikhil's True Mate.

"I will be taking one Nekeok and one human," Luol informed him.

"But there is only one deep-repair unit," Onp said frowning.

"The second has been brought down from the Defender to speed up the process."

"But..."

"Why only one?!!" Mac demanded and both males looked at her in shock.

"I'm sorry, Mackenzie?" Luol frowned down at her. He hadn't realized she was here. "Why only one what?"

"Why only one of my people? You know they need the deep-repair unit more than the others!"

"I..."

"They need it, Luol!"

"I know they do, Mackenzie, but so do the others, and your males will require a great deal more time in the unit. So much time that I would be able to treat two or three of the others. And with the supply ship arriving in four days..."

"What does that have to do with anything?"

"The others..." Luol's gaze traveled to the others in the room. "They will be leaving on the ship so they can return to their families and homes while you..."

"While we will be remaining here," she finished for him.

"Yes, for now at least."

"What do you mean for now?"

"I only meant until we discover where your home world is. Your concern for your people is admirable, Mackenzie, and I support it, but there are also others that have suffered."

Mac found she couldn't argue with that. They weren't the only ones that had suffered, but at least the others knew and understood what was happening to them, then and now, while her friends didn't.

"Then at least start letting them use the educator," she argued back. "There is so much they don't know or understand. You have no idea what it feels like to not understand what is being said to you. To not know how this world works and why. They can't even understand what I am saying to you right now."

Looking behind her, Luol saw she was right. All her people were standing there staring at them with a combination of confusion and fear. How would he feel if he suddenly found himself in their world and couldn't communicate?

"I can not properly attend to two beings in the deep-repair units, and also monitor another using the educator."

"Then I'll help you," Mac told him.

"What?" Luol's eyes widened in shock.

"I said. I. Will. Help. You. Let me go find out who wants to go first."

∞ ∞ ∞ ∞ ∞

"What's going on, Mac?" Craig asked as soon as she returned.

"The Kaliszians have brought down another deep-repair unit so they can start treating you guys the way they have me. It's a bed that closes around you." She saw their confusion. "The only thing I can compare it to is an MRI bed. It scans you then fixes whatever needs repaired while replenishing whatever has been depleted from your system. It will take some time."

"How much time?" Craig demanded.

"I was in it two times totaling almost twelve hours."

"Why two times?" Paul asked.

"Luol wasn't sure how my system would react to the unit so he erred on the side of caution."

"But you didn't have any problems. Right?" Jen asked concerned.

"I didn't," she reassured her. "Luol is also going to start applying their educator to you, one at a time, so you can know what I know."

"How long does that take?" Craig asked.

"A couple hours. So who wants to go first?" she asked looking at each one of them expectantly then frowned when no one immediately volunteered. "Guys?" she prompted.

"I'll go," Craig and Paul said at the same time.

"Great, then let's go," Mac said

"Paul..." Eric grabbed his hand.

"Someone needs to do this, Eric. It will be fine," Paul squeezed his hand reassuringly then looked at Mac. "Let's go I'm ready to understand all this shit!"

∞ ∞ ∞ ∞ ∞

Luol was still slightly shocked as he sealed the door of the medical unit. Onp had vigorously tried to deter Mackenzie from accompanying him, but when it came to the battle of wills, Mackenzie was the surprising victor. He found himself smiling as he remembered how flustered Onp had become when Mackenzie had told him that the only way he could stop her from leaving the area was if he physically restrained her and she was *sure* that wouldn't upset Nikhil at all.

Turning, he found Mackenzie talking quietly not to the two males she'd introduced as Paul and Craig, but to the Nekeok that was going to be treated by the other repair unit. Moving closer, he was surprised to find she was comforting the male.

"Is there a problem, Mackenzie?" he asked moving to her side. Nekeok's were a somewhat short-tempered species that could strike out when irritated. While they were small by Kaliszian standards, they were still larger and stronger than humans.

"No. I was just reassuring Blag that he had heard correctly. The supply ship will be here in four days. He's anxious to get back to his wife. They have been notified that he's alive, right?"

"I... I do not know," Luol admitted.

"Well, we need to find out," she told him. "Blag's wife was with offspring when he was taken, and he is very concerned about her."

"I will contact the General after they are in the repair unit. I am sorry, Blag," Luol turned to the Nekeok whose name he hadn't even known, "that I never thought to inquire."

"It is to be expected," the Nekeok replied, and it had Luol frowning.

"What do you mean?" Luol demanded.

"Kaliszians are only ever concerned with themselves. It is what caused the Great Infection," Blag said moving toward one of the repair units. "If it weren't that the Zaludians were stealing a resource you might need, you never would have even bothered freeing us."

"That's an untruth, Blag," Luol denied.

"Is it?" Blag challenged. "Then tell me why were you on the other side of the empire for so long fighting the Ratak, when you should have been defending us from the Ganglians? The planets the Ratak were trying to claim hold vast mineral resources that you can trade with the Tornians for food. It is the only reason you care about them. They have no indigenous life, no people, just minerals."

Luol opened his mouth to argue, then snapped it shut, finding that in this, Blag was not wrong. Then he watched Blag jump up on the unit. "Yet you are trusting me to treat you?"

"You may be a selfish species, but you have honor. You would never harm one in your care." With that, Blag laid down and closed his eyes.

Mac's eyes widened as she listened to the exchange and wasn't sure what surprised her more, Blag's accusation, or that Luol didn't deny it. She was also glad that Paul and Craig couldn't understand what was being said. She didn't need them questioning what she didn't understand herself yet.

"Mac, what's going on?" Paul's question had her pulling her gaze from Blag and Luol.

"Luol and Blag were just talking about Luol contacting his family." While she didn't lie, she didn't tell them everything that was being said. She needed them to trust what she was telling them. She just hoped she was right. "Watch and you'll see what Luol is going to do, and then you can decide which one of you wants to use the repair unit and which one will use the educator."

"I'll do the repair unit," Craig immediately spoke, moving closer to watch what Luol was doing.

Mac wasn't surprised that Craig had chosen the repair unit. It wasn't because he was fearless in the face of the unknown, because he wasn't, he just didn't like not being first. She looked to Paul, who just rolled his eyes.

"I'm fine with the educator. It would be nice to know what everyone else is saying," he leaned in close to Mac so only she could hear his next words. "Then I will also know what else they just said."

"Paul..." her eyes searched his.

"It's okay, Mac. I trust you. Craig might not, but then he's been trying to get close to you since you met, and you've kept shooting him down even when things were really bad."

"I wasn't interested in him then and I'm not now."

"That was pretty obvious from the way you were kissing that Nikhil," Paul gave her an understanding smile.

"Mackenzie?"

Luol's voice saved her from having to reply, and she turned to him. "Would you explain to your male that I need him to lie down on the bed?"

"He's not my male," she denied in Kaliszian, causing Luol to raise an eyebrow at her but she moved toward him.

"Craig, you need to get on the bed and lie down just like Blag did," she told him in English. "The unit will start to scan you once it closes." She watched Craig's eyes widen as the cover began to close and she knew he was beginning to panic. "It's okay, Craig, just relax and breathe. It's not going to hurt or be painful. You can even move around if you want."

"It doesn't knock you out?" Craig asked.

"No, but you can sleep if you want." She looked up and saw Luol had finished working the control panel of the unit.

"Is there a problem?" Luol asked her in Kaliszian.

"No, I think Craig just thought the unit would knock him out."

"Knock him out?" Luol frowned at her not understanding the word.

"Make him sleep," she clarified.

"Oh, well I can, if you think he would be more comfortable that way."

Mac looked to Craig and could see he was struggling with being in the closed unit. She understood. She hadn't liked it either, not after the cramped conditions of the mine. "It might be best if you did. I don't think he'll be able to stay in the unit otherwise."

Moments after saying the words, she watched Craig's body relax and his eyes close.

"Well that was quick," Mac said.

"It helps when severely injured warriors are brought in."

"I thought your portable repair unit was able to treat severe injuries in the field," Mac said.

"That unit can only fully repair non-life threatening injuries. The most severe must be treated with this unit. The portable unit makes it possible for most to make it to one."

"That's why you didn't want to bring the second one down." She now understood.

"Yes, but the Defender isn't going to be leaving orbit so if something were to happen, the injured would just be brought here. Do not worry, Mackenzie. All will be fine." Luol checked the readings on both units then looked to Paul. "Is he ready for the educator?"

"Paul?" Mac turned to look at him. "Ready?"

"Ready."

Chapter Thirteen

Mac sat next to Paul holding his hand as Luol explained to him, in Zaludian, what he was doing and why, and what he would feel. After a tense nod from Paul, Luol put the educator on him. For a moment, Paul's grip tightened around Mac's hand, and then it relaxed.

"He is now in a deep sleep," Luol told her. "It will be several hours before he wakes."

"I'll stay with Paul so you can see to Craig and Blag if you tell me what I need to watch for."

"Agitation mostly. It means he is fighting the information the educator is trying to give him."

"Why would that happen?" she asked giving Paul a concerned look.

"We don't know for sure, but believe it is either because the educator has somehow triggered a bad memory, or the chemical composition of the recipient's brain is just unable to absorb what it is receiving. While it's rare, it can cause permanent harm if not corrected."

"Oh, so maybe you should stay here, and I'll sit with Craig and Blag."

"You would not understand the readings the units are giving you and would be unable to adjust them," Luol told her quietly.

"I'm sorry, Luol." She looked up at him, her eyes full of regret.

"For what?"

"For demanding that you treat so many at the same time. I didn't realize the risks..."

"But you were right, Mackenzie," he told her kindly. "Your people need to be able to understand what is happening. If I expected there to be any problems, I would have refused. And it is truth that even General Rayner has no power to sway me when it comes to what is best for those I treat."

"Really? Not even the most feared and powerful General Rayner?" She'd learned that from the educator.

"General Rayner is feared and powerful for a reason, but he is also honorable and would never intentionally harm one under his care."

"You truly believe that?"

"Yes."

Mac was silent for a moment, watching Paul lying there so peacefully. "I need to thank you, Luol."

"For what?" he asked frowning at her.

"Nikhil told me that you asked your Ashe to obtain and send coverings for me on the next supply ship."

Luol gave her a warm smile. "That was no hardship for her. My Maysa loves to go shopping, especially for young females."

"I'm a young female?" she asked raising an eyebrow at him. She knew for a Kaliszian, a young female referred to one under the age of eighteen, who was not yet considered fully mature. "I don't think Nikhil sees me that way."

Luol's cheeks started to flush. "It was the only way I could describe your size to Maysa. I did not mean to infer..."

"I was just teasing you, Luol," she said smiling at him. "I take it your females are larger than me."

"When they reach their maturity, yes, but before that, they come in different sizes."

"One being mine."

"Yes. Maysa and I only have male offspring, so she was very excited to spend my credits on something other than 'boring male coverings', as she refers to them. "

"Still, it was such short notice and..." Mac trailed off. Why hadn't she realized? Nikhil had told her some of their females would offer their friendship to males for extra food or credits. Of course, he would have to pay for her coverings. How much she didn't know. Could he afford them? That was something else she didn't know and then she had gone and asked for more.

"Mackenzie, is something wrong?" Luol asked.

"I... nothing. I just realized there was something I need to talk to Nikhil about. So you think Paul will be okay with me watching him?"

"Yes. Now I need to check on Craig and Blag."

"Alright. Oh, and don't forget to check to see if Blag's family has been contacted."

"I won't."

∞ ∞ ∞ ∞ ∞

Luol frowned at the readings the deep-repair unit was giving him for the human called Craig. While the repair unit was replenishing the same nutrients as it had in Mackenzie, his weren't nearly as depleted as hers, and his weight loss didn't seem as extreme. Why was that, if they had all experienced the same things up until she was discovered? Making a few adjustments, he turned his attention to Blag's unit.

"How much longer?" Blag asked as he watched Luol.

"You are doing well," Luol told him absently.

"That's not what I asked!" Blag fired back.

"Another hour."

"Where is Mackenzie?" Blag demanded.

"She's in the other room sitting with her friend." Luol saw Blag's gaze searching behind him.

"They are a strange species," Blag finally muttered.

"Did you ever interact with them in the mine?"

"No."

"You never saw them?" Luol found that hard to believe. The mine wasn't that big.

"Only in passing. The Zaludians separated us by species. I can't believe a female was able to survive there, especially one as kind and as delicate as Mackenzie."

Luol raised an eyebrow at Blag's words. Nekeoks were a species that few intentionally dealt with because of their temperament, but they were loyal to those that earned their respect. It seemed that Mackenzie had earned Blag's with just a few kind words. It was something he hadn't given Blag.

"She is an exceptional female," Luol agreed, moving to where Blag could see him easier. "If you are resting comfortably, I will go contact the General and see if your wife has been notified."

"I am fine. Go!" Blag ordered impatiently and turned his gaze back to the ceiling.

Luol gave Blag an annoyed look at his order and subsequent dismissal of him. He was about to tell him he could go to Daco when Luol remembered that Blag's wife had been with offspring when he was abducted. Spinning on his heel, he went to contact Treyvon.

∞ ∞ ∞ ∞ ∞

Nikhil watched as the sparring match between Gulzar and Nroa progressed, his expression revealing none of his satisfaction at how well Gulzar was doing against the Elite Warrior. The male had great potential and Nikhil knew it wouldn't be long before Gulzar attained the Elite status he so desired. All he needed was more experience, which was suddenly apparent when Gulzar overextended himself. Nroa swept Gulzar's feet out from under him, and the tip of his sword was at Gulzar's throat before he even landed on his back.

The two warriors stared at each other for a moment, both breathing heavily, their bodies gleaming with sweat before Nroa withdrew his sword and held out a hand. Gulzar gave him a frustrated look but reached up and took it, allowing Nroa to pull him to his feet.

"It will come, Gulzar," Nroa reassured the younger warrior. "You're just letting your impatience get the better of you."

Gulzar nodded his head in agreement. "Thank you for your insight and advice, Warrior Nroa."

"Good. Again," Nroa ordered, and they began.

'Yes,' Nikhil thought, 'Gulzar will make a fine Elite Warrior.'

"It won't be long," Treyvon said stepping up next to Nikhil.

"No, it won't. He will make a fine addition to your Elite Warriors."

"Agreed. How is your True Mate today? I was informed you did not take her to last meal."

"She rested through it. I thought to wake her, but Luol assured me her body knew what it needed and to let her rest."

"Was Luol correct?"

"Yes. She woke well rested and hungry."

"That is good. Has she agreed to be your Ashe yet?" Treyvon asked looking to the bead that Nikhil still wore. The only bead a male was able to freely offer a female.

"I... I have not yet asked her," he hesitantly admitted. "She has been through so much and is still adjusting to wearing my True Mate bead since it is not the way of her species. I wanted to give her time to adapt before I asked her for more."

"You can't think she would refuse you?!!" Treyvon gave him a disbelieving look.

"We have had... misunderstandings, because of our differences. I do not want there to be one when I make my request."

"Are there many differences?" Treyvon asked quietly.

"Yes."

"I..." The ringing of Treyvon's comm stopped him from asking more. Stepping away from Nikhil, he answered.

"General, this is Luol."

"What is it?" Treyvon demanded.

"A request has been made to know if the families of the survivors have been notified of their status."

"By who?"

"By Blag, a Nekeok. His female was with offspring when he was taken. He is concerned about her welfare."

"A *Nekeok* disclosed this to you?"

"No, he disclosed it to Mackenzie, who told me."

"A Nekeok spoke to Nikhil's Ashe?" Treyvon turned his gaze to Nikhil and saw he had moved to give Gulzar more instruction.

"Yes. He was very respectful to her," Luol quickly reassured him.

"I see. All I can state as truth is that I contacted the Minister in charge of the Nekeoks' home world when they were discovered and gave them the names of the survivors. Whether they contacted their families, I do not know."

"I see. I will relay that information, General, but I don't believe it will appease Blag."

"It will have to, for it is all the information I have."

"Yes, General."

Luol looked up from his comm to see Mackenzie silently watching him through the open doorway of his office. It was obvious she had heard both sides of the conversation, and she wasn't happy about it. "We've done all that is required, Mackenzie."

"Then you should be *required* to do more," she fired back quietly, still holding Paul's hand. "How would you feel if it were Maysa and she didn't know that *you* were alive?"

Luol suddenly felt a kinship with Blag and it shamed him to realize he'd never considered it before. If it were his Maysa that needed to be contacted, he would be tearing down the walls until he was able to reassure her.

"I will see what I can do."

Mac nodded then turned her attention back to Paul. He was lying there so still that it worried her. Had she been that still when she'd worn the educator?

"Yes," Luol replied, and she realized she had spoken out loud, "and Nikhil was just as worried then as you are now."

"He was?"

"You doubt this?" Luol frowned at her. "You doubt your True Mate's commitment to you?"

"I... if it weren't for this," she touched the bead in her hair, "would we even be having this conversation? I've only known Nikhil two days, Luol. Love doesn't happen in two days!"

"It does if it is true," Luol told her. "Is yours?"

"How am I supposed to know that? After everything that's happened, how am I expected to trust that what I'm feeling is real? For either of us? Nikhil is relying on this bead. How can he know it's not a mistake? That it's not just because you've never met a human before?"

"Mackenzie. The Goddess gifted the Kaliszians with the True Mate bead to end the conflicts that arose between males over who their True Mate was."

"What?"

"Was this not in the educator?" Luol frowned.

"No."

"I'm sorry, Mackenzie. I did not realize our ancient tales were not included in the educator." Luol took a deep breath then began.

"Kaliszians are a warrior race. It is our nature to fight for what we want and to defend what we have. Our mates were what we would fight the most violently for. It became a problem when more than one male laid claim to the same female."

"But wouldn't the female just choose then?"

"You do not know our males," Luol told her with a wry grin. "One would never just accept that the female he desired had chosen another. Not without proof."

"But the Dasho bead..."

"Can be offered to any male and as long as the male accepts and wears it, he is her Dasho."

"For as long as..."

"Yes, the Dasho and Ashe beads are the only ones that a Kaliszian can remove."

"They're like wedding rings," she whispered.

"Wedding rings?"

"It's a tradition on Earth that many follow where a male and female will exchange rings. They are worn around a specific finger." Mac touched her left ring finger. "It symbolizes they are committed to one another."

"An unbreakable commitment?"

"No. It can be broken if one or both decides to."

"It is the same way with the Ashe and Dasho beads which is what caused so many deaths and so much pain and suffering. The Goddess finally took pity on us and gifted us with the True Mate bead. An outward and irrefutable sign of who's one True Mate is. It stopped the conflicts, at least until the Great Infection struck."

"That's when you stopped finding your True Mates," she whispered.

"Yes, and we did not even realize it at first as our attention was on trying to save our dwindling food supply and feed our people."

"You didn't notice?"

"No, not until many years later," Luol's eyes glowed slightly brighter as he looked at the bead she wore. "It is why seeing you wear Nikhil's True Mate bead is so important. It gives us all hope that we might finally find ours."

"I... but Maysa..."

"I believe... No I know Maysa is my True Mate, yet my bead won't accept her." Luol touched the bead he still wore, his eyes full of hope. "Perhaps now it will."

Paul's slight movement had them both looking at him.

"The educator has finished." Luol reached down and removed the device. "He will wake momentarily."

Mac squeezed Paul's hand as his eyes slowly opened and he looked at her. "Hi," she whispered in Kaliszian.

"Hi," he replied in Kaliszian. "That didn't take long."

"I thought the same thing, but it's been two hours, Paul."

"Really?" Paul looked to Luol for confirmation.

"Yes," Luol responded, also in Kaliszian. "Can you answer a few questions for me?"

"I can try," Paul told him.

"Do you know where Crurn is?"

"You mean the planet where the Emperor of the Kaliszian Empire resides?"

"Yes."

"It's three days from here," Paul answered.

Luol smiled at Mac then looked back to Paul, "That is correct. You have absorbed the educator's information. How are you feeling?" Luol asked as he helped him sit up.

Paul swung his feet to the floor, took a deep breath, and thought for a moment before responding. "Good."

"How's Craig doing?" he asked standing.

"He needs, at least a few more hours in the repair unit. I will contact someone to escort you back to your area and bring someone else back."

"Are you okay with that, Paul," Mac asked rising to stand by him.

"Yeah, I'll see who wants to go next."

Entering the outer room, they saw Blag rising from the repair unit. Apparently it had completed healing him.

"Blag, are you ready to return to your people?" Luol asked.

"Yes," Blag responded shortly.

"I checked with General Treyvon and was informed he contacted your Minister."

"Minister Klueh?!!" Blag spat. "That means my Ashe still does not know I am alive."

"You don't believe Klueh contacted her?" Luol couldn't hide his shock.

"Of course not. I am not Kaliszian, just a species that lives within your Empire." With that, Blag turned and walked away.

∞ ∞ ∞ ∞ ∞

Nikhil was enraged, his fist leaving an impression in the solid steel door of the medical unit that he was locked out of. He'd nearly drawn his blade on Onp when he learned his Mackenzie was no longer where he'd left her. Now he was unable to enter where she was, and heads would roll for it. He lifted his fist to pound again when the door suddenly slid open.

"Nikhil." Luol took a step back allowing the enraged warrior to enter.

"Where is she?" Nikhil growled threateningly.

"Mackenzie is in my office sitting with the human called Eric while he uses the educator."

"She isn't supposed to be here. She is supposed to be where I left her. Where she is safe."

"I'm safe here," Mac announced, walking out of Luol's office hearing Nikhil's words.

"Mackenzie," he breathed. Shouldering his way passed Luol, he pulled her into his arms needing to feel her in them, needing to know she was safe.

"I'm fine, Nikhil." She rested her hands on his chest and was surprised at how hard his heart was pounding. He'd really been worried. "I'm really okay, Nikhil."

"Goddess, Mackenzie." He lowered his head to capture her lips for a quick, hard kiss. "Don't do that to me again. I've only just found you."

"But wouldn't you have known if I was in trouble?" She pulled back slightly. "Because I wear your True Mate bead."

"But I don't wear yours," Nikhil admitted hoarsely.

"What?" She gave him a confused look. "But the educator said the bead connected us."

"That's what happens when the beads are exchanged," Luol said softly from behind Nikhil. "As you have no True Mate bead to give Nikhil, the connection is not complete."

"Nikhil?" She looked up at him questioningly.

"I have to touch the bead you wear to know your condition," he admitted.

"Why didn't you tell me that?" she asked.

"I hadn't had the chance to and..."

"And?"

"And I hoped, that given enough time, the full bond would still form."

"I see." She pushed against his chest putting some space between them. "So you lied to me."

"I did not lie to you, Mackenzie," he instantly denied.

"You just didn't tell me the truth." This time, she shoved hard against his chest and as his arms fell away, she moved out of his embrace. "That's not going to work for me, Nikhil. If I can't trust in you, believe in you, and have you tell me what I need to know, then this," she grabbed her hair that held his bead and it swung out as if it meant to return to him, "is meaningless."

"Don't say that!" Nikhil exclaimed. The heart in his chest that had just begun to settle started pounding even harder than before.

"Why not? It's the truth!" Mac felt her heart break at the devastated look on Nikhil's face. He thought she couldn't feel his pain because he didn't wear her True Mate bead but he was wrong. He'd touched her soul with how gently and carefully he had cleansed her, and how he kept putting her needs first. But none of that mattered if he wasn't honest with her.

"You are my True Mate, Mackenzie," he told her reaching for her again, but she stepped farther away, and he slowly dropped his arms.

"Yes, but you might not be mine since you don't wear my bead and that's what you didn't want to tell me, isn't it?"

"I... yes... some might see it that way," he reluctantly admitted, "but I don't. We have bonded, Mackenzie. I don't need a bead to tell me that. I feel you here." He touched his chest where his heart was still pounding so hard that it seemed to be trying to fly to her, knowing it was safe in her care.

Mac felt her eyes fill at Nikhil's heartfelt words. She could hear his truth in them and it made her want to reach out and comfort him, but she needed that truth to permeate more than just their relationship. She needed it to filter through their entire life. There was so much she still didn't know or understand and if she couldn't rely on Nikhil to tell her, who could she?

"I need to get back to Eric," she told him, turning to re-enter Luol's office.

"Eric?" Nikhil questioned.

"He is the human male currently using the educator," Luol informed him quietly. "Mackenzie insists on sitting with them, so they are not alone as I see to the treatment of those in the deep-repair unit."

"You leave her alone with other males?" Nikhil growled.

"I leave her alone with males that she knows and trusts. She has already spent a great deal of time alone with them, Nikhil. She is loyal to them. They are her friends, and they have bonded because of what they have survived together. That is something you are going to have to deal with and accept if you want your mate to be truly happy.

"They let her be taken, Luol, let her be harmed."

"And she seems to hold no animosity toward them for it. Perhaps you need to find out why." Luol walked away to check on the two in the repair unit.

∞ ∞ ∞ ∞ ∞

Nikhil stood in the doorway of Luol's office, ignoring the way his massive shoulders pressed against the frame, and watched his mate sit beside another male holding his hand. His first instinct was to storm across the room and pull her away from the male. She was his. His mate. She should never touch another male. But he knew that would be wrong. That it would drive his mate even farther from him. He tensed as she lifted a hand to gently tuck a strand of the male's hair behind his ear. But as he watched, he realized she wasn't touching the other male the same way she touched him. Yes, there was feeling in the touch, but it wasn't a caress.

Moving across the room, he pulled over a chair and sat down heavily on the other side of the couch. "You care about this male," he said quietly.

"Eric."

"What?"

"His name is Eric, and yes, I do." She lifted her gaze to his. "Very much. Just like I care for all the others."

"Explain to me why."

"What do you mean why?"

"They let the Zaludians take you, Mackenzie." While he spoke quietly, there was no doubting the rage behind his words. "You were harmed because they didn't protect you. How can you still care about them?"

"Is that all you see? How you found me?" She shook her head and looked back to Eric. "You just don't understand."

"Then make me understand." He leaned forward, his elbows resting on his knees. "I need to understand, Mackenzie."

"They protected me, Nikhil, when they didn't have to."

"Didn't..."

"They didn't know me. I wasn't one of their group. I was just their guide. The one they trusted to lead them up the mountain and bring them back safely. I failed."

"They can't blame you for what the Ganglians did, Mackenzie."

"They could have, but they didn't. Instead they protected me. When we first got to that mine, the Zaludians took half of us to the cave where we lived and the other half they put to work in the mine. I was put to work. I collapsed when we got back to the cave, and they took the other group. I didn't know what I was going to do. We saw how the Zaludians beat a Jerboaian to death when he collapsed, and then they beat the one that tried to protect him."

"We heard they would do that," Nikhil said quietly.

"You heard right, and as much as I didn't want to die that way, I knew it was going to happen because there was no way I could do that type of physical work... so did the guys. When the Zaludians returned with the other group, they brought food and told us we had fifteen minutes. I didn't eat because I knew I'd be dead soon and it would just be a waste of food the others needed." Her eyes began to fill with tears, and she ran the back of her hand over Eric's gaunt cheek before she continued. "The Zaludians returned and as I rose to go with my group, Eric pushed me down and went in my place."

"He..."

"He was in the group that had just returned from the mine. His only thought should have been to rest until they came for him again. Instead, he took my place."

"He worked back to back shifts?"

"Yes, and when he returned, one of the other guys took his place. They never let me return to that mine, Nikhil. Do you understand now? They all did what they could to protect me."

"And the Zaludians never noticed?"

"As long as they had six bodies they didn't care."

"Then how...?"

"Did they discover me?"

"Yes."

"My fault. You see, I discovered a crack in the back wall of the cave and J..." she cut herself off, realizing she had almost

224

told him about Jen. "I would hide in there whenever we heard the Zaludians coming just to make sure they wouldn't realize I was female. On that day, one of the guys had gotten a bad cut, and I was treating it since I had medical training, when a Zaludian suddenly walked in. Because of the condition of my coverings, he realized I was female. All the guys rose up to protect me, but I told them not to fight."

"What?!!" Nikhil couldn't believe it. "Why?"

"Because they couldn't have won," she told him. "All that would have happened was that the Zaludians would have killed them, and I would have been taken anyway. So I went willingly."

"You were injured." That had been bothering Nikhil all along because there was no reason for the Zaludians to beat her, especially if they were planning on selling her to a Pleasure House.

"That's because once I was far enough away from the guys, I tried to escape. I almost made it outside, but then the one with the red beads caught me. He was the one that beat me."

"You tried to save yourself."

"Of course. I wasn't just going to let them *take* me. Not without a fight."

"You are a fighter, aren't you, my Mackenzie." Nikhil ran a large, rough knuckle carefully over the soft skin of her cheek removing the tear that had escaped her beautiful brown eyes. "One would never guess it because of your size, but I am coming to believe you are the strongest female I have ever met."

"A bigger untruth you have never told, Nikhil Kozar," she said but tipped her head into his touch giving him a sad smile, "but thank you."

"It is not an untruth, Mackenzie, for it takes one truly strong to survive what you have. But it is also for that reason that I never want you to have to be that strong again. I want to take care of you, want to keep you safe."

"I'm not strong, Nikhil, but that doesn't mean I'm weak either. I only survived because I wasn't alone and because I had people I could trust and rely on helping me."

"I want to be one of those people that you trust, Mackenzie. Someone you know you can rely on no matter what."

"Do you?"

"Yes."

"But it works both ways, Nikhil. You have to trust and rely on me too, and you haven't been doing that."

"I... " Nikhil gave her an abashed look. "You are right, my Mackenzie, and I have no excuse except to say that it is not the Kaliszian way, and I am still adjusting to having a True Mate. A very strong, very beautiful, very small True Mate," he finished softly.

"God, if you two get any sappier, I'm going to need a shower," Eric groaned causing them both to look down at him in shock as he reached up to pull off the educator.

"Eric, no!" Mac grabbed his arm stopping him before her gaze flew back to Nikhil. "Get Luol," she ordered.

Nikhil was immediately up and out of the room at her command.

"What's wrong, Mac?" Eric asked.

"Nothing I just want Luol to be the one to remove the educator, Eric. He's the Healer. I don't want to risk you being hurt."

"Nikhil seems like a good guy, Mac," Eric told her quietly, lowering his hand.

"He is."

"Then why are you giving him such a hard time?"

Before Mac could respond, Nikhil and Luol were returning.

Chapter Fourteen

Nikhil sat next to Mackenzie as they ate their midday meal. She'd refused to leave the medical area saying she needed to be there when Craig woke. Nikhil wanted to argue with her. He wanted to take her to their quarters so they could be alone. He wanted to pull her into his arms and kiss her. Instead, he had retrieved two meals, and they were silently eating them in Luol's office.

"What's wrong, Nikhil?" she asked putting her half-eaten meal aside.

"Nothing," he picked up the pouch and handed it back to her. "Finish your meal."

"I'm full. You can finish it or Craig can when he's out of the repair unit." She set it back down on the table then rising onto her knees, she cupped his jaw with her hands and she turned him to face her. "What's wrong?"

Nikhil looked into her warm, brown eyes and saw her concern for him. What had he ever done to deserve that? Reaching out he tucked a strand of her hair behind her ear, the tips of his fingers caressing her silky skin.

"Nothing is wrong, Little One. I had just been hoping to have some time alone while we enjoyed our meal."

"But we're alone now."

"In our quarters," Nikhil added quietly. "I wanted to hold you."

Mac's eyes widened slightly then a mischievous smile crossed her lips right before she swung a leg over his thighs and wrapped her arms around his neck. "How's this?"

"Mackenzie," Nikhil's eyes flew to the open door even as his hands gripped her hips pulling her tightly against him.

"What?" she asked, pressing a kiss to his strong, square chin.

"Someone might see us."

"So?" she asked, pulling his head down so her lips could reach his. "You're my True Mate, aren't you?"

"Yes," he growled trying to capture the lips she'd pulled away from his.

"So why is it wrong for someone to see us kissing?"

"It's not," he told her and lifting a hand gripped the back of her head, holding her still. "It's what I want to do after we kiss that others aren't allowed to see."

With that, he captured her lips for a hard, deep kiss.

Mac rose up on her knees, her arms wrapping around his head as she sunk into the kiss. Goddess, the man could kiss. Her hips involuntarily moved against his washboard abs as their tongues sparred and she suddenly realized Nikhil had been right. They should have gone to his quarters because she wanted to do more than just kiss him, a lot more.

"Ahem," followed by the clearing of a throat had Mac and Nikhil breaking apart to find Luol standing in the doorway. "Sorry to interrupt," he said not looking sorry at all, "but the repair unit is about to finish, and I'm about to wake the male... Craig up. I thought you would want to be there."

"I do," Mac said her cheeks flushing.

"Then I suggest you finish your... midday meal and meet me at the unit," Luol told her, his lips twitching as he tried not to smile and walked away.

Mac buried her face in Nikhil's neck for a moment before lifting her gaze to his. "Next time we go to your quarters for midday meal."

Nikhil gazed down at her, trying to regain some control over his body. Goddess, all he wanted to do was strip her bare and plunge his throbbing shaft into her. He knew her channel was slick and wet. She was ready to take him because her covering had risen as she rose to her knees and it had been those soft folds she'd rubbed against his abs that the vest didn't cover. All he had to do was release himself, and they would be one. He looked into her eyes and saw the desire in them. Desire that told him she wouldn't stop him if he did, but he also saw her need. Her need to be there for one that had been there for her.

"We will," he growled then slowly set her on her feet. "And we will be taking last meal in *our* quarters tonight."

"Agreed," she whispered, noticing the way he stressed the word 'our.' "Thank you for understanding."

As they turned to walk out, Nikhil reached for his comm that had started to beep and after a short discussion, returned it to his waist.

"Mackenzie..."

"You have to go," she said.

"Yes."

"It's alright."

"I want you to remain here in medical until I return for you." He put a gentle hand on her cheek tipping her gaze up to his. "Vow it to me, Mackenzie."

"I'll stay here until you come and get me." When he just stood there, she added, "I vow."

∞ ∞ ∞ ∞ ∞

The sound of the repair unit opening was the first thing that registered in Craig's mind. The next thing was the sound of Mac's voice softly talking to someone in a language he didn't understand.

Mac.

He would know that husky voice anywhere.

It reached into his dreams and reminded him that he was still a man.

But what was she saying?

Who was she talking to?

Turning his head toward the sound of her voice, his eyes flew open and there she was looking up at the Kaliszian called Luol.

"Mac..." he croaked out, surprised at how dry his throat was.

"Craig." Mac turned her gaze to him, a gaze full of warmth and happiness for him. "How are you feeling?" she asked in English.

"Thirsty," he told her and watched as she immediately turned to get him what he needed.

"Here." She put a hand behind his head lifting it to help him drink.

"How long was I out?" he asked after he drained the glass.

"Almost five hours."

"Five?!!" Craig gave her an astonished look. It hadn't felt that long to him. "I don't even remember falling asleep."

"That's because Luol gave you something to help with that."

"He drugged me?" Craig arrowed straight up turning furious eyes to Luol.

"I told him to, Craig," Mac quickly defended Luol, who couldn't understand what was being said. "You needed to relax and let the unit work, and you weren't. It was my call."

"You were out when you were treated?" He was going to be pissed if she said no.

"Yes," she told him. "Now you need to start speaking in Zaludian so Luol can help you."

"Where's Paul?" he demanded, but it was in Zaludian.

"He's back with the others. So is Eric, who also used the educator while you were being treated," she told him.

"Both of them?"

"Yes," Luol answered him this time, "and they tolerated it very well with no side effects. Now how are you feeling?"

Craig took a minute to think about it. "Good. All those aches and pains are gone." He lifted a hand and saw that all the scars he'd accumulated in the mine were gone too, and turned stunned eyes to Luol.

"Yes, the repair unit took care of those and any others you had on your body. It also replenished all the nutrients that you were deficient in. The only thing I found unusual was that your system was not as deficient as Mackenzie's had been even though you were held the same amount of time." He looked to Craig hoping for an answer, but all he found was Craig staring hard at Mackenzie.

"Mackenzie, would you know why?" Luol asked quietly.

"No," she said softly before pulling her gaze away from Craig to repeat more strongly, "No, Luol, I don't know why that is. Maybe I was just deficient to begin with or maybe it was because of the beating I took."

"Beating?!!" Craig jumped off the bed then grabbed her upper arms giving her a hard shake. "What beating?!! Are you telling me that fucking Kaliszian *beat* you?!!"

Before Mac could recover from Craig's sudden move, Luol grabbed him by the throat and threw him across the room.

"Luol!" Mac grabbed his arm, stopping him from going after Craig. "Stop!"

"You are the True Mate of a Kaliszian," Luol growled. "No one attacks you!"

Mac couldn't believe how hard Luol's voice had become or how brightly his eyes were glowing. She'd never seen him act like this. He'd always been so caring and gentle with her, and that's when she realized that while he claimed to be Kalbaughian, he was still a Kaliszian warrior.

231

"He wasn't attacking me, Luol," she said trying to calm him.

"Look at your arms, Mackenzie," Luol spit out.

She did and was surprised to see that bruises were already forming there. "Craig didn't mean to," she said defending Craig. "He was just surprised. I never told them that the Zaludians had beaten me. He thought I meant Nikhil."

"What?" Luol finally looked at her. When the human male had jumped off the bed of the repair unit, he had reverted to his language, and Luol hadn't been able to understand what he was saying.

"He thought Nikhil had harmed me. He was just reacting."

"Nikhil would never harm you."

"I know this. Craig doesn't. It's going to take time for all of us to adjust and accept these changes, Luol."

"I see." Luol's gaze returned to Craig, who was slowly getting up, his eyes never leaving Luol. "Then I apologize to you, Mackenzie, for not keeping you from harm. It seems my time as a Healer has dulled my reflexes."

"They didn't seem dull to me," Mac told him putting a careful hand on the still bulging bicep of his arm. "I didn't realize that you were more than a Healer, Luol, that you were also an Elite Warrior."

"It has been many years since I have been an Elite, but yes, I am still a Warrior. I would never be allowed to treat them if I was not."

"Mac, what's going on?" Craig asked, holding his right arm as he watched Luol warily.

"In Zaludian, Craig," Mac said glaring at him, and after a moment he repeated the question. "Luol was defending me."

"From who?" Craig asked.

"From you! He thought you were harming me," she looked at the darkening bruises, "and I guess he was right."

"Shit, Mac! I never meant to hurt you! You know that!"

"I wouldn't have thought so but here's the proof, and if Nikhil sees it, he'll do a whole lot worse to you than what Luol did." She saw Craig pale and swallow hard then looked to Luol. "You can make these disappear, can't you?"

"I could but Nikhil needs to be informed," Luol said still watching Craig.

"No, he doesn't. It was an accident, and it's never going to happen again. Is it, Craig?" she asked giving Craig a hard look.

"No... of course it's not! I never intended..."

Mac ignored the rest of what Craig was saying and turned her gaze back to Luol and switched to Kaliszian. "Please, Luol. Nikhil doesn't need to know about this. We already have so much to get through, so much to understand about one another. You know he will never be able to understand or accept this." She lifted a bruised arm. "He'll kill Craig."

"As he should," Luol told her, his eyes having not yet lost that hard glow.

"Which isn't going to help in getting my people to trust you. We've survived the Ganglians. We've survived the Zaludians. Are you telling me that after surviving all that, the Kaliszians are going to be the ones that finally kill us? All because we don't understand your rules? Because we tried to defend one another? Was Blag right? Do you only care about Kaliszians?"

Luol jerked back as if she had struck him with the full strength of an Elite warrior. "No! That is not what I'm saying. Mackenzie, you know it isn't."

"Then help me." She held out her bruised arms to him.

"Fine, but if it happens again, Nikhil will be informed." He waited for her to nod.

"If it happens again," Mac's hard gaze shot to Craig, "Nikhil can have him after I'm done with him."

Luol looked at her in shock then began to laugh. "I believe Nikhil would be truly upset then because you wouldn't leave anything for him."

"That's right."

"Mac?" Craig asked in Zaludian. "What's going on?"

"Luol has agreed to treat my bruises so my Mate won't see them and kill you," she told him bluntly.

"What?" Craig paled.

"If Nikhil saw this and knew you'd done them, he'd kill you." She let that sink in for a moment before continuing. "You may not like this, Craig, but Nikhil is my True Mate and the only male I want, and nothing is ever going to change that. I know you were always trying to get something going between us even before the Ganglians took us. I told you no then, and I'm telling you no now. I'll always be grateful for you helping to protect me, but that's all I'll ever feel for you; gratitude and friendship. If you can't accept that, then stay away from me." She looked to Luol. "Where do you need me?"

Luol just stared at her for a moment then smiled. Oh yes, the Goddess had chosen the perfect mate for Nikhil. She was going to be just what the massive warrior needed.

"Let's go into my office and I'll treat you with the handheld unit." He looked to Craig. "Then I'll treat that break in your arm."

"You broke Craig's arm?" Mac's gaze flew to him and for the first time noticing just how gingerly Craig was holding his arm.

"He landed badly," Luol said with a dismissive shrug.

"You need to treat him first, Luol."

"No. You are first, Mackenzie. His injury was caused because of his lack of control. He waits. Otherwise, I notify Nikhil," Luol threatened.

"Alright. Fine," Mac said testily moving toward his office.

∞ ∞ ∞ ∞ ∞

After that, the rest of the afternoon was relatively quiet. She'd given Craig the remainder of her food packet, much to Luol's displeasure, once his arm was repaired. Craig then insisted on being the next to use the educator. Mac knew Luol thought it was because Craig was trying to make up for what had happened, but she knew it was because Craig was something of a control freak. He would never be able to stand that Paul and Eric would understand something that he didn't.

Craig had become their unspoken leader after he'd been the one the Ganglians had forced the educator on. There was no other reason for it, but no one had challenged him about it either. Not that there was much 'leadership' needed in the mine. The Zaludians were in charge, but now that they were free, it seemed he was trying to assume control.

Mac sat with him just as she had with Paul and Eric, but once he was under, she let go of his hand. Another Nekeok had arrived along with Tyler which surprised her. She'd thought either Paul or Eric would have come back, and she said as much.

"They felt that since they had both used the educator, that someone else should be treated so it would be fair to everyone," Tyler told her.

And there in lay the difference between Craig, Paul and Eric. Paul and Eric thought of how others would feel. Craig not so much.

"Where's Craig?" Eric asked.

"Using the educator," she told him and they exchanged a knowing look. "So are you ready to feel better?"

"Definitely. Where do you want me?" he asked looking to Luol.

"On the bed," Luol told him and explained to him, as he had Craig, what was about to happen. But this time, he informed the male that he could 'knock him out' as Mackenzie had said.

"Mac?" Tyler looked at her. "What do you think?"

"I think you won't feel as claustrophobic when the cover closes if you let Luol give you something."

Luol could see that the male called Tyler seriously considered what Mackenzie had said before slowly nodding his head. "Knock me out, Doc," he said, then lay back on the bed.

"Doc?" Luol looked to Mackenzie for clarification as the cover on the deep-repair unit closed and began to treat Tyler.

"It's an Earth term for Healer," she told him.

"I see." As he continued to watch her, she raised a questioning eyebrow. "You never left the side of the other males once the educator was on."

"No."

"Is there something about this Craig that I should know about?"

"No. It's fine, Luol. Honestly." At his confused look, she corrected. "My vow."

"You need to let Nikhil know if Craig gives you problems, Mackenzie. It is his duty and honor to protect you."

"Honor?"

"Of course. To have a True Mate is the greatest honor the Goddess can give a male. It shows she finds him worthy."

"Shouldn't that be my choice? If I find Nikhil worthy I don't care what anyone else thinks, not even a Goddess." She saw she had shocked Luol. "Humans don't have True Mate beads that we can rely on, Luol. It would be nice if we did." She lifted

Nikhil's bead to look at it. "It would make it so much easier, but then again maybe not."

"What do you mean?" Luol frowned at her.

"I mean, and please don't take offense at this, but you say Maysa is your True Mate, even though she doesn't wear your True Mate bead."

"She is," Luol told her angrily.

"But do others believe that?" she questioned. "That she is your True Mate? That she would never remove your Ashe bead?"

Luol opened his mouth then snapped it shut because he knew some males had tried to lure his Maysa away when he was gone. "Are you saying this doesn't happen on your Earth?"

"Oh it does, but we don't have this 'sign from the Goddess' that we've met our Soul Mate. Our True Mate. We have to take it on faith and trust and believe. If I wasn't wearing this," she jiggled the bead she was still holding at him, "would any of you honestly believe I was Nikhil's True Mate? Would Nikhil? He might have offered me his Ashe bead, but what if his True Mate bead suddenly ended up on someone else... What would he do? What would *you* do?"

Luol gave her a lost look.

"Exactly. You rely on this when maybe you should just trust and rely on what you feel instead."

∞ ∞ ∞ ∞ ∞

Luol sat in his office later that night, after Nikhil had come to collect Mackenzie, and let himself truly think about what she had said. Their society revolved around their beads. Their past, present, and future were displayed there for all to see, including their worth and value to society. He'd never questioned it before, but now he did. All because of one small human female. If his True Mate bead ever transferred to another, he knew his heart would shatter, knew his Maysa's would shatter too. Would he stay with his Ashe and the life they had created together or would he abandon her for another?

Without a thought, he reached out and entered the code that would connect him to his Maysa.

"Yes?" a soft voice answered.

Her beautiful face, that had creases on one cheek from where she'd been sleeping appeared on his screen and Luol suddenly realized just how late it was on Crurn.

"Luol? Is that you?" Eyes that a moment ago had been blurry with sleep sharpened and filled with fear. "Luol! What's wrong? Are you hurt?"

"No! No, Maysa. I'm sorry I called so late. I didn't realize what time it was there."

"That doesn't matter. What is wrong, my love? You are well?"

"I am fine. I just missed seeing your beautiful face." His words had the fear fading from her eyes. Fear she rarely revealed to him.

"We just spoke yesterday," she told him settling deeper into their bed.

"Yesterday was a lifetime ago," he murmured.

Maysa stilled. "There is something wrong. Tell me."

"Not wrong, I just find myself questioning things I never have before."

"What kind of things?" she asked.

"Our beads," he finally admitted.

"Our beads?" She sat straight up in bed. "Why would you question our beads? They are a gift from the Goddess."

"Are they?" he asked.

"Luol, what's brought this on?"

"I've been treating a human female."

"The one Nikhil's True Mate bead transferred to?" she asked. "The one I sent coverings for?"

"Yes. They do not have Suja beads in their world."

"They don't? Then how do they know who is who in their society? Who their True Mate is?"

"Mackenzie says they have to take it on faith and trust, that there is no outward sign."

"Mackenzie..."

"She has requested that I not use the title," he told his Ashe.

"What? Why would she do that?"

"She had requested it before she had used the educator. I do not know if she understands the significance for us and I have not informed her differently. Nikhil will do that when he finally offers her his Ashe bead."

"He hasn't done that yet?" Maysa couldn't hide her shock.

"No. Mackenzie has had much to deal with since her rescue. I believe Nikhil is waiting until she has recovered more fully."

"That's male thinking. A female would want him to offer his bead."

"A Kaliszian female would. She is a human female."

"She sounds intriguing."

"You would like her, Maysa. She is very intelligent and questions many of the things we just accept."

"Like our Suja beads." Maysa finally began to understand what had Luol questioning their beads. Her Dasho had a very inquisitive mind.

"Yes."

"What did she question?"

"That we only believe we've found our True Mate if our bead transfers to them."

"I see." Sadness filled Maysa's eyes knowing he was referring to how neither of their True Mate beads had transferred to the other, not even after all these years. "She doesn't realize how blessed she is."

"She believes it should be *her* choice," Luol told her quietly.

"She doesn't want Nikhil for her True Mate?" Maysa could understand the hesitation if this human female were truly as small as the coverings she sent indicated. Nikhil was the largest Kaliszian warrior in the Empire.

"Oh she does, but she finds it unacceptable that we only believe it because of the bead," Luol paused then continued. "She then asked me a question, and it shames me to say I don't know the answer."

"What question, Luol?" Maysa whispered.

"What I would do if my True Mate bead suddenly transferred to a female other than you?"

Maysa felt her breath catch and tears filled her eyes. "You would have to go to her."

"No!" Luol's chair hit the wall as he surged to his feet. "No! *You* are my Ashe. You are the mother of my offspring. *You* are the True Mate of my heart. No other could ever take your place for me, and if yours ever transferred to another male.... I would kill him, Maysa," he admitted his eyes glowing brightly. "I would fight to keep you."

"Luol..."

"Just the thought of it has me wanting to cut off my True Mate bead."

"No! Luol, no!" Maysa exclaimed reaching out to try and touch him through the screen.

"I will not lose you, Maysa."

"You are not going to. You are the True Mate of my heart too, Luol. Nothing, not even a bead, could ever change that."

"Vow it, Maysa!" he demanded, his eyes still glowing. "Vow it to me!"

"I vow it, Luol. There is only you in my heart."

Chapter Fifteen

Mac lifted her head from Nikhil's chest to stare down at his sleeping form. They'd barely made it into their quarters before Nikhil was tearing her coverings off. Damn, nothing had ever turned her on more than that amazing green glow that filled Nikhil's eyes as he looked at her. It was like the hottest, softest touch as it moved over her body and she felt it in the deepest part of her soul. How was that possible?

A part of her wanted to cut the True Mate bead out of her hair just to see if it was what was causing these incredible feelings, but another part of her screamed in protest. The bead meant something to Nikhil, and she didn't know what it would do to him if she removed it, and she would never intentionally harm him.

Fingering the bead that was causing all this confusion and heartache, she searched her soul for answers. She hadn't done that in a long time. Not since her grandpa had died and she'd had to decide what to do with her life. She'd come to accept that she probably wasn't going to have a happily ever after story, not with a man at least. She lived in a small town, had known most of the men there all her life, and except for Derek back in high school, none of them had ever attracted her. Most men wanted some tall, thin, beautiful woman who knew what to say and how to dress. Men like Craig. She knew the only reason he was fixated on her was because she was the only female available.

She had her mountain and while she was sometimes lonely, she had at least been content.

Then the Ganglians had shown up, and she'd lost her mountain.

A small smile grew on her lips as she looked down at Nikhil. But she'd found a mountain of a man and that was a trade she'd willingly take every day of the week and twice on Sunday.

She felt the questions and chaos in her mind and soul settle then fade away. She wanted Nikhil because *she* wanted him. Bead or no bead. He was kind and gentle, was sweet and huge. He was protective, and he was everything she never knew she wanted.

Yes, they had only known each other a few days, and had met under horrendous circumstances, but still she knew and trusted him and that trust ran soul deep.

She remembered her mother telling her how she and her father had met back when they'd still been a happy family.

It was love at first sight, Mackenzie. I just knew it in my soul. Your dad was it for me.

Mackenzie hadn't understood half of her mother's words then, but she had felt the happiness and truth behind them. How had she forgotten that?

That's how she'd felt from the first moment she'd woken up to Nikhil carrying her out of that mine. Her soul had known she was safe and she was supposed to be. Why was she questioning it now because she wore some stupid bead?

"What is wrong, Mackenzie?" Nikhil's deep voice had her looking into his softly glowing eyes.

"Nothing is wrong. I'm just thinking."

"About this?" He moved the hand that had been circling her waist, holding her securely against him, to her fingers that were still touching his bead.

"Yes."

"It bothers you. To wear my bead?" His eyes dimmed with hurt.

"Not in the way you are thinking." She pushed herself up to rest her elbows on his chest, knowing he could easily handle her weight.

"Then in what way?" he asked, and when she didn't immediately answer, the arm still around her waist tightened. "I need you to tell me truth, Mackenzie, as much as you need me to tell you mine."

"I know. I just don't want my truth to hurt you or harm you. Never you, Nikhil."

"And you think it will."

"Yes. Because my ways, my beliefs, and traditions are not yours or your people's."

"So I will learn them, but I can't do that if you do not tell me what they are. So what were you thinking?"

"I was thinking about cutting off your True Mate bead," she told him honestly.

"What?!!" Nikhil roared, nearly knocking her off the bed as he reared up.

"Nikhil!" she cried out, grabbing his shoulders as she felt herself start to fall. His arms immediately caught her, but the look in his eyes was pure devastation.

"You do not wish to be my mate!" The anguish in his voice tore at her soul.

"That's *not* what I'm saying!" She framed his face with her hands. "Nikhil! Let me explain!"

"There is nothing to explain! Only when a mate finds the other one completely unworthy will they cut the bead from their hair."

"*That's NOT what I am saying!*" she yelled at him. "Do you honestly think I could consider you unworthy after what we just did together?"

244

Nikhil froze from lifting her off him to get out of bed. "Then what are you saying?"

"I'm saying that I hate that the only reason everyone accepts me as your True Mate is because of some stupid bead! That I hate knowing the only reason I'm with you right now is because of it. And I'm saying that I hate the fact that you would have just left me with Luol and walked away if it weren't for the same damn bead!" Tears were running down her face by the time she finished.

"You think I would have abandoned you... if not for my bead..." Nikhil whispered.

"Yes!" she all but screamed at him.

"And this bothers you..." He used one of his rough thumbs to gently wipe away her tears.

"Of course, it *bothers* me! I don't need some damn bead to know how I feel about you. To know that I love you. I feel it here," she touched the place where her heart was," and I feel it in my soul. I *know* you are my other half, but you wouldn't if..."

Her words were cut off by Nikhil rolling her onto her back and silencing her with a hard kiss that went on and on.

"I would never have abandoned you, my Mackenzie," Nikhil told her when he finally pulled away just far enough to let her breathe. "I couldn't have, bead or no bead. The moment I held you in my arms, I felt a contentment that I did not understand. There were others that could have taken you to Luol. I should have let them and stayed with my warriors. It was my duty, but my place... My place was with you. Only you."

"That's only because of the bead," she argued.

"I didn't know it had transferred, Mackenzie. A Kaliszian has to see his True Mate bead on a female before he knows. I never saw it and never would have if Luol hadn't pointed it out to me before he closed the deep-repair unit. I was feeling all this long before that."

"You didn't know?" she asked hopefully.

"No." His lips brushed hers as he continued to speak. "I will confess that I will be forever grateful that you wear my bead, for without it others would try to steal you away from me. They would never believe one as amazing and beautiful as you could have true feelings for me."

"You would clobber anyone stupid enough to try," she said giving him a wobbly smile.

"I would kill them, Mackenzie." Nikhil's words were flat, hard and direct. "You are mine and only mine."

Mac reached up to grab the braids that had fallen over each of his shoulders, as her concerned brown eyes looked up into his. "Would you really kill for me, Nikhil? One of your own people? A Kaliszian?"

"I would kill the Emperor himself if he were to try and take you from me, Mackenzie. Kaliszian or not. It does not matter. You are mine. Not because of my bead, but because *you* say you are."

Mac felt her eyes fill again knowing Nikhil was telling her truth, but she still had to ask. "Even though you will never wear my True Mate bead? Even though I will never have a Dasho bead to offer you?"

"Even so, Mackenzie. I don't need an outward sign that you are mine, but..." he trailed off.

"But?" she asked, her gaze searching his.

"But I would still like to offer you my Ashe bead," he told her quietly. "I greatly desire you to be my Ashe, for you to willingly and knowingly accept it and all that it means."

"What does it mean... to you, Nikhil?" she asked quietly.

"It means *you* have chosen *me*. That you have found me worthy and love me as much as I love you."

"You love me?"

"With all my heart and soul, Mackenzie. For I am nothing and my life is meaningless without you in it now."

Nikhil slowly rolled, sitting up he lifted her so she was straddling him before he removed his Ashe bead, and slowly presented it to her.

"Mackenzie Wharton, will you be my Ashe? I vow if you accept this bead that I will always provide and care for you, that I will protect you with my life. I will love you with all my heart and soul, and when the Goddess calls my name to enter the Promised Land, I will still fight to remain at your side."

"Nikhil..." Mac reached out taking the bead as she searched her mind for what her response should be. Finding nothing, she gave him her words. "I, Mackenzie Wharton, accept *you*, Nikhil Kozar, as my Dasho and True Mate. With or without your bead, I am yours and only yours. I will love you with all my heart and soul, and when the Goddess calls my name to enter the Promised Land, I will fight to remain at your side."

Mac leaned forward, meaning to seal her vow with a kiss, only to have Nikhil stop her.

"Put it on first," he whispered, his eyes glowing.

"Help me. Show me where," she whispered back.

"It goes here," Nikhil told her indicating the ends of the strands of hair that held his True Mate bead. He was surprised to find the hair had already started to braid even without her wearing a Suja Clip or an Elemental Bead. The bead was halfway up the strand, displaying for all to see, how strong their bond already was. Together they set the Ashe bead in the proper position, and it immediately attached.

"That really is so cool," she whispered, watching as the green swirls on the white bead began to move as if it felt her pleasure at being Nikhil's Ashe.

"Cool? That is good?" Nikhil asked.

"Very good," she assured him. "Now, I think the moment needs to be commemorated with something more than a kiss."

"More?" Nikhil asked, not sure what she was talking about but trusted his Ashe and True Mate.

"Yes," she gave him a secretive smile. "Now I want you to lean back and just enjoy."

Mac began at his hard square chin, refusing to let herself kiss his lips because she knew if she did she would become distracted from her mission. Slowly, her lips followed the path of the tense muscles running down his neck giving them each little licks and nips.

"Mackenzie," Nikhil said in a strained voice.

"I want to show my Dasho how much I love him, Nikhil. Will you let me give you something I'll only ever give to you?" She waited until Nikhil gave her a jerky nod then let her lips continue their journey.

She'd never gotten to really explore Nikhil's incredible body. Oh, she'd touched and kissed it, but Nikhil was such a large, dominant male that she'd always given in to his demands and needs, but not this time. This time, she wanted to be the one in charge. Would he allow it?

Kissing her way over the bulging muscles of his massive chest, her hands skimmed his shoulders, then down the arms still holding her. Reaching a hard, flat nipple she sucked it deep into her mouth and couldn't contain the small smile when she felt his body jerk beneath her. After circling it with her tongue several times, she worked her way to the other one, giving it the same attention as her hands moved down along his sides.

Bracing her hands on his thighs, she slid her lower body down between his legs as she kissed her way along the hard muscles of his chiseled abs, only lifting her mouth when his shaft bumped her chin. She'd been here once before, but Nikhil had pulled her away and taken over before she'd been able to complete what she wanted to do. Not this time.

Her gaze took in his long, heavily-veined shaft, inhaling his unique scent deep into her soul. This was Nikhil at his most basic. A powerful male who was still gentle, was spicy yet comforting, with just a hint of danger. Easing back slightly, her eyes took in the glistening bead of pre-cum hanging from the tip of his engorged head. Her tongue reached for it just as it started to drip down his slit. Following its path, she made sure she got it all. Her effort was rewarded with more of his spicy essence pulsing out.

"Mackenzie!" Nikhil rose back up, meaning to pull her from his shaft when the look in her eyes stopped him.

"Not this time, Nikhil. This time, I want to love you first. Let me." Her hot breath flowed over the head of his cock the way her desire for him flowed through her body.

"Let you what?" he choked out, her heat burning him.

"Love you." Her eyes never left his as she opened her mouth as wide as she could and took him in.

"Mackenzie!" he called out hoarsely, his hips involuntarily bucking into her hot, moist mouth.

Mackenzie took advantage of the movement taking him even deeper. With each pass, her tongue caressed the thick, pulsating vein along the underside of his shaft, her body responding to its primitive beat by flooding her channel with need, preparing her for him.

"Goddess, Mackenzie!" Nikhil's fingers sunk deep into her hair, watching as her mouth rode his shaft. He'd never seen anything as erotic in his life as his Mackenzie's lips wrapped around his shaft, her cheeks hollowing out as she sucked him.

"Don't stop, Mackenzie," Nikhil pleaded, his breath ragged as his hips pumped faster and deeper into her mouth. He could feel his balls tightening and knew he wasn't going to last much longer. But before he could pull her away, Mackenzie did what he thought was impossible, and took all of him deep into her throat and swallowed. It was too much and with a shout, his body exploded, shooting his seed down her throat.

Nikhil fell back onto the bed, pulling his Mackenzie up with him, unable to believe what she had just done. Never in his life had he heard of a female doing what she had, not even the most experienced of pleasure workers. He was a Kaliszian warrior, larger than any other, and no female had ever been able to take all of him.

Mackenzie lay across Nikhil's heaving chest feeling downright smug that little old her had this huge, amazing male breathless and trembling. She knew he wasn't going to be down long, but she was going to enjoy it while she could.

"You, my Mackenzie, are a dangerous female," he told her when he could finally speak again.

"Really?" she asked, her eyes sparkling up at him.

"Yes, and in a few more minutes I'm going to show you just how dangerous I am."

"I can't wait." She lay there just enjoying the moment when she thought of something.

"Nikhil?"

"Yes, my Mackenzie?"

"There is something on Earth that we exchange as an outward sign that we have committed ourselves to another."

"There is?" Nikhil asked lifting is head to gaze at her.

"Yes."

"What is it?"

"Rings. We exchange wedding rings."

"Rings?"

"Yes, they usually match and are worn by both the male and female. We wear them on this finger." She touched the ring finger on her left hand.

"It is permanently attached?"

"No. It is more like your Ashe bead. It can be accepted or declined and even after it's been accepted, it can be returned if one changes their mind."

"What are these rings made of?" he asked.

"They are usually metal, either gold, silver, or platinum, some have jewels in them. It depends on what the couple wants."

"And you would like us to... exchange these rings?"

"Yes," she gave him an uncertain look. "Would that be okay? I mean I guess I don't know if Kaliszians have things such as rings. I haven't seen anyone else wearing them."

"It is not common, but I have heard of some females adorning themselves with what you have described."

"Why isn't it common?"

"Because most of our minerals and jewels are used to purchase food supplies from the Tornians. Only the worthiest can amass the credits needed to obtain them for themselves."

"Oh... I never thought of that..." She shook her head. "It doesn't matter then. It was just a thought."

"I will see what I can do," he told her.

"No, Nikhil, don't worry about it. I don't need to see my ring on your finger to know you are mine. Wearing your beads is enough for me." She remembered something from earlier in the day. "Nikhil?" she asked her gaze searching his.

"What is it, Mackenzie?"

"The coverings you asked Luol's Ashe to get for me..."

"What about them?" he asked.

"Can you afford them?" she asked, chewing on her bottom lip.

"You question whether I can provide for you?" The satisfied, relaxed expression that had been on his face disappeared.

"I... I guess I just don't know. I assume you can afford the coverings you had Luol's Ashe get for me. Otherwise you wouldn't have gotten them, but then I asked for more and I shouldn't have done that. I mean I have no idea what things cost here, and it's not like I have anything of value to contribute."

"Nothing of value?!!" Nikhil roared rolling her onto her back as rage filled him. "You are valuable! To me, you are the most valuable thing in the universe to me!"

"I know that," she looked up at him, surprised by his move but not worried, not scared, "but we both know that's not what I'm talking about. I'm new to your world, and I want to be able to contribute, to help you, to be your partner. I don't want to be a burden."

"Mackenzie." Nikhil lowered his forehead to hers, his anger leaving him as quickly as it had come when he realized what was really worrying his Mackenzie. She was worried how her being in his life would affect him. Her only concern was for *him*. "The cost of the coverings will not be a problem, not even the extra ones."

"You're sure?"

"I vow it to you." Nikhil didn't know what to expect when he gave her that vow, but it wasn't the smile that slowly grew on her face that started his heart pounding faster. Or the way her body began to move beneath him causing his shaft to harden.

"Well, I'm glad we got that out of the way... so are you ready to show me just how dangerous *you* are?" she asked wiggling her eyebrows at him.

Nikhil couldn't stop the growl from escaping his throat as he lowered his mouth to his mate. "I am a *very* dangerous male, and even if it takes all night, I will prove it to you."

"Lucky me..." she whispered, and those were the last coherent thoughts she had for a very long time.

∞ ∞ ∞ ∞ ∞

Luol was still staring at the dark screen, fingering his True Mate bead, long after he finished his call to his Maysa. Never in his life had he felt so conflicted. The True Mate bead was supposed to be a gift. That's what he'd told his Mackenzie. A gift from the Goddess that had stopped the bloodshed that occurred when males fought over the same female. But now he saw it as a curse for he would kill any male that tried to take Maysa from him.

Choice. That's what Mackenzie believed she should have.

Faith.

Trust.

Those were the things the Kaliszian people offered to the Goddess, but it seemed not to their Ashes or True Mates. In all the years since he'd chosen Maysa as his Ashe, and she had accepted, neither of them had ever asked the other what they would do if their True Mate beads transferred to another.

Why?

Because they were afraid of the answer they would receive?

He knew Maysa was faithful to him, as he was to her. But was that faith?

He thought he had already trusted her with his deepest darkest secrets, but now he realized he hadn't. Not until tonight, when he'd told her what he would do if her bead ever transferred to another. He had expected her to rage at him, had expected her to tell him that he would be killing her real mate, but she hadn't. She had agreed that she would always be *his* True Mate, no matter the bead.

Luol felt his eyes fill, remembering the belief and trust his Maysa had in him. He was enough for her, bead or no bead. She wanted him and only him. Goddess, that was the biggest blessing he could ever receive.

He was about to rise, to take this new revelation to rest with him, when he remembered Blag and how his Ashe didn't even know he was alive. Sitting back down, he entered a code. It was time to show the Nekeok that Kaliszians did care about those under their protection.

Chapter Sixteen

Mac found she was still smiling days later as Nikhil escorted her to the survivors' area. The two of them had grown so close in the last few days, and as they had, the fact that she was keeping Jen's existence from him began to gnaw at her. It's why she'd asked Nikhil to bring her here. Everyone was finally healed and had used the educator, everyone except Jen. They'd managed to keep her hidden as different warriors brought them to Luol and Mac hadn't corrected them, but now she needed to convince Jen to let Mac reveal her presence.

She nodded to Onp as they entered the area. The warrior had taken the new duty assigned to him very seriously. She'd never seen him treat any of the survivors with anything less than respect. She'd even over heard several of the guys talking to him, and he'd readily answered all their questions. As he returned the gesture, Nikhil's comm beeped and after giving his arm a reassuring squeeze, she made her way over to her friends.

"Nikhil," he answered.

"Squad Leader, I need you and your warriors to report to the transports immediately," Treyvon informed him.

"Has something happened?" Nikhil demanded, his gaze going to Mackenzie.

"I will inform you when you arrive."

Nikhil wanted to argue, to know if his Mackenzie was at risk, but he knew he couldn't. "Yes, General. I will contact my warriors immediately."

Mac had been talking to Paul, and while she hadn't heard what was said she could sense something was wrong. Moving to Nikhil, she put a hand on his chest. "Nikhil?"

"I must report for duty, Mackenzie," he informed her regretfully. "I want you to remain here until I return."

"Is there something wrong?"

"I do not know," he told her honestly.

"I'll stay here, Nikhil," she immediately reassured him. "It's going to take a while for the guys to shave and for Paul to cut their hair. Thank you for letting me borrow a few of your knives."

"You are sure he knows how to use them?" He looked at Paul, who was inspecting one of the smaller blades Mackenzie had convinced him to allow them to use.

"Yes, Paul just told me he could when I showed them to him."

"I will be back as soon as I can, Mackenzie," he told her pulling his gaze back to her.

"I know." She rose up on her toes and gave him a gentle kiss when he leaned down. "Go, Nikhil. I'll be fine."

Giving her a stiff nod, he turned on his heel and left pausing only long enough to speak to Onp.

"With your life, Onp," he growled.

"With my life, Nikhil," Onp vowed.

∞ ∞ ∞ ∞ ∞

"Is everything okay, Mackenzie?" Paul asked as she returned.

"I'm sure it is," she told him. "Nikhil just has to report for duty. He had planned on staying to make sure you didn't kill yourself with those," she joked, gesturing to the blades in his hands. "So can you really shave with those?"

"I'd prefer a straight razor, but these will do." He ran his hand over his own scruffy face. "I'll start with me, get a feel for the weight and balance of the blade then see who trusts me enough to shave them."

Mac smiled as he walked toward the cleansing room because she knew everyone there would trust him. Turning she went to find Jen.

∞ ∞ ∞ ∞ ∞

Nikhil and his squad assumed their seats on the shuttle as it took off, then silently looked to General Treyvon waiting for him to inform them what was going on.

"We have intercepted a Zaludian transmission emanating from the last mine we searched," Treyvon informed them.

"We missed someone?" Nikhil questioned, and couldn't help but wonder if it was because he hadn't been there.

"Unknown as of yet," Treyvon told them. "It seems only to be transmitting mining data and could be an automated signal sent at a predesignated time. We will search every inch of that mine until we find the source of the transmission, and what, or who triggered it."

"Yes, General," they all responded.

∞ ∞ ∞ ∞ ∞

Parlan couldn't help but smile as he watched the transports lift off and disappear over the horizon heading for the mine and the transmission he'd been able to activate remotely, thanks to the help of his friend. The plan was working perfectly and soon all those that had disparaged him would suffer. He couldn't wait to see how the strong and mighty Nikhil handled the loss of his Ashe and True Mate, and couldn't wait to see how Rayner explained how the first base reestablished on Pontus was attacked while he was in command of it. Everyone would assume it was the will of the Goddess who still hadn't forgiven Rayner for what his ancestor had done.

Humming happily to himself, he finished his last tour on the wall. Soon the Zaludians would arrive under the guise that they were the resupply ship. They would use the codes and passwords he had supplied to fool the Defender that was patrolling the space above them. They would then attack the survivors' area killing all beings there before anyone could stop them.

When tomorrow dawned, the Kaliszian Empire would be entering a new era. A stronger, brighter one where those that should be ruling were. And he, Parlan Spada, would be one of them.

∞ ∞ ∞ ∞ ∞

"So are you finally going to tell me?" Jen asked.

"Tell you what?" Mac turned on the cot, so she sat facing Jen.

"What this is all about." Jen reached up freeing the braid Mac had tucked behind her ear and the beads that were on it.

"They're called Suja beads," Mac told her quietly.

"Suja beads." Jen frowned at the word. "These are what the Kaliszians wear in their hair."

"Yes. They designate a Kaliszian's place in their society, their ancestry, and reveal their achievements," Mac told her knowing that since Jen hadn't used the educator, she wouldn't know any of this.

"They tell all that? They aren't just for decoration?"

"No. This one," she touched the bottom bead, "this one is called an Ashe bead. Ashe means Lady in Kaliszian. Nikhil offered it to me a few days ago, and I accepted it." She gave Jen an uncertain look as she continued. "It makes me his wife."

"What?!!" Jen screeched, then dipped her head as everyone looked their way. Lowering her voice she repeated. "What?"

"I'm Nikhil's wife," Mac told her again.

"I... ah... but why?"

"What do you mean why?"

"Why would you marry him? Did he force you?"

"Of course not!" Mac instantly denied. "Nikhil would never do that!"

Jen just stared at her friend, trying to decide if she was telling her the truth. They'd had only each other to rely on for so long that it had gotten to the point where they could finish the other's sentences and knew what the other one was thinking. She could tell Mac wasn't lying to her now. "Then why didn't you want to tell me?"

"Because I wasn't sure how you'd feel about it... after Todd... I was worried it would upset you."

Jen felt her throat clog with tears at the mention of her husband. God, she wished he were here with her, helping her. But he wasn't, and she had to go on without him. Straightening her shoulders, she forced back her tears. "Do you love him, Mac?" she asked.

"With all my heart," Mac instantly responded, and Jen could see the love shining in her friend's eyes. "I can't explain it, Jen, but I feel it. Here," she touched the spot on her chest where her heart was, "and now that I've found him, I can't imagine my life without him in it. I know we're going to have some rough times. After all we still have a lot to learn about each other. We're two different species, and then, of course, there's the fact that he's male."

That last comment brought a small smile to Jen's lips. She remembered the times she'd struggled with Todd, and they'd known each other a lot longer than Mac had known this Nikhil. "Then I'm happy for you, Mac."

"You are? You're sure?"

"Yes, but does it really matter what I think?"

"Of course, it matters. You're my best friend and the closest thing to a sister I've ever had. I wouldn't have made it through all this if it weren't for you."

"That's a lie. If it hadn't been for me, you would have headed back down the mountain like you originally planned, and you wouldn't even be here. You'd still be on Earth. Safe."

"Maybe, but I don't regret staying. I've found my place, Jen, and while I will always regret what had to happen to get me here, I'll never regret that I am. I found my Soul Mate. My True Mate." She looked down and touched the True Mate bead in her hair.

"Is that another Ashe bead?" Jen asked quietly.

"No. This is one Nikhil's True Mate bead," Mac told her quietly and the love was easily heard in her voice.

"True Mate bead? Nikhil offered that to you too?" Jen asked.

"No, Kaliszians can't offer their True Mate bead," she told her.

"Then how are you wearing it?"

"It's kind of hard to explain, Suja beads aren't alive, not in the way we think of things being alive, but they kind of are, and like I said, different ones mean different things. The height of the bead on the braid is also important."

"In what way?"

"The height of any bead indicates the importance, worthiness, or strength of what the bead represents."

"So Nikhil's True Mate bead being more than halfway up your braid indicates..."

"That our bond is very strong and that he loves me as much as I love him."

"I'm happy for you, Mackenzie." Jen reached out to squeeze her hand. "Honestly. We've all been through hell and seem to have lost something of ourselves because of it, but you... you've found something very special and very rare. Cherish it. Hold it close to your heart and never let it go. Because when you lose it," this time Jen couldn't stop her tears from falling, "when you lose it, you lose a piece of yourself that you can never get back."

Mac wrapped her arms around Jen pulling her close. She didn't even have to look up to know that the guys had closed ranks around them, blocking them from everyone else in the room.

"If you love him, Mac, hold on to him. Fight to keep him, to stay with him. Fight with everything you are."

"I will, Jen. I swear to the Goddess I will, but I need you to be there with me, helping me. I can't do this alone. We've been through too much together not to be there for each other now. We're the only human females in this entire universe, and I can't do this without you."

"You can."

"Okay, then I don't want to." She gave Jen a small smile. "I told Nikhil about how humans exchange rings instead of beads."

"You did?" Jen couldn't stop herself from looking at the finger where her rings once rested.

"Yes, I wanted him to wear my ring since I have no Dasho bead to offer him."

"Dasho bead?" Jen frowned.

"It's the bead a female Kaliszian offers to a male making him her husband."

"He's agreed to marry you," Jen couldn't keep the astonishment out of her voice "In a human way?"

"Yes. He's willing to commit himself to me, verbally. It's not something Kaliszians do. They rely on this bead instead." She touched her True Mate bead again.

"You don't like that. Why?" Jen asked, frowning at her.

"Because it takes away your responsibility, your commitment, and trust for the other person. Would you have married Todd, trusted him, based solely on a bead transferring to him?"

"No," Jen told her quietly, "I wouldn't have, but it seems *you* have."

"No, I didn't. I argued with Nikhil about it. I even threatened to cut it off."

"You did?"

"Yeah, I didn't care if I was wearing the first True Mate bead to transfer in five hundred years or not. *I* was going to decide who I loved, who my Soul Mate was and if the Goddess didn't like it that was just too bad."

"And you chose Nikhil."

"Yes."

"And Nikhil chose you."

"Yes."

"You know I can't stand beside you, Mac. The Kaliszians don't even know I'm here."

"You could if you let me tell them about you," Mac raised her hand to stop the argument she knew was coming. "There's no danger to you here, Jen. No one's going to force you to do anything you don't want to do, but you *need* the deep-repair unit. You know you do. You've seen for yourself how much better the guys are doing after being treated. You're fading away right before our eyes, and I can't stand it. Not when there's something I can do about it."

"There's no reason for me to..."

"That's bullshit and you know it! You still matter, Jen!"

"For what?!! To be a charity case?!! I won't be that, Mac!"

"Who's asking you to be?!! Damn it, Jen, you kept us alive in that mine! How, I'll never know, but you made it so the food they gave us was enough. We survived!"

"Not all of us," Jen said quietly, and the pain in her voice had tears rolling down Mac's face.

"And that wasn't your fault, Jen."

"Wasn't it? I was the one that refused to leave that damn ring in the tent."

"So? There was no way you could have known what was going to happen."

"Those damn rings shouldn't have mattered so much."

"Of course, they should have. The man you loved gave them to you.

"Fuck that! *He* should have mattered more."

"And he did. *You* fought for him, Jen. Only you."

"Yeah, and I lost..." The fight went out of Jen's voice. "You should have let me die, Mac."

"No. You were meant to survive, Jen. So you could save the rest of us."

"And now?"

"And now you have to survive so you can make it right with your sister."

"Kimmy," Jen whispered.

"Yes, Kimmy. Remember her? You need to survive so you can get back to her."

"Even if we can get back, she hates me. She has every right to."

"She doesn't. You're her sister, the only family she has left. She's going to want you back."

"You think so?"

"I know and..." Mac trailed off as she looked behind Jen.

"What?" Jen swung around fearing the worst, only to have a smile break out across her face as Paul walked out of the cleansing unit, his hair trimmed and his face clean-shaven. "Paul..."

Mac couldn't believe how good Paul looked. If it weren't for the weight loss, she'd say he looked as good as he did the day she first met him. "Damn, Paul, if we weren't both married I'd be all over you."

"Yes, well he's all mine, Mackenzie Wharton, so you keep your hands off him," Eric said walking up to his husband. "I always said you cleaned up good."

"Yes, well you're next," Paul said wiggling his knife at Eric. "I've been waiting years to have you at my mercy. So come on, it's time to make you amazingly handsome again."

"Like I haven't always been," Eric argued, but he willingly followed Paul into the cleansing room.

"God, those two never get old," Mac said laughing.

"You should have seen them at Todd's and my wedding."

"A good time?" Mac asked.

"The best," Jen confirmed. "They did this dance that stole the show."

"And that didn't bother you?"

"Me? No. Todd, maybe, but then Todd always liked to be the center of attention. As long as it made him look good."

"Jen..."

"Mac, we've been together too long, you know all my secrets. Todd wasn't perfect, but he didn't deserve to die that way. He was my husband, and I will honor him."

"I know, Jen, but you need to honor him by surviving, and you can't do that if you don't let Luol treat you."

"I'll think about it." She squeezed Mac's hand. "Seriously, I will."

∞ ∞ ∞ ∞ ∞

Nikhil had his blaster drawn as he made his way through the mine, the confines of the walls making it impossible for him to use his sword. So far they'd discovered nothing but empty caves. Stepping in to search the next one, he felt his heart start to pound as he recognized it from Mackenzie's description. This cave was where the Zaludians had kept his True Mate. This was where she'd had to learn to survive with males that, while they had protected her to a point when it came right down to it, they had let her go.

He moved to the back of the cave searching for the crevice she said she'd used to hide in. Finding it, he could understand why the Zaludians had never found her. From the front, it looked like any other wall. It wasn't until you got right up next to it that you saw the narrow opening. How had his Mackenzie managed to fit in there? Nikhil tried and couldn't even get one leg in.

"Find something, Squad Leader?"

Nikhil turned to find Treyvon standing at the cave's entrance. "No, General, just checking something." Nikhil moved toward the entrance. "This area is clear."

"This is where the humans were kept," Treyvon told him.

"I know."

"How? I didn't think you made it this deep into the mine."

"I didn't. Mackenzie described it to me." The sound of the General's comm beeping stopped Nikhil from saying more.

"Rayner."

"We found it General," Gryf's voice came over the comm.

"Where?" Treyvon demanded.

"In the main Zaludian cave," Gryf told him tensely. "You're going to want to see this."

"On my way."

∞ ∞ ∞ ∞ ∞

Treyvon watched as Gryf connected their interface device to the Zaludian computer sending the transmissions. They'd found no one in the mine and no evidence that anyone had been there since they'd left. All the seals and alarms were still intact and armed.

"Was it preprogrammed, Gryf?" Treyvon asked.

"No. This unit received a signal yesterday telling it to start transmitting that signal. It was also instructed not to try to hide or encode the transmission."

"They wanted us to discover it," Treyvon said thoughtfully, looking at the unit.

"I believe so," Gryf agreed.

"Why? For what purpose? It wasn't a trap," Treyvon looked around the room, "there's no one here." Treyvon's comm went off again. "Rayner!"

"General, this is Warrior Gulzar."

"What is it, Gulzar?" Treyvon asked impatiently, his mind on other things.

"General, I wanted to inform you that the resupply ship is on its final approach."

"What? Why would you contact me about that?" Treyvon demanded.

"I... General, you ordered that you be informed immediately of all ships coming near Pontus."

"Yes, but..." Treyvon trailed off and began to frown. He'd just talked to Darzi the Captain of the Fenton, last night. Darzi was an old friend and had contacted him to let him know they'd gotten delayed leaving Crurn and would be late arriving. That wasn't the Fenton approaching! "Notify the Defender and put the base on high alert!"

"General?" Gulzar questioned.

"That's not the Fenton! Get everyone notified. Now!" As Treyvon gave the order, he heard the first explosion come over the comm. "Gulzar!" When all he received was static, he snapped his comm closed. "Fuck! I want everyone back to the transports! Now!"

∞ ∞ ∞ ∞ ∞

Mac couldn't help but smile as one by one the guys allowed Paul to shave and cut their hair. It was amazing to see the difference it made in them. Each one came out standing a little straighter, their shoulders thrown back a little farther. They were rediscovering who they once were.

"They look good, don't they?" Mac said smiling at Jen.

"They do, but..."

"But what?" Mac asked.

"Why are those Kaliszians staring at them like they have two heads?"

"What?" Mac's eyes flew to where Onp and Nroa were standing by the doors and saw Jen wasn't wrong. The Kaliszians were staring at the guys with such a look of shock and horror that she almost laughed. She needed to explain to them what was happening and why.

"For a Kaliszian, the ultimate punishment is to have their hair cut off. It removes their Suja beads, removing their identity. It is reserved for only the most abhorrent of offenses."

"Really?"

"Yeah. You should have seen Nikhil's reaction when I first got here and commented that mine was such a mess that I should just cut it."

"Not good I take it."

"No. Not good at all. I'd better explain to Onp and Nroa that this is normal for humans. That the guys aren't being punished for something." Giving Jen's arm a squeeze, she rose and crossed the room.

That's when all hell broke loose.

∞ ∞ ∞ ∞ ∞

Nikhil didn't bother to sit as the transport shot off the ground in a maneuver typically reserved for only dire combat conditions. His fingers tightened around the structural beam that was constructed from the strongest metal the universes had to offer, leaving deep depressions.

"Who?" Nikhil fired the question at his General and friend.

"I don't know," Treyvon responded angrily. "Or why. Defender! What have you got?"

"General, it's a Zaludian ship, heavily armed."

"How the fuck did it get past you?!!"

"They had all the proper codes and passwords, General, including a false visual projection that only dropped when they armed their weapons."

"Where are they attacking?" Treyvon demanded.

"The base, General."

"Return fire!" he ordered.

"They've already landed within the compound, General. If I fire now, *I* will destroy the base!"

"Fuck!" Treyvon turned to the pilot, "Get us there! Now!"

"Yes, General!" the pilot responded.

"Why would the Zaludians attack?" Gryf questioned over the roar of the engines. "We know they've been here now. It's not like they can resume mining."

"They want something." Treyvon's mind was racing, narrowing down all the possibilities and he didn't like the few that remained. He looked to Nikhil.

"Mackenzie," Nikhil said through stiff lips. "They had planned on selling her to a Pleasure House."

"True," Gryf said, "and while her uniqueness would have brought a high price, it doesn't warrant this level of attack."

"It might if she were breeding compatible with the Tornians," Treyvon told him quietly.

"What?!!" Nikhil moved toward Treyvon. "What are you saying?!!"

"The female, the one that was with Emperor Vasteri when he crashed, was similar in size and skin tone to your Mackenzie, Nikhil."

"She's human?" Nikhil asked.

"I don't know for sure. Vasteri stayed very close to her, and I only interacted with her for a short time. Vasteri claimed her as his Empress," Treyvon informed him.

"That still doesn't mean..." Gryf started.

"I've heard a rumor that she is with offspring," Treyvon said, "which means..."

"That the Tornians will be searching for more like her," Nikhil responded.

"Yes," Treyvon nodded.

"You think the Tornians are behind this?" Gryf questioned in obvious disbelief.

"No. The Tornians are an honorable race. If they were going to attack, *they* would attack, not send Zaludians. But that doesn't mean the Zaludians don't see an opportunity here. If Mackenzie was truly breeding compatible with the Tornians then..."

"Then she would be the most valuable female in the universe and there are those in the Tornian Empire that would pay whatever was asked to obtain her," Nikhil finished through clenched teeth.

"Yes," Treyvon agreed.

"How long ago did you hear this rumor about the Empress?" Nikhil demanded.

"Right before we discovered the humans."

"And you didn't tell me?!!" Nikhil growled threateningly, his hands fisting. "When you learned Mackenzie was my True Mate and that there might be a threat against her?"

"There was no threat. It hasn't been confirmed yet that the Empress is with offspring or even that she is human! Nikhil! Do you really think I would knowingly allow harm to come to the first True Mate the Kaliszian Empire has seen in over five-hundred years, let alone *yours*?!!"

Nikhil knew Treyvon; he was an honorable male that Nikhil had always admired and felt fortunate to call him friend. He was also loyal to his warriors and people, always putting them before his own needs. He would never knowingly allow Nikhil's Ashe to be harmed. He forced himself to calm. "No. You of all males would never allow a female to be harmed."

"We won't let them take her, Nikhil," Treyvon told him. "She is yours."

"She is," Nikhil agreed, reaching up to touch the empty braid that had once held his Ashe and True Mate beads. Goddess, how he wished he wore Mackenzie's so he would know if she were okay."

"The base is in sight, General," the pilot informed them, and all eyes looked on in horror at the smoke and flames that were rising from the survivors' area.

"Goddess," Gryf whispered."

"Battle Stations!" Treyvon ordered.

∞ ∞ ∞ ∞ ∞

The first explosion knocked Mac off her feet as she crossed the room to talk to Onp and Nroa. The second had her curling up into a ball, trying to protect herself from all the flying debris as the outer wall of the room was blown out.

Carefully, Mac moved to sit up and took in the devastation that only moments ago had been a room full of people. The exterior wall that had opened into a small, walled area was gone, and those further out were only rubble. As the smoke and dust began to clear, she saw a ship was landing.

"Mackenzie!" Onp suddenly materialized at her side. "Are you injured?"

"I... I don't think so," she said slightly dazed trying to take in all the destruction she was seeing. "What's going on?"

"Then come, we must get you out of here!" He told her, ignoring her question as he pulled her to her feet.

"Get me out?" she asked looking around in horror at the mangled bodies.

"Yes. We are under attack! We must get you to safety."

"No, we need to help the injured." She jerked her arm out of his hold, her eyes frantically searching where Jen had been. All she found was turned over cots. "Jen!" she screamed starting to run across the room. "Where are you?!!"

"Mackenzie, no!" Onp shouted, knocking her down when blaster fire suddenly filled the room. Rolling, he pulled his blaster and returned fire. "Go!" he ordered still firing. "Find some place to hide until we can get you out of here."

Mac immediately obeyed, crawling toward where she'd last seen Jen, ignoring the glass that was cutting into her skin.

"Jen!" she screamed. "Jen!"

"Over here," a faint voice called back.

"Jen!" she called out again moving toward the voice. "I'm coming, Jen"

Mac had just moved another cot out of her way to find Jen huddled back in a corner when she saw Jen's eyes widen in fear before she screamed out a warning. "Mac! Behind you!"

Mac swung around and screamed out in horror at the Zaludian moving toward her. *Oh my God!* Her mind screamed. *It's the Zaludians! She couldn't let them take her! She'd never survive it again!* She crab-crawled back away from him as fast as she could, but she didn't get far before the Zaludian grabbed her by the throat and lifted her off the floor.

Mac clawed at the hand holding her but only managed to shred her fingers on the spiked glove covering it. Her mind screamed for Nikhil as the room began to dim and darkness started to invade her vision.

"No!" Mac barely heard the enraged scream, but she was suddenly dropped and she sucked in a much-needed breath. Rolling over, she meant to run, but instead, she froze when she saw Jen on the Zaludian's back, stabbing him repeatedly with one of Nikhil's blades.

The Zaludian reared back in pain, frantically reaching behind him to pull Jen away before throwing her against the wall. Her head hit with a sickening thud, and she collapsed into a boneless heap on the floor.

"Jen!" Mac screamed, but the Zaludian was on her again, this time swinging his fist and Mac's world went black.

Chapter Seventeen

The transport had barely touched down behind the Zaludian ship before Nikhil had opened the hatch, a blaster in one hand, his sword in the other. He jumped out and was running toward the survivors' area. They'd all heard the comms from Onp and Nroa calling for reinforcements, saying they were under direct attack and taking heavy casualties. He prayed to the Goddess that his Mackenzie wasn't one of them.

More Zaludians poured out of their ship trying to slow them down, but Nikhil just carved a path through them, never more thankful for his massive size and strength. Any that got close, he ended with his sword. Those further away he cut down with his blaster. No one was stopping him from getting to his Mackenzie's side.

He had just reached what had been the exterior wall of the building when he heard his Mackenzie's scream and saw a Zaludian strike her in the face, the sharp spikes of his gloves shredding her delicate, pale skin.

"No!" his roar was filled with all the rage and pain that filled his soul as he watched her head snap back. He fired at the Zaludian, sending him to meet Daco, then reaching his Mackenzie's side dropped his weapons, catching her before she hit the ground.

"Mackenzie!" he whispered as her ravaged face fell back over his arm. He didn't notice how Onp, Nroa, Gryf, and Treyvon instantly formed a protective circle around them. Didn't notice that the human males and Nekeoks were fighting the Zaludians with anything they could find. His entire focus was on his Mackenzie.

"Get her to Luol!" Treyvon ordered. "Onp, Nroa, Gryf, clear a path."

"General, the base is not secure," Gryf informed him.

"Which is why Onp and Nroa will accompany Nikhil and make sure he and his Ashe get to medical. Gryf, you will remain with me, and we will finish eradicating this filth from our planet."

"Agreed, General," Gryf responded, and he started clearing the path to what had once been the entrance to the area.

Nikhil swept Mackenzie up in his arms and relied on those he most trusted to protect them both on their way to medical. "Hold on, Little One," he whispered.

∞ ∞ ∞ ∞ ∞

"Hold on, Little One..."

The words whispered through her mind, and her soul reached out for them. She needed them, him to survive, but he and the words faded away.

"Nikhil!" she cried out, but Nikhil didn't respond. Someone else did.

"Why do you call out for the one you thought to refuse?" a melodic voice questioned.

Mac spun around to find the most stunningly, beautiful woman she had ever seen standing just a short distance behind her, and instinctively she knew she was the Goddess.

"What?" she questioned.

"Why do you call out for the male you thought to refuse?" she asked again.

"I never refused Nikhil!"

"You thought to refuse his True Mate bead. It is the same as refusing him."

"It is *not* the same! This," she grabbed the strand of hair holding the bead, "has nothing to do with what I feel for Nikhil!"

"Then I will remove it." The Goddess reached out and was shocked when her hand was slapped away.

"You will not touch it!" One instant Mac found herself growling at the Goddess, the next there was an explosion and she was flying across the floor. The largest male she had ever seen was leaning down over her, his glowing eyes glaring at her. He was even larger than Nikhil, and while his eyes glowed like a Kaliszian, his long, dark hair covered his entire head, and his skin seemed to change colors like a chameleon.

"Raiden!" the Goddess exclaimed.

"She *harmed* you!" he growled.

"I shouldn't have tried to remove her True Mate bead," the Goddess was immediately at his side.

"That matters not! No one harms you!"

"Then tell her to keep her hands to herself," Mac found herself saying, her anger replacing her fear.

The male gave her a shocked look before he stood and an amazing smile transformed his scowling face into one that stole her breath. He was the most handsome male she had ever seen.

"Thank you," he told her, his deep voice seeming to fill the universe.

"He's mine," the Goddess said, stepping between them and the temperature of the room dropped drastically. "*My* mate."

It was a struggle, but Mac was finally able to pull her gaze from the male to look at the Goddess. "Good. Great. Fine. I've already got a male, and he's all I want."

"Really? Then why did you threaten to cut off his True Mate bead?"

"Because I don't need it to know he's mine." Mac's gaze ran over her. "I see *you* don't wear a True Mate bead. Are you sure he," she nodded toward Raiden, "is your True Mate?" she asked raising a questioning eyebrow.

Mac wasn't prepared for how dark everything suddenly became or how the ground beneath her shook, but she felt the rage emanating from both of them.

"You dare question our bond!??" they both roared.

"Sucks, doesn't it?!! To have others question your commitment all because of some bead!"

Raiden was the first of the two to calm, and he gave her a considering look. "You are very brave for one so small."

"Am I?" Mac asked.

"Yes. Few are willing to stand up to me," Raiden told her.

"Perhaps that's because you knock them on their ass first and ask questions later," Mac told him.

"Perhaps." Raiden took a step back, extending his hand to help her up. Mac took it and with that touch understood so much more than she had before. With his touch, he allowed her to see how he and the Goddess fell in love, how a lower God named Daco destroyed the people he had left behind to be with his mate, and how they suffered. Daco hadn't been able to drive Raiden out of the memory of the Kaliszian people as he had hoped though, but they had nearly destroyed themselves trying to find what Raiden had, a True Mate. Because of that, Raiden and the Goddess had created the True Mate bead.

Gasping at the onslaught of information, she ripped her hand from his.

"Now you see," he told her.

"Yes, but the bead you created no longer brings comfort or peace to the Kaliszian people," Mac told him quietly.

"What do you mean?" Raiden demanded.

"When you," she looked to the Goddess, "cursed the Kaliszians with the Great Infection, you didn't just kill the plants that feed their bodies, you killed what they needed to feed their souls! Their True Mates."

"Impossible!" The Goddess moved to stand in front of her mate, her eyes blazing into Mac's.

"But it's true. I am the first person your True Mate bead has transferred to in nearly five-hundred years."

"No!" The Goddess stumbled back looking up at her mate in horror. "Raiden, that can't be true! It was never what I intended."

"I know, my love. I know," he said, pulling her into the safety of his arms.

"What *did* you intend?" Mac asked. "Because from what I have seen you meant to destroy those you once held dear."

"I was in such a rage when I learned what Emperor Berto did to his young female offspring... How others allowed it... I wanted to punish them, make them hurt as much as I did, as those young females had."

"You caused the Great Infection," Mac said quietly.

"They caused it!" she immediately fired back, and then her shoulders slumped. "But I created it."

"Goddess..." Raiden wrapped comforting arms around her. "We can not undo what has been done."

"Why not?" Mac asked. "You are Gods, aren't you?"

"Because the offenses were *real* and until those that allowed them to happen prove they have recovered their honor, I can do nothing!"

"How does an *entire* race prove they are honorable?!!" Mac demanded. "That's impossible!"

"It's not about the entire race. It's about those that caused the original crime."

"Five-hundred years ago?!!" Mac looked at her in shock. "They're dead!"

"But their descendants aren't! It only takes one, from each species, to end what I have wrought!"

"But..."

"I am trying to bring all those together that can do this, but I need your help."

"My help?"

"Yes, you are a caretaker, one that protects the land and what grows on it. The Kaliszians will need you."

"That makes no sense. Nothing grows in the Kaliszian Empire because of *you*!"

"This is true, but because of you and those with you, I have been able to sow the first seeds of change. I need you there when they begin to appear."

"You're saying life is going to return to Pontus? To the Kaliszians?"

"Yes, but before that happens, I have to correct a great harm. The Kaliszian people need to know they still have True Mates. That I have not forsaken them."

"But how?" Mac questioned.

"You will see." The Goddess touched the braid that held Nikhil's True Mate and Ashe beads. "Love well, Little One. May you find as much happiness with your True Mate as I have with mine."

With those words, the Goddess kissed Mac gently on the forehead and Mac's world went dark.

∞ ∞ ∞ ∞ ∞

Nikhil pressed his forehead against the cool glass of the closed deep-repair unit, wishing he were touching his

Mackenzie instead. Luol had taken one look at the bloody mess in Nikhil's arms and rushed them to the unit, activating it to it's highest level.

"She will recover, Nikhil," Luol tried to reassure him. "You got her here in time."

"It should never have happened," Nikhil said. "I have failed her."

"You haven't," Luol quickly denied.

"Her face," Nikhil's voice broke and he turned devastated eyes to Luol. "Her beautiful face. He struck her, Luol."

"I saw that, but you can thank the Goddess that the Zaludians never use Tornian steel in their gloves. The unit will repair the damage. She won't even have a scar. Her skin will be as beautiful and as flawless as before."

"How much longer?" Nikhil demanded, his gaze returning to Mackenzie, struggling to see her through the thick, white vapor that was swirling in the tube.

Luol knew for Nikhil it felt like an eternity since the unit had closed, separating him from his Ashe, but it had been less than thirty minutes. Mackenzie's facial injuries had been extensive, and he wasn't going to rush the unit. He knew Nikhil was struggling with not being able to see her, but Luol had introduced a strong sedative into the unit. He didn't want Mackenzie waking while the unit was still closed. He wanted the first thing she saw to be Nikhil. She would need him as she struggled through the memory of the attack.

"It won't be much longer now," Luol assured him. "She is responding well."

"She'll never forgive me, Luol. I have broken my vow to her."

"What?"

"I vowed to keep her safe, that the Zaludians would never harm her again."

Luol understood Nikhil's concern a Kaliszian warrior never gave his vow unless he meant to keep it. It was a matter of honor. For him to not keep it was one of the few offenses that could destroy the True Mate bond. But Mackenzie was unlike any other female he had ever met, and he did not think she would see it that way.

"No one could have known the Zaludians would be desperate enough to return and attack."

"That does not matter," Nikhil muttered.

"I believe it will to your Mackenzie. She is a very special female, Nikhil."

"She is, but even she has her limits."

"I do not believe this will be one of them." The signal from the unit had Luol looking back to the control panel to see it had finished and was about to open.

"Luol?" Nikhil looked to him.

"She will be awake shortly. Stay close to her, Nikhil. The first thing she will remember is being attacked by the Zaludians. She is going to need to see you to know she is safe."

Nikhil held his breath as the tube retreated and he got his first glimpse of his Mackenzie. Her hair was still a matted, bloody mess as were her coverings, and while there was still blood on her face, all the damage caused by the Zaludian's fist was gone.

"Thank you, Goddess," Nikhil whispered with a shuddering breath as he lowered himself onto his forearms, his forehead coming to rest on hers. "Thank you."

"Nikhil?"

Mackenzie's faint, hesitant voice had him pulling back just far enough to look down into her beautiful, brown eyes filled with confusion. "I'm here, Mackenzie. You are safe."

"Where..." Suddenly it all came back to her, the explosions, the Zaludians, the studded fist coming at her and the pain. She jerked in Nikhil's arms, crying out in fear, her feet trying to gain leverage as her gaze flew behind him searching for her attacker.

"They're gone, Mackenzie." Nikhil wrapped his arms around her, pulling her close knowing why she was afraid. "The Zaludians are gone. You are safe."

"They are?" she asked looking up at him, her gaze full of fear. "I am?"

"Yes."

"Vow it," she demanded, but when he hesitated her eyes widened. "I'm not safe... they're still here!"

"No!" Nikhil denied, his arms tightening around her holding her still. "They aren't!"

"Then why won't you give me your vow?!!" she demanded.

"Why would you still believe it, believe me, after I have failed you so completely?" he questioned and felt Mackenzie go completely still.

"What?" she asked looking up at him.

"I failed you! I left you unprotected, and you were harmed! The Zaludians harmed you!"

"Nikhil..." she reached up framing his face with her hands. "How can you possibly think that?"

"Because it is truth!" he told her.

"No, it's not!" she denied. "You left me in the middle of a military base surrounded by armed warriors. How is that unprotected?!!"

"Because I wasn't there and you were harmed! I broke my vow."

"Nikhil..." Mac's eyes shined up into his with unshed tears. She knew how seriously Nikhil took those vows he gave her.

"You think I would blame you for an attack no one could have predicted?"

"Of course. You are the most precious thing in my life. I should never have left your side."

"And you are the most precious thing in mine," Mac told him, "and nothing is ever going to change that, especially not some stupid attack by the Zaludians. I will always believe in you, Nikhil, always trust in you and your vow. It's like your love for me, strong and unending. Give me your vow."

Nikhil felt his own eyes fill with his True Mate's words. He hadn't lost her. She was still his."

"Always," Mac whispered, and he realized he'd spoken out loud.

"I vow to you, Mackenzie. The Zaludians are gone, and they will never harm you or any of your people again."

"I know..." she pulled his head down and kissed his lips. "I know we are all..." Suddenly, she remembered she hadn't been the only one harmed and she jerked back in Nikhil's arms. "Oh my God! Jen!"

"What?" Nikhil frowned down at her. He and Mackenzie had lain in bed every night, and she told him about every male that had been treated. There had been no one named Jen.

"Jen! We have to get to Jen!" she pushed at Nikhil's shoulders trying to get him to let her up. "He threw her against the wall after she jumped on his back trying to protect me."

"*She?!!*" Nikhil's gaze flew from Mackenzie to Luol and saw he was just as shocked.

"Yes! She! Oh God, we have to get to her. She hit that wall so hard! She hasn't been treated by the repair unit yet!" Mac covered her mouth with a trembling hand. "Oh God, Nikhil! I have to get to her! She stopped that Zaludian from taking me!"

Nikhil stood, ripping his comm from his belt. His eyes remained fixed on Mackenzie as he contacted Treyvon. "General!"

"What is it, Nikhil? Has your Ashe recovered?"

"Yes, General, but she has just informed me that the humans have been concealing another female. That the female was seriously injured during the attack!"

"What?!!" Treyvon's shout echoed off the walls even through the comm.

"Are you still in the survivors' area?" Nikhil demanded.

"Yes! I will find her! Tell Luol to have a repair unit waiting!"

"Yes, General!"

"Nikhil..." Mackenzie's eyes remained locked with his and she could see the hurt in them.

"You lied to me, Mackenzie."

Mac's eyes widened at how hard and cold Nikhil's voice had become. "I didn't!"

"You just did not tell me truth," he fired back. "Is that not something you said was unacceptable to you?!!"

"Yes! But this is different." When Nikhil would have moved away from her, she grabbed his arm. "You didn't tell me about something that was personal that affected *us*. You and me!"

"And this doesn't affect us?!!" he looked at her in total disbelief.

"No! Not like that! This was about someone else! The guys protected Jen, just like they did me. When you rescued us, all they did was continue to protect her because they didn't know how you would treat her, and they couldn't risk it!"

"*You* knew we would never harm her!" Nikhil shouted at her.

"I did!" Mac told him, wincing slightly that he was shouting at her; not because she thought he would hurt her, but because she knew *he* was hurting. "I tried to convince Jen to let me reveal her presence. That's why I wanted you to take me there while you were gone. So I could try again, but *she* wasn't ready, Nikhil, and I couldn't force her."

"How badly is she injured?" Luol demanded from the control panel of the other repair unit.

"From today, I don't know." Mac felt her eyes start to fill as she remembered what had happened. "I barely saw her jump on that Zaludian's back before she started stabbing him with one of Nikhil's blades. I was clawing at the hand that was wrapped around my throat," Mac's hand went to her throat as she remembered. "Jen made him drop me, but then he ripped her off his back and threw her against the wall. She hit it so hard... and when she hit the floor she didn't move. I don't know how she managed to stop him. She'd been so severely injured in the mine. Broken bones.... scars... "

"What?!!" Both males looked at her in shock.

"I don't know how she survived," Mac whispered, her tears flowing down her face. "I did what I could, but when she started to run a fever I thought we were going to lose her."

Before they could question her further, Treyvon shouted as he came rushing into the room carrying something wrapped in a gray cape.

"Luol!" he roared.

"Oh God! Jen!" Mac was up and moving to her friend.

"Get back!" The rage in Treyvon's snarled words had Mac stumbling back in shock and Nikhil pulled her protectively behind him.

"Do not attack my Ashe!" Nikhil snarled back. Stepping forward he bumped his chest against the General.

"She put a female at risk!" Treyvon roared at him.

"Stop it! Both of you!" Mac shoved her way past the two males to get to Jen. "None of that matters right now. What matters is Jen. Luol?" She looked up at the Healer with pleading eyes.

"I need to see how badly she's injured before I activate the unit, Mackenzie." Luol moved to Jen and couldn't contain the gasp of horror at what was revealed when he pulled back the hood that had fallen over the female's face. While there was no sign of recent injury, her face was ravaged with healed scars that could only have been caused by the spikes of a Zaludian glove. "She was able to recover from this? In the mine?"

Luol's question had the arguing males looking at Jen and they immediately ceased fighting.

"This and more," Mac told him, her tears starting again. "They threw her into the crevasse with all the other dead bodies. She shattered her ankle on the way down, and there are more scars on her body from where the rocks sliced into her." Mac opened the cape further, revealing them to Luol.

"Goddess..." Mac wasn't sure who said that.

"Can you help her, Luol?" she asked looking to the Healer.

"I will do all I can for her, Mackenzie." He immediately moved back to the control panel. "Step back I need to start treating her immediately if I'm going to save her. She is fading fast."

"Oh God!" Mac's trembling fingers covered her mouth as she leaned back into Nikhil's arms when she felt them envelop her in comfort. "She's been in such pain, Nikhil. Every day I saw it, but she never gave up. None of us would have survived without her.

They all watched as the unit closed and a dense blue vapor filled it.

"What's that?!!" Mac questioned.

"It's to ease her pain and help her stay relaxed while the unit works. I don't want her waking while the unit is still running. She might harm herself."

"Do you know how long?" Mac asked.

"Your first treatment took nearly six hours, Mackenzie," Luol informed her.

"It did?" Mac hadn't realized that.

"Yes. She, I believe, will take much longer." His fingers continued to fly over the controls as he spoke. "I vow I will do my best for her, Mackenzie, and while I do, you need to go with Nikhil and rest."

"I can't do that!" she immediately denied. "I need to stay with Jen."

"There is nothing you can do for her right now." Luol's fingers finally stopped moving, and he gave her a hard look. "You need to rest and recover from your own injuries, or you will be no good to her when she wakes."

"I'm fine," she told him but even as she said it, she let Nikhil tighten his embrace.

"You are not," Luol told her bluntly, then looked to Treyvon whose gaze was still locked on the closed repair unit.

"Nikhil, you are relieved of your duties," Treyvon told him in a hard voice. "See to your Ashe. That's an order."

"Yes, General," Nikhil replied, and before Mac could protest, swept her up in his arms and carried her away.

∞ ∞ ∞ ∞ ∞

Mac curled up into Nikhil's arms and let him carry her away from her friend. She knew Luol was right. There was nothing she could do for Jen right now. She needed to regain her strength if she was going to help Jen when she woke. She knew

Nikhil was still upset with her, knew there was still a lot she needed to explain. That's why she was surprised when instead of carrying her to the couch he carried her into the cleansing stall and set her on her feet.

"Nikhil?" she looked up at him questioningly.

"You can not rest covered in blood," he told her curtly, starting to pull her stained covering up.

"Nikhil..." she put a hand on his arm stopping him. "I'm sorry. I'm so sorry I didn't tell you, but it wasn't my secret to reveal."

"You didn't trust me!" For the first time, he revealed the depth of the hurt her secret had caused him.

"I do! God, Nikhil! You have to know I do!" She gripped his face, pulling it down so he could see the truth in her eyes. "With my *life*! With my *soul*! "

"Then why not with *this*?!!" he asked.

"Because it wasn't *my* secret to tell! It wasn't about *me*! You saw Jen, saw what she suffered, what she's had to survive, and there's more." Her thumbs covered his lips to stop him from speaking. "But that's for Jen to tell. It's her story. Don't ask me to betray that trust... because I would, if *you* asked me to. If *you* needed me to. There isn't anything I wouldn't do for you, Nikhil. Don't you know that?"

Nikhil stared down at his Ashe. His True Mate. Could he truly fault her for being so loyal to one of her own? A female. A female she had obviously bonded with in the way he had with many of his warriors. He was demanding something of her that he wasn't certain he could give her in return. What did that say about *him*?

"Do not break your vow, my Mackenzie. When she is ready for it to be known, it will be, but I must ask you this. Are there any other females hiding?"

"No! It was just Jen and me. I vow it!" Sealing her vow, she pressed her lips against his and wrapped her arms around his neck.

For a moment, Nikhil didn't respond, and Mac thought she had lost him but then he groaned, and his arms wrapped around her and he lifted her off her feet. She immediately wrapped her legs around his waist and held on.

Nikhil ravished her mouth. He couldn't believe how close he had come to losing her, and not just because of the Zaludians. He had reacted badly finding out she was keeping something from him. He'd yelled at her, had nearly lost control, but she hadn't run from him, hadn't feared him. She'd trusted him not to harm her even then. He needed to deserve that trust and thinking only of his own needs and desires was not the way.

Ripping his mouth away from hers, he stared down at the darkness that was flowing from her hair with the force of the shower. Darkness caused by the blood she'd lost when she'd been injured. That was one thing the deep-repair unit couldn't compensate for. Yes, it could replace the blood, but it took time for the body to reabsorb what it had lost.

"Nikhil?" Mac looked up at him questioningly.

"I need to care for you, Mackenzie. I need to show you how much I love you and that I will never harm you."

"I know this, Nikhil. You don't have to prove anything to me," she searched his glowing green eyes and saw that he felt he did. As his size had been held against him his entire life, he needed to show her he could still be gentle and caring. Slowly, she unwrapped her legs from around his waist and let him lower her to the floor.

"Alright, but I'm not letting go of you," she told him, wrapping her arms around his waist. "I need you close."

Nikhil would never complain about his Mackenzie's hands on him, but he stilled, hearing the tremble in his mate's voice. "Mackenzie?"

"I was so scared, Nikhil," she whispered burrowing into his chest. "When I realized it was the Zaludians that were attacking."

Nikhil hated the fear he heard in her voice. Hated that he hadn't been there for her when she needed protected. He also knew that she needed to voice that fear before she could heal. Slowly, he began to work the cleansing liquid into her hair and listened.

"Paul was just coming over to talk to us. He'd finished shaving and cutting all the guys' hair, and wanted to know if either of us wanted our hair trimmed."

Nikhil had to call on all his control to stop himself from growling his displeasure at her cutting any part of the amazing mass his fingers were now in.

"We all heard the first explosion but didn't know where it was coming from. We didn't realize we were under attack. Not until the exterior wall blew out and the Zaludians started storming in. I couldn't believe it. I don't think any of us could. The Jerboaians took the worst of it. They were the closest to the wall. Once the Zaludians were inside, they seemed to take a moment and then they zeroed in on us. They were looking for us... for me." She looked up at him, fear filling her eyes again. "Why were they looking for me, Nikhil?"

"We do not know for sure," he told her truth as he continued to cleanse her hair, because this concerned her and she had the right to know. "Treyvon believes it might have something to do with the Tornians."

"The Tornians? But why? I've never even met one."

"I know." Gripping her head, he carefully tipped it back rinsing away the foam as his thumbs gently removed the remaining blood on her face.

"Then why?" she asked, looking him in the eye.

"It seems not long ago the Tornian Emperor discovered a female that might be breeding compatible with them."

"Breeding compatible?" Mac frowned, then remembered that for the Tornians the Goddess' Great Infection had caused fewer and fewer females to be born. That now, according to the educator, Tornian males now outnumbered their females two hundred to one and that they were unable to breed with any other known species. "But that still doesn't explain why me."

"Treyvon briefly met the female, here on Pontus, when the Emperor's shuttle crashed. He said that while her appearance was very different than yours, that you were still similar to her in skin tone and size."

"He thinks she's from Earth," Mac whispered, lifting her arms as Nikhil removed her stained covering.

"He does not know. All he knows is that the Ganglians captured both of you. He had never seen one like her before, but if she is breeding compatible and if the Zaludians or Ganglians have made that connection, then you would be extremely valuable to them."

"Because they could sell me to males desperate to have offspring," Mac whispered, in horror.

"Yes," he told her honestly.

"Nikhil..."

"That will never happen!" he told her seeing the fear in her eyes. He couldn't stand it. Lifting her off her feet, he captured her lips in a hard, deep kiss.

"Nikhil..." she gasped into his mouth. "I need you. I need to feel you inside me," she wrapped her legs back around his hips and wrapped her arms around his head. "Please."

Nikhil knew he could never refuse his Mackenzie, especially when what she was asking for was him. Pressing her against the wall, he hooked an arm under her ass lifting her up as he pulled back just far enough to free himself from his pants. Setting the head of his shaft at her entrance, he gripped her tiny waist and slowly lowered her onto him.

Mac gasped as she felt Nikhil begin to fill her. Goddess, he was it so large... she knew that, but it still surprised her every time they made love and it turned her on. He stretched her tight channel to the point that she could feel the heavy beat of his heart pulsing deep inside her, making them truly one.

"Nikhil!" she cried out, ripping her mouth from his as she took all of him.

"Mine! You are mine, Mackenzie! Only mine!" he growled as he slowly began to thrust in and out of her, groaning at the way her channel clung to his shaft trying to suck him back in as he pulled nearly completely out of her. Unable to stop himself, he thrust back in as deeply as he could, needing to connect with her in the most primitive of ways. He could already feel his balls pulling up, and he wanted to fill her with his seed, wanted to claim her, to make sure no male ever doubted that she was his. He wanted his seed to take root and for her to bear his offspring. He wanted everything he had never thought he could have. "Goddess, Mackenzie!"

Mac couldn't believe the feelings that were flowing through her, and she knew they were all coming from Nikhil through the True Mate bead she wore. Reaching out, she grasped the braid that had once held that bead and felt an extra jolt of love and connection that sent her into a powerful orgasm that had her screaming out her pleasure as Nikhil exploded inside of her.

∞ ∞ ∞ ∞ ∞

Nikhil lay beside his Mackenzie in their bed, an arm thrown across her waist keeping her close as he watched her sleep. Goddess, he shouldn't have taken her like that. Especially after all she'd been through that day. He should have just cleansed her and let her rest... but he couldn't regret it, he'd never regret it.

"You'd better not," she told him sleepily.

"What?" he asked and watched as she struggled to open her eyes far enough to gaze into his.

"You better not regret it," she told him. "If you do, I'll kick your ass."

"How... how did you know I was thinking that?"

"Because you said it, dummy." Her eyes started to close again.

"I didn't. I just thought it." Nikhil's whisper had her eyes opening again.

"You had to have said it, otherwise how could I have heard you?"

"Because that is the other secret Kaliszians have always kept about their True Mate bead. When exchanged, they allow them to not only feel what the other is feeling, but also speak to them in their minds.

"What?" she gave him a confused look.

"Only True Mates, ones they have exchanged their beads and have the deepest of bonds, can hear the other's thoughts."

"But we didn't..." Mackenzie's words trailed off as her gaze went to Nikhil's braid that once held his True Mate and Ashe bead. Now, halfway up that braid was a green bead with amber swirling through it.

Nikhil's gaze followed hers and came to rest on what she was holding in her delicate hand, and he felt his heart stutter. There, attached to *his* braid, his Ashe's fingers lovingly caressing it, lay the most beautiful bead he had ever seen. It was a lighter green than the one she wore, and it swirled with warm amber instead of the white of his, but he still knew what it was. It was impossible. She wasn't Kaliszian, but he was wearing her True Mate bead. *He* was wearing it.

"Nikhil? How is this possible?"

"I do not know, but I can only thank the Goddess that it has."

"The Goddess?" she whispered.

Something in his Mackenzie's tone had him giving her a hard look. "Mackenzie, what aren't you telling me?"

"I thought it was a dream," she whispered.

"What are you talking about?"

"Meeting the Goddess... and her mate. We, umm, really didn't get along all that well."

"What?!!" Nikhil didn't try to hide his shock.

"She challenged what I felt for you, that it was truth because I didn't believe in the bead."

"You don't?" he asked.

"I believe in *you*, Nikhil, with or without your bead. But I will always love, cherish and protect it, just as I will you for the rest of my life." She looked at her braid that held his True Mate and Ashe bead and smiled at what she somehow knew would be there.

A Dasho bead.

Reaching up, she removed the amber bead with white swirls running through it and looked to her Nikhil.

"Nikhil Kozar, will you be my Dasho? I vow if you accept this bead that I will always love and protect you with all my heart and soul and that when the Goddess calls my name to enter the Promised Land, I will still fight to remain at your side."

Nikhil felt his breath stall. He'd come to accept that he would never wear her Dasho bead. He'd thought he was fine with it, but now he realized how much he had wanted to wear her bead.

"Mackenzie Wharton, I accept you as my Ashe, as I have before and always will with or without wearing your bead. You are my love, my heart, and my soul, and if the Goddess tries to welcome me into the Promised Land without you, I will refuse and always remain at your side."

Wrapping his fingers around hers, together they brought the bead closer, and it seemed to jump from their fingertips to firmly affix itself halfway up his braid.

Mac stared at the bead for a moment then looked into Nikhil's eyes. "I love you, Nikhil. With or without those beads, you are the only one I was meant for, the only one I will ever love. Now," she gave him a teasing smile, "show me how much you love me."

Epilogue

The Supreme Commander of the Kaliszian Defenses stared down at the female lying so peacefully on the repair unit bed and felt the most extreme rage filling him. Luol had refused to move her, stating that her condition was so fragile that he wouldn't risk not being able to immediately close the unit, if needed.

Her injuries had been healed, as that was what the unit did, but still she refused to wake. Luol had also told him that the worst of her injuries, the broken bones that had healed in the mine, were irreparable, that they would still cause her pain.

That was unacceptable to him. No female should ever have to suffer. Especially not this tiny, fragile-looking creature that he couldn't seem to pull himself away from. She was too vulnerable, too beautiful. He'd never seen a female that rivaled her beauty and knew that what ever it took to keep her safe he would do it... or die trying.

∞ ∞ ∞ ∞ ∞

Michelle has always loved to read and writing is just a natural extension of this for her. Growing up, she always loved to extend the stories of books she'd read just to see where the characters went. Happily married for over twenty five years she is the proud mother of two grown children and with the house empty has found time to write again. You can reach her at m.k.eidem@live.com   or   her   website   at http://www.mkeidem.com she'd love to hear your comments.

∞ ∞ ∞ ∞ ∞

Made in the USA
Middletown, DE
10 August 2018

Lifting the Veil over Eurocentrism

Dr. M. Reese

Lift the Veil

all the best,

Exodus
6:8-9

Joseph Evans

Lifting the Veil over Eurocentrism:
The Du Boisian Hermeneutic of Double
Consciousness

Joseph Evans

AFRICA WORLD PRESS
TRENTON | LONDON | CAPE TOWN | NAIROBI | ADDIS ABABA | ASMARA | IBADAN

AFRICA WORLD PRESS
541 West Ingham Avenue | Suite B
Trenton, New Jersey 08638

Book design: WibTaye Publishers
Cover design: Saverance Publishing Services

Library of Congress Cataloging-in-Publication Data

Evans, Joseph (Joseph Norman)
  Lifting the veil over eurocentrism : the Du Boisian
hermeneutic of double consciousness / Joseph Evans.
    pages cm
  Includes bibliographical references and index.
  ISBN 978-1-59221-956-8 (hard cover) -- ISBN 978-1-59221-
957-5 (pbk.) 1. Eurocentrism. 2. Civilization, Modern--
European influences. 3. Du Bois, W. E. B. (William
Edward Burghardt), 1868-1963--Criticism and
interpretation. 4. Du Bois, W. E. B. (William Edward
Burghardt), 1868-1963--Political and social views.
5. Racism. I. Title.
  CB430.E93 2013
  320.56'9--dc23
                              2013046154

Table of Contents

࿇

Forethought

❧

I trust the Spirit, and by the Spirit I trust what I hear and see, and what I think, touch and feel. I am a follower of Jesus of Nazareth and, among others; I am an admirer of Du Bois, Fanon, Nkrumah, Thurman and Baldwin. By the Spirit, and for different purposes, their words breathe the breath of liberation. Of Baldwin, I understand that "I know, that in any case, that the most crucial time in my own development came when I was forced to recognize that I was a kind of bastard of the West; when I followed the line of my past I did not find myself in Europe but in Africa. And this meant that in some subtle way, in a really profound way, what I brought to Shakespeare, Bach, Rembrandt, to the stones of Paris, the cathedral at Chartres and to the Empire State."[1]

Indeed Baldwin's words are saturated in Du Boisian thought that explains, if not embraces, double consciousness; and Baldwin's words express an other-wise worldview; a worldview that is African and African American; a worldview that belongs to people of color; a worldview that shapes our collective double consciousness. Double consciousness forms our worldview, how we hear, see, think, touch and feel and how we share a collective consciousness and interpretation. Thus a collective consciousness and interpretation are the seedbeds for my Du Boisian hermeneutic of double consciousness.

Like so many others who have traveled this way, and as you read this book, like so many others who have traveled this way, you will discover this species of hermeneutic grows from a collective struggle to lift the veil over Eurocentrism. Nkrumah said of the Eurocentric veil: "For centuries, Europeans dominated the African continent. The white man arrogated to himself the right to rule and to be obeyed by the non-white; his mission, he claimed, was to

---

1.   James Baldwin, *Notes of a Native Son* (Boston, Massachusetts: Beacon, 1955), 6-7.

'civilize' Africa. Under this cloak, the Europeans robbed the continent of vast riches and inflicted unimaginable suffering on the African people."[2] Nkrumah's courage, then, is an informant, and his courage will remain in memoriam.

As with Nkrumah, the Du Boisian, I trust the courage of the Spirit and therefore I have written what has taken me a lifetime to declare. Therefore, I declare my spiritual, psychological, intellectual and cultural independence from the veil over Eurocentrism. To lift the veil over Eurocentrism, I declare a deep commitment to define myself; and therefore, I no longer permit Eurocentrism to do so. Independent of the insular Eurocentric veil, and by the Spirit, I declare that it is necessary that I break away from Eurocentrism and that I freely and responsibly interpret my world, its texts and principally the Scriptures. For Jesus of Nazareth's sake, I declare that this is a necessary democratic act.

Now it was about the sixth hour, and there was darkness over all the earth until the ninth hour. Then the sun was darkened, and the veil of the temple was torn in two.
Luke 23: 45

---

2. Kwame Nkrumah, Milestone Documents. "Kwame Nkrumah: I Speak of Freedom." Accessed June 11, 2013. http://www.milestone-documents.com/documents/view/kwame-nkrumah.

Preface

❧

Lifting the Veil over Eurocentrism: The Du Boisian Hermeneutic of Double Consciousness has four chapters, and an afterword. Chapter 1 is entitled "Double Consciousness: The Du Boisian Hermeneutic." In this chapter, I present my thesis argument, which is that Eurocentrism has hegemony over interpretation and, as a result, this hegemony has forced black folks to live within the veil of Eurocentrism. In so many words, black folks have been subject to interpretation that posits that black folks are inferior to whites in every way. Thus, I have grounded my argument in W.E. B. Du Bois's lifetime engagement in the battle over interpretation.

Du Bois enters the battle in the last decade of the nineteenth century and continues through every stage of the twentieth century until his death in 1963 (and the battle continues into the second decade of the twenty-first century). It is within this sociopolitical, socioeconomic and intellectual context that Du Bois published *The Souls of Black Folk*. As much as anything else, *Souls* is a book about refuting hegemony over interpretation in order to create rhetorical and narrative space for blacks to become the subjects, heroines and heroes of their own stories. Du Bois understood that this would lead to black liberation and equality but this liberation struggle continues.

Du Bois's major premise that he presented in *Souls* is: the twentieth century's largest problem is located in the color line, "the relation of the darker to the lighter races of men" and this "problem" is a psychological and spiritual one. Interpretation, then, is psychological and spiritual. Interpretation is at the heart of the psychological and spiritual awareness of Africans, African Americans, and people of color. Pyschospiritual awareness is black folks' universal response to Eurocentrism. This is the context that shapes double consciousness. In Chapter 2, "From Behind the Sorrow Songs: Du Boisian Double Consciousness," I begin with Du Bois's interpretation of African American sorrow songs. For

Du Bois, these sorrow songs or spirituals help reveal that African Americans have created their own narrative and interpretation which is not Eurocentric in form. Instead, I assert that African American narrative and interpretation is informed by double consciousness; which makes these, other-wise forms and species, separate from Eurocentric narratives and interpretations. Instead African American narratives and interpretation greatly unveil double consciousness as a key to understanding what life for the socio-marginalized is like within the veil.

Chapter 3 is entitled "The Du Boisian Hermeneutic of Double Consciousness and Frantz Fanon." In this chapter I contend that wherever Eurocentrism is located double consciousness emerges among people of color. Also I attempt to persuade readers that the Du Boisian hermeneutic of double consciousness is a pan-African invention. In order to do so, I present Frantz Fanon's literary work to further explain the dynamics of double consciousness. Fanon was African born and therefore he adds invaluable insights into the psychological effects of double consciousness and how it functions in different social and geographical locations. What is more, Fanon employs a psychological lens to ground double consciousness in the psyche of people of color who were and are relegated in the Algerian socio-margins.

In Chapter 4, "A Different Way to Tell the Story: The Du Boisian Rhetorical Strategy," I contend that the Du Boisian hermeneutic of double consciousness is the informant of rhetoric and narrative (and every other discipline) for Africans, African Americans, and people of color and that double consciousness shapes an Afrocentric or pan-African narrative. In the Afterword, I offer final reflections about Du Boisian thought, its historical development and its intellectual influences upon African American, African and people of color's shared narrative, rhetoric and interpretation. I contend too that Du Boisian thought grows out of a nearly universal invisibility for people of African descent which I believe has created a kind of forced intimacy and a global parochialism. It is these conditions that created the necessity of double consciousness.

I could not have written this book without several people providing constructive criticism, support, and prayers. Robert Reid is the chair of the Department of Communications at the

University of Dubuque. He was the first to read Chapter 1, and his insights gave me a good path forward. Robert is a friend who affirmed this project from the start and said that my thesis was unique and forward thinking. Lucy Hogan, the Hugh Latimer Elderdice Professor of Preaching at Wesley Theological Seminary, read some of the chapters and offered sage advice that made me aware that double consciousness could be located in women of European descent as well as women of color. Her careful tutelage led to the inclusion and treatment of womanists' and feminists' claims. Ronald Allen is the Nettie Sweeny and Hugh Th. Miller Professor of Preaching and New Testament at the Christian Theological Seminary. Ron shared his deep "Coltrane"-like commitment and his understanding and appreciation for the African American prophetic tradition and culture. Ron fully grasped the connection between biblical and cultural hermeneutics with jazz and blues interpretations. Ron boldly told me that he knew of no one who had written about the hermeneutics of double consciousness.

Dale P. Andrews is the Distinguished Professor of Homiletics, Social Justice and Practical Theology and John McClure is the Charles G. Finney Professor of Preaching and Worship at Vanderbilt Divinity School. Dale and John added so much to refining my research and writing. Dale's understanding of the black church is unquestionable, and John's insight into the psychological nature of double consciousness, which he acknowledges, parallels his other-wise hermeneutic. Dale and John have made this book stronger.

T. Vaughn Walker, WMU Professor of Christian Ministries and Professor of Black Church Studies at Southern Seminary, is the single most important of the many professors who shaped my vocational formation. He remains a mentor and friend. He too has read several parts of the manuscript. His largest contribution, however, is his gentle reminder that I must stay true to my heritage and commitment to the nature of Scripture throughout this book project and certainly my ministry. Robert Ellison is a Visiting Professor of Rhetoric and Composition at Marshall University. Robert has made several key editorial changes that make the manuscript read with precision, propriety, and with a purity of words.

I offer special acknowledgments to Kassahun Checole, publisher of Africa World Press and Red Sea Press. Dr. Checole immediately recognized the value of the manuscript and understood that this book makes a contribution to the ongoing conversation and, yes, debate that surrounds the inclusion of people of color in the paradigm shift in hermeneutics.

I must thank Patricia, my wife, for her constructive criticism, support and continuous prayers. From the beginning she has never wavered. In fact, she has read and listened to every word of every chapter and offered several editorial suggestions. She has done this for more than five years--the length of time that it took to research, write and complete this project. Her contribution is above and beyond the call of duty.

I did not know at the beginning of this project that I would become a Du Boisian thinker, which has made me intellectually and socially aware of his impact on the pan-African worldview. Du Bois's hermeneutic of double consciousness is the point of departure that informs every aspect of the prophetic black life. I unapologetically associate myself with the Du Boisian prophetic tradition as a committed Christian thinker.

Chapter One: Double Consciousness: The Du Boisian Hermeneutic

I walk through the churchyard
To lay this body down;
I know moon-rise, I know star-rise;
I walk in the moonlight, I walk in the starlight;
I'll lie in the grave and stretch out my arms,
I'll go to judgment in the evening of the day,
And my soul and thy soul shall meet that day,
When I lay this body down.
Negro Song, "Wrestling Jacob"

They that walked in darkness sang songs in the olden days—Sorrow Songs—for they were weary at heart. And so before each thought that I have written in this book I have set a phrase, a haunting echo of these weird old songs in which the soul of the black slave spoke to men. Ever since I was a child these songs have stirred me strangely. They came out of the South unknown to me, one by one, and yet at once I knew them as of me and of mine. Then in after years when I came to Nashville I saw the great temple builded of these songs towering over the pale city. To me Jubilee Hall seemed ever made of the songs themselves, and its bricks were red with the blood and dust of toil. Out of them rose for me morning, noon, and night, bursts of wonderful melody, full of the voices of my brothers and sisters, full of the voices of the past.

W. E. B. Du Bois[1]

---

1. W. E. B. DuBois, "Of the Sorrow of Songs," *The Souls of Black Folk: Essays and Sketches* (Chicago: McClurg, 1903) 250-51.

The twentieth century begins with the seminal publication of *The Souls of Black Folk* written by a then unnoticed intellectual, W. E. B. Du Bois. For more than a century, this book has shaped public racial debate in social, political and religious spheres. Du Bois declared that "The problem of twentieth century is the problem of the color-line, the relation of the darker to the lighter races of men."[2] This excerpt indicates that Du Bois is informed by a pan-Africanist's worldview and that he understands the role that racial classifications play in Western racial, economic and political constructs.

These cultural constructs are embedded in, reinforced by, and influenced by Eurocentric aesthetic interpretations and claims of *de facto* superiority over all other cultural norms. For most American whites, these constructs are nearly invisible and unnoticed. For many of them, it always has been this way, and therefore; they are not aware of how this unholy trinity gives them social advantages that citizens otherwise do not enjoy or socially qualify to receive. These advantages are passed on to other generations, thus causing undue and inappropriate psychological effects on both whites and blacks. What remains astonishing is that this kind of cultural bias continues to fester and ensue whereby resentment and guilt continue.

These psychological effects have not only bruised blacks in America but also people of color wherever Eurocentrism is established. Eurocentrism is cultural hegemony with global tentacles. In this context, Du Bois crafted *Souls* as a thoughtful response to these and other social arrangements. Du Bois knew this and used *Souls* to challenge people of the dominate classes and establishment to listen against their hearing. For Du Bois, this was perhaps the only way for people conditioned by Eurocentric claims to understand the pain and suffering that is associated with Eurocentric or Western thought that excludes people of color globally.

In this way, I have identified Du Bois as a seer. I do so because Du Bois was among the first to articulate that an inappropriate relationship among race, economics, and politics (this trinity may be expanded today to include class) emerged in Western thought

---

2.   Ibid., "Of the Dawn of Freedom," 10.

that afforded unfair advantages for a disproportionate number of citizens, namely people of European descent. As a nonecclesial prophet, Du Bois believed socioeconomic and sociopolitical advantages were unchristian and unethical when contrasted with the American ideal that informs democracy.

As a response, Du Bois sought ways to dismantle this irreligious and unethical construct. And he found ways to give socially marginalized citizens a voice by lifting the veil that cloaked these kinds of advantages. Others, who also perceived this relationship as unethical, chose to communicate in similar ways. For these reasons and others that will be discussed in this chapter, I define these men and women as a part of the Du Boisian prophetic tradition, and I call them Du Boisian rhetor-preachers: those who employ rhetoric attached to the biblical tradition to persuade and inform their audiences through morally ethical suasion.

The Battle over Biblical Interpretation

Du Bois modeled the Du Boisian prophetic tradition for rhetor-preachers when he framed the twentieth century's problem as the color line, and I believe that the color line is still the problem facing people of the twenty-first century. The color line's stubbornness spills into our battle over biblical interpretation. On one hand, the white pole is informed by Eurocentric aesthetics, interpretations, and assumptions. On the other hand, the second pole of color is informed primarily by traditions and beliefs from African soils that are still very much alive and adapted into African American communities and other peoples of color.

By interpretation divided at the color line, I mean that biblical interpretation is embroiled in cultural politics that too often reflect hegemonies, worldviews, conventions, and biases that are culturally limited and serve to reinforce the social power of the majority culture, but offers no universal vision. For Du Boisian preachers and scholars, then, to preach and teach a Theo-ethic-centric Bible, they must forge ahead and bridge the interpretation divide. To do so, they must appropriate a hermeneutic that I call the Du Boisian hermeneutic of double consciousness. This is an interpretation of biblical texts through the lens of those who are marginalized by the dominating classes' aesthetics, interpretations, and assumptions.

The interpreter informed by double consciousness understands how the text looks through the eyes of both the Eurocentric majority interpreter and of the community that has been marginalized and dominated by the majority group. Double consciousness empowers the Du Boisian interpreter to read a text in such a way as to make it an instrument of liberation and no longer a rationale for oppression.

Like the dominating cultures of the nineteenth and twentieth century, twenty-first-century worldviews continue to force marginalized people of color into an invisible status, which further continues to minimize their culture and aesthetic. In this century, however, it is people of color's cultural aesthetics, interpretations, and assumptions that provide unique, fresh and different insights into biblical interpretation. By reconsidering the public career of W. E. B. Du Bois and how he interpreted his poles in one world, as well as contrasting his poles with the biblical traditions, we find a credible point of departure for the Du Boisian hermeneutics of double consciousness.

Reconsidering W.E. B. Du Bois and Hermeneutics

Here at the outset, I concede that not all preachers, whether black or white, will appreciate the Du Boisian hermeneutic. It is not for those who do not discern their call from God to be within the prophetic tradition. However, I do contend that a Du Boisian worldview is important to a species of twenty-first-century preachers and scholars' hermeneutics when they see themselves in the prophetic tradition. I believe that these preachers will benefit by reconsidering what Du Bois intended for his audience when he published *Souls*.

In *Souls*, Du Bois begins each of his essays with well-known and well-worn Western, Eurocentric, canonical epithets. Just beneath those familiar epithets are obscure musical bar graphs without lyrics. The inclusion of the bar graphs adds mystery to Du Bois's writings. He engages in deliberate manipulation of his readers' curiosity. For many of his readers, Du Bois knows that the musical bar graphs are beyond Eurocentric cultural aesthetics, interpretations, and assumptions; thus, the mysterious meaning of the bar graphs remains beyond many readers' experiences.

It was not until *Souls'* last essay that Du Bois solved the riddle of the musical bar graphs. Du Bois discloses to his readers that African American aesthetics, interpretations, and assumptions had begun to emerge to form a rhetorical tradition that later is located in a similarly informed literary tradition. For example, he knows Negro Spirituals, which he calls Sorrow Songs; these songs or Spirituals are what the musical bar graphs mysteriously represented. Du Bois introduces his audiences to the Sorrow Songs as a part of the emerging African American cultural canon.

These *Songs* are not just songs; indeed, they are historical and social interpretations that chronicle the African American journey and our search for justice and harmony among all people. The *Songs* are equal in heritage to the Eurocentric cultural aesthetics, interpretations and assumptions. What Du Bois expresses remains important today. Few scholars from the majority culture will acknowledge the contributions that scholars and preachers of color have made to the academy, church, and world. Clearly, Du Bois understood Eurocentrism and its refusal to acknowledge African and African American scholarship. For these and other reasons, in adroit fashion, Du Bois reveals to his audience that he is literate in Eurocentric and African American aesthetics and canons. This indicates that Du Bois considers himself as culturally biformational. That is, Du Bois can interpret language, texts, and people in multiples. This provides for us a glimpse at the formation of Du Boisian double consciousness and how it evolves into a hermeneutic system.

Du Bois strategically places Eurocentric epithets alongside Africentric ones, which demonstrates that he has appreciation for Eurocentric cultural aesthetics, interpretations, and assumptions. He also wants to expose his audiences to the emerging people of color's cultural aesthetics, interpretations, and assumptions that draw different conclusions about various subjects and the nature of people. What is of import, however, is that Du Bois possesses a bifocal cultural lens, which I identify with human genius that originates from the social margins—the cultural seedbed for double consciousness. Du Bois's bifocal lens features prominently in *Souls*, especially when we notice that he has given the world a book of parabolic essays.

Du Bois and the Nature and Purpose for Biblical Religion

I concede that it is unusual to identify Du Boisian scholarship as religious in nature. I also concede that it is unconventional to claim that Du Bois's public career parallels the Hebrew prophetic tradition. However, recent scholarship has reconsidered Du Bois's religious nature. Jonathon S. Kahn notices that Du Bois often "constructively relies on religious images and notions as levers for fashioning political sensibilities, deploying 'divinity'—religious language, ideas, and form—to give expression to his discontent." [3] Kahn argues that Du Bois does this in part because he knows that rhetorically, religious language is mysterious and aesthetic. It is a categorical language that defines and accepts otherwise unclear perceptions of reality.

For Du Bois, then, "Religion serves as an agitating agent; it enables him to imagine ideals but only by evincing and articulating the imperfect more clearly. Ideals for Du Bois are dialectically grounded in unflinching acknowledgement of limitations and infirmities."[4] Kahn's thesis can be summarized in the following way:

> My suggestion is that Du Bois's religious spirit is rooted in its peripatetic instability. Du Bois's idiosyncratic use of religious vocabulary produces a reverent form of discontent that comes from critical questioning, from challenging dogma, and from attempting to tie the tradition to future demands. This is the promise of divine discontent.[5]

Perhaps unintended, Kahn by implication has associated Du Bois with the Hebrew prophetic tradition: The Hebrew prophets spoke against imperial powers such as Assyria, Babylon, and Persia (Daniel 10). Like the Hebrew prophets, Du Bois longed for holistic redemption and justice. Evidence points us toward his professional

---

3.   Jonathon S. Kahn, "Divine Discontent as Religious Faith" in *Divine Discontent: The Religious Imagination of W. E. B. Du Bois* (Oxford: Oxford University Press, 2009), 8.
4.   Ibid., 9.
5.   Ibid.

and literary careers whereby he spoke against Eurocentric and American sociopolitical and socioeconomic powers, because he sees that they were not inclusive of all people irrespective of racial heritage. This is in direct contradiction to American democratic values. For Du Bois, the function of the prophetic tradition is its concern with contemporary social systems; those who employ the prophetic tradition become advocates on behalf of people who are enduring particular injustices within those social systems.

Edward J. Blum, another recent Du Boisian scholar argues that Du Bois did not attempt to hide his religious nature. In fact, "Anyone who looks for religion in Du Bois's canon will find it in abundance and will discover a deeply spiritual Du Bois." Blum continues:

> Du Bois penned in an unpublished personal reflection. This "religiousness" had few social or personal outcomes; it failed to improve life for African Americans, and hence was fundamentally irreligious to Du Bois. True faith, Du Bois declared, would show the "eternal connection of Christianity and Latin, of godliness and mathematics, of morality and geography." Du Bois did not want religion to be absent from scholarly life or social life. He wanted faith to have a direct and positive impact on what individuals learned and how they lived.[6]

Kahn and Blum have characterized Du Bois as a nonecclesial prophet. Redemption and justice for Du Bois are holistic. To live a religious life, then, is to become attractive, that is, educated, informed, and actively participating in their pole (informed perspectives) in the one world where individuals find themselves.

In Du Bois's formative years, it is highly unlikely that he was not exposed to Lewis Tappan or Charles Finney's evangelical, abolitionist Christianity or the fire and brimstone revivals with Pentecostal fervor that he would experience during his Fisk years,

---

6. Edward Blum, "Rethinking Du Bois: Rethinking Race and Religion" in *W. E. B. Du Bois: American Prophet* (Philadelphia: University of Pennsylvania Press, 2007), 11.

as a student and later as a supportive critic.[7] On the other hand, and early on, Du Bois was exposed to orthodox New England mainline Christianity. This background enabled him to understand Eurocentric religion from the inside. For Du Bois, religion and education were inseparable. This cultural perspective perhaps may be shared commonly among Episcopalian and Congregationalists congregations. For Du Bois, this seems to be true. Once Du Bois stated that "My grandmother was Episcopalian and my mother Congregational. I grew up in the Congregational Sunday School."[8]

The first two chapters of *Dusk of Dawn* provide readers with a sense of Du Bois's personal piety and cultural understanding of Christian faith. With an air of a New England Victorianism, Du Bois associates himself with this kind of understanding of faith, something that is a deeply personal matter; something that is not worn outwardly on someone's sleeve. The evidence of conversion for a Du Boisian Christian is that one believes that she or he is called to a particular assignment not only in words, but also in deeds. In this way, a person is believed to have been possessed by Christian faith and is a follower of Jesus.

Du Bois was able to further ground his religious experience when he began to understand Christianity through Alexander Crummell, a nineteenth century Episcopal minister and intellectual who is considered the father of pan-Africanism. In the following excerpt from "Of Alexander Crummell" included in *Souls*, we get a sense of how Du Bois perceives Crummell:

> I saw Alexander Crummell first at a Wilberforce commencement season, amid its bustle and crush. Tall, frail, and black he stood, with simple dignity and

---

7. See "Revolution" in *Dusk of Dawn*, 282. What is important, Du Bois advocated for an African American president of Fisk University (1924). At the same time, Du Bois was fully immersed in the Pan African movement. This may be the single informant for his outrage over Fisk's president remaining a person of Eurocentric origin and cultural orientation. Du Bois writes, "How far can a Negro college, dominated by white trustees and a white president and supported by white wealth, carry on in defiance the wishes an best interests of its colored constituency?"

8. Ibid., 10.

8

unmistakable air of good breeding. I talked with him apart, where the storming of the lusty young orators could not harm us. I spoke to him politely, then curiously, then eagerly, as I began to feel the fineness of his character, his calm courtesy, the sweetness of his strength, and his fair blending of the hope and truth of life. Instinctively I bowed before this man, as one bows before the prophets of the world. Some seer he seemed, that came not from the crimson Past or the gray To-come, but from the pulsing Now, - that mocking world which seemed to me at once so light and dark, so splendid and sordid. Fourscore years had he wandered in this same world of mine, within the Veil.[9]

---

9. Du Bois, "Of Alexander Crummell" in *The Souls of Black Folk*, 159-160. Also see *W. E. B. Du Bois: American Prophet*, 131-32. Though I have included a lengthy excerpt, I suggest that it further demonstrates that Du Bois was a professing Christian and an Episcopalian. Like Du Bois, Alexander Crummell was an Episcopalian:

In the early 1970s a young sociologist set out to learn more about the legendary Du Bois. Dorothy Yancey, a professor at Georgia Institute of Technology in Atlanta and later president of Johnson C. Smith in Charlotte, North Carolina, wanted to know what Du Bois' students and colleagues thought of him. On locating ten of his former Atlanta University students and colleagues, she found a number of surprising facts. Du Bois would bring coffee and cookies to his graduate seminars; he was never without his cane; he rarely remembered a student's name, even well into the semester. When interviewing Samuel Usher, Yancey received perhaps her most shocking reflection. Usher reminisced that as a college student, he was convinced that his history and sociology professor was an Episcopalian. And, if this faith was good enough for Professor Du Bois, it was good enough for young man Usher. He spent his entire career in the church in part because of Du Bois.... What moved Samuel Usher to become a minster? Perhaps it was the prayers that Du Bois shared with his classes, prayers that invoked a social gospel and called for an alliance of all oppressed peoples.

Although Du Bois depicts Crummell as a cosmic hero, what is important to my thesis is that readers notice that Du Bois is attracted to Crummell's intellectual prowess and that he appreciates Crummell's pragmatic understanding of sociopolitical and socioeconomic limitations imposed upon him by social establishments and systems. For Du Bois, the only story that provides historical precedence for such conditions and a language is one that universally expresses these conditions is Holy Scripture. Second, due in part to his admiration for and identification with Crummell's worldview and prophetic vision, Du Bois evidently perceived that his capacities where similar to Crummell's. A persuaded Du Bois began to discern his call to a particular assignment. His prophetic call and assignment was specifically to work toward the eradication of racism.

Moreover, Crummell serves for Du Bois as an example of how genius grows noticeably from the social margin. Du Bois was a victim of racial discrimination, as was Crummell. Yet, Du Bois saw in Crummell a person who was called to serve marginalized people, groups, and classes as their advocate. A second point of import, Du Bois identified himself with Crummell's worldview and found that it provided a basis for self-affirmation. Like Crummell, Du Bois became a public intellectual religionist. He was called to be a prophetic seer.

Du Boisian Rhetor-Preachers as Prophetic Seers

In this way, I am able to reconsider Du Bois as a rhetor-preacher, someone who employs religious language to express the presence of transcendence. Du Boisian rhetor-preachers are called to use prophetic religious language, namely that of the Bible. These preachers believe that biblical language transcends the here and now. Their use of biblical language is because of their belief that this sacred language is the Word incarnate and that it offers glimpses of an alternative reality, which is often counterintuitive to what is considered the norm. It is a prophetic invention that grounds eschatological hope; it is an ethical claim of what "ought to be" or "what should be" instead of what is. By taking their lead from Du Bois, the Du Boisian rhetor-preachers engage in the eschatological Hebrew prophetic tradition and, like Du Bois, the Du Boisian rhetor-preachers are seers.

As seers, Du Boisian rhetor-preachers reconsider Du Bois's *Souls* as parabolic sermons used for public and civic discourse. These "sermons" are effective on public platforms and in sacred pulpits. With his first sermon in *Souls* (the first essay), Du Bois subtly introduces his understanding of double consciousness. He defines it in this way, "One ever feels his twoness, an American, a Negro; two souls, two thoughts, two unreconciled strivings; two warring ideals in one dark body, whose dogged strength alone keeps it from being torn asunder."[10] For this to emerge, Eurocentric culture must join others in redefining a world where a new form of community can exist.

In these few words, Du Bois explains double consciousness and points toward the existential worldview of African Americans and people of color across political, social and religious boundaries. More so, these observations are reinterpreted to express the inner strivings and the pyschospiritual heart and soul of people of the African Diaspora. In this context, I have located a shared worldview among peoples in our one world who are separated by cultural aesthetics, interpretations, and assumptions.

I have stated that two poles exist in one world. The Eurocentric worldview pole represents the dominating culture's beliefs that their contributions to the world at large are superior to all others. They assume that they alone have invented Western culture, which implies that other cultural contributions are insignificant and metaphorically absent and invisible. On the other hand, the worldview of persons of color represents their beliefs that their cultural contributions to the world at large are assumed to be equal to all others. They have not assumed to have invented Western culture alone, and they refuse to accept that their contributions are insignificant and absent and invisible.

The Du Boisian Hermeneutic and Its Parallels with Postmodern Hermeneutics

The Du Boisian hermeneutic provides people of color a way to resist hegemonies and invisibility in the world and in its texts. In so many words, this hermeneutic boldly states that there is another

---

10. W. E. B. Du Bois, "Of Our Spiritual Strivings" in *The Souls of Black Folk*, 3.

way to interpret, and therefore it provides for interpreters another point of departure to make different assumptions that include people of color in the world around them. I primarily focus on African American culture and worldview, and its distinction as representative of people's "other-wise" interpretation. By other-wise, I mean those who employ "other-directed textual analysis that could be used in support of an ethical perspective on homiletical theory." [11]

African American people or "other-wise people" comprise a well-chronicled example of how a different textual interpretation can become a model for forming a different hermeneutic that will influence pulpit speech for decades to come. People of color have learned to interpret what non-people of color think of them and alongside what people of color think of themselves. This, in brief, is Du Boisian double consciousness, the hermeneutic system of other-wise people.

Postmodern hermeneutics is the other-wise hermeneutic. It is the description of the hermeneutics of double consciousness, or what I have called the Du Boisian hermeneutic. I should note that it already functions in multiple voices, multiple faces, and multiple places. I am, however, connecting the dots that already exist between Du Bois's double consciousness and the social sciences (history, sociology, psychology, literature, politics, economics, etc.) with contributions that the Du Boisian double consciousness makes to a particular biblical hermeneutics. I appropriate Du Boisian double consciousness to explain how people of color pervasively interpret the world, its texts (and our own texts), and how we incorporate our personal experiences to understand. Because of our globally shared double consciousness, people of color are uniquely the quintessential other-wise people who provide relevant ways to interpret biblical texts.

---

11. John McClure, *Other-wise Preaching: A Postmodern Ethic for Preaching* (Saint Louis: Chalice Press, 2001), ix. Also see Jacque Derrida, *Of Grammatology* (Baltimore and London: Johns Hopkins University, 1976); idem, *Speech and Phenomena, and Other Essays on Husserl's Theory and Signs* (Evanston, IL: Northwestern University, 1973); idem, *Writing and Difference*, trans. Alan Bass (Chicago: University of Chicago, 1978).

Hermeneutic interpretation takes place in a sociohistorical context and, more narrowly, a communal context.[12] For effective preaching, then, it is necessary to underscore that an organic relationship exists among hermeneutics, rhetoric, and homiletics. First, I begin with hermeneutics, the science and art form of interpretation that begins with a worldview. Second, hermeneutics is an informant for rhetoric. Supported by their hermeneutic, people of color develop a rhetoric that expresses their understanding of nature that aids them in refuting unfair human structures of power. Third, because hermeneutics is the point of departure for developing rhetoric; it is the informing overlay and point of departure for developing a homiletic theory.

In other words, rhetoric informs methodologies, and I contend that rhetoric also strengthens homiletic theories. As Henry Mitchell writes, "Preaching is carried out in the idiom, imagery, style, and worldview of a particular people."[13] By homiletics, I mean an artful study of preaching that closes communication gaps between preachers', listeners', and readers' communal poles within our one world and biblical texts.[14] By communal poles, I mean that which shapes particular pyschospiritual, sociopolitical, and socioeconomic systems. By and large, communal poles of the world create a particular way that a group may understand itself.

---

12. Henry H. Mitchell, *Black Preaching: The Recovery of a Powerful Art* (Nashville: Abingdon Press, 1990), 15. See *Habermas and the Public Sphere*, Craig Calhoun (Cambridge: MIT Press, 1999), 473-474. Jurgen Habermas believes that hermeneutics is a communal interpretation, "I think there is an everyday-life hermeneutic, an ethical reasoning of ourselves as those who are embedded in a particular life history, in particular historical conditions."
13. Mitchell, *Black Preaching*, 11.
14. "Homiletics Coming of Age," *in Concise Encyclopedia of Preaching*, ed. William H. Willimon and Richard Lischer. (Louisville: Westminster John Knox, 1995), 249. Robert Stephen Reid's definition for homiletics in *The Renewal of Preaching in the Twenty-First Century: The Next Homiletics*, by David J. Randolph with commenting by Robert Stephen Reid (Eugene, OR: Cascades, 2009), 15, parallels my own: "Homiletics is the creative and critical discipline that understands the homily as a type of discourse absolutely sui generis and in which the relationships consistent with the unique character of the homily are identified, developed, and expressed."

13

What I have defined as communal poles of one world parallels that which Paul Ricoeur says: "Hermeneutics then, is simply the theory that regulates the transition from structure of the work to the world of the work. To interpret a work is to display the world to which it refers by virtue of its arrangements, its genre, and its style."[15] According to David J. Randolph, "Traditional hermeneutics is the study of the interpretation of the Bible while in the New Hermeneutic it becomes also the interpreting of life in the light of the Bible."[16]

By Du Boisian hermeneutics of double consciousness, I mean an artful study of how Du Boisian preachers interpret biblical texts through bifocal if not multifocal lenses and poles. These preachers take into account how listeners and readers hear and how they understand biblical texts and how these texts intersect with their communal poles in our one world. For people of color and for people informed by Eurocentric culture who choose to employ this species of hermeneutic, I contend that double consciousness is where the two poles—our world and the biblical world—intersect.[17] I further contend that Du Boisian hermeneutics functions through a communal "preunderstanding" that informs how the rhetor-preacher communicates, how listeners and readers understand, and why biblical texts remain our ancient contemporary.[18]

---

15. Paul Ricoeur, "Metaphor and Reference" in *The Rule of Metaphor: Multi-disciplinary Studies of the Creation of Meaning in Language* (Toronto: University of Toronto, 1975), 220.

16. "Hermeneutics is the interpretation of the Bible. For many years it has dealt with the question what the text meant. A New Hermeneutic has turned attention to what the text means that has far-reaching consequences." (*The Renewal of Preaching*). *Also see The Renewal of Preaching, 1st ed.,* "The contribution of the new hermeneutic to a new homiletic can be far-reaching," 17.

17. "Hermeneutics" in *Concise Encyclopedia of Preaching*, 175-76. See *The Renewal of Preaching in the Twenty-First Century.*

18. Ibid., 31. Also see "Hermenuetics" in *Concise Encyclopedia of Preaching*, "Schleiermacher attempted to communicate the understanding of Scripture, he discovered that his audience already had some understanding of the material. He called that a "preunderstanding" and realized that it had to be taken into account. The interaction

What Randolph describes as "the interpreting of life in the light of the Bible," I describe as Du Boisian hermeneutic cues. These cues are cultural aesthetics that greatly determine how we view race, economics, and politics, which in turn influence religion, law, medicine, art, literature, and other institutional spheres, all of which inform our worldviews. I further suggest that the Du Boisian hermeneutic cues are primarily noticed in the African American aesthetic, namely rhetorical and literary traditions, spirituals, the blues, jazz, and other communal poles that shape worldviews that grow out of cultural marginalization.

These hermeneutic cues further help to shape African American rhetoric. This is foundational to biblical African American homiletic theory.[19] Thus the Du Boisian master lens is a lens of marginalization. Although historically, Eurocentric hermeneutics (of the West) tends to overlook the margins, I suggest that the Du

---

between interpreter and the text is the beginning of a circle that widens to include those to whom the interpretation is addressed," 79.

19. Cleophus J. LaRue, *The Heart of Black Preaching* (Louisville: Westminster John Knox, 2000), 16. LaRue referring to David Kelsey's *The Uses of Scripture in Recent Theology* (Philadelphia: Fortress Press, 1975), writes that "Kelsey makes two very important foundational interpretative claims. First, he argues that every faith community brings its own particular template of master lens to scriptural interpretation. Second, he claims that our decisions about how to construe scripture is not based solely on a close study of biblical texts but on a prior decision in which we imaginatively try to grasp the essence of Christianity." Third, LaRue is correct to say, "While Kelsey did not specifically cite a black theologian or preacher in his work, I argue that blacks also see a pattern in scripture to which they ascribe wholeness, and that pattern—a sovereign God who acts in concrete and practical ways on behalf of the marginalized and powerless—is the primary component that lends itself to distinctiveness in their preaching. This foundational biblical hermeneutic provides us with a means for understanding the sense in which exposition of scripture and the life of situations of blacks come together consistently and creatively in black preaching." What I describe is the "hermeneutic circle." See Gustavo Gutierrez, *A Theology of Liberation: History, Politics, and Salvation*, trans. Sister Caridad Inda and John Eagleson (Maryknoll, NY: Orbis, 1973), 4.

Boisian hermeneutic lens has become the primary lens of the West. As Alvin Padilla writes,

> Indeed the whole world has come to our doorstep. Learning to live well in the diverse culture of North America is no longer an option but a necessity. The U.S. Census estimates that in 2050 the proportion of whites in the population will be only 53%. Our children will live and serve in a society in which their classmates, neighbors and fellow disciples of Christ will be equally divided between whites and people of color. As new people move into our cities and local communities, the communities undoubtedly will change. The changes could be haphazard and filled with misunderstandings, hurt feelings and even violence, or the changes could permit all to reinvent and reinvigorate themselves for the better.[20]

Padilla provides a picture of the two worlds though I prefer two poles in one world and how they will interface with each other. As the West grapples with its new existential realities, people will continue to sense their vulnerabilities because of the failure of Western mythologies to sustain Western hegemonies. The Du Boisian hermeneutic of double consciousness that informs an other-wise rhetoric offers an alternative response and presents what I will later discuss as a different meta-narrative.

It should go without comment that these poles are on a collision course with race, economics, and politics, because the collision is with authentic pan-Africanism. It is important for all preachers to understand what the cultural shifts are revealing about what constitutes a different West. As Padilla has indicated, the two poles are numerically disproportionate. The people of color's pole makes up the majority of the world's populations who are mostly sociomarginalized people. Because of globalization, these shifts will continue to expose the West (North America and Europe) to different kinds of interpretation. Thus, whether all preachers will

---

20. Alvin Padilla, "A New Kind of Theological School: Contextualized Theological Education Models" in *Africanus Journal vol. 2, no. 2, (November 2010), 5-6.*

appreciate or employ this species of hermeneutic, it remains important for all preachers to understand how other-wise people interpret and understand the world.

The Formation, Function, and Definition of the Du Boisian Hermeneutic of Double Consciousness

To develop a Du Boisian hermeneutic first is to understand that it is a hermeneutic of double consciousness and, second, preachers must also understand that the Du Boisian hermeneutic philosophically is a branch of rhetoric, namely dialectic. Aristotle in "The Rhetoric of Aristotle: Book 1" begins with these words: "Rhetoric is the counterpart of Dialectic [that is, the art of public speaking and the art of logical discussion are the co-ordinate, but contrasted, processes]; both have to do with such knowledge, things that do not belong to any one science."[21]

In short, "Dialectic and Rhetoric for all make some attempt to sift or to support theses, and to defend or attack persons."[22] In a real sense, dialectic provides for the Du Boisian rhetor-preachers a tool to refute competing claims about various subjects as Aristotle indicated. Dialectic as refutation is the point of departure for forming African American aesthetics, interpretations, and its assumptions. In addition, dialectic lends itself to refutation for self-defense, which is a vitally significant survival tool for marginalized people. It presents for them a way to demonstrate that they understand the dominant culture's thesis. This is noticed consistently in African American rhetoric, sermons, and literature. You will see this thematic pattern later in David Walker's "Appeal" and Robert Young's *Manifesto*.[23]

---

21. *The Rhetoric of Aristotle* ed. Lane Cooper (Englewood Cliffs, NJ: Prentice Hall, 1932), 1-5.
22. Ibid., 1.
23. David Walker, *To the Coloured Citizens of the World: But in Particular, and Very Expressingly to Those of the United States of America* (New York: Hill and Wang, 1965). Robert Alexander Young's "The Ethiopian Manifesto, Issued Defense of the Blackmans' Rights, in the Scale of Universal Freedom" was published in New York City in February 1929 in *A History of the Negro People in the United States*, Vol. 1 (Secaucus, NJ: Citadel, 1973), 90-93, ed. H. Aptheker.

Walker's and Young's pamphlets serve as examples of how marginalized persons learn to employ the "masters' tool" to create an antithesis dialectic argument. Dialectic is refutation, redress, and argument. It is a language for critical thinkers who think as rhetor-preachers in the Du Boisian prophetic tradition, those who seek to create an alternative perception of reality. In this way, marginalized rhetors create dialectical tension in the dominant culture's thesis; they demonstrate what a Eurocentric thesis merits but strategically proceed to reveal its flaws. Of course, this has social implications, because those who employ this strategy cause public debate to take place in all public and private spheres of influence.

Du Boisian dialectic is a difficult system for Eurocentric interpreters to grasp. Few interpreters in the dominant culture have engaged in critiques of themselves outside of their cultural philosophical box. For example, the American health care debate has political constructs. The public debate has been solely a Eurocentric argument. This is a narrow consideration that is bereft of democratic solutions. In other words, there is no rhetorical space provided for other-wise interpretation. These constructs do not permit ideologues to move past their ideological impasses. I suggest this is an example of what "gridlock" in Washington symbolizes. That is, the dominating culture's worldview has minimal capacity for transcendence or "other-wise" imagination of what could be.[24]

Dialectic points out these ideological impasses and is another feature of the Du Boisian hermeneutic. This serves a pragmatic function that may become a part of the traditional hermeneutics of the Western establishment if preachers and orators who are informed by Eurocentric culture are willing to struggle with adapting and appropriating this hermeneutic. The cultural struggle to adapt the Du Boisian hermeneutic is not exclusive to whites, however; the struggle to adapt this hermeneutic is also for blacks

---

24. The Patient Protection and Affordable Care Act (H.R. 3590) "Obama care" was passed into law by the House on October 8, 2009. The House passed the bill with a vote 219-212. The Senate passed the bill with a 60-39 on October 24, 2009. The bill went to conference and passed on March 21, 2010; President signed the law two days later. See Public Law 111-148 – 111th Congress.

and browns who do not necessarily agree or understand this kind of hermeneutic.

Those of all colors and races who do not consider themselves called to prophetic proclamation may resist or consider this kind of hermeneutic outside of their scope of ministry. This is due, in part, because many seminary-trained minorities (including women), have been trained in Eurocentric theology, interpretation, and homiletic theory. Therefore, for many, the Du Boisian hermeneutic may hinder preachers and ministers who are not prepared to interpret texts by a different criterion of interpretation that addresses a different sociocultural thesis that is outside of their hermeneutic domain.

Nevertheless, at this point, I want to define the Du Boisian hermeneutic of double consciousness as more a system than simply a method. Methods are to be followed, whereas systems are discovered. Systems are organic and already exist, as is the case for the Du Boisian hermeneutic of double consciousness. I identify its characteristics as follows: (1) double voice, (2) pyschospiritual awareness, (3) deferred understanding of meaning, and (4) dialectical tensions. As I previously mentioned, the Du Boisian hermeneutic of double consciousness, whether knowingly or unknowingly, functions in multiple voices, multiple faces, and multiple places, which gives the Du Boisian hermeneutic of double consciousness a pan-African point of departure.

Again, it is my objective to connect the dots between Du Boisian double consciousness' contributions to social sciences with the potential contributions that Du Boisian double consciousness can contribute to biblical interpretation. The following pages are my attempt to present to Du Boisian preachers a point of departure for employing the Du Boisian hermeneutic.

Double Consciousness as Hermeneutic Informant in Luke 15

As an illustration of the double consciousness in action, I employ Du Bois's double consciousness as the hermeneutic informant when preparing a message on the "Parable of the Sheep, Lost Coin, and Son (Luke 15)." In this parable, Luke constructs his narrative by placing his theological claims underneath his telling of his story that involves Jesus, the Pharisees, Scribes, and the marginalized. Luke creates a mood that subtly reveals the Pharisees' and Scribes' disapproval of Jesus, in part because Jesus gave access and attention to those who were socially marginalized (vv. 1-3).

What else can be determined at this point? The Pharisees and Scribes represented the Hebrew establishment, but Jesus aligns with the sociomarginalized. Luke wants his audience to know that Jesus understood how the representatives of the establishment perceived their power, and how the establishment's power socially deprived the poorest citizens. Jesus further wants the sociomarginalized to know that he understands their need for an agent to give them a voice. In order to communicate to the underclasses and underprivileged that he knows what their oppressors think and feel about them, Jesus employs something similar to double consciousness. Thus, Jesus spoke on their behalf—the oppressed, the powerless—relating a parable about justice and redemption.

In short, Jesus explained to the Pharisees and Scribes that they had valued a lost sheep and a lost coin more than addressing human suffering; that is too often members of a privileged social order do, whether knowingly or unknowingly. They place valuing material possessions above appreciating the values and equality of every human life. Luke wants his audience to see what Jesus sees, namely that the Pharisees and Scribes lost sight of the underclasses and underprivileged people of Israel. A Du Boisian hermeneutic helps me to recognize that Jesus admonishes the establishment for valuing things more than people.

When read in this way, the sociomarginalized have been given voice; they have experienced positional justice. By this I mean that many people who live in socially deprived conditions need sociopolitical and economic interventions. In this instance, their human conditions have not changed, but spiritually and emotionally they have experienced justice. They know that they are adjudicated and acquitted. This leads to redemption, which provides a poetic vision of hope. What is more, I am sure that this example of interpretation resonates among people of color, those who are globally sociomarginalized.

Double Consciousness and Double Voice

Sigmund Freud associates double voice with double meaning, or what he defines as a play on words. He actually associates double voice or double meaning with "wit." Freud writes, "If we delve more deeply into the variety of 'manifold application' of the same word, we suddenly notice that we are confronted with forms of 'double meaning' or 'play on words' which have been known for a long time and which are universally acknowledged as belonging to the technique of wit."[25] For Freud, wit belongs to the psychological and social aspects of communication, and wit used in this way helps us to understand how humans encode and decode a message.

What if Luke's Jesus is employing the technique of "wit" in his telling of the "Parable of the Lost Sheep, Coin and Son"? What if, for Luke, Jesus' wit is double voice, which means creating texts that address both the dominating classes and sociomarginalized? What if Luke's Jesus is using the technique of "wit" as a vocabulary of the marginalized to speak both to and against the dominating classes? Double voice usually functions through a deliberate, but nuanced, repeating theme as is the case in Luke 15:7, 10, and 32. Although this is subtle, Luke's Jesus employs double voice techniques when he says, "Just so, I tell you, there will be more joy in heaven over one sinner who repents than over ninety-nine righteous persons who need no repentance" (v. 7), and again, "Just so, I tell you, there is joy before the angels of God over one sinner who repents" (v. 10); and in the passage of the Prodigal Son (v. 32), "It was fitting to celebrate and be glad, for this your brother was dead, and is alive; he was lost, and is found."

By use of the Du Boisian hermeneutic, I am able to locate Luke's Jesus' rhetorical double voice strategy in a repetitive pattern: celebration, joy, and recovery of things of value, namely people; nothing is more valuable than a human body and soul. This is an example of what Henry Louis Gates, Jr., calls "Tropological Revision," a repetition to highlight contrasting difference in a conventional interpretation and the emerging interpretation of an

---

25. Sigmund Freud, "Technique of Wit" in *The Basic Writings of Sigmund Freud*, trans and ed. A. A. Brill (New York: Modern Library, 1995), 617.

other-wise people.[26] The Pharisees and Scribes' interpretation is conventional and traditional, but quite different from the interpretation that the common people heard from Jesus.

The repetitious words are hidden arrangements of organization and meaning that expressed emphatic joy and celebration about redemption, pyschospiritual and sociospiritual justification, and recovery of human bodies. In recognizing nuanced and adroit syntactical strategies, one can understand the powerful existential and reflective role that double consciousness, as double voice, plays in interpretation. By existential role, I mean that double voice helps interpreters sense how marginalized people decode their present conditions. Also, by reflective, I mean that double voice helps interpreters sense how marginalized people decode their present conditions. Also, by reflective, I mean that double voice confronts the dominant classes with critical reflection on language usages and alternatives to traditional interpretations of meaning. Thus, like Du Bois's Gentile readers (In *Souls*, Du Bois employs Freudian wit and calls his readers Gentle Readers), we sense differences between traditional interpretation and that of Jesus then and now.[27]

In the last episode of the parable, where Jesus tells his audience about the Prodigal Son, I am informed by the vernacular of the signifying monkey. Jesus is combative and employs double voice to confront the establishment. He creates telling contrasts, those between the religious, wealthy, and the common Poor's lifestyles. By way of double voice, we are able to see that the establishment

---

26. Henry Louis Gates, Jr., *Signifying Monkey: A Theory of African-American Literary Criticism* (Oxford: Oxford University Press, 1988).
   The black tradition is doubled voice. The trope of the Talking Book, of double voice texts that talk to other texts, is the unifying metaphor within this book. Gates lists four sorts of double voice textual relations: Tropological Revision, The Speakerly Text, Talking Texts, and Rewriting the Speakerly (xxv-xxvi).

27. See W.E. B. Du Bois, "Forethought" in *The Souls of Black Folk* (New York: Bantam 1989), xxxi. I believe Du Bois is signifying by saying "Herein Lie buried many things which if read with patience may show the strange meaning of being black here at the dawning of the Twentieth Century. The meaning is not without interest to you Gentle Reader;" which I believe, Du Bois, here, is employing double voice. In this context, Du Bois could have said, "Gentile Reader."

enjoyed a certain level of social and financial status; they had the means, and they had the power to kill a fatted calf and celebrate new birth or recovery of faith, justice, and social redemption.

In order to contrast and compare, I have employed Freudian wit to understand how the others who were listening to Jesus seemed to feel when he told his parable to them. Jesus knew that his listeners could not financially afford such lavish celebrations. Instead, the common people in the text (and they represent the majority of the world's people today) could only imagine what it meant to have such socioeconomic power and status to do what they willed. As a result, they no doubt understood that Jesus was admonishing the Pharisees and Scribes for not taking the responsibility for seeking the salvation and welfare of estranged and neglected people.

Luke's parable is an example of how double voice functions. In this instance, it points toward dominating classes' indifference toward sociomarginalized people that renders them invisible. This, in part, explains the strange and empty gaze we see often in the faces of throngs of marginalized peoples across America and the world. For the sociomarginalized, then, this experience results in psychospiritual awareness of self-worth.

Double Consciousness and Psychospiritual Awareness

Closely related to double consciousness is psychospiritual awareness, another characteristic of the Du Boisian hermeneutic. Psychological awareness helps us to understand sociomarginalized people's sense of inferiority that is imposed upon them by the dominating classes' cultural "preunderstanding of self" and worldview. To borrow a metaphor from Du Bois, this is an example of life within the veil. In the "Forethought" of *Souls*, Du Bois writes, "I have stepped within the Veil, raising it that you may view faintly its deep recesses, the meaning of its religion, the passion of its human sorrow, and the struggle of its greater souls."[28] What does this mean? Du Bois points us toward impressions of a subculture that exists within the cultural veil and within the cultural West. In other words, socially marginalized cultures function underneath the larger culture and are unnoticed

---

28. DuBois, "Forethought" in *The Souls of Black Folk*, xxxi.

primarily by the cultural main.[29] In addition, people of color learn how to survive in both poles within the one world. This indicates that a part of the biformation of the sociomarginalized subculture has a psychospiritual orientation.

Houston Baker, Jr., in his book *Turning South Again*, has provided an insightful interpretation of Du Bois's use of the metaphoric veil that I am appropriating to describe psychospiritual awareness. Baker's emphasis is on associating the "veil" with performance, parochialism, and the human body:

> The "veil" is Du Bois' metaphor for what might be thought of as the "edge" of the performative frame, the dissonant rim where safe, colored parochialism is temptingly and provisionally refigured as anguished mulatto cosmopolitan. The "veil" hands in the performative moment like a scrim between dark, pastoral, problematic folk intimacy with black consciousness, and free-floating anxieties of the public mulatto modernism that subjects one to the "white gaze." The "veil" is the counterpart, in cognition or mental life, to the lynched "member" of the somatic or bodily screen. The veil hangs as maddeningly and terrifyingly as the lynched body, between the white world and public emergence of a modern *blackness*.[30]

The veil for Baker functions as a place of forced intimacy among the sociomarginalized that is informed by anxieties about public life and the constant mental fear of public embarrassment. This, he believes, is the emergence of modern blackness or African American psychospiritual formation. Another way of rephrasing

---

29. See DuBois, "The Colored World Within" in *Dusk of Dawn*
30. Houston A. Baker, Jr., *Turning South Again: Re-Thinking Modernism / Re-Reading Booker T.* (Durham, NC: Duke University, 2001) 53. Baker writes "The psychological dynamics, anxieties, phobias, and panic of publicly performing such scientific magic of social change can only be understood in the context—the frame—of the mind of the virulently white supremacist South," 57.

this is Du Bois's metaphoric language: hate, doubt and despair.[31] This is an expression of self-loathing that often harasses people of color. I am certain this kind of analysis can be made about the people of modern-day Palestine, Afghanistan, Yemen, Algeria, and, yes, Egypt, Syria, Libya, Turkey, and Tunisia, to name contemporary examples.

Another way of understanding double consciousness as it relates to the Du Boisian hermeneutic, and similar to Henry Gates's assumptions, is cultural politics—namely, social constructs of difference. By this I mean that Du Bois understood culture as a local invention (within the veil); therefore, culture is always political. As Charles Lemert explains, "When cultures come into contact with each other on the borders and battle lines of social differences, they always rub each other the wrong way."[32] Thus, double consciousness is also a function of social constructs—the very nature and purpose of politics.

The interweaving of psychological and social dimensions of double consciousness is a principle part of the Du Boisian hermeneutic. It is validated by what Evans Crawford has called a biformation process. An excerpt from his book *The Hum: Call and Response in African American Preaching* provides a thorough definition of the process:

> The biformative process and its consequent creative marginality would have been an inevitable part of Howard Thurman's spiritual development as a black man in America. That is why I prefer to call the process of preparation for preaching that I observed in Thurman and that I am exploring in this book "spiritual biformation." That term keeps before us the particular legacy of being black in America and its impact upon the homiletical musicality of African American preaching traditions.[33]

---

31. See Du Bois, "Of Alexander Crummell" in *The Souls of Black Folk*, 159.
32. Charles Lemert, "Cultural Politics in the Negro Soul" in *The Souls of W.E.B. Du Bois* (London: Paradigm, 2004), 75.
33. Evans Crawford and Thomas Troeger, *The Hum: Call and Response in African American Preaching* (Nashville: Abingdon Press, 1995), 19. I further believe that Howard Thurman also validates W.E.B. Du Bois

Although Crawford locates biformation in the theological development of Thurman (which I believe is Thurman's masterful amalgamation of social and psychological aspects of spiritual formations), Crawford primarily sees this as a psychological formation as much as anything else. When he prefers to call the process "a preparation for preaching," he is speaking of a commonly held worldview and, thus, a shared hermeneutic among African Americans. What is more, Crawford concedes that "All of this is perhaps another way of saying what Henry Mitchell meant in his early writings when he spoke of the black minister as bicultural."[34] Of course Crawford and Mitchell are influenced by Du Boisian double consciousness.

The difference, however, that I am suggesting is that biformation and bicultural awareness are informants for the psychospiritual awareness that is inherent in the Du Boisian rhetor-preachers' interpretation, thus connecting people of color globally to a similar hermeneutic process. What was conceived of necessity for black (African and African American) survival provides insight into the sociomarginalized understanding of their perceived inferior self—that is, their social caste or social location.

Du Boisian rhetor-preachers, and those like-minded who employ double consciousness to inform their hermeneutic, linguistically connect the populations of the two poles in our one world. Because of an awareness of the social conditions that provide a hermeneutic context, Du Boisian rhetor-preachers can locate psychospiritual awareness in biblical texts. Psychospiritual awareness also has a relationship with defining social location.

Psychospiritual and Social Location

Another aspect of psychospiritual awareness is social location. The Du Boisian hermeneutic is located in the devaluation of human bodies, the point of departure for all other social marginalization. For example, a devaluation of black bodies serves as a nexus for understanding double consciousness as psychospiritual and social aspects that influenced our necessity to

---

as a prophetic voice; see his *Jesus and the Disinherited* (Boston: Beacon Press, 1976).

34. Ibid.

pay close attention to social location. Social location is well accepted and cited in the antebellum period. Consider the conditions associated with the peculiar institution of the American slavery system, which was a misrepresentation of biblical literature, namely the words attributed to the Apostle Paul. Ephesians 6:5-6, "Slaves, be obedient to those who are your masters according to the flesh, with fear and trembling in the sincerity of your heart as to Christ," was used often to quell slave rebellions and the slaves' inner strivings and cravings for obtaining their freedom, human dignity, and equality.

A closer reading of verse 6, however, provides different insights into the previous verse: "[N]ot by the way of eye-service, as men-pleasers, but as 'slaves of Christ, doing the will of God from the heart." It seems that Paul thought that physical slavery was the perversion of spiritual allegiance to Christ. I am not concerned however with a complete exegesis of the Pauline thought on this subject. It is used here to exemplify hegemony over biblical interpretation during the peculiar institution of slavery. In this way, we can grasp the weight of psychospiritual and social inferiorities and how they influence interpretation.

What if Luke's parable is reconsidered in light of misrepresentation of interpretation by dominating classes? And what if the members of the sociomarginalized people understood Jesus to say that their human bodies were as valuable as their dominators'? Because Jesus was familiar with how human and cultural constructs form, he employed linguistic patterns to communicate truth through the art of the parable.

He first identified with their (assumed) inferiority status, which I associate with psychological and social status and, second, connects psychological and social wellness with human souls' spiritual and social redemption. I can imagine that Jesus winked his eyes toward the sociomarginalized people, and, in the twinkling of his eyes, they hear him say, "I understand your plight; do you understand that I do?" Thus, to be freed from multiforms of slavery is, first, to understand its nature and holistic grip, and, therefore as a result, achieve psychological, social, and physical freedom on the road toward spiritual redemption and salvation.

By using a Du Boisian hermeneutic as an overlay of this Lucan text, Du Boisian rhetor-preachers can grasp psychological significance and social location in biblical texts; then they can sense the presence of the Spirit as the healer of people and particularly those of marginalized statuses. According to Gates, "Du Bois's most important gift to the black literary (interpretive) tradition is, without question, the concept of duality of the African American, expressed metaphorically in his related metaphors of 'double consciousness' and the 'veil.'"[35]

Psychological well-being is at the heart of social location and central to Du Bois's employment of double consciousness that grew out of the veil. As Arnold Rampersad puts it:

> The most striking device in *The Souls of Black Folk* is Du Bois's adoption of the veil as the metaphor of black life in America. Mentioned at least once in most of the fourteen essays, as well as in the "Forethought," it means that "the Negro is sort of a seventh son, born with a veil, and gifted with second-sight in this American world—a world which yields him no true self-consciousness, but only lets him see himself through the revelation of the other world." If any single idea guides the art of the *The Souls of Black Folk*, it is this concept, which is anticipated the noted fictional conceit, developed by Ralph Ellison, that blacks are invisible to the rest of the nation.[36]

By "second-sight," Rampersad means double consciousness. Further he points out that Du Bois believes that, because the dominating classes have imposed permanent inferiority status on to African Americans (and quite possibly the majority of the world's population) psychologically, then, they have no true self-consciousness, but only see themselves through the revelation of the larger society. As you shall see later in this chapter, this is an indication that the Du Boisian hermeneutic is a species of dialectic.

In effect, what Rampersad suggests is a perception of invisibility or nonvalue for people of color in the American human family. Rampersad is correct as far as he goes; I suggest, however, that his

---

35. Gates, "Introduction," in *The Souls of Black Folk* (New York: Bantam, 2005), xix.
36. Ibid., xx-xxi.

construct is applicable to all sociomarginalized conditions in which people find themselves enslaved globally. Again, this means that Du Boisian rhetor-preachers must appreciate double consciousness and psychospiritual formations because they are interpretive constructs for developing a Du Boisian hermeneutic. By this I mean that Du Boisian rhetor-preachers, those who employ this kind of hermeneutic must inform the dominating classes that they too, are enslaved as long as others remained marginalized. In addition, the Du Boisian hermeneutic employs deferred understanding of meaning as one of its functions to communicate this message.

Double Consciousness and Deferred Understanding of Meaning

If hegemonic, hierarchal social and racial classes diminish the value of human personalities and bodies, then the latter are rendered as invisible. Rampersad indicated in the previous excerpt, citing what Ralph Ellison conveyed in *The Invisible Man*, that blacks can remain invisible in the larger culture and society. It follows, then, that understanding of meaning for the establishments' culture may be deferred, because their interpretations and assumptions are without outside critique that can be provided by people of color.

I do not suggest that multiple meanings exist; I do assert that an understanding of meaning is multilayered. As Sallie McFague puts it, "The Story is thick, not transparent; like a painting, it is looked at not through."[37] Thus I place understanding on one hand and meaning on the other. I further suggest that biblical textual interpretation is not fixed. I also suggest, however, that biblical textual truth is fixed indeed, and textual truth is what exegetical preachers seek to discover. If so, there is an intermediate relationship between understanding and meaning.

Often, memories of past events trigger truth claims in the present. This is a function of a psychological moment that I closely

---

37. Sallie Mc Fague, *Speaking in Parables: A Study in Metaphor and Theology* (Minneapolis: Fortress Press, 2007), 5.

associate with phenomenology.[38] The events at Congo Square are a phenomenological example. The dancers in antebellum New Orleans moved among the assembly as a direct, but adroit, poetic response to their social conditions. Their dancing was human language symbols, or extended metaphor, which conveyed an intermediary relationship between the dominating classes' understanding and meaning. In this instance, there was a socioeconomic, political, and psychological distance between understanding and meaning about African and African American equality.

The meaning that dancers intended to reveal is that all people are intrinsically equal. Congo Square dancers created art forms that subtly suggested that their equality will be revealed in light of future cultural understanding (which leads to acceptance). "Poetic language," as Ricoeur reminds us "is no less about reality than any other use of language but refers to it by means of a complex strategy which implies, as an essential component, a suspension and seemingly an abolition of the ordinary reference attached to descriptive language."[39]

It follows, then, that the Du Boisian hermeneutic is a complex theory that locates certain truth claims in the margins. Second, interpretation in general is not fixed, but in fact only is revealed truth. In the Congo Square dancers' case, however, they controlled meaning; understanding had not been fully revealed to the dominating classes. Thus the dancers created an art form that would cause a trigger later, a memory of an event(s) that passes through individual and collective memories and suddenly, understanding of meaning in the present is no longer deferred. In this way, we understand revealed truth because of a clearer understanding of past memories that produces meaning in present tenses.

Understanding of meaning may be deferred until an observer's comprehension is prepared to see and feel what is being placed before her or him as significant. I am aware that this closely sounds

---

38. Paul Ricoeur, "Personal Memory, Collective Memory" in *Memory, History, Forgetting,* (Chicago: University of Chicago Press, 2006), 101-02.

39. Ricoeur, "The Metaphorical Process as Cognition, Imagination, and Feeling in *Critical Inquiry* 5, no. 1. (Autumn 1978), 143-59.

like reader-response, and it may be. Reader-response often develops in communities of minds, those who share a similar worldview, preunderstanding, and social expectations. However, I know also that readers impose meaning into texts (and on to people) that simply is not there.

This further makes the argument for the Du Boisian hermeneutic, which I believe grew out of marginalization similar to the events in Congo Square. It is the Du Boisian hermeneutic that provides for Du Boisian rhetor-preachers, a hermeneutic system that helps them look for revisions and corrections in interpretation and its assumptions. It is dominating cultural hegemony over interpretation and assumptions that relegate marginalized people into dark cultural recesses that may hinder many from hearing the redemptive and salvific message.

An example of the relationship between double consciousness and deferred understanding of meaning is captured in a performance headlined by Wynton Marsalis. In the aftermath of Hurricane Katrina, Marsalis returned to his native New Orleans. He came with his trumpet. He came with a band called Odadaa! and a Ghanaian drum master who taught him African bell patterns, rhythms, and melodies of the *Ga* people. "Most importantly, he taught me," Marsalis said, "that music has meaning in all of our cultures." [40]

Marsalis came to New Orleans with the Jazz at Lincoln Center Orchestra, and with their support, he employed a species of a pan-African hermeneutic. His hermeneutic system afforded him rhetorical space to employ human-language symbols (extended metaphors). Instead of following the contours of a Eurocentric narrative where Anglo Americans remain the subject, Marsalis

---

40. Yacub Addy is well known globally as a Ghanaian drummer; he was a special guest alongside Odadaa!, a percussionist and vocalist. Both played with Wynton Marsalis and the Jazz at Lincoln Center Orchestra during the Montreal Jazz Festival in 2007. They performed Marsalis' new album *Congo Square*; see "Wynton Marsalis isn't Congo Square's star, and that's Ok," in *The Times Picayune* (April, 24, 2009). Marsalis debuted *Congo Square* in Congo Square (Louis Armstrong Park), on April 23, 2006. See Chapter 2, section titled "Du Boisian Double Consciousness, Congo Square, and Ragtime Jazz" for more about Congo Square.

paralleled the same hermeneutic system and rhetorical strategy that Du Bois presented in *Souls*. In so many words, Marsalis presented an alternative metanarrative where the subject was multivoiced with multifaced expressions.

The Du Boisian hermeneutic and rhetorical strategy that I have identified in *Souls* is a democratic protest against racial, economic, and political hegemony. In a similar way, Marsalis accomplishes nearly the same thing by creating visual images of what jazz represents, which are expressions of democratic protest against Eurocentrism's hegemony. Marsalis maintains Du Bois's strategies but replaces *Souls* with his interpretation of the Congo Square events. Like *Souls*, however, Marsalis presents the Congo Square events as democratic protests against hegemony. By so doing, he resists Eurocentrism's conventional aesthetics, interpretations, and assumptions. Instead, Marsalis applies his own inventions and becomes a participant in democratic protests. "Democracy is a form... in which all the citizens take part in distributing"[41] He came to his native New Orleans to perform his current music recording, which was prophetically entitled *Congo Square*.[42]

The Ghanaian drum master Yacub Addy was the co-writer of the music that appears on the Congo Square recording. According to Addy, "Wynton wanted the music to represent the people who would have been in Congo Square back when Africans were playing there and to include two basic human conditions: peace and war. Just like anywhere in the world, there would have been children, women, men and elders there; there would have been peace, and there would have been conflict."[43]

Moreover, Marsalis musically wanted to create an event that would communicate an ongoing, living narrative. This was accomplished in the syntactical arrangement of his music:

> We used two pieces we had started developing in our original collaboration. The first is a combination of New Orleans Second Line parade music and the Ga processional Kolomashi, which was created as protest

---

41. *The Rhetoric of Aristotle*, 44.

42. Wynton Marsalis's *Congo Square* was planned and recorded before Hurricane Katrina.

43. See Yacub Addy's official website: www.yacubaddy.com

music during Ghana's independence struggle. It follows Wynton's vocal protest about Katrina in "Ring Shout." The second is "Place Congo," where I combined one of my father's medicine rhythms, Bamai, a rhythm of Ga Akong, with a composition Wynton wrote for the orchestra. I mention these because they are examples of adding my tradition to existing jazz pieces and showing how specific and sometimes unexpected traditions go naturally with jazz, if you have the ears to hear it.

We also included a libation, an African-style prayer. Because of the many people who died in Katrina, and the many Africans who performed in Congo Square and also passed so many years ago, it was very important in our tradition that we pour the libation and pray to honor their spirits.[44]

Marsalis' syntactical pattern is deliberately nuanced and adroit. Like Du Bois's mysterious musical bar graphs, these patterns may be mysterious to those unfamiliar with African and African American cultural traditions, but discernibly familiar to those who share his cultural poles that inform his pan-African worldview.

In this way, Marsalis creates interpretive and rhetorical space to shape his story with African and African American traditions giving his story human voices. His living story is an amalgamation of African and African American traditions that I have located in the processionals namely, the Ghanaian Kolomashi and New Orleans Second Line, the African American Ring Shout, "Place Congo" and a musical rendition of a libation prayer. The Congo Square recording's songs are sermonic movements similar to Du Bois's parabolic sermons that appear in *Souls*. What is of import here? Like Du Bois, Marsalis refuses to employ Eurocentric forms to tell his story. Instead, he employs a species of a pan African hermeneutic and rhetoric in order to do so.

If the Du Boisian hermeneutic of double consciousness is a pan-African invention, the hermeneutic then is to refute Eurocentric myths and assumptions. An example of this is Marsalis addressing the meaning of the Congo Square events. Marsalis was

---

44. Ibid.

successful in his effort to revise misleading historical interpretation associated with Eurocentric spheres of influence. Thus, Marsalis reconstructed Congo Square historically, reinterpreted the events, and employed something similar to the Du Boisian understanding of deferred understanding of meaning. What is more, Marsalis honors three people groups; namely, Katrina's sufferers, African Americans, and Africans who passed through antebellum Congo Square. These syntactical arrangements create presence and mystery befitting the musical event and the historical occasions that took place there.

Double Consciousness and Dialectical Tension

A final consideration for this species of hermeneutics is to address dialectical tensions that are identified in biblical texts (further implying ethical constructs and theology). As Rampersad suggested, "the Negro is sort of a seventh son, born with a veil, and gifted with second-sight in this American world—a world which yields him no true self-consciousness, but only lets him see himself through the revelation of the other world."[45]

Because the Du Boisian hermeneutic of double consciousness is dialectic, Rampersad reminds us that sociomarginalized human conditions are associated with the veil, "but only [his social condition] lets him see himself through the revelation of the other world."[46] In so many words, this is dialectic. Rampersad is correct to suggest that many African Americans and people of color plausibly invent their cultural constructs in response to European interpretation. Since Rampersad made his claims about the interpretation of the metaphoric veil, other African American theorists and scholars have proffered cultural theses independent of Eurocentric thought. Instead African and African American thinkers such as Molefi Kete Asante trace African American interpretations to its African roots.

I assert that Rampersad's interpretation of the metaphoric veil withstands more recent scholarship, because Rampersad's insight into the psychology of African Americans parallels my understanding of dialectical tension that functions in this context. Put another

45. See Gates, "Introduction" in *The Souls of Black Folk* (2005 ed.), x.x.
46. Ibid., xx.

34

way, I consider that dialectical tension, which I have located in the Du Boisian hermeneutic, is also located in rhetorical refutation. Thus, dialectical tension serves a dual function in the Du Boisian hermeneutic. On the one hand, recognizing dialectical tension in texts presents challenges to theological certainty. For those of us who employ the Du Boisian hermeneutic of double consciousness, we may see competing choices in biblical texts that result in our having to choose ethical motifs to ground our conclusions. This does not mean that our conclusions are always correct, but we certainly attempt to be plausible. On the other hand, dialectical tension is an informant to our hermeneutic because it enables interpreters to formulate theological and ethical motifs. From these motifs, Du Boisian preachers and scholars are empowered to assert that certain principles take shape from these motifs.

Again, the events in antebellum Congo Square are an example of how dialectical tension functions (which includes Marsalis' interpretive revisions). First, it functions as a challenge or as democratic acts of protests that are disguised in music and dance. Those who danced and performed in Congo Square participated in deferring meaning until a later time. Still, the original audiences were exposed to forms of dialectical tension. The very democratic acts of protest often were misunderstood, but the art began to form an alternative hermeneutic and metanarrative that eventually resulted in a different social awareness. For this to happen, later, confluences of significant events began to birth understanding of the Congo Square dancer s' intentions to reveal truth. As you can see, dialectical tension hermeneutically is a part of double consciousness. Choices over interpretation have to be made. They, however, may need revision over time and distance traveled away from the event. This strangely sheds more light on a text and its subject.

It bears repeating then, that Du Bois' term "double consciousness" is metaphoric but signifies or bears reference toward otherness. Furthermore, it is important to note that a metaphor's primary purpose is to change or alter our understanding of meaning. I would add that identifying the function of metaphors in texts, biblical or otherwise, does not necessarily indicate a definite meaning of something, but merely points interpreters toward a closer reading. This gives interpreters (preachers) restricted choices within reason. I am aware that recent Eurocentric biblical scholarship is moving toward claims that interpreters are not bound to authorial intention or even textual authority.

The Du Boisian Hermeneutic and the Metaphoric Process

Let me say that locating metaphors in texts uniquely locates dialectical tensions. This maintains the integrity of the metaphorical process. By metaphoric process, I am informed by Ricoeur's "The Metaphorical Process as Cognition, Imagination, and Feeling." Ricoeur argues that metaphoric phrases have two constitutive functions: the psychological and the semantic; together these functions form a metaphoric process. Ricoeur characterizes "image" and "feeling" as metaphors' for psychological theory. Ricoeur means by semantic theory that metaphors can "provide untranslatable information and, accordingly, into metaphors claim to yield some true insight about reality."[47] In this way, I acknowledge semantics as a valuable tool for understanding, in part, the formation of the Du Boisian hermeneutic of double consciousness.

Again, consider the parable in Luke 15. I suggest that Luke's Jesus is telling a parable that makes use of metaphoric process to disclose embedded dialectical tension and its apparent relationship with double consciousness. I do not consider it necessary that Jesus had to encounter literally a shepherd who left behind the ninety-nine sheep to look for the one, nor do I believe that Jesus intended for readers to rely on an actual occurrence in which a woman lost a coin and found it. What is more, I do not consider it necessary that an historic figure (a wealthy man's son) left home under disrespectful circumstances, eventually "came to himself" and, afterward, returned home filled with contrition (v. 17).

I do consider it necessary to point out that Luke's Jesus told this parable and that the parable is filled with dialectical tensions that provide alternative readings of reality in order to express support for the *summum bonum*—the highest principles for the highest ethical choices. By using metaphoric process to disclose

---

47. Ricoeur, "The Metaphorical Process." 143.

embedded dialectical tensions, Luke's Jesus presents ethical choices for the Pharisees and Scribes to reconsider their theology and exegesis that Jesus proved to be insensitive, if not insolent. In any case, their exegesis and theology were not applicable for affirming that all people are intrinsically equal under the light of truth and the intention of God.

By employing a metaphoric process with this in mind, I find dialectical tension (double consciousness) in Jesus' parable. This provides an explanation for how the Congo Square performers, these pre-Du Boisian interpreters, utilized the metaphoric process. They did this by creating dialectical tension as an ethical construct. In each of these instances, they use metaphors to create dislocations of conventional and traditional ways of interpretation and provide space for otherness which is of extreme import for understanding the meaning of sociomarginalization. Second, whether it is physical, musical, oral or written language, the metaphoric process passes outside itself to facilitate transcendence and transformation. [48]

In effect, Congo Square performers are an example of the Du Boisian hermeneutic of double consciousness. Their contributions are invaluable for reinterpreting Jesus' parabolic formula. Ricoeur's metaphoric process is similar to that of Jesus' metaphoric process. In any case, metaphoric process reveals dialectical tension between understanding and meaning.

The Metaphoric Process, Double Consciousness and Extended Metaphor

Another characteristic of metaphoric process is extended metaphor. In fact, I do not know of any authentic African American preaching tradition that does not make use of this characteristic of the metaphoric process. According to Cleophus LaRue, "extended metaphors are helpful because they allow for preachers a wider sphere in which to act. For example, it would greatly limit our understanding of God's power to proclaim that the sole metaphor in black preaching is God as liberator."[49] LaRue

---

48. Ricoeur, "Metaphor and the Semantics of Discourse" in *The Rule of Metaphor*, 74.

49. LaRue, *The Heart of Black Preaching*, 27-29.

is correct to suggest that African American preachers intuitively, perhaps because of existential sociomarginalized conditions, are reluctant to place arbitrary limitations on the mysterious providential hand of God. In response, many African American preachers employ extended metaphors and poetic language to express motifs that otherwise they cannot explain adequately. This is a justification for why many African American preachers are attracted to biblical parables.

Sallie McFague notes, "Current scholarship sees the parable as an extended metaphor also, that is, as a story of ordinary people and events which is the context for envisaging and understanding the strange and extraordinary."[50] McFague sees extended metaphors theologically, as a way to see the story theologically beyond the human story. As an example she employs Luke 15, the parable of the Prodigal Son:

> To say then, that a New Testament parable is an extended metaphor means not that the parable "has a point" or teaches a lesson, but that it is itself what it is talking about (there is no way around the metaphor to what is "really" being said). Thus to say that the parable of the Prodigal Son is a metaphor of God's love suggests that the story has meaning beyond the story of a human father and his wayward son, but that only through the details, the parable itself, are we brought to an awareness of God's love that has the shock of revelation. If the story of the Prodigal Son tells us about that love, it does so indirectly, for the story itself absorbs our interest. We do not, I think naturally allegorize it (is the father "God"? is the feast a symbol of "the kingdom"?). The story is "thick," not transparent; like a painting, it is looked at, not through. William Wimsatt, the literary critic, says that a stone sculpture of a human head refers to a particular human head, to be sure, but what interests us—and what may ultimately illumine our appreciation of that "real" head—is concentration on the carved head before us. The story of the Prodigal Son is a sculpture, a metaphor, of something

---

50. McFague, *Speaking in Parables*, 5.

we do not know much about—human becoming and God's extraordinary response.[51]

McFague suggests that a parable is employed to reveal otherness, "The world of the parable, then, includes, it is, in fact both dimensions—the secular and the religious, our world and God's love. It is not that the parable points to the unfamiliar but that it includes the unfamiliar within its boundaries."[52]

Though McFague is speaking principally from a theological perspective, I have noticed a parallel with the Du Boisian hermeneutic. It is clear that McFague has insisted that dialectical tension exists between the world's poles, those closed and those that are transcendent. What is more, her hermeneutic and theology depend on extended metaphors as a central means for conveying bridges to cross toward understanding and meaning.

Hermeneutically, I agree with LaRue, too, because I understand metaphors to limit interpreters from assuming and predicting that God will act the same each time. Preachers of color rightly have cautioned against the flawed assumption that "God" can be put in a box. As Larue writes, "A God who acts mightily in a host of ways in various situations has much more elasticity and is more inclusive [which is represented] by the various extended metaphors likely to be found in a black sermon." [53] In short, preachers who employ the Du Boisian hermeneutic of double consciousness as their point of departure are aware that their textual interpretation must be revisited each time he or she prepares to preach, not assuming that their previous interpretation is correct. There is always room for further illumination.

Conclusion

The Du Boisian hermeneutic of double consciousness is an invention by those whose poles of one world originate within sociomarginalized conditions. This is the genesis for Du Bois's metaphoric veil. To understand how it functions and its significance, the first step is to recognize the social conditions that

---

51. Ibid., 5.
52. Ibid., 5-6.
53. LaRue, *The Heart of Black Preaching*, 27-29.

formed it. No other literary expression that I have read explains this as clearly as does "Of the Meaning of Progress," the fourth essay in *Souls*. The essay's lead character is a young girl, who is eager to receive formal education to satisfy the natural yearnings of any human heart. Her name is Josie. Du Bois recalls that:

> She was a thin, homely girl of twenty, with a dark-brown face, and thick, hard hair... She seemed to be the centre of the family: always busy at service, or at home, or berry-picking; a little nervous and inclined to scold, like her mother, yet faithful, too, like her father. She had about her certain fitness, the shadow of an unconscious moral heroism that would willingly give all of life to make life broader, deeper, and fuller for her and hers. I saw much of this family afterwards, and grew to love them for their honest efforts to be decent comfortable, and for their knowledge of their own ignorance. There was with them no affection. The mother would scold the father for being so "easy"; Josie would roundly berate the boys for carelessness; and all knew that it was a hard thing to dig a living out of a rocky hill side side-hill.[54]

Du Bois hints that he would again see Josie's family. Ten years would pass, however, before Du Bois returned to the blue hills of east Tennessee, where he found that little had changed and that life continued within the veil: "We had a heap of trouble since you've been away." Jim, one of Josie's younger brothers, was accused of stealing wheat by Farmer Durham. Jim escaped the stones hurled at him, but refused to run from the constable. He was charged with thievery and was placed in stockades. The family responded, "It grieved Josie, and great awkward John (her older brother) walked nine miles every day to see his little brother through the bars of Lebanon jail."

Du Bois tells us that "Josie grew thin and silent, yet worked the more." Her father grew old, and Josie worked the more and this

---

54. Du Bois, "Of the Meaning of Progress" in *The Souls of Black Folk*, 46-47.

time in Nashville, for a year. She earned ninety dollars to furnish a new house, making it a home.

> When the spring came, and the birds twittered, and the stream ran proud and full, little sister Lizzie, bold and thoughtless, flushed with the passion of youth, bestowed herself on the tempter, and brought home a nameless child. Josie shivered and worked on, with the vision of school days all fled, with a face wan and tired—worked until, on a summer's day, someone married another; then Josie crept to her mother like a hurt child, and slept—and sleeps. [55]

Du Bois captured this sense of the tragic in "Of the Meaning of Progress." He characterized sociomarginalized life and its symbolism as a palpable, pulsing reality. Du Bois created the significant importance of "now," which I trace to his understanding of Crummell's pan-Africanism, another way to describe African influence on multiculturalism. It is a multivoiced, multifaced, and a multiplaced worldview and a social condition that breeds ignorance, anger, and, eventually, the death of hope. It also breeds democratic protest which is an identification of hope. This tension between fate and faith remains our ancient contemporary. Josie's life is an example of cultural identity, and her life is representative of African and African American contemporary life within the veil. The veil is filled with hurt and pain. This is Du Bois at his best; his literary expression of double-consciousness serves as the seedbed for my Du Boisian hermeneutic.

The story I have told follows a similar path. A part of the story that I have told, I have asserted that Congo Square is a plausible example for the Du Boisian hermeneutic of double consciousness. This cultural worldview reflects a common hermeneutic that, according to Du Bois, evolves into something pan-African. Today, however, we can revise Du Bois's claim and say that pan-Africanism is the seedbed for any attempt to forge a multicultural hermeneutic. It too is shared by people of color and is identifiable in multivoices, multifaces, and multiplaces. The Du Boisian

---

55. Ibid., 52.

hermeneutic of double consciousness symbolizes a cultural response to marginalization; it also functions as an alternative to traditional views held by those of dominating cultures and classes. As I previously mentioned, the Du Boisian hermeneutic is shared by people of color, including their artists, writers, musicians, and Du Boisian rhetor-preachers.

Establishment preachers who will learn to employ the Du Boisian hermeneutic of double consciousness must first learn to "listen against their hearing." This is an invaluable first step toward transforming communities into advocates for justice and redemption. It is also a powerful way to nurture trust among biblical believers. I have been in cross-cultural settings where listening against my hearing has been the most powerful tool that I have had in my possession. I have learned to use it as I continue to discover that African Americans and, particularly, the African American middle class have increasing influence in the American story. The African middle class, however, must affirm its allegiance to pan-Africanism over and against the negative effects, influences, and stereotypes that Eurocentrism has placed upon African and African Americans and all others who are children of the Diaspora.

Chapter 2: From Behind the Sorrow Songs: Du Boisian Double Consciousness Emerges

&

> What are these songs, and what do they mean? I know little of music and can say nothing in technical phrase, but I know something of men, and knowing them, I know that these songs are the articulate message of the slave to the world. They tell us in these eager days that life was joyous to the black slave, careless and happy. I can easily believe this of some, of many. But the heart-touching witness of these songs. They are the music of an unhappy people, of the children of disappointment; they tell us of death and suffering and unvoiced longing toward a truer world, of misty wanderings and hidden ways.
> W. E. B. Du Bois[1]

"Of the Sorrow Songs," foreshadows W.E.B. Du Bois's development of double consciousness. For his many eavesdroppers, Du Bois's interpretation of the sorrow songs provides a glimpse into what shapes black people's self-image and unconsciousness, thus the Du Boisian veil. From within the veil, Du Bois points toward an inner spiritual and intellectual path that reveals strength that possesses black folks. It is dogged as Josiah Young captures in *Dogged Strength within the Veil*, where he explains

---

1. W.E.B. Du Bois, "Of the Sorrow Songs" in *The Souls of Black Folk* (New York: Bantam, 1989), 187-8. The first edition was published in 1903 by McClung publishing.

how double consciousness shapes common pathos among people of color: it is life within the veil.[2]

Thus the New Englander, the aloof Victorian Du Bois, whose emotions too often are masked behind his outward ardent reticence, finds full expression within the sorrow songs. These songs are a gift from those who suffered and whose words offer the world an expression of bluesy art and literature, an art and literature that belongs to the priestly function. Like his predecessors' and contemporaries' dogged strength, Du Bois employs a bluesy language that expresses a priestly function that he experiences as a collective, communal catharsis and purging. Du Bois, then, acknowledges that he is a part of the blues culture, and he uses sorrow songs to speak through him, to him, and of him. He is transformed.

Though these songs are accused of primitiveness, Du Bois appropriates them to form an alternative language that translates Eurocentric, ex-cathedral, academic definitions into earthier and pedestrian definitions. By definitions, I mean that Du Bois provides a different interpretation of African American doggedness that describes how African Americans, Africans and other people of color survive Eurocentrism, and, second, by definitions I mean that Du Bois appropriates sorrow songs so that he may draw a map and construct a road for those who want to travel within the veil. Later, however, I will explain how these sorrow songs are the point of departure for the blues, and how the blues are a part of the authentic African American aesthetic.[3] Indeed, sorrow songs are possibly the initial authentic American aesthetic. I will suggest that African American aesthetics (spirituals, blues and jazz, etc.), resist highbrow Eurocentric academic categories and critique.

---

2. Josiah Ulysses Young, III, *Dogged Strength within the Veil: Africa Spirituality and the Mysterious Love of God* (New York: Trinity Press, 2003).

3. Sorrow songs are also the *raison d'être* for gospel music. See Wyatt Tee Walker, *Somebody Is Calling My Name: Black Sacred Music and Social Change* (Valley Forge, PA: Judson Press, 1979).

The Du Boisian Hermeneutic Influence on Black Liberation Theology

Keeping in mind that I suggests that Du Bois employs the blues an aesthetic that for him, serves as a window into African American liberation, I believe then, that Du Bois, must be considered as the father of black theology, and that his contributions to our understanding of double consciousness is black theology's point of departure. Through the ethical theology of Howard Thurman and the liberation theology of James H. Cone, black theology and double consciousness continue to take shape in the collective black consciousness. It forms, because Du Boisian double consciousness is a pan-African invention. Due in part to Du Bois's early writings, the emergence of Afrocentric ethics and black liberation theology is accepted by clergy who serve progressive black churches.

Howard Thurman, a former Dean of Marsh Chapel at Boston University, shaped his theology that was informed by Du Boisian thought. Because of Thurman's Christology, which seems to focus on the humanity of Jesus, we recognize a radically different interpretation of Jesus of Nazareth. What emerges from Thurman's theology is a *raison d'être* for the Du Boisian prophetic tradition, which is a critique of Eurocentrism. Thurman understands the blues sensibility and, for this reason, his bluesy jazz sensibility grew out this context. Thus, Thurman's critique fulfills a prophetic function that demands an- other-wise interpretation. For this reason, I identify him among those in the Du Boisian prophetic tradition.

Since 1968, James Cone, a systematic theologian, has taught at Union Theological Seminary in New York. He is Du Boisian, and he recognized our need to construct a black theology. His theology has shaped our interpretation and perspective about the possibility that God affirms the intrinsic value of Africans, African Americans, and people of color. In fact, Cone's black liberation theology and empowerment motifs seem to surface and parallel the sociopolitical movements in the 1960s of African Americans and other people of color. Cone's first contributions surfaced during the post-civil rights struggles.

Alongside the post-civil rights struggles which are the 1960s and early 1970s black resistance and militancy, Cone shaped a black theology out of what were then the current social and political contexts which began a sea change in the American body politic. Although Cone's theology is prophetic by nature (by this I mean he, too, has a jazz sensibility), it is shaped by his critical memory that informs his blues sensibility.

According to Cone, the blues "do not deal with abstract ideas that can be analyzed from the perspective of objective reason," and "they are not propositional truths about the black experience."[4] Thus "it is necessary to view the blues as a state of mind in relation to the Truth of the black experience."[5] Later, Cone adroitly makes a similar claim about how a species of black preachers view the Scriptures and how they deliver their sermons. "In regard to biblical literalism, it is of course true that slaves were not biblical critics and thus were unaware of European academic reflections on the origins of biblical writings emerging in response to the Enlightenment. Like most of their contemporary [preachers] they accepted the inerrancy of scripture."[6] Cone goes on to explain, "Traditionally, the black preacher was literal only about what he [she] believed God would do for the people. The very literalism of black religion supported a gospel of earthly freedom."[7] In so many words, Cone points out that African American folk culture has a philosophical relationship with existentialism.

The Similar Nature of the Sorrow Songs and the Blues

Like the blues, sorrow songs are an existential expression that chronicles an experience that people of color continue to share. The sorrow songs grew out of a state of marginalization that occurs when centuries of cultural hegemony impose and support illegitimate claims for Eurocentric culture superiority. Therefore, for Du Bois, the sorrow songs express what otherwise he could not say but only feel. Because the spirituals or sorrow songs have unlimited expression, they are culturally elastic and timeless. They

---

4.   James Cone, *The Spirituals and the Blues* (Maryknoll, NY: Orbis, 1972), 102.
5.   Ibid.
6.   Ibid., 36.
7.   Ibid., 37.

are, then, the original language of double consciousness, which I trace to the sorrow songs, the blues, and the jazz.

The blues are universally understood by most people of color, because, by nature, they are secular-sacred music. The blues are secular expressions about human inequality and a daily struggle to survive vile conditions. The sorrow songs are sacred expressions about God knowing about the vileness of inhumane conditions experienced by black people, but God will deliver them eventually from their oppressors. This is a faith, fate, doubt, hope motif, which is dialectic, but together they are a holistic invention of bluesy-churchy music that mirrors black existence. This holistic invention is heard in Jimmy Smith's bluesy jazz organ, and his interpretation of his music places black people squarely within the existential tradition. This secular-sacred music represents a worldview that informs the spirituals (sorrow songs), gospel music, the blues, and jazz.

> Black music, then, is not an artistic creation for its own sake; rather it tells us about the feeling and thinking of a people of African descent, and the kinds of mental adjustments they had to make in order to survive in an alien land. For example, the work songs were a means of heightening energy, converting labor into dances and games, and providing emotional excitement in an otherwise unbearable situation. The emphasis was on free, continuous, creative energy as produced in song. A similar functional is applied to the slave seculars, ballads, spirituals as well as the blues.[8]

What Cone writes about is black music's influential role in African American culture. In fact, Cone indirectly reinforces my thesis: that is, to interpret the blues and jazz is to trace them toward double consciousness. What is more, black music is a hermeneutic cue that demonstrates how (black) art imitates double consciousness. It reveals sociological and political pathways into the pyschospiritual conditions that black people face—life within

---

8.   Ibid., 98.

the veil. Cone, then, captures the essence of the holistic cohesiveness that is present in the African American psyche.

This lack of life quality that blacks experience is defiled absurdity, which causes many people of color to constantly grapple with their choices. They must choose between love, hope, hate, doubt, and despair. They must choose courage over fear in order to quench their deep thirst for racial justice against a cup that black folks know is mingled with unmitigated hegemony. To counter this absurdity, many people of color have turned toward faith in religious otherness.

This absurdity also plunges blacks deeply into cultural skepticism, which leads to nihilistic conclusions about the quality of black life. I trace sacred and secular black nihilism directly toward the ill-effects that I associate with Eurocentrism and that are heaped upon people of color. I trace this forward toward hip-hop culture and its explicitly nihilistic rap music lyrics as will be shown later in this chapter. By this I mean, because of marginalization, African Americans and people of African descent feel—that is, Christians, Muslims, Jews, agnostics, or atheists alike —because of Eurocentrism, all experience similar marginalization, and, as a result, all employ a similar hermeneutic of double consciousness.[9]

In this instance, however, I am addressing, primarily, "divinely inspired" Eurocentric religious claims endlessly made about their culture, classes, and communities. In particular, because of their puritanical obsessions with hegemonic inspiration, many whites believe that Eurocentrism grants Anglo people of European descent a status of "God's elect and predestined," which is another way to claim permanent superiority. As early as the pre-Civil War period, blacks refused to believe this kind of preordained propaganda. What is present in black folks' literature and secular lyrics in their slave songs is what I would characterize as evidence:

> The secular songs of the slavery were non-religious,
> occasionally anti-religious, and were often called devil

---

9. See David Walker's *Appeal, in Four to Those of the United States of America Articles: Together With Preamble to the Color Citizens of the World, But in Particular, and Very Expressingly,* ed. Charles M. Wiltse (New York: Hill and Wang, 1930).

songs by religious folk. The seculars expressed skepticisms of black slaves who found it difficult to take seriously anything suggesting the religious faith of white preachers.[10]

Slaves decoded and resisted the slave master's singular message, reinforced by many of the dominate culture's preachers, where people of color are doomed to servitude by the Divine Other. At the taproot of the slave and people of color's culture is dialectical tension.[11] The blues then grew out of dialectical tension, which leads to existential tensions between two poles in one world: one white and the other of colors. After slavery, for example, emancipation brought broken families, Jim and Jane Crow, black codes, and total destruction of political policies that have far-reaching implications, such as legal sentencing of black males either into prisons and sanctions for those who harm black males sometimes resulting in their murders.[12]

Billie Holiday sings about this in "Strange Fruit," "Southern trees bear a strange fruit / Blood on the leaves and blood on the root / Black bodies swinging in the southern breeze / Strange fruit hanging from the popular trees."[13] Holiday's voice still haunts and echoes the pain-filled moral failure of reconstruction policies, which supposedly were aimed at reforming the American South. It did not happen. What did happen, however, was that American

---

10. Cone, *The Spirituals and the Blues*, 98.
11. Melva Wilson Costen, *African American Christian Worship* (Nashville: Abingdon Press, 2007), worldview and interpretation is: From the African taproot, the early shapers of Black folk religion forged a Christian worldview, or "sacred cosmos," that permeates all of life. Everyday living is not separate from worship. The reality of human corruption, oppression, and inequality anywhere in the world provides a hermeneutical principle, a lens through which the Word of God is seen, heard, understood, felt, and interpreted in worship.
12. See Michelle Alexander, *The New Jim Crow: Mass Incarceration in the Age of Colorblindness* (New York: The New Press, 2010).
13. "Strange Fruit" was a poem written by Abel Meeropol, a Jewish high-school teacher from the Bronx, about the lynching of two black men. He published under the pen name Lewis Allan, derived from two children he lost in their infancy. See David Margolick, *Strange Fruit: Billie Holiday, Café Society, and an Early Cry for Civil Rights* (Philadelphia: Running Press, 2000), 25-27.

blacks faced abject poverty and pyschospiritual realities that came with this condition as heard in this blues passage, "never had to have no money befo, And now they want it everywhere I go."[14]

Thus, a pyschospiritual hangover left by slavery and lynching informs a blues sensibility. The bluesy characteristics of black life are traced to nihilistic conditions, which are an ongoing existential threat to people of color. These conditions further shape the contours of the bluesy language of people of color that informs how they tell their tragisaga stories about their human condition. The blues are the indigenous folk story and a language "of the people." Because the blues belong to the people, they are a replica of the spirituals and humanism. From both perspectives, however, the blues serve as a priestly function, which is purging and catharsis. The blues tradition expresses the sentiments of the masses and reassures them that their feelings about their experiences are not absurd, but in fact, it is their living conditions that remain absurd.

Double Consciousness Informs James Cone's Blues

I now turn our attention toward finding an authentic interpretation for the blues. I insist that this interpretation parallels how people of color interpret their texts, whether written, oral, or living. This means that the blues are an expression of "shared experience." James Cone, a brilliant theologian whose canonical works have contributed to black liberation theology, is of interest to me. His work in this area grounds our search for a definition. In *The Spirituals and the Blues*, Cone deftly makes a case that "authentic interpretation" is an indigenous folk linguistic, and that it informs cultural hermeneutics and theology. As Cone seems to do, I claim that hermeneutics emerge from an indigenous experience. Thus, hermeneutics informs rhetoric, theology and homiletics (and all other disciplines).

Cone recounts his shared experiences growing up in Bearden, Arkansas. In fact, Cone interprets spirituals and the blues as nearly the same expression and genre:

---

14. Cone, "O freedom! O freedom! O freedom over me!" *The Spirituals and the Blues*, 41.

It is simply not possible to grow up with Arkansas blues and spirituals of Macedonia A.M.E. Church and remain unaffected by the significance of blackness in the context of white society. I run therefore convinced that it is not possible to render an authentic interpretation of black music without having shared and participated in the experience that created it. Black music must be lived before it can be understood.[15]

Cone suggests that an "authentic interpretation" of the spirituals and the blues belongs to a particular culture, and a more narrowly, authentic interpretation belongs within a shared setting, time and space and the blues' meaning, belongs to a particular audience, to a particular communal group. For Cone, only those who find these events unique can place significance and value upon their shared experiences. It is like being present at a black picnic and hearing someone tell the younger members of the family, who are struggling to understand the relevance of the story, "you had to be there, junior; you had to be there." People must live in a similar context, time, and place to claim that they have a commonly shared experience.

Context, then, for "authentic interpretation" drives meaning toward commonly held interpretation of an event that is significant to groups of people. These common experiences are at the taproot of Cone's romantically remembered blues. In other words, his blues are not understood critically and not considered historical-empirical facts. Instead, Cone's blues are poetic interpretation and therefore aesthetic in form (it is a blues sensibility). In this way, Cone is able to construct spirituals and blues theology that take shape as something remembered about a specific, special experience, shared by people in a particular setting, time, and space. I add that hermeneutic formation takes a similar path.

Cone's spirituals and blues are an example of how cultural hermeneutics function and how communal experiences shape interpretation. Experience, around which worldview depends and forms, is the significant factor in developing a system for hermeneutic interpretation. I suggest further that cultural

---

15. Ibid., 3.

hermeneutics informs all disciplines. In both instances, these disciplines gain credibility because of their appreciation for authentic interpretation in the tradition of a blues sensibility.

Indeed, I take Cone's blues sensibility seriously. That is, only those who possess an authentic interpretation are those who experience events in a particular context. I also ask, "Can there be any critical reflection or theoretical theory based on a blues sensibility?" If my reading of Cone is correct, then the answer is yes and no. Terry Eagleton, author of *After Theory*, rightly says that we cannot return to "pretheoretical innocence" and those who attempt to do so are in for disappointment. In this way, Cone is correct as Eagleton explains:

> If theory means reasonably systematic reflection on our guiding assumptions, it remains as indispensable as ever. But we are living now in the aftermath of what one might call highbrow theory, in an age which, having grown rich on the insights of thinkers like Althusser, Barthes and Derrida, has also some way moved beyond them.[16]

Cone is entirely correct to suggest that his spirituals and his blues are beyond highbrow theory because they are his spirituals and his blues. He reminds us, "They are not propositional truths about black experience."[17] I suggest that these same principles apply to cultural hermeneutic interpretation in any tradition.

Eagleton, however, is correct to point out that it is impossible for cultural interpretation to escape some formal reflection, critique, and borrowing. Because of this, I must add a positive corrective to Cone's views. When I borrow from theorists who depend on "soft objectivism," I am able to trace an authentic interpretation toward the blues tradition. Indeed this is similar to what Eagleton suggests and that is a historical connection exits between generations. "The generations that followed after these path-breaking figures did what generations that follow usually do. They develop the original ideas, added to them, criticized them and

---

16. Terry Eagleton, *After Theory* (New York: Basic Books, 2003), 1-2.
17. James Cone, *The Spirituals and the Blues*, 102.

applied them."[18] Thus, Eagleton provides a nexus for those who interpret Cone's blues as a segue toward the evolution of a jazz sensibility.

For now, however, a blues sensibility is the hermeneutic taproot for the people of African descent's tragisaga story. Interpretation in this tradition is not highbrow or Eurocentric. If any Eurocentric label is associated with a blues sensibility, it would be a poststructuralist's theory, something that moves beyond modernity and colonialism. A blues sensibility and a jazz sensibility, as will be explained in a discussion about *Du Boisian Double Consciousness, Congo Square and Ragtime Jazz* is something other-wise and may be the best way to express postmodern interpretation. What is important here, the blues remains the theological and political language "of the people." By this, I mean that the blues interpretation includes suffering and liberation. Human suffering is priestly and liberation is abolitionist and prophetic and I claim that both are Christological.

The Priestly Hermeneutic Function and the Blues

The problem with suffering remains our contemporary nemesis. Biblical theodicy writers were challenged to explain human suffering's existence. One only has to look to one of Job's soliloquies to see this (Job 10:18-22). Still, these writers demonstrate their integrity by acknowledging that suffering is humanity's constant companion. The Psalmist decried:

> My God, my God why have You forsaken me? Far from my deliverance are the words of my groaning. O my God, I cry by day but You do not answer me; And by night, but I have no rest (Psalm 22:1-2).

In comparison, the Gospel writer said:

> And He [Jesus] began to teach them that the Son of Man must suffer many things and be rejected by the elders and the chief priests and the scribes, and be killed, and after three days rise again (Mark 8:31).

---

18. Terry Eagleton, *After Theory*, 2.

These Old and New Testament passages parallel if not converge as priestly and prophetic proclamations. In the first passage, I locate a community that shares a worldview about human suffering. The writer's inspiration and impetus for writing this Psalm is in part an expression of a shared communal experience and the need for catharsis and purging. This is a priestly function; this is a blues sensibility; this is a Du Boisian perspective of the role of the sorrow songs.

Informed by this ancient Hebrew sociohistorical context, the Gospel writer knows well that Hebrew culture experiences priestly catharsis and purging collectively. Thus, we know that the writer interprets Psalm 22:1-2 as a national condition. This is bluesy. It is similar to Cone's blues indigenousness to Bearden, Arkansas. The psalmist's lamentation parallels African roots and echoes the isolating influences that slavery has had upon people of color. Cone believes "The origin of the blues is difficult to determine. Most experts agree that they probably began to take form in the late nineteenth century. But the spirit and the mood of the blues have roots stretching back into slavery days and even to Africa."[19] If this is true, then, Psalm 22 is a forerunner of a blues sensibility. Indeed, I believe clearly that a blues sensibility is present in this Psalm, and I believe too that I have located a Hebrew communal preunderstanding of human suffering that influences interpretation similar to what Cone claims about people of African descent.

The text from Mark demonstrates that Mark's audience is informed by the Hebrew community's preunderstanding of human suffering. However, it moves beyond ancient understanding and sees more. It becomes a reference to Jesus' suffering for all communities. This I take into consideration when I interpret the contexts of Psalm 22:1-2 and Mark 8:31. In the latter text, the Gospel writer sees the priestly and prophetic function wedded when Jesus said, "and after three days [I] rise again." In this way, Jesus' suffering is a vicarious experience of atonement that we feel inside and outside of the Hebrew community. What is important? These texts speak of a priestly function, and the second text (Mark 8:31) speaks of priestly and prophetic functions fulfilled in Jesus. In my view, both texts are bluesy and Christological.

---

19. James Cone, *The Spirituals and the Blues*, 98.

The blues language is also political. It is important to declaim that a blues sensibility is also a language of liberation as are the spirituals. Notice communal resistance to their social conditions in the lyrics of this eschatological spiritual:

> Children, we shall be free
> When the Lord shall appear.
> Give ease to the sick, give sight to the blind,
> Enable the cripple to walk;
> He'll raise the dead from under the earth,
> And give them permission to talk.[20]

James Cone writes, in effect, "Deception was not only present during slavery but is still with us today, and it will continue to exist as long as there are white people in power who define the law and order according to white supremacy and black inferiority. This simple fact seems to have been overlooked by even the most sensitive white interpreters of the blues."[21] Thus overlooked in the blues is sociopolitical resistance. If by implication only, resistance is expressed in the spiritual: "give ease to the sick, give sight to the blind, Enable the cripple to walk." Though this spiritual and many others deceive the dominate culture's understanding of the docile slaves, so be it. A slave community understood sociopolitical, cathartic, purging, and liberating language.

At this point, I readmit double consciousness into this discussion. Cone indirectly makes a strong case for it. Double consciousness dominates and permeates African American worldview and interpretation. It is located also in the blues and particularly in the blues' lyrics that creatively speak against Eurocentrism and its cultural hegemony. Double consciousness informs a blues sensibility; it remains the spool and thread that best expresses the shared significance the Hebrew community has with people of African descent.

---

20. James Cone, *The Spirituals and the Blues*, 34.
21. Ibid., 19.

Double Consciousness and Howard Thurman's Jazz Sensibility

As previously mentioned, I believe that Du Bois is the father of black liberation theology. I believe, too, that Howard Thurman connects Du Boisian thought with other black theologians' contributions that challenge the black church. Moving forward, it is helpful to realize and acknowledge their contributions to the broader church traditions—black, white, and other-wise. I want to narrow Du Boisian thought in this context to double consciousness. Thurman's point of departure for the prophetic function is double consciousness and how it shapes people of African descent's worldview. For that reason, I identify him with the prophetic Jazz tradition.

Thurman's theological writings, poetry, and sermons provide for the academy and church rich, sage, and prophetic insights into the mysteries of human nature and the religion of Jesus. The rich insights from Thurman's *Jesus and the Disinherited*, I characterize as theological ethics or, put in another way, a sense of what "ought to be."[22] Thurman has written a commentary that explains the pyschospiritual nature of Du Bois's book of parabolic sermons, *Souls*. I further characterize Thurman's book as an apology for people of color's wretched fight for survival against nihilism, this ever present and looming condition that threatens the psyche of African Americans and other people of color.

Cornel West reminds us that "*Nihilism is to be understood here not as a philosophical doctrine but there are no rational grounds for legitimate standards or authority; it is, far more, the lived experience of coping with a life of horrifying meaninglessness, hopelessness, and (most important) lovelessness.*"[23] West, describing black America, makes sense:

> Nihilism is not new in black America. The first African encounter with the New World was an encounter with a distinctive form of the Absurd. The initial black-struggle against degradation and devaluation in the enslaved

---

22. Howard Thurman, *Jesus and the Disinherited* (Boston: Beacon Press, 1976).
23. Cornel West, *Race Matters* (New York: Vintage Books, 2001), 22. West's italics.

circumstances of the New World was, in part, a struggle against nihilism. In fact, the majority enemy of black survival in America has been and is neither oppression nor exploitation but rather the nihilistic threat—that is, loss of hope and absence of meaning is preserved, the possibility of overcoming oppression stays alive. The self-fulfilling prophecy of the nihilistic threat is that without hope there can be no future [,] that without meaning there can be no struggle.[24]

West characterizes black America as bluesy and, alongside Thurman's *Jesus and the Disinherited*, similarities rise—namely these writers see the effects of socimarginalization destroying hope among people of color. Therefore, *Jesus of the Disinherited* is bluesy too; it addresses the "whys" for nihilism in African American life, but Thurman locates prophetic leaven hidden within the African American psyche (Luke 13:18-21). Leaven for Thurman signifies hopeful possibilities that empower the imagination of those who possess a jazz sensibility. Simply described, the book is easy to read, and Thurman demonstrates his grasp on rhetoric and composition by his employment of perspicuity of style, precise clarity, and propriety of word choice, purity of language.[25]

In *Jesus and the Disinherited*, you will notice similarities between Du Bois's poetic expressions about people of color's nihilistic struggle, but we cite hopeful possibilities that are hidden leaven in his eulogy to Alexander Crummell. Crummell's travails appear in *Souls*, a depiction of Crummell's life within the veil. Du Bois writes of Crummell, "Three temptations he met on those dark dunes that lay gray and dismal before the wonder-eyes of the child: the temptation of Hate, that stood out against the red dawn; the temptation of Despair, that darkened noonday; and the temptation of Doubt, that ever steals along with twilight. Above all, you must hear of the vales he crossed, - the Valley of Humiliation and the Valley of the Shadow of Death."[26]

---

24. Ibid., 23.
25. Perspicuity, precision, propriety and purity are all elements of Hugh Blair's Belle Lettres. See *Lectures on Rhetoric and Belle Lettres*, Southern Illinois University Press.
26. Du Bois, *Souls*, 159.

Although Thurman published *Jesus of the Disinherited* forty-six years after the first publication of *Souls*, I suggest that Thurman uses his book to compliment and supplement many of the original themes Du Bois first introduces in *Souls*. The themes in *Jesus and the Disinherited* are: (1) Jesus, An Interpretation, (2) Fear, (3) Deception, (4) Hate, (5) Love and an Epilogue. These themes address the Jesus' socioreligious response to human nature.

Like Du Bois (and Frantz Fanon), Thurman expresses the pyschospiritual grip that sociomarginalization has upon on people of color—life within the veil.

> A profound piece of surgery has to take place in the very psyche of the disinherited before the great claim of the religion of Jesus is presented. The great stretches of barren places in the soul must be revitalized, brought to life, before they can be challenged. Tremendous skill and power must be exercised to show the disinherited the awful results of the role of negative deception into which their lives have been cast. How to do this is perhaps the greatest challenge that the religion of Jesus faces in modern life.[27]

This passage expresses the challenges that the religion of Jesus faces in Thurman's chapter entitled "Deception" in *Jesus and the Disinherited*; indeed, life within the veil. In the proverbial mirror, it reflects a learned and conditioned behavior that is psychological deception. Before social advancement for sociomarginalized people occurs, Thurman is correct to recommend to a very sick patient immediate, radical, psychological and spiritual surgery in order to remove a life-threatening malignancy. This is the central reason why Thurman concedes that life for people of color is parochial and, among other things, psychologically limited by Eurocentrism. It is bluesy, it is challenging, and it is another way for us to understand how double consciousness metastasizes inside people of African descent's worldview, and how people of color interpret texts.

---

27. Thurman, "Deception" in *Jesus and the Disinherited*, 68.

As mentioned earlier, it is difficult and nearly impossible to rise above these kinds of environmental circumstances when a person is constantly struggling to survive, whether that struggle is on the level of physical survival, subsistence, or simply for dignity as Thurman writes:

> This is really the form that the dilemma takes. It is not solely a question of keeping the body alive; it is rather how not to be killed. Not to be killed becomes the great end, and morality takes its meaning from that center. Until that center is shifted, nothing real can be accomplished. It is the uncanny and perhaps unwitting recognition of this fact that causes those in power to keep the disinherited from participation in meaningful social process. For if the disinherited get such a new center as patriotism, for instance—liberty within the framework of a sense of country or nation—then the aim of not being killed is swallowed up by a larger and more transcendent goal. Above all else the disinherited must not have any stake in the social order; they must be made to feel that they are alien, that it is a great boon to be allowed to remain alive, not to be exterminated.[28]

While sitting in a popular coffee house located on Capitol Hill in Washington, DC, I noticed a man beside me reading *Christian Ministry* by Charles Briggs, a nineteenth-century Calvinist preacher.[29] At first I did not disclose that I had read the book during my seminary years. I engaged him on his terms as he explained what he had reasoned from the content of the book. After a while, he asked me if I had read it. I admitted that indeed I had. He asked me what my thoughts were about the puritanical preacher's theological claims. Gently but firmly, I told him that I thought Eurocentric theology was deeply limited and flawed for twenty-first-century realities. Perhaps I offended him. He responded, "Well, I'm not going to change my theology."

---

28. Ibid., 69.
29. See Charles Briggs, *Christian Ministry: An Inquiry Into Its Causes of Insufficiency* (New York: Seeley, Burnside and Seeley, 1844.

I understood his response. As a white American male, he must have felt put upon and that I was capitalizing on the latest white male bashing so often heard from the liberal left. This causes reactionary behavior, which is conditioned, and it surfaces as a social and political orientation commonly shared among white evangelicals. Too often many white evangelicals confuse homogenous ideologies with theology, and therefore from this premise I suggested that this self-described fellow preacher had determined that he was right and chose to dig in and stand his ground.

This, of course, is precisely the problem. In his religion, there is little room for a broader perspective and maybe not room for transcendence. As offended as I perceived him, in turn he must have believed that I was equally offended by my retort; perhaps I was. He may have heard in the tone of my voice, "Oh yes you will, if you want your Christian proclamation to be taken seriously by the majority world of people."

Though he seemed surprised by my authoritative answer, I am sure that he was not going to change immediately. There is a species of white evangelical Christians that finds it hard to entertain that others may have something to add to what has already been said, but I'm sure also that I challenged his reality just a little bit.

I have cited a personal illustration that relates to Thurman's incisive perspective about those (both black and white) unduly influenced by Eurocentrism. Those who indulge are convinced by convenience as Thurman said; some hold on to unmitigated power "to keep the disinherited from participation in meaningful social process." Still, Thurman sees prophetic hope in the religion of Jesus. I hear Thurman's optimism. If people of color find dogged strength to persevere toward something larger than one's environmental circumstances, she or he can forge toward a transcendent goal; this is what the religion of Jesus means.

This is an example of how a blues sensibility's significance serves as segue and transformation toward jazz interpretation. As I mentioned earlier, jazz interpretation sees hope in the face of many obstacles and challenges. This hope, however, is fading as Cornel West prophetically warns. He is correct to point out that nihilism is increasing daily in the black world. At the time of this writing, I believe there remains but a small window of time to perform radical spiritual surgery that is needed in the Eurocentric church, academy, and the body politic. This last claim is at the heart of the work of Du Bois, Thurman, and Cone and, later in this chapter, you will see that Michael Eric Dyson makes similar contributions to the Du Boisian prophetic tradition.

Du Boisian Double Consciousness, Congo Square and Ragtime Jazz

At this point, my intention is to explore double consciousness and its relationship with jazz. I have located their shared taproot in the Congo Square events where we can see African American double consciousness and jazz emerge as an alternative or otherwise interpretation (and a narrative) to Eurocentrism. For those who preach in the Du Boisian tradition, and for those who employ the Du Boisian hermeneutic of double consciousness, they must be aware of how double consciousness functions as a hermeneutic in texts. By tracing jazz toward double consciousness, I identify the Du Boisian hermeneutic.

The two Du Bois essays that I cite below are "Negro Art and Literature" and "The American Folk Song." In both essays, Du Bois poetically chronicles the contributions that he ascribes to black genius. In the first passage I point to what some viewed as a public spectacle, but you will see that, among other things, the "Bamboula" dance was a democratic act in the public square, and, in addition, I make the claim that double consciousness informs the dance. In the second passage, I make a similar claim that double consciousness is present in the early formation of jazz.

From "Negro Art and Literature"

Beyond the specific ways in which the Negro has contributed to American art, stand[s] undoubtedly his spirit of gayety and the exotic charm which his presence has loaned the parts of America which were spiritually free enough to enjoy it. In New Orleans, for instance, after the War of 1812 and among the free people of color, there was a beautiful blossoming of artistic life which the sordid background of slavery had to work hard to kill. The "people of color" grew in number and waxed wealthy. Famous streets even today bear testimony of their old importance: Congo Square in the old Creole quarter where Negroes danced the weird "Bamboula" long before Coleridge-Taylor made it immortal and Gottschalk wrote his Negro dance; Camp Street and Julia Street took their names from the old Negro field and from the woman who owned land along the canal. Americans and Spanish both tried to get the support and sympathy of the free Negroes.[30]

From "The American Folk Song"

Little beauty has America given the world save the rude grandeur God himself stamped on her bosom; the human spirit in this new world has expressed itself in vigor and ingenuity rather than in beauty. And so by fateful chance the Negro folksong the rhythmic cry of the slave—stands today not simply as the sole American music, but as the most beautiful expression of human experience born this side the seas. It has been neglected, it has persistently been mistaken and misunderstood; but notwithstanding, it still remains as the singular spiritual heritage of the nation and the greatest gift of the Negro people.[31]

What is important? In the first passage, Du Bois points out that the first authentic American aesthetic grew out of the art and commerce of free people of color. The early people of color did find signs of free expression; it was also true that many people of color were slaves in New Orleans in 1812. If all are not free, then no one is free. This provides a sociohistorical context for the emergences of the Bamboula dance. It was an act of democratic protest that revealed how free and slave people of color shared a common worldview, which is double consciousness. Indeed the point of departure for double consciousness is protest for democracy; these shape the aesthetic contours that make jazz.

---

30. W.E.B. Du Bois, "Negro Art and Literature" in *The Gift of Black Folk* (Garden City Park, NY: Square One publishers, 2009). 136.
31. Ibid., "The American Folk Song" and also see "Of Sorrow Songs" in Du Bois, *Souls*, 186.

In the second passage, we sense the common folk story or the black folks' narrative forming out of the common "rhythmic cry of the slave," and I agree with Du Bois that the black folks' narrative "stands today not simply as the sole American music, but as the most beautiful expression of human experience born this side the seas."[32]

What is significant about the two passages? "Negro Art and Literature" expresses that people of color grew in number and waxed wealthy in a similar fashion as did the Hebrew people during their time in bondage and slavery in Egypt (Ex.1:8-13). The biblical account provides a narrative context and reason for why black folks in New Orleans resisted and protested for democracy. Although some of them owned property, this did not guarantee for them any political rights. Needless to say, political rights are only one part of the Du Boisian unholy trinity: race, economics, and politics.[33] Second, in "The American Folk Song," Du Bois comments, "this new world has expressed itself in vigor and ingenuity rather than in beauty." I translate "vigor and ingenuity" to mean markets, commerce, scientific discoveries, all arms of capitalism.

This affords Du Bois rhetorical space to charge white Americans with materialism and Eurocentric pursuits of wealth instead of developing an authentic American aesthetic. By default then, African Americans offer America its authentic cultural aesthetics, which are very important for developing a national ethos, rhetoric, and interpretation of that narrative. Thus, the "authentic interpretation" that Cone pursues is Du Boisian because it points toward America's authentic interpretation which the blues provides.

In the events of Congo Square, Du Bois identifies protestant defiance in the behavior of "people of color." Second, in "The American Folk Song" (this passage also appears in "Of the Sorrow Songs" in *Souls*), Du Bois speaks of American beauty as a "rude grandeur God himself stamped on her bosom," but the human experience of beauty that America possesses is a national gift

---

32. Ibid.
33. See W.E.B. Du Bois, *Dusk of Dawn: An Essay Toward An Autobiography of A Race* Concept (Piscataway, New Jersey: Transactions Publishers, 2011), 47.

provided by the genius of Negroes. Du Bois, in but a few words, demonstrates his understanding of a dialectic relationship between beauty and defiance. This relationship informs people of color's worldview; namely, that symmetrical beauty coupled with defiance points toward harmony and justice. In short, to coexist with everyone, people of color understand equality is assured only by their constant pursuit of democracy.

Free People of Color, Slaves of African Descent, Their Democratic Protest

In pursuit of democracy, free people of color alongside African American slaves coalesced around beauty and defiance to form democratic protest. Through use of vocals, musicians, and rhythmic, hypnotic patterns they called the juba and with a dance they called the Bamboula they protested against their socioeconomic and political conditions:

> Whites were shocked by what they saw; intricate vocal choirs, massed groups of musicians playing rhythmic slapping patterns called the juba to the slow sensual gyrations known as Bamboula.[34]

From the sociomargins, authentic democratic genius surfaces in America.[35] This shows how Congo Square dancers served as

---

34. Gary Giddens and Scott DeVeaux, *Jazz* (New York: Norton, 2009), 77.
35. Bryan Crable, "Race and Rhetoric of Motives: Kenneth Burkes' Dialogue with Ralph Ellison" in *Rhetoric Society Quarterly* 33, no. 3 (Summer 2003), 5-25. In the conclusion of his essay, Crable attempts to create a synthesis by referring to universal truths shared between Ellison and Burke. Thus he makes this statement: "Specifically, we would ground our theoretical effort in the assumption shared by both men: the significance of human symbol use (and mis-use)." By this, I associate Congo Square dances with Ellison and Burke's human symbols, but I ground these human symbols as protests disguised as metaphors that communicated dormant meaning. Why was the meaning dormant? Because of semantics, the dominant culture did not perceive truth grounded in their understanding of what dancing was for; that is, for the dominant culture, dance is for entertainment.

human language symbols of American democratic protests. By sociomargins, I mean a social location for people groups identified as "other-wise"; unequal and disqualified by something undemocratic.

At a glance, some of the early observers thought the Congo Square dance performances were solely a public spectacle and for entertainment. Others were not sure. As previously mentioned, "whites were shocked" by the dancing black bodies flailing in mysterious motions.[36] Those who danced in Congo Square were human language symbols, which I define as semiotics (or semantics, syntactic and pragmatics) of jazz—like hermeneutic interpretation.

Through mysterious motions, however, what resulted is these dances gave multiple voices to black folks' communication theory. A function of the Congo Square dancing was semantic appropriation as described by Henry Louis Gates and Mikhail Bakhtin, "as a double-voiced world, that is, a word utterance in this context, decolonized for the black purposes by inserting a new semantic orientation into a word which already has and retains its own orientation."[37]

These dances, however, were human symbols of protest, created in the semantics of the creative genius of the sociomarginalized peoples. See Henry Louis Gates, Jr., "A Myth of Origins: Esu-Elegbara and the Signfying Monkey" in *The Signifying Monkey: A Theory of African-American Literary Criticism* (Oxford: Oxford University Press, 1988), 50.

36. Giddens and Deveaux, "Congo Square, Creoles of Color and Uptown Negroes," 77.

37. Gates, "A Myth of Origins," 50. Gates provides a passage from Bakhtin, work:

> The audible of double-voiced word is therefore meant to hear both a version of the original utterance as the embodiment of its speaker's point of view (or "semantic position") and the second speaker's evaluation of the utterance from a different point of view. I find it helpful to picture a double-voiced word as a special sort of palimpsest in which the upper-most inscription is a commentary on the one beneath it, which the reader (or audience) can know only by reading through the commentary that obscures in

Why is this significant? In the Congo Square dances, I am able to locate semantics, double voice, social location, and signifying in particular. What is more, these parallel Du Boisian double consciousness. Thus, double consciousness is located in the Congo Square dancers' mysterious motions. Their bodies in motion are transformed into living metaphors (which signifies *intertextuality*). A second function that I am able to locate in the Congo Square protests are forms of signification, or what Gates describes in black folks' vernacular as signifying. In this instance, dancing in Congo Square signifies an organized protest movement, with sociopolitical messages that go far beyond spectacle and entertainment.

I contend that in addition to the aforementioned, these dances are living examples of how an analysis of social location helps Du Boisian interpreters to identify the presence of double consciousness in biblical texts.

Semantics, double voice and signifying are examples of how interpretation of meaning may remain dormant or deferred until a particular culture evolves.[38] That is, Congo Square dancers

---

the very process evaluating. See Ferdinand de Saussure, *Course in General Linguistics*, ed. Charles Bally and Albert Sechehaye, trans. Wade Baskin (New York: McGraw-Hill, 1966), 71. Also see quoted in Gary Saul Morson *The Boundaries of Genre: Dostoevsky's Diary of a Writer and the Traditions of Literary Utopia* (Austin: University of Texas, 1981), 108.

38. Gates, "A Myth of Origins," *The Signifying Monkey*, 25. What I refer to as dormant meaning, Gates describes as intermediate meaning. That is, "The text, in other words, is not fixed in any determinate sense; in one sense, it consists of the dynamic and intermediate relationship between truth on the one hand and understanding on the other," 25. Species of black preaching use tropes and metaphors to communicate nuanced, if not deferred, meaning; this is consistent with my claim that a rhetorical act can be an example of dormant meaning. For example, I associate my use of dormant meaning with Perelman's comments about dormant metaphor, "This strength [dormant metaphors] is due to the fact that it obtains its effect by drawing on a stock of analogical material that gains ready acceptance because it is not merely known, but is integrated by language into the cultural tradition." What Perelman describes, functions in rhetoric that originates in marginalized subcultures. See his "Dormant Metaphors"

performed as living semanticists; they created a living subtextual narrative or what is more commonly called intertextuality. Prophetic critique of double consciousness then is visualized and on display and, what is more, it greatly depends on a relationship between intertextuality, semantics, double voice, signification, social location, deferred understanding of meaning, and other dimensions of Du Boisian hermeneutic of double consciousness.

As previously mentioned, analysis of social location identifies the presence of double consciousness. Consider the social location of those who performed in Congo Square. They were sociomarginalized across class (free Africans and slaves of African descent). They shared a common location and worldview and therefore they employed double voice and signification art, a disguise that helped them to protest against their oppressors. To avoid punitive action from their oppressors, the art of the Congo Square vocalists, dancers and musicians deferred their oppressors' understanding of meaning. By this, I mean that the Congo Square performers understood their cultural *difference*.

With the power of *difference*, nuance and mystery and through the power of dance, they created an attractive, but alternative text. It was immediately perceived as culturally different from that of the dominant class's culture. It made the dominant class's text unattractive, undesirable and from that point forward unsustainable. Those interlopers became the interrogators of the living text. The Congo Square vocalists, musicians, and dancers discovered that deferred understanding led toward cultural synthesis. As a result of the newest synthesis, the dominant culture began to gradually change, and, therefore, the Congo Square dancing served as an example for how double voice and signification have a role in a different cultural interpretation.

In 2007, I observed then presidential candidate Barack Hussein Obama campaign as a change agent. A majority of Americans and world citizens viewed him in a similar way. After his election, it was time for President Obama to implement his promised change. To change the American body politic is to challenge the American

---

in Chaim Perleman and L. Olbrechts-Tyteca, *The New Rhetoric: A Treatise on Argumentation* (South Bend, IN: Notre Dame University Press, 1969), 9. 404.

dominant culture's values system (which is Eurocentrism). Obama presented our contemporary cultural thesis as unattractive, undesirable, and unsustainable to postmodern audiences. As a response, Obama proposed to Americans new possibilities and new benefits associated with a new vision or new cultural thesis; his new thesis is cultural *difference*. Some American citizens rightly viewed Obama's different American culture as antithetical to the status quo, but cultural *difference* is democracy enfleshed.

Cultural *difference* is indeed democracy but it is more; it is the seedbed for pyschospiritual transformation. Pyschospiritual transformation translated into policies that challenge sociopolitical, socioeconomic, and sociotheological underpinnings of dominating Eurocentric American values, mores, and traditions is called "mainstream values" by the establishment. To manage his American cultural transformation, Obama employs the power of *difference*, nuance, and mystery disguised in a metaphoric Congo Square dance.

The Bamboula dance of public policy transformation is a hypnotic rhythm; it is a kind of juba. Obama uses the juba to present an alternative text (narrative) for American culture. Obama's alternative text signifies cultural *difference* and some American citizens have not immediately understood it. For those who do not readily understand the symbolism of the performers, then, fullest meaning is deferred. In order for these citizens to understand later, they will have to embrace a hermeneutic of *difference* to follow Obama's jazz-like Congo Square "Bamboula and juba" dance, which I trace toward double consciousness.

Black Bodies and Double Consciousness

For Congo Square dancers, the employment of their bodies was the only resource available to organize and implement their protest events. This serves as sociohistorical and sociopolitical points of departure for our understanding of the role that African American music, literature, art, and other rhetorical acts share in hermeneutic formation. Thus, the Du Boisian hermeneutic of double consciousness formation creates synergy that demands democracy. Semantics, double voice, signifying, social location, and intertextuality— together they are informants of double consciousness that informs this hermeneutic.

In this context, the Congo Square dancers are human language symbols that perform as living democratic protests. This is a strong indication that the Du Boisian hermeneutic tradition redefines American democratic tradition. This hermeneutic formation begins in the deepest sociomargins of African American culture. What is more, because of intertextuality, a different subtext and commentary of the culture at large emerges. This subtext that I identify as intertextuality informs African American religious music, art, dance, and pulpit oratory. All of these shape an African American prophetic worldview, which I locate in the Du Boisian prophetic tradition.

As previously mentioned, the Du Boisian prophetic tradition is the taproot of what I argue shares the same context as jazz. Birthed in Congo Square, both are synonymous with protest, resistance, and democracy. The Du Boisian tradition, like jazz, comments on the dominating culture, and the Du Boisian tradition offers commentary on dominating cultural norms.[39] What is more, the Du Boisian prophetic tradition, like that of the jazz tradition, asks similar questions about epistemological points of departure that constitute Eurocentrism. It follows then, that people of color question Eurocentric classifications that afford people of noncolor *de jure* and *de facto* advantages that are embedded in Eurocentric hegemony. The United States Constitution is an example. From the beginning, people of color have engaged in a dialectic struggle for

---

39. In my description of the Du Boisian hermeneutic of double consciousness, I have employed what I refer to as pyschospiritualism as a central characteristic. This is a way to analyze dominant and marginalized cultural standings. It is interesting, however, that I am able to associate with Chaim Perleman in at least two ways, which are argumentation and pathological. Perleman's "The Theory of argumentation which is the aid of discourse aims at securing an efficient action, on minds might have been treated as a branch of psychology." Second and of specific interest for me, Perleman treats pathology as transposition, emphasizing the symmetry (Put yourself in his place!) provides a basis for what is deemed to be a well-founded application of the rule of justice..." argumentation and pathology as I present Perleman here are points of entry into double consciousness and a hermeneutic of suspicion; two key parts of my hermeneutic and homiletic system. Perleman and Olbrechts-Tyteca, *The New Rhetoric*, 9, 222.

equality. As a result, Du Boisian interpretation is an expression of dialectic tension, which often is located in dissent. Moreover, Du Boisian dissent frequently leads to democratic debate, but always Du Boisian dissent is an expression of interpretation that seeks to make crooked places straight in the process and pursuit of democracy.[40]

Therefore, the Du Boisian prophetic tradition refutes Eurocentrism and redefines democracy. I suggest that the Du Boisian prophetic tradition is intrinsic to the very meaning (though often deferred) of American democracy and that the Du Boisian tradition makes again the crooked places straight in the progress of sociopolitical and pyschospiritual transformation for the majorities as well as the marginalized in Eurocentric culture.[41] *A hermeneutic that includes these characteristics is the kind of hermeneutic that points all preachers and homiliticians of all cultural points of departure forward in the twenty-first century.* By its very nature, this hermeneutic addresses diverse musings; it serves human strivings and leanings for equality.

Once this kind of hermeneutic theory, and what it embodies, is grasped, it presents a way forward for Du Boisian preachers. This means that this hermeneutic signifies a new approach and creates a different way to comment on Eurocentrism. Like the organized dissimilarities cited in Congo Square, this hermeneutic embraces

---

40. Isaiah 45:2 (My translation).
41. A second primary text for this project is *The Souls of Black Folks*. Du Bois provides the clearest written insight in the psychological and spiritual integration for black folks. What is more, he demonstrates similar needs for other people and in the face of (Western) culture, which is rapidly becoming nihilistic. Therefore, I will address pyschospiritualism as a part of my approach to homiletics; hermeneutically it functions in the double consciousness not only for African Americans, but also for Euro-Americans. An example is the predominately-white audiences who attended black performances by artists such as Miles Davis and Otis Redding. Vicariously, through these performers whites experience pleasure and pain and liberation and protest against their own hegemonic strongholds on democracy (Eurocentrism). Ironically, I have cited that many whites did not understand the democratic protest hidden in the art of dance, specifically at Congo Square, but during jazz concerts and soul performances, indeed whites began to understand their needs to feel something other than good about themselves.

dialectical tension in the world. Like a jazz composition, dialectical tension may be left unresolved, sometimes for generations, sometimes forever, but it gives democratic voice to its aficionados.[42]

I want to remind us, that jazz grew out of democratic resistance against dominating cultural cachets, mores, and traditions that discredit human equality. Du Bois writing in "American Folk Music" draws parallels between spirituals, Bamboula, and jazz; and when referring to jazz, he clumsily describes jazz as "ragtime" and later as "ragtime jazz."

> It is to be noted that whereas the chief characteristic of ragtime is rhythm, the chief characteristic of the spirituals is melody. The melodies of "Steal Away to Jesus," "Swing Low, Sweet Chariot," "Nobody Knows de Trouble I See," "Couldn't Hear Nobody Pray," "Deep River," "O, Freedom Over Me," and many others of these songs possess a beauty that is—what shall I say? Poignant. In the riotous of Ragtime the Negro expressed his irrepressible buoyancy, his keen response to the sheer joy of living; in the spirituals he voiced his sense of beauty and his deep religious feeling.[43]

What is clear, Du Bois expresses the religious nature that belongs to African American music, dance and art, and I will add secular and sacred oratory. By implication, Du Bois expresses also that the African American aesthetic grew from double consciousness. To be sure, dominating culture causes to congeal among people of color, a psychological and spiritual collectiveness to form.

---

42. Perleman and Olbrechts-Tyteca, *The New Rhetoric*. I will refer to this volume repeatedly. In this instance, I want to point readers and researchers toward Perleman's work in "Breaking of Connecting Links and Dissociation," 411. Perelman's study of new rhetoric parallels black folks' preaching and its phenomenological power.
43. Du Bois, "The American Folk Song" in *The Gift of Black Folk*, 130.

Double Consciousness and Its Relationship with Fear and Hatred

As I indicated earlier, nihilism is increasing daily in the black world. Thus I believe it is necessary to address two universal human emotions—fear and hatred—that I associate with nihilism. Fear, I believe, leads to hatred. These emotions too often cause misunderstandings in racial dialogues that are intended to find ways and means toward reconciliation. In addition, fear and hatred distort worldviews and, as a result, hermeneutics.

> The ever-present fear that besets the vast poor, the economically and socially insecure, is a fear of still a different breed. It is a climate closing in; it is like the fog in San Francisco or in London. It is nowhere in particular yet everywhere. It is a mood which one carries around with [herself] himself, distilled from the acrid conflict with which his [her] days are surrounded. It has roots deep in the heart of the relations between the weak and the strong; between the controllers of environment and those who are controlled by it.[44]

Thurman describes fear as an emotion that is "closing in," like a fog. He describes fear also as an expression of economic and social insecurity, and he rightly asserts that fear is rapidly closing in on our Eurocentric-culture. Fear, however, has moved far beyond this. Today fear is a nihilistic psychological condition. If we read Thurman's prophetic insights about fear through a nihilism lens, we are able to understand what is current and happening in our contemporary settings. His second assertion suggests a class struggle over poverty, citing those who control environments and those controlled by them. Of course, poverty is perceived to be a "colored problem" but we know that poverty has no racial boundaries; sadly, however, social responses to poverty do. These social responses, reliant on misguided perceptions, become complex racial and class political struggles.

---

44. Thurman, "Fear" in *Jesus and the Disinherited*, 36-37.

Unfortunately, "Hatred cannot be defined. It can only be described."[45] I suggest that this is due to sociomarginalization that breeds hatred outside and inside life—within the veil, and, what is more, unfortunately, hatred informs double consciousness. Thurman's chapter "Hate" in *Jesus and the Disinherited* remains relevant in our contemporary times. Thurman believes rightly that hatred of other people stems from a lack of fellowship with those hated:

> Hate is another of the hounds of hell that dog the footsteps of the disinherited in season and out of season. During times of war hatred becomes quite respectable, even though it has to masquerade often under the guise of patriotism. To even the casual observer during the last war it was obvious that the Pearl Harbor attack by the Japanese gave many persons in our country an apparent justification for indulging all of their anticolored feelings. In a Chicago cab, enroute to the University from Englewood, this fact was dramatized to me. The cab had stopped for a red light. Apropos of no conversation the driver turned to me, saying, "Who do they think they are? Those little yellow dogs think they can do that to white men and get away with it?"[46]

This story told by Thurman is alarming on many levels. The first was the cabdriver's assumed solidarity with Thurman. Though Thurman does not readily state that his driver was a white person of European descent, it is plausible. On the other hand, Thurman, an African American listening to a European American casting aspersions upon Japanese immigrants would have been vastly unusual. To accept this reading assumes that the driver was willing to overlook his (or her) racial differences with Thurman to hate the Japanese.

If we examine Thurman's social location, we may learn much from this episode. Thurman was a man who possessed the highest academic credentials that a university system bestows, and,

---

45. Ibid., 75.
46. Ibid., 74.

presumably, Thurman's credentials were different from those of his cabdriver. By reading the passage this way, Thurman is saying either that the cabdriver was willing to overlook Thurman's credentials to discredit the Japanese, or, because of the cabdriver's skin privilege, he or she felt that no inhibitions were warranted. If this is an accurate close reading, Thurman's credentials did not matter and did not change the feeling of superiority that the driver possessed. Thus a sense of racial superiority supersedes class distinctions. What is more, a sense of racial superiority gives an individual or a group permission to embrace whomever and to discredit whomever in order to reinforce their worldview.

A second dilemma, plausibly, is not one of racial inequality but, in fact, a dilemma that is rooted in a class struggle. Let us assume that Thurman and the cabdriver are members of the same racial classification, and that Thurman's social class was higher than that of his driver. This is plausible because of the driver's apparent and immediate assumed comfort with Thurman; the driver takes this for granted, and he or she assumes permission to vent against Japanese immigrants. It is further plausible to read the passage this way, because the cabdriver fears that the Japanese immigrant population is gaining on him or her, he or she feels threatened, after all at the time of Thurman's observations, blacks were clearly on the lowest economic rung of the American social ladder.

If this is the closest reading, the driver assumes fellowship with Thurman because they are members of the same racial classification. If this is so, it also gives the driver a perception that they may spew their fear and hatred of Japanese immigrants without morally rational justifications. If I read Thurman's story correctly, same racial classification assumes a similar worldview and further assumes that same racial classification supersedes difference in socioeconomic class distinction.

Finally, what seems of import here is that Du Boisian interpreters must take social location and context seriously to make the best hermeneutical choices. Because of skin privilege, whites assume superiority over blacks despite social class distinctions. Because of skin inferiority (though strangely, this too is skin privilege), blacks assume equality with blacks despite social class distinctions. In each of these ways to interpret Thurman's passage, I point out that I am able to locate double consciousness.

Tupac's Nihilism and Du Boisian Conclusions

As mentioned earlier, "Nihilism is not new in black America" and it is increasing daily. In response to this claim, I intend to trace forward the Du Boisian hermeneutic of double consciousness to Michael Eric Dyson's groundbreaking contributions. By employing Dyson's analysis of hip-hop culture, I locate double consciousness and note that it is similar to other species of black expressions such as sorrow songs, the blues, and jazz genres. Dyson found his voice and hit his intellectual stride in his writings on hip-hop culture. He appropriates from rhetoricians what they refer to as black folks' death and mourning narrative, which informs his analysis of Tupac Shakur's tragisaga life.

The art form that made Tupac a household name is commonly called "rap." What may not be well known is that "rap" is a pan-African invention. Rap too was birthed in a sociopolitical setting, similar to today's immigration controversies. When rap music emerged in its sociopolitical context, it too held our national attention (nothing new about that). What is more, rap found an audience at a time of declining institutional spheres for the black counterpublic. This occurred during our national transition from civil rights, to post civil rights, and more narrowly from the Black Power movement to hip-hop itself:

> Moreover, the impact of that other important piece of 1965 legislation, the Hart-Celler Immigration Act, which eliminated country-specific quotas on immigration, complicated the very idea of a "black" community. Between 1960 and 1984 some 604,104 immigrants from the Anglophone Caribbean and 141,109 from Haiti would come to the United States, great[ly] affecting the form and content of black cultural expression. Among the new arrivals was DJ Kool Herc, a Jamaican immigrant, who introduced us to the "break beat" and aided in the creation of the genre of music called rap. [Michael] Dawson goes as far as to say that "taken together, the disintegration of the institutional bases of black counterpublic since the early 1970s and increasing black skepticism regarding the existence of a bundle of issues and strategies that define a black agenda should lead us to question whether we can

assert that a subaltern counterpublic exists—and if it does, now how healthy is it?"[47]

The break beat is similar to the Bamboula dance and juba, a counterclockwise step that emerges during Congo Square. The break beat signifies an alternative beauty and defiance motif that provides a critique of the black establishment's failure to prepare the hip-hop generation for a transfer of social leadership. The break beat fills this void in the Public Square and sphere. This context shapes Tupac's worldview and our understanding of hip-hop's militancy.

I trace hip-hop to Black Panther culture. Dyson writes of Tupac's "revolutionary roots" in "The Son of a Panther: A Postrevolutionary."[48] According to Dyson, "Tupac was the hip-hop James Baldwin: an excruciatingly conscientious scribe whose narratives flamed with moral outrage at black suffering." Thus, born and conditioned by his mother and his godfather, Black Panther Elmer "Geronimo" Pratt's ideology, Tupac learned to invent rap lyrics that demonstrated his understanding and youthful outrage over imposed socioeconomic and sociopolitical disparities created by Eurocentrism.

Tupac indeed represents a generation of African American youth and their obsessions, if not their romantic perversions with death and materialism. Dyson writes that "Panther purists claim that Tupac's extravagant materialism and defiant hedonism are the death knell of political conscience, the ultimate sellout of revolutionary ideals."[49] Tupac's materialism and "thug fantasies"— gangsterism, financial malfeasance, and "brutal factionalism"— were all signs of his internal conflict between Black Panther revolutionary ideals and the fruits of financial successes in Eurocentric culture. In short, because of his double consciousness, Tupac found it hard to serve two masters. In both instances, "Tupac is the conflicted metaphor of black revolution's large

---

47. Eddie Glaude, Jr., *In a Shade of Blue: Pragmatism and the Politics of Black America* (Chicago: University of Chicago Press, 2007), 147.

48. Michael Eric Dyson, "The Son of a Panther: A Post revolutionary," *Holler If You Hear Me: Searching for Tupac Shakur* (New York: Basic Civitas Books, 2001), 47-67.

49. Ibid., 49.

FROM BEHIND THE SORROW SONGS ⧕

aspirations and failed agendas."[50] In sum, Tupac's motivation is unsustainable and fatalistic.

Of course this is generational, pyschospiritual nihilism. And, what is more, Dyson accurately locates in hip-hop culture a relationship between nihilism and double consciousness. "To borrow W.E.B. Du Bois's notion of dual consciousness, in Tupac's two warring ideals were (w)rapped in one dark body. Now the question to ask is: 'Could Tupac's dogged strength alone have kept him from being torn asunder?'"[51] Hip-hop's rap music is today's sorrow songs, the blues, and jazz that points toward today's double consciousness. It is post-civil rights, and it is something that mirrors the Black Power (nationalist) movement. Like the genres that precede it, sociomarginalization is its seedbed. Unlike its predecessors, however, hip-hop is rightly granted a different and distinct culture and status. I believe these other African American genres also signified different and distinct cultures that are different from Eurocentric culture. Historically, however, their equal status among cultures has not been recognized.

I have included a long excerpt from Dyson's chapter "But Do the Lord Care" because I believe that Dyson captures the pulse of the hip-hop culture's worldview. In this excerpt, you will see the impact of Tupac's artistic expression, which identifies the hip-hop generation's shared experiences and that further points toward double consciousness:

> When Tupac was murdered, Baptist pastor Reverend Willie Wilson received calls from a couple of local radio station personalities. "Reverend, can you do something?" they asked. "We're getting a flood of calls from young people who are in such grief and pain." Wilson agreed to hold a memorial service for the slain rapper in his Washington, D.C., church. It drew youth from across the city who were, in Wilson's words, "befuddled, bewildered, lost, [and] disillusioned." In Wilson's mind, the service would give "these young people a place to channel their feelings." Wilson's eulogy may have startled some in the

---

50. Ibid., 49.
51. Ibid.

religious community and beyond. "Hip-hop artists in many instances are the preachers of their generation, preaching a message which, too often those who have been given the charge to preach prophetic works to the people have not given," Wilson said at the service. "The Tupacs of the world have responded in many instances have reflected... that Scripture that comes to mind: 'If you don't speak out, then the rocks will cry out.' I think in a very real sense these pop artists are the rocks that are crying out with prophetic words." About Tupac's role in what might be termed a postindustrial urban prophecy, Wilson was clear: "He was their preacher, if you will, who brought a message that [young people] can identify with, related to what was real, that spoke to the reality of the circumstances, situations [and] environments they have to deal with every day."[52]

Reverend Wilson's claim that Tupac and the "Tupacs," are (secular) preachers of their generation (as were Curtis Mayfield and Bob Marley and as Sade is) for many young people. Indeed, the contemporary Tupac's message is startling to their audiences and critiques alike. It is understandable then, to see that Tupac's message certainly was startling for many ordained preachers and faithful parishioners.

Wilson is correct also in his prophetic leanings. What Wilson sees in hip-hop is its cultural critique of Eurocentrism. This is no different from the role that cultural critics have seen in social function of sorrow songs, the blues, and jazz. Historically their role is a sociopolitical critique of our past and present culture. There were many who did not embrace their sacred-secular cultural interpretation and message. This happened and continues to happen, in part, because many people do not recognize the significance of some hip-hoppers' prophetic message. (Though these claims are important, I do not compare their prophetic utterances and observations to biblically inspired eschatological claims.)

---

52. Ibid., 201-202.

Like their predecessors, a hip-hop rapper's message does not affirm Eurocentrism, which seeks to set our cultural norms and expectations, and, for people of color, Eurocentrism attempts to shape our acceptable social behavior and our willingness to accept our cultural limitations—life within the veil. In fact, it is important to remember that like sorrow songs, the blues, and jazz, hip-hop's rap was born out of resistance to Eurocentric hegemony.

This brief but necessary analysis offers a path toward the Du Boisian hermeneutic of double consciousness. And in this way I am able to identify and locate the hermeneutic in our current culture. Indeed Dyson presents a complex Tupac who personifies secular-sacredness and, at the same time, a nihilistic humanness that fights for hope and transcendence. Dyson provides balance, however, when he refers to Bishop T.D. Jakes' views on Tupac. Jakes sees Tupac squarely in the domain of the blues' side of the Du Boisian hermeneutic and rhetorical tradition. Dyson writes, "According to Bishop T.D. Jakes, Tupac's messages were certainly prophetic, but in a way that revealed his pain and suffering not in a manner that helped society clarify its direction. Tupac's message was "so prophetic that in many ways" it warned of the 'inevitable outcome.'"[53] Jakes then means that hip-hop culture identifies similar challenges that are historically present and face every generation of people of color.

Hip-hop's response, however, is different, and it is louder, venting, and vulgar. Indeed Jakes openly admits that Tupac's outspoken lyrics and language do not reflect his Christian tradition, which I believe is overly informed by Eurocentrism's underpinnings. Because of this, I do not think that he sees hip-hop's relationship with Black Power rhetoric that precedes it. What is important to note, however, is that each generation's suffering increases, and thus their crying aloud is louder, and their lyrics and language are angrier and more desperate.

I understand Tupac's rap lyrics as communal-collective catharsis and purging. In this way Tupac's rap lyrics parallel Du Bois's view of the role of sorrow songs. Tupac is crying out through his lyrics, which express "pain and suffering," which parallels the Psalmist's expressions located in Psalm 22.

---

53. Ibid., 208.

Dear Lord
As we down here, struggle for as long as we know
In search of a paradise to touch (my nigga Johnny J)
Dreams are dreams, and reality seems to be the only place to
go
The only place for us
 I know, try to make the best of bad situations
 Seems to be my life's story
 Ain't no glory in pain, a soldier's story in vain
 And can't nobody live this life for me
 It's a ride you all, a long hard ride.[54]

Jakes does see Tupac's lyrics as fulfilling a prophetic function, but he also sees Tupac's songs as void of helping society or what Jakes characterizes as the failure to "clarify its direction."[55] Prophetic talk is identifiable because people recognize its relevance, its significance, and that its impetus is spoken "for the people." Recently we recognize a revival of spoken word recitals in secular and sacred spaces; these recitals belong to the prophetic tradition.

Prophetic speech speaks of possibilities outside of parochialisms that limit black folks' lives. For this to occur, however, the preacher and artist must risk being misunderstood by the majorities and the minorities, and ironically they must risk being understood by majorities and the minorities as well. Tupac was understood by those with whom he was communicating. Those who shared his anger and double consciousness embraced his message.

Tupac, Double Consciousness, Congo Square and the Black Body

Because I am rethinking the literal devaluation of the black body through symbolism, I have taken the liberty to relocate Tupac's black body into Congo Square. I suggest that his interpretation parallels characteristics of the Du Boisian

---

54. Tupac Shakur, "Black Jesus," 2PAC+OUTLAWZ, *Still I Rise*, 1999, Interscope Records, 4904132.
55. Michael Eric, Dyson, *Holler If You Hear Me*, 208.

hermeneutic of double consciousness.[56] I place his black body among the other black bodies, namely among the Congo Square performers: the dancers, vocalists and musicians. I further assume that Tupac shared their cultural worldview and experiences that inform and shape double consciousness.

The Congo Square performers created democratic protests with their black bodies disguised in dance performances, songs, and music. Earlier, I emphasized that these performers became living metaphors and semantics.[57] Their artistic performances signified that it was only their bodies that they could employ in order to communicate their human equality. In a very similar way, the hip-hop artists follow a parallel pattern. When rap artists take to a stage, they participate in a long tradition of democratic protest. In a real sense, these rap artists transform their stage into a Congo Square event. It is a cultural ritual of affirmation and reminiscent of the Bamboula dance and the juba. The performances are free-flowing like jazz; the lyrics are bluesy—even nihilistic and predicated upon cultural "preunderstanding." Strangely, however, though too often the lyrics are nihilistic, the performances remain cathartic and purging experiences. This provides a bluesy hope in the face of doubt, despair, and the shadows of death. Always a rapper's performance is an act of beauty and defiance wrapped in their swagger, swerve, and flailing black bodies swaying to the beat that belongs to hip-hop.

The black body's beauty is captured in hip-hop's rapping break beat sounds that are similar to the Bamboula and juba—again a counterclockwise movement. Hip-hoppers' swaggering black bodies' movements are a signal of a countercultural movement that is taking place beneath the mainstream's noses. Of course, this is like a prophetic parable. According to the writer of the Gospel of Mark, Jesus said, "To you has been given the mystery of the

---

56. I have determined that the Du Boisian hermeneutic of double consciousness's characteristics is as follows: double voice, deferred understanding of meaning, social location, pyschospiritualism, and dialectic tension.

57. See in this chapter's notes 22- 27. I have argued that Congo Square dancers are living metaphors and semantics. They are living texts that point toward double consciousness. Congo Square is described by Giddens and DeVeaux in *Jazz*, 77.

Kingdom of God, but those who are outside get everything in parables" and, he continues, "and that while seeking, they may see and not perceive, and while hearing, they may not understand, otherwise they might return and be forgiven" (Mk. 4:11-12).

The rap artist's hypnotic rhythms are like those of the original Congo Square performing cast. And like the Congo Square performers, hip-hoppers' rap music also defers meaning and employs intertextuality to encode their message that is decoded by persons who share a similar sociomarginalization and worldview and hermeneutic grid. The black body in a swaying movement is a kind of beauty that signifies leanings toward harmony, which can be understood as democracy.

The black body's defiance is what Dyson identifies in his chapter "I Got Your Name Tatted on My Arm." The tattoos represent defiance and swagger. Tattoos that cover nearly all parts of the human body startle our conventional understanding about the human body's sacredness. At the same time, the tattoos reveal what Tupac understood about his body; he understood that his body was placed under sociopolitical and economic limitations; that his body and all other black bodies were subjugated to the Jim and Jane Crow traditions, mores, and myths that undergird Eurocentrism's hegemony. What is desecration to the body to many of us, for hip-hoppers tattoos are their personal defiance against authoritarian power. I empathize with hip-hoppers. I recognize that many of them are crying out for justice that is similar to Buddhist monks during the Vietnam War.[58] In protest against brutalization caused by warring factions, they set themselves on fire. Their defiance became a work of art something, strangely poetic and peculiarly beautiful.

In the following excerpt, Dyson shares a conversation that he had with Johnnie Cochran, the late attorney of O. J. Simpson fame, about Tupac:

> "One day he had his shirt on," Johnnie Cochran remembers of an early encounter with his then new client

---

58. Since the early 1970s, the images of the Buddhists monks are forever seared into my memory, and these memories have disturbed my social and political consciousness.

Tupac Shakur. "He took his shirt off, and across his stomach he had 'thug life' on it. There's all this writing. It [was] all over the place. I would kid him about not coming to court with a lot of jewelry and stuff on. He was a very handsome boy, very handsome. He had earrings too, you know; that is the style. But he had all this writing on his body. I asked, 'Why do you put all that stuff on your body? Is that necessary?'"[59]

Cochran, the consummate professional, could not keep from being fixated on Tupac's body tattoos. Cochran makes an effort to emphasize that Tupac was handsome, but it was the countercultural expressions of the tattoos that dominated his impression of him. Tupac made his body a symbol of beauty and defiance; perhaps it was his cry for democracy's promise of harmony and justice.

The tattoos on Tupac's back were indeed his lament, searing Exodus 18:11 into his skin, "Now I know that the Lord is greater than all the gods; for in the very thing in which they behaved proudly, He was above them." Was this not Tupac's way of acknowledging God and his awareness of God's presence? It seems so, and it also seems that Tupac understood, like many others of his generation, that his life was quarantined; his life—within the veil. But despite Tupac's cultural veil and his parochial limitations, God is. God sets boundaries, and God is above all gods, including hip-hop's god of materialism and Eurocentrism's failure to recognize the worth and equality that is intrinsic in all bodies, including the black body.

Tupac's God, like the very God revealed in Hebrew Scriptures, is the Sovereign ruler above all men and things. If this is Tupac's consciousness, he knows that he is equal to all men and only inferior to God. Because of Tupac's acknowledgment and awareness of God, he knows that his giftedness is God-given. He also knows that his giftedness is a muted violin inside the veil. This muting causes the so-called angry black male. When the divinely gifted violin is muted, it becomes hatred of self. In comparison,

59. Dyson, "I Got Your Name Tatted on My Arm" in *Holler If You Can Hear Me*, 231.

83

self-hatred present in the black male is what Thurman describes as an informant for double consciousness.

In this way, anger is passed to every generation of black males, largely because of limitations placed upon them by cultural mores reinforced by Eurocentrism. Tupac, then, symbolizes his generation of angry black males. Despite his financial success, what informed his social consciousness and his awareness was his designated social location. In other words, the location of his black body is similar to those located in Congo Square. Social location shaped the contours of Tupac's worldview and interpretation. As Dyson suggests, Tupac understood this, "thousands if not millions, of young black males believed his body was their body."[60] Tupac's identification with their pain was on display in the public square and eventually in the public sphere, knowingly making him a public spectacle. "Tupac stopped being a star and had become a grammar: His moves, gestures, and performances were a startlingly faithful articulation of their conflicted, confused inner lives [conflicted lives of double consciousness]. Much of his art insisted that their bodies were his. It was if he were saying, 'I will be your sacrificial lamb. I will suffer for your sake, in your place.'"[61]

Of course this sounds like Dyson believes that Tupac thought of himself as a messiah figure. It is true that Tupac's black body was devalued and is symbolic of the strange fruit, *The Cross and the Lynching Tree* about which James Cone writes.[62] I suggest, however, that more than likely, Tupac did come to realize indeed that he represented many African American males—most of whom whose names and identities would remain anonymous and invisible. But Tupac was not the first to understand this phenomenon, this sense of physical, psychological, and emotional lynching.

Well before Ralph Ellison's *Invisible Man*, Du Bois suggested in *Souls* that Alexander Crummell accepted a similar position. Of Crummell Du Bois said:

> So he grew, and brought within his wide influence all
> that was best of those who walk within the Veil. They who

---

60. Ibid., 233.
61. Ibid., 233-4.
62. See James Cone, *The Cross and the Lynching Tree* (Marykoll, NY: Orbis, 2012).

live without knew not nor dreamed of that full power within, that most men should not know. And now that he is gone, I sweep the Veil away and cry, Lo! The soul to whose dear memory lined beneath his snowy hair; lighting and shading, now with inspiration for the future, now in innocent pain at some human past. The more I met Alexander Crummell, the more I felt how much that world was losing which knew so little of him. In another age he might have sat among the elders of the land in purple-bordered toga; in another country mothers might have sung him to the cradles.[63]

Du Bois's words are eulogy, an ode to Crummell's intellectual prowess, his character and dogged strength of perseverance and faith. First, Du Bois's poetry attracts us to the story of Crummell. Du Bois's Crummell moves inside and outside of the veil and brings along with him to the other world the best of the genius that originates from the sociomargins, life—within the veil. Crummell is bifocal and metaphorical because he moves among the "lampstands" (Revelation 2:1).

Although Crummell is gifted like many black men and women and despite the limitations that the veil placed upon him, he was granted providence and grace while others were not. Du Bois associates Crummell's life alongside what visionary John the Revelator said of Jesus. John depicts a resurrected Jesus moving among the lampstands, inside and outside the poles of the world. By analogy, Du Bois wants these lampstands to symbolize the two poles where Crummell lived. This is what shapes the contours of Crummell's double consciousness.

Because of socially comparative conditions, Tupac's double consciousness strangely parallels that of Crummell, making Congo Square a universal condition. Tupac, however, may have had less social reinforcements than did Crummell. Thus it is understandable that Tupac expresses his anger loudly. He moves inside and outside the veil and among the lampstands, and, as does Crummell, he sees an alternative side of life. He chooses, then, and he regulates himself to life—within the veil. By whatever means, Crummell and

---

63. Du Bois, "Of Alexander Crummell" in *Souls*, 167.

Tupac accept their social location despite their advantages bequeathed to them by Sovereign grace.

Unlike Dyson, however, I do not see Tupac obsessed with a messiah complex. Instead, I see him struggling to share in the Du Boisian prophetic tradition alongside those men and women who understand the absurdity of Eurocentrism's limitations imposed by racial strata and classification. Like Du Bois who rightly saw Crummell's deep love of man and his prophetic expression of courage, I make a similar claim about Tupac's body located in Congo Square. Though his self-destructive behavior was anything but Du Boisian, Tupac also shared similarly with Crummell and Du Bois's deep love of man and prophetic expression of courage.

Conclusion

People of color continuously live in sociomarginalized conditions that cause dialectic tension to persist and inform the black psyche. This dialectic tension results in double consciousness. Before many others, Du Bois understood the formation of double consciousness and therefore he responded. What Du Bois understood about double consciousness, he sought to explain its constant presence with people of color. He sought to explain how it shapes the contours of the daily life existences of people of colors. Du Bois along with others (such as Dr. Wyatt Tee Walker who wrote *Somebody is Calling My Name*), chronicled black folks' worldview and the early formation of black hermeneutics. Walker observes, "If you listen to what black people are singing religiously, it will provide a clue as to what is happening to them sociologically."[64] Thus I contend that tracing African American hermeneutic expression through sorrow songs, the blues, and jazz continues in the species of hip-hop's rap music. In so many words, double consciousness surfaces in the black psyche, formed through constant shared doggedness of sociomarginalization.

What Walker traces through African American religious music experience, Du Bois in "Of the Sorrow Songs" introduces the formation of double consciousness to the world. What is more, he contends that black genius is at the heart of these songs, and that

---

64. Walker, *Somebody is Calling My Name*, (Valley Forge, Pa: Judson Press, 1979, 17.

these songs are representative of black folk s' common experience in the world. Also the sorrow songs reveal a system of thought which informs a shared sociomarginalized cultural worldview. It is this worldview that is shared among the oppressed of the human race. That is to say, similar expressions are made by people of color across the world.

The Du Boisian hermeneutic of double consciousness, then, is meant to be understood as a pan-African invention. It is an interpretive expression that crosses geographical and political boundaries. This happens because Eurocentrism remains the constant oppressive cultural system that hinders people of color. By way of dialectic, double consciousness is refutation that leads to democratic protest as an artistic, adroit expression of beauty and defiance, which is the response of people of color to Eurocentric hegemony.

Chapter Three: The Du Boisian Hermeneutic of Double Consciousness and Franz Fanon

In the metropolis of the modern world, in the closing of year of the nineteenth century, there has been assembled a congress of men and women of African blood, to deliberate solemnly upon the present situation and outlook of the darker races of mankind. The problem of the twentieth century is the problem of the colour line, the question as to how far differences of race, which show themselves chiefly in the colour of the skin and the texture of the hair, are going to be made, hereafter, the basis of denying to over half the world the right of sharing to their utmost ability the opportunities and privileges of modern civilisation.

To be sure, the darker races to-day the least advanced in culture according to European standards This has not, however, always been the case in the past, and certainly the world's history, both ancient and modern, has given many instances of no despicable ability and capacity among the blackest races of men.

To the Nations of the World[1]

W.E.B. Du Bois

These epigraphs appear in a W.E.B. Du Bois address before the initial Pan African Congress (1900) entitled "To the Nations of the

---

1. "To the Nations of the World" in *W. E.B. Du Bois: A Reader ed. David Levering Lewis* (New York: Henry Holt and Company, 1995), 639. In 1919, W.E.B. Du Bois is credited for organizing the meeting. It is said that 57 delegates attended this congress meeting from 15 different countries. The United States and Great Britain denied some of its citizen's attendance by denying them their passports.

World." Three years later, these same phrases reappear but in similar revised forms in *The Souls of Black Folk*'s first –two Du Boisian parabolic sermons, "Of Our Spiritual Strivings" and "Of the Dawn of Freedom (1903)." Important to my thesis then, is to make clear that as he did in "To the Nations of the World, Du Bois follows a similar rhetorical and hermeneutic path in *Souls:* "The problem of the twentieth century is the problem of the colour line." This remained the Du Boisian proposition that he presents consistently throughout his career; his ongoing fight against Eurocentrism.

This Du Boisian proposition then, is that Eurocentric thought, values, mores, opinions and traditions or Eurocentrism, is grounded in a notion that its thoughts and accomplishments provide for grandiose claims of cultural superiority over previous and current non-Eurocentric cultures and secondly, that people of color are the central liability and singular blight on Eurocentric's highly refined self-definition. Thus, the Du Boisian proposition is supported by these two premises: the first premise is that Eurocentrism always makes itself the positive subject. As a result of this positive depiction, what is always positive is the dominate culture's invention of the white subject; and the white subject is always afforded space to define people of color negatively. In response people of color must refute Eurocentrism, its claims and define themselves. In so many words, for people of color then, refutation of Eurocentrism is important; and it gives a reason for why a person of color's hermeneutic and communication theory is dialectic.[2]

---

2.   Molefi Kete Asante, *The Painful Demise of Eurocentrism* (Trenton, NJ: African World Press, Inc, 1999). Asante publishes this book of essays just before the turn of the century. In this way, I sense his effort to be considered prophetic. This passage that I include however, is to reinforce that my content is deliberate and against Eurocentric hegemony; not against people of European descent.

> To speak of the demise of Eurocentrism is not the same as to speak of the demise of Europe or of Europeans. Eurocentrism in its most extreme form has not generated an entire cacophony of voices that have been arrayed against the best interests of international cooperation and mutuality. It has generated a view toward the world of

Eurocentrism and the context it shapes and forms, informs Du Bois's public career that began during the decline of colonialism and the rise of post-colonialism or Eurocentrism. This occurred at the turn of twentieth century, the time when Du Bois understands that tentacles of Eurocentrism had deeply reached into the psyche of people of African descent. With this in mind, DuBois crafts *Souls* and *Darkwater* as parabolic stories or parabolic sermons to manipulate his audiences to *listen against their hearing*.[3]

Those who interpret *Souls* in this way are careful to notice that Du Bois has employed "the color line" phrase to bring attention to the negative reinforcement that Eurocentrism places against people of color, namely; racial, economic and political conditions that are globally imposed upon them. By globally, I mean that people of color continue to endure socio-marginalization in the larger geopolitical and geo-economic context which Du Bois located in the twilight of modernity (the span of time between his major publications: "To the Nations of the World," *The Souls of Black Folk, Darkwater and Dusk of Dawn*). What is of interest, Du Bois makes clear that deliberate manipulation of racism, economics and politics is associated with colonial hegemonic power.

This provides for us a context that I suggest shows that *Souls* was never meant then, to be interpreted as an American problem alone. That is, *Souls* was not to be interpreted solely as an American master/slave narrative. Instead, *Souls* was intended to clarify that Eurocentrism is the chief global impediment. *Souls* therefore, is a pan-African critique and refutation of Eurocentrism. It is a book of sermons and its motif is liberation from tyrannical Eurocentrism which is "the basis of denying to over half the world the right of

---

domination, hegemony, and control. Every aspect of gross Eurocentrism seems articulated toward this end, ultimately the subverting of international relationships. Thus, slavery, apartheid, Nazism, segregation, imperialism, intellectual arrogance, racial murders, and military and technological domination have been expressions of Eurocentrism.

3. I have made this claim because Du Bois employs highly symbolic, metaphoric religious language to communicate his argument against Eurocentrism.

sharing to their utmost ability the opportunities and privileges of modern civilization."[4]

The Du Boisian Response to Eurocentrism

In "To the Nations of the World," and other texts, Du Bois addresses racial inequality. Where racism is a nihilistic personal choice, Eurocentrism is a nihilistic cultural construct which forms Eurocentric institutional behavior which of late, has become a caricature of itself. Eurocentrism (as I define it) is systemic and globally organized; it is sanctioned by socioeconomic and sociopolitical power; and it targets socio-marginalized people of color and poor people of non-color. These people become collateral damage.

To think as a Du Boisian preacher, it is clear that Eurocentrism goes beyond Anglo North American and European institutions.[5] It is biased, and an oppressive, global construct. For Du Boisian preachers, then, what remains to be confronted is how the world's citizens will dismantle de jure and de facto Eurocentrism, and secondly, what remains is how to insure that those who have experienced Eurocentrism's collective and collateral damage is compensated.[6]

---

4. W. E. B. Du Bois, "To the Nations of the World," 639.
5. I have defined Du Boisian preachers as women and men who are called to the prophetic. They are jazz preachers; those who ask questions about democratic values and democracy's reach toward equality.
6. David Levering Lewis, in the following, he attempts to place Du Bois' rhetoric in a historical context: For a few pregnant moments, rhetoric and platitudes yielded to prophecy. Yet, however edifying the prescient, the statement was not intended to signal some radical change in their thinking about Queen Victoria's legitimate over lordship. Du Bois's passage in "To the Nations of the World" in which he called "as soon as practicable [for] the rights of responsible self-government to the black colonies of Africa and the West Indies," was bold but not unprecedented and was not to be interpreted as demand for independence from the British Empire. The independence of African peoples from European suzerainty seemed in 1900 a prospect incalculably far in the future, even to a clairvoyant Du Bois. Moreover, any clarion call to the demise of the British

Eurocentrism furthermore, is what Du Bois describes in *Dusk of Dawn* as a premeditated manipulation and exploitation of the proletariat's personal racial views which too often results in unsubstantiated fears of racial, gender and other *difference*. What occurs next is difficult to describe but I believe that our current hegemonic world system, commonly known as Eurocentrism is similar to King Nebuchadnezzar's dreadful dream recorded in Daniel 2-7. Its New Testament equivalent is similar to what John the Revelator discerned on the Isle of Patmos in Revelation 13. I identify Eurocentrism as an apocalyptic self-perpetuating system. Franz Fanon, writing in *A Dying Colonialism* makes this related statement about what I have called a self-perpetuating system which is Eurocentrism:

> The new relations are not the result of one barbarism replacing another barbarism, of one crushing of man replacing another crushing of man. What we Algerians want is to discover the man behind the colonizer; this man who is both organizer and the victim of a system that has choked him and reduced him to silence.[7]

Fanon, writing about Europe, hanging on to power over colonized nations, provides an accurate historical depiction of what we now commonly refer to as the emerging phenomena of Eurocentrism. I associate Fanon's claims with biblical apocalyptic language that prophesies the coming world empires, which I believe points toward an amalgamated culture that is Eurocentrism. And as Fanon has written, those who have organized these empires; they have eventually become its victims and are choked to silence. These world empires create systems that describe Daniel's four beasts; "The first was like a lion and had eagles' wings. Then as I looked its wings were plucked off, and it was lifted up from the ground and made to stand on two feet like a man, and the mind of a man was given to it" (Dan. 7:4).

Empire would have been impolitic and severely reprimanded by the London hosts of these genteel Pan-Africanists," 251.

7.   Franz Fanon, *Dying Colonialism* (New York: Grove Press, 1959), 32.

In comparison, what John writes about the fourth beast, I interpret as an amalgamation of the previous three major empires. The fourth beast has become a superstructure, commonly known as the Roman Empire, the cultural seedbed for Eurocentrism. "And I saw a beast rising out of the sea, with ten horns and seven heads, with ten diadems on its horns and blasphemous names on its heads. And the beast that I saw was like a leopard; its feet were like a bear's and its mouth was like a lion's mouth... (Rev.13:1-2). I interpret these verses as an accurate description of the fourth amalgamated beast.

More recently in a *New York Times* opinion editorial entitled, "Dr. King Weeps from His Grave," Cornel West, a radical democrat, warns America about Eurocentrism which I considered as a parallel to biblical and historical evidence of the fall of world empires. He writes that in order to change this course of history that threatens America, we must face this amalgamated beast which is Eurocentrism. The structure of Eurocentrism is what Dr. King called militarism, materialism, racism and poverty. In the following excerpts, West focuses his attention on recapitulating King's amalgamated beast as dysfunctional markets, oppressive oligarchic and plutocratic greed:

> ...I have said in our national tour against poverty, the recent budget deal is only the latest phase of a 30-year, top-down, one-sided war against the poor and working people in the name of a morally bankrupt policy of deregulating markets, lowering taxes and cutting spending for those already socially neglected and economically abandoned. Our two main political parties, each beholden to big money, offer merely alternative versions of oligarchic rule.
>
> King's response to our crisis can be put in one word: revolution. A revolution in our priorities, a re-evaluation of our values, a reinvigoration of our public life and a fundamental transformation of our way of thinking and

living that promotes a transfer of power from oligarchs and plutocrats to everyday people and ordinary citizens.[8]

Of course any rhetoric that threatens Eurocentrism as an economic monopoly is certainly to be recast as an attempt to redistribute wealth. For America's Eurocentric establishment, this is a red flag. That is when questions rise about oligarchs and plutocratic power. Those who raise these issues historically have been demonized immediately as Socialists, Marxists and worst, Communists (but it could be biblical Christianity Acts 2:41-47). In response to what I would characterize as a prophetic critique of our economic system, we hear the Eurocentric establishment, ideological labels that are meant to be negative. These labels are controlled by the establishment and therefore, these labels do not and cannot define people of color and what they may think. These labels should not fund Du Boisian preachers precisely because they are labels that belong to Eurocentrism.

Whether people are labeled Capitalists, Socialists, Marxists or Communists, these labels are Eurocentric inventions and constructs. In other words, Eurocentrism controls the debate and conversation. In short, Eurocentrism determines the definitions and thus the subject remains "the white subject." When this occurs, all debate is closed and denies rhetorical space for "otherness" to define the culture or even themselves. When people of color use Eurocentric language and definitions which too often reinforces negative images of people of color; they have no voice; they cannot be heard.

West's opinion editorial is an example of the Du Boisian prophetic tradition. It takes strength, love and courage to speak against what can only be understood as tyranny against the majority of people of the world. West correctly sights oligarchs and plutocrats as waging an economic war against the proletariat, "poverty is an economic catastrophe, inseparable from the power

---

8. Cornel West, "Dr. King Weeps from His Grave" in *The New York Times* (August 26, 2011). This editorial was written for the Inaugural of the Martin Luther King, Jr., memorial. When West refers to our "national tour against poverty," he is referring to Tavis Smiley and his bus tour to emphasis the large masses of American currently who are suffering poverty.

of greedy oligarchs and avaricious plutocrats indifferent to the misery of poor children, elderly citizens and working people."[9]

Neither King nor West prophesies that the end of American world influence has to be eminent. Both however, demand democratic inclusiveness. Indeed for those who disproportionately benefit from Eurocentric hegemony in all of its forms, democratic inclusiveness threatens their social status in all of its recognitions. On the other hand, democratic inclusiveness deepens democratic love which guarantees democratic change. West however, does trace World Empire to unfettered and unregulated markets and corporations that trump sound moral judgment, "Market-obsessed nihilism – the corporation as the embodiment of absolute will – is the Achilles' heel of American democracy that parades as its crown jewel Free – market fundamentalism has for so long been the precondition of American democracy that we have rendered it sacred – an unexamined fetish that we worship."[10]

When considered this way, I suggest that Eurocentrism morphs into Eurocentric institutional behavior. Again I have defined this as a self – perpetuating system. Indeed it has a life of its own and therefore Eurocentrism is only *passively* influenced by the proletariats' personal fears. When the United States for example, has faced civil or economic crisis, Eurocentric institutional behavior changes course for self-preservation. The 2008-9 executive ʻand legislative government bail outs of Wall Street investors occurred as a response to the American and European financial meltdown. Eurocentric institutional behavior disregarded the white proletariat's objections to protect its own Eurocentric interests.

For self-preservation, Eurocentric institutional behavior manipulates the proletariat's fears. Their fears are often misguided rage toward people of color. Eurocentric institutional behavior then, benefits from irrational behavior of people. Because of the irrationality and misguided fears of the proletariat, Eurocentric institutional behavior only seems to mirror irrational people's xenophobia, but in fact, its policies are used as a disguise for its

---

9. Ibid.
10. Cornel West, *Democracy Matters: Winning the Fight Against Imperialism* (New York: The Penguin Press, 2004), 40.

invisible agenda, which is self-preservation, that further marginal-izes people of color and people of non-color alike, or as Fanon writes in the *Wretched of the Earth*,

> The Western bourgeoisie, though fundamentally racist, most often manages to mask this racism by a multiplicity of nuances which allow it to preserve intact its proclamation of mankind's outstanding dignity [or in so many words, the system does not claim its own victims].[11]

Of course this irrationality is cultural bigotry which leads to institutional hegemony on both the Eurocentric liberal left and conservative right.[12] Lewis R. Gordon describes this as "the superstructural context of the First World, the world in which 'world' is constituted as a one-way mirror. In that world, only its reflection is seen." To see an example of this bigotry that Lewis describes, one only has to observe a political debate that takes place in the United States Congress between Democrats and Republicans. It is a one way mirror as Lewis puts it.

Current Eurocentric political debates are debacles that often are called "gridlock in Washington." This so called "gridlock" is reinforcement of Eurocentrism. These failed policies continue, because there is no "otherness" participating. Without "otherness,"

---

11. Robert Bernasconi, "Casting the Slough: Fanon's New Humanism for a New Humanity" in *Fanon: A Critical Reader*, 114.

12. Lewis R. Gordon, "The Black and the Body Politic: Fanon's Existential Phenomenological Critique of Psychoanalysis" in *Fanon: A Critical Reader* eds. Lewis R. Gordon, T. Denean Sharpley-Whiting and Renee T. White (Oxford: Blackwell Publishers, 1996, 74. The following excerpt describes the Eurocentric position, a kind of debate that takes place among Eurocentric peoples of non-color, an example of ideological and institutional hegemony. "To speak of politics today, especially with regard to metaphors lie within body politic and body politics, is to encounter an underlying feeling of wasting time. For as the chatter digresses, and as the common, *perfunctory interplay of attempting to articulate 'both sides' plays itself out,* the impatient revolutionary call emerges with existential force" 'So, my friends, what is to be done?'" I have added italics to emphasis my position that interpretation of events is limited to Eurocentrism; it by deliberate design mutes otherness.

Eurocentrism avoids dialectic and remains a non-transcendent closed system that is threatened by *difference*. Although nothing changes, by default these policies continue to grant myriad but unfair privileges to Eurocentric people of non-color.[13]

Manning Marble, commenting on Du Bois, has made a similar observation, "Du Bois perceived racism, 'the color-line,' as a fully global phenomenon, undergirded by a political economy of modern capitalism. The Jim Crow system in the United States was just a subsidiary of that larger global system of racialized exploitation and empire."[14] In fact, "He [Du Bois] recognized early on that structural racism [Eurocentrism] on the global scale could not be overturned without a coordinated mass democratic effort by people of African descent, Asians, and other racialized minorities situated at Western capitalism's oppressed periphery."[15]

If Manning is correct, then, Eurocentric global oppression and marginalization is systemic and organized; which means that people of color globally, experience similar degradations, humiliations and various limitations. It is plausible then, to assume that people of color have been forced to see the world through an oppressive lens. At the end of that lens is Eurocentrism. What else Eurocentrism does is that it forces people of color into a shared status of socio-marginalization. Because of this, Africans and other people of color have formed a similar hermeneutic of resistance, which can be located in their dialectic worldview.

Racialism then, is Eurocentrism. It is systematic hegemony shared by Anglo North American and European institutions that bends its philosophical, legal, economic, political and theological constructs toward Eurocentrism with far reaching implications. What is of import here is that Eurocentrism is globally socioeconomic, sociopolitical and socio-racially organized. This of course is a restatement of what Marable describes; the *Jim Crow* as a window into a larger "global system of racialized exploitation and empire."

---

13. W.E.B. Du Bois, *Dusk of Dawn: An Essay Toward An Autobiography of a Race Concept* (Piscataway, NJ: Rutgers - The State University, 2011), ix.

14. Manning Marable, *W.E.B. Du Bois: Black Radical Democrat* (Boulder, CO: Paradigm, 1986), xxxi.

15. Ibid.

Currently, then, Eurocentrism is a universal socio-marginalized colonial construct that continues to disguise itself to dominate people of color in post-colonial culture. As a response and as a result of the continuation of Eurocentrism, double consciousness continues. In other words, the Du Boisian phrase "the problem of the colour line" must be reconsidered in the context of Eurocentrism. Today double consciousness funds a collective dialectic response to Eurocentrism. What is more, double consciousness is a pan-African lens that serves as the point of departure for people of color's collective worldview and shared interpretation of events, and texts, those that are oral, written, or living. I call this pan-African phenomenon the Du Boisian hermeneutic of double consciousness.

Du Boisian Double Consciousness and Pan-Africanism

The inaugural Pan African Conference was held on July 23, 24 and 25, 1900, it convened in London's Westminster Town Hall. Numerous societies and organizations were represented at the congress, including, Aborigines Protection Society and the Society of Friends, along with several African representatives and six American representatives.[16] Du Bois spoke during the congress's closing session. David Levering Lewis has made comment about the orality of Du Bois' address, his speaking tone, and his style of delivery, "the grave cadence and crisp diction prefigured momentous phrasings that would reappear slightly changed in *The Souls of Black Folk*."[17]

---

16. David Levering Lewis, *W.E.B. Du Bois: Biography of Race* 248. The six African American delegates were as follows: Thomas Calloway, Anna J. Cooper, W.E.B. Du Bois, Ada Harris, Bishop Alexander Walters,

17. Ibid., 250-1. I have included a lengthy quotation of Du Bois' "To the Nations of the World":
    The problem of the twentieth century is the problem of the colour line, the question as to how far differences of race…are going to be made, hereafter, the basis of denying to over half the world is right of sharing to their utmost ability the opportunities and privileges of modern civilization. To be sure, the darker races are today the least advanced in culture according to European standards. This has not, however, always been the case in the past, and certainly the world's history, both ancient

Although Du Boisian double consciousness was not yet fully formed, Du Bois introduces the world to his theory in "To the Nations of the World" address. He frames it in this way, "the question as to how far differences of race, which show themselves chiefly in the colour of the skin and the texture of the hair, are going to be made, hereafter, the basis of denying to over half the world the right of sharing their utmost ability the opportunities and privileges of modern civilisation." What may be observed from this excerpt? Eurocentrism invents a false and debilitating dichotomy that is capable of harassing people by "the colour of the skin and the texture of the hair." I am suggesting this kind of dichotomy demands that people who are shaped and conditioned by Eurocentrism remain permanently divided from people of *difference*.

People of color represent *difference* which necessitates Du Boisian double consciousness. People of color in turn; embrace their imposed *difference*, and use it as a defense against Eurocentrism's colonial and post-colonial oppression (Later you will see an example of this in the Algerian woman's veil). Among people of color, Eurocentrism has created a commonly shared worldview and interpretation informed by a response of resistance to hegemonic, cultural marginalization. Like Du Bois, Du Boisian preachers must identify the problem of the color line in their contemporary context and draw attention to issues that are similar to those Du Bois raises in "To the Nations of the World" and ask questions related to why Du Bois repeats the "color line" phrase in *Souls*. In both instances, Du Bois is suggesting that Africans and

---

and modern, has given many instances of no despicable ability and capacity among blackest races of men. In any case, the modern world must needs remember that in this age…the millions of black men in Africa, America, and the Islands of the Sea, not to speak of the brown and yellow myriads elsewhere, are bound to have great influence upon the world in the future, by reason of sheer and physical contact….If, by reason of carelessness, prejudice, greed and injustice, the black world is to be exploited and ravished and degraded, the results must be deplorable, if not fatal, not simply to them, but to the high ideals of justice, freedom, and culture which a thousand years of Christian civilization have held before Europe. See also the following footnote to cite this historic speech.

their descendants located in various places share a similar existential condition; namely that Eurocentrism is a hegemonic superstructure that marginalizes people of color globally. In this way, we can understand the genesis of pan-Africanism.

Du Boisian Pan-Africanism

Du Boisian pan-Africanism was inspired by Henry Sylvester Williams' foresight into the eventual unification of Africans and people of color. In November 1899, Williams, a Trinidadian barrister, describes this forthcoming unification by introducing the phrase, Pan-Africanism.[18] Du Bois appropriates William's foresight and translates his phrase, pan-Africanism, into an organized anti-colonialism world movement. Like Williams, Du Bois prophesies the end of colonialism. Du Bois' address "To the Nations of the World" then, is philosophically pan-African. And we know that pan-Africanism eventually becomes transformative, and it became the twentieth century's catalyst for the civil rights and post civil rights – black power movements.[19]

---

18. According David Levering Lewis, Henry Sylvester Williams, a Trinidadian barrister was "One of the most visionary colored men of his generation, he was cultured, dedicated, and globe-wandering, but he would be practically forgotten when he died aged forty-two, see *W.E.B. Du Bois: Biography of Race*, (New York: Henry Holt and Company, 1993), 248. An explanation for Pan-Africanism, according to Lewis is as follows: "Pan-Africanism came with the Zeitgeist, an inevitable, derivative idea, at once circumspect and revolutionary. It was another movement exploding into the twentieth century like a stick of dynamite – Pan Hellenism, Pan-Germanism, Pan-Slavism – with the Irish, Afrikaners, Armenians, Serbians, and other historic 'races' already lighting fuses for the new country.," 248.
19. Manning Marable, *W.E.B. Du Bois: Black Radical Democrat* (London: Paradigm Publishers, 1986). Marable is among the most thoughtful of the African American social history intellectuals, whom I heavily rely on to shape a narrative of Du Bois in this chapter. It is important to note, the Pan-African movement began years before the London meeting of 1900 by many notable African American scholars among them, African American clergy scholars. Marable commented that [W.E.B.] Du Bois growing affinity for "Pan-Negroism" and the cultural image of Africa was shared by many Afro-American intellectuals in the 1890's. A.M.E. Bishop Alexander Walters and

Thus Du Boisian understanding of Eurocentrism claims that Eurocentrism deliberately presents a negative connotation of people of color – globally. As a response to Eurocentrism, and as I stated, the Du Boisian hermeneutic of double consciousness is pan-African. It is dialectic resistance; it is a response to Eurocentrism which is primarily a colonial system that lingers in post-colonial racialism and hegemony. Whenever Cultural Revolution is taking place such as the Arab spring or currently in Syria, dialectic functions as resistance that invents different interpretation and rhetoric.

Today Culture Revolution includes gender equality (as Franz Fanon will explain). Nevertheless, I have identified that the Du Boisian hermeneutic of double consciousness manifests in different cultures in different shapes and forms. What is similar and remains a common theme however, is this hermeneutic is dialectic in form, it is a response to Eurocentrism and its devastating effects over people of color.

To further make this argument, other voices emerge as co-labors. Du Boisian preachers must advance their understanding of the Du Boisian hermeneutic of double consciousness and that the hermeneutic is a shared and collective phenomenon among people of color. To demonstrate this collective perspective of shared interpretation, I have located the Du Boisian hermeneutic of double consciousness, its gradual movement and variations, in other regions of the world. I have limited that location to regions that interest Franz Fanon. To accomplish this I am funded by Fanon, his work, his contributions, and those whose comments parallel Fanon's contributions toward the Du Boisian hermeneutic of double consciousness, which epitomizes my understanding of Eurocentrism and its effects on people of color.

[Alexander] Crummell participated in the Chicago Congress on Africa in August 1893. The week-long conference featured a presentation by A.M.E. Bishop Henry M. Turner, who urged Afro-Americans to emigrate to the [African] continent. Another conference on African affairs was sponsored by the Stewart Missionary Foundation and held at Gammon Theological Seminary in Atlanta in December 1895," 38.

The Du Boisian Hermeneutic of Double Consciousness and Franz Fanon

As mentioned earlier, the Du Boisian hermeneutic of double consciousness is resistance dialectic to Eurocentrism and therefore, and as a result, this hermeneutic empowers people of color entangled in the American master/slave narrative. In other regions of the world; this hermeneutic empowers people to resist the colonizer/colonized narrative. The latter narrative is similar to the one that Franz Fanon employs.

Fanon's life was a fleeting comet. He burst into the world's consciousness with unwavering courage, and he left it as a "flaming tail." His life was filled with dogged protest, passionate resistance and letters. Fanon, a psychiatrist, was born on June 20, 1925 in Martinique; he died in Bethesda, Maryland in 1961. Because of his parent's African middle – class status, Fanon was afforded studies in French academies that were unavailable to most members of his race.

In 1953, Fanon accepted a post as head of the Blida-Joinville Hospital in Algiers. There Fanon experienced a kind of intellectual and social baptism. Informed by a different consciousness, Fanon was able to see the struggles of marginalized people. He joined the struggle with absolute devotion and he immersed himself into liberation that later would form emerging motifs.[20] In this way, Fanon joins himself with Du Bois.

What is of interest here, however; is the very way that Fanon's work parallels Du Boisian double consciousness. Whereas Du Bois' primary point of departure for double consciousness is an emphasis of the human social condition; Fanon's emphasis is on the human psychological condition; both are non-ecclesial prophets who experience the human condition from their social location.

So that we may consider Du Boisian double consciousness from Du Bois and Fanon's social locations, two passages are included. The first is Du Bois' definition of double consciousness and the second is Fanon's which is similar to that of Du Bois:

---

20. Lewis R. Gordon, T. Denean Sharpley – Whiting and Renee T. White "Introduction: Five Stages of Fanon Studies" in *Fanon: A Critical Reader*, 2-3.

After the Egyptian and Indian, the Greek and Roman, the Teuton and Mongolian, the Negro is a sort of seventh son, born with a veil, and gifted with second sight in this American world – a world which yields no true self-consciousness, but only lets him see himself through the revelation of the other world. It is a peculiar sensation, this double consciousness, this sense of always looking at one's self through the eyes of others, of measuring one's soul by the tape of a world that looks on in amused contempt and pity. One ever feels his twoness – an American, a Negro; two souls, two thoughts, two unreconciled strivings; two warring ideals in one dark body, whose dogged strength alone keeps it from being torn asunder.[21]

There is, in the *Weltanschauung* of colonized people, an impurity, a defect that forbids any ontological explanation. Perhaps it will be objected that it is so with every individual, but that is to mask a fundamental problem. Ontology, when admitted once and for all that it leaves existence by the wayside, does not permit us to understand the being of the black. For the black no longer has to be black, but must be it in front of the white. Some critics will take it on themselves to remind us that this situation is reciprocal. We respond that this is false. The black has no ontological resistance to the eyes of the white. Overnight the Negroes have had two systems of reference with regard to which they felt the need to situate themselves. Their metaphysics, or, less pretentiously, their customs and the earnestness with which they are discharged, were abolished because they found themselves in contradiction with a civilization of which they were ignorant and which imposed itself on them.[22]

When Du Bois and Fanon's definitions of double consciousness are considered as synthesis, what emerge are similar conditions of the black world which Floyd W. Hayes refers to as "negative social

---

21. W. E. B. Du Bois, *The Souls Black Folk*, xxiii-xxiv.
22. Franz Fanon, *Black Skin, White Masks* (New York: Grove Press, 1967), 109-10.

and cultural contractions."[23] What is more, Hayes has identified "a contradictory and ambiguous consciousness upon black people's struggle to exist within the absurdity of America's anti-black culture."[24] Contradictory and ambiguous consciousness indeed suggests the bifurcated identity of people of color does exist and in fact, it may be a "shattering of the self or the psyche." In both instances, Du Bois and Fanon suggest that shattering of the social and psychological self is premeditated socio-marginalized circumstances which facilitate the nature of people of color's existential conditions that is double consciousness.

There are further parallels for how Du Bois and Fanon understand double consciousness; both definitions are deeply rooted and grounded in existentialism. Du Bois' "the Negro is a sort of seventh son, born with a veil, and gifted with second sight in this American world – a world which yields no true self-consciousness, but only lets him see himself through the revelation of the other world" is a romantic expression of African Americans seemingly set a apart as a cosmic race of prophets who are gifted in second sight. The gift of second sight however is accompanied by passion of suffering.

On the other hand, Fanon's "Ontology, when admitted once and for all that it leaves existence by the wayside, does not permit us to understand the being of the black. For the black no longer has to be black, but must be it in front of the white" are explanations for the ill effects of Eurocentrism on the psyche of people of color. Thus, I can locate Du Bois' and Fanon's definitions of double consciousness as similar; Du Bois' point of departure is social conditions – within the veil (social location) and Fanon's point of departure is psychological conditions – within the veil (again social location). By expressing African Americans as "a seventh son, born within a veil," Du Bois is referring to ontological limitations and similarly, these ontological limitations are noticed in Fanon's statement, "For the black no longer has to be black, but

---

23. Floyd W. Hayes, III, "Fanon, Oppression, and Resentment: The Black Experience in the United States" in *Fanon: A Critical Reader*, 19. These two excerpts appear in Hayes's essay to emphasis that double consciousness imposes cultural and psychological negative and cultural contractions.
24. Ibid.

must be it in front of the white" further limits self-consciousness and self-determined identity. It is clear; Du Bois and Fanon have framed psychological and sociological pathologies as existential conditions that develop double consciousness.

Du Boisian preachers, informed by these psychological and sociological pathologies and existential conditions, must define African American worldview as a well chronicled representative of people of color's constant existential fight against nihilism. One only has to read closely "Of Alexander Crummell" to hear Du Bois make this point. Du Bois characterizes Crummell's vocational life as a fight against nihilism: "Three temptations he met on those dark dunes that lay gray and dismal before the wonder-eyes of the child: the temptation of Hate, that stood out against the red dawn; the temptation of Despair, that darkened noonday; and the temptation of Doubt, that ever steals along with twilight. Above all, you must hear of the vales he crossed,--the Valley of Humiliation and the Valley of the Shadow of Death."[25]

Du Bois epitomizes the social effects that the American master/slave narrative has over African Americans and by implication people of color in other regions of the world. Of course this has been reinforced by the white subject and white mythologies that is content with people of color defined in a negative connotation. Du Boisian preachers must understand the master/slave narrative which is an invention of Eurocentrism.

Fanon, however, makes a distinction between the American slave/master narrative and the Colonizer and the Colonized. Nevertheless, like North American people of African descent, Fanon's colonized people too suffer from Eurocentrism which has influenced the negative existential condition that is associated with people of color in other regions of the world. For Fanon, existentialism that affects colonized people of color takes on slightly different contours and shapes than those located in Anglo North America's Eurocentrism. Fanon grounds these differences in psychological constructs. Nevertheless, what remains constant in other regions people of color remain – within the veil.

---

25. W. E. B. Du Bois, "Of Alexander Crummell," in *The Souls of Black Folk*, 215.

Du Boisian Hermeneutic of Double Consciousness and the Veil

What can only be considered as literary genius, Fanon describes how the Du Boisian veil functions in the colonized Algerian society. Fanon's "Algeria Unveiled" indicates his familiarity with Du Boisian use "of the Veil" metaphor. He shows how double consciousness functions in Algerian life – within the veil. Fanon, in this way, expresses how Eurocentrism imposes socio-marginalization: human restrictions and political limitations in every sphere that makes Eurocentrism the fourth beast.

The veil oftentimes called the *haik* that the Algerian woman wears is generally associated with an Arab cultural costume and society at – large.[26] Beyond the Algerian woman, the veil belongs to Tunisian, Moroccan and Libyan national societies. According to Fanon, "For the tourist and the foreigner, the veil demarcates Algerian society and its feminine component...The [Algerian] woman seen in her white veil unifies the perception that one has of Algerian feminine society... The Algerian woman, in the eyes of the observer, is unmistakably 'she hides behind a veil'"[27]

The Eurocentric view of the Algerian woman is homogenous. For those who are proponents of Eurocentrism, she is an oppressed figure in Algerian indigenous culture. According to Fanon, Western oligarchs and plutocrats thought "Lets win over the women and the rest will follow" that is, Algerian resistance to outsiders will desist.[28] To further infiltrate Algerian resistance to Eurocentrism, the veil was made a sociopolitical symbol of Algerian backwardness when compared to Eurocentric superiority. To lift the status of the Algerian woman, and to destroy Algerian resistance to colonizers, the fourth beast sought to lift the Algerian woman's veil.

It is obvious, Fanon wants us to fully grasp that those who are employees of the beast, deliberately set out to destroy Algeria's customs, traditions and values. In the following excerpt Fanon

---

26. Fanon describes the haik , in *Dying Colonialism*. Its "Arab name for the big square veil worn by Arab women, covering the face and the whole body," 36.
27. Franz Fanon, "Algeria Unveiled" in *A Dying Colonialism*.
28. Ibid., 37.

explains how ironically, Eurocentric worldview misunderstands the Algerian woman's self-consciousness. Thus Eurocentric thought assumes that the Algerian woman's veil is limiting and demeaning if not dehumanizing but on the contrary, the veil that the Algerian woman dons is filled with symbolism that honors her and affirms her self-consciousness and certainly her veil defines her prominence and status in Algerian society:

> Beneath the patrilineal pattern of Algerian society, the specialists described a structure of matrilineal essence. Arab society has often been presented by Westerners as a formal society in which outside appearances are paramount. The Algerian woman, an intermediary between obscure forces and the group, appeared in this perspective to assume a primordial importance. Behind the visible, manifest patriarchy, the more significant existence of a basic matriarchy was affirmed. The role of the Algerian mother, that of the grandmother, the aunt and the "old woman," were inventoried and defined.
>
> This enabled the colonial administration to define a precise political doctrine: "If we want to destroy the structure of Algerian society, its capacity for resistance, we must first of all conquer the women: we must go and find them behind the veil where they hide themselves and in the houses where the men keep them out of sight."[29]

Thus the beast's strategy was to convert "the woman, winning her over to the foreign values, wrenching her free from her status, was at the same time achieving a real power over the man and attaining a practical, effective means of destructuring Algerian culture."[30] In the next two excerpts, Du Boisian preachers should be aware of the sociological and psychological synthesis that is associated with double consciousness:

> Between Me and the other world there is ever an unasked question: unasked by some through feelings of

29. Ibid., 37-38.
30. Ibid., 39.

delicacy; by others through the difficulty of rightly framing it. All nevertheless, [do] flutter round it. They approach me in a half – hesitant sort of way, eye me curiously or compassionately, and then, instead of saying directly, How does it feel to be a problem? They say, I know an excellent colored man in my town; or, I fought at Mechanicsville; or Do not these Southern outrages make your blood boil? After these I smile, or am interested, or reduced the boiling to a simmer, as the occasion may require. To the real question, How does it feel to be a problem? I answer seldom a word.[31]

For Du Bois, the question is "How does it feel to be black in America?" For Fanon, the question is "How does it feel to be black in Algeria?" For us, the question is "How does it feel to be black in the world?" Thus each question demonstrates the white subject's effectiveness over and against black attitude. It is these questions that trace Eurocentrism and how it presents challenges to black self-consciousness in a global context.

The Algerian man, for his part, is the target of criticism for his European comrades, or more officially for his bosses. There is not a European worker who does not sooner or later, in the give and take of relations on the job site, the shop or the office, ask the Algerian the ritual questions: "Does your wife wear the veil? Why don't you take your wife to the movies, to the fights, to the café?"[32]

What is indicated here? In two different regions, countries and historical time periods, Eurocentrism asserts itself as superior over all other cultures and races. Notice its rhetorical strategy is to divide and conquer.

An illustration of the divide and conquer rhetorical strategy, is depicted in the notion of Eurocentrism's superiority which Du Bois expresses in "Of Our Spiritual Strivings" where the black and

31. W.E.B. Du Bois "Of Our Spiritual Strivings" in *The Souls of Black Folk*, 2-3.
32. Fanon, "The Algerian Woman" in *A Dying Colonialism*, 39.

white characters' conversation is controlled by the white subject who controls racial relations and interpretation (this is the rhetorical strategy perfected). As I have mentioned earlier Eurocentrism is systemic and organized and this is obviously seen in Fanon's Du Boisian anecdote, "Does your wife wear the veil? Why don't you take your wife to the movies, to the fights, to the café?" Again, the white subject asserts itself in order to control racial relations and impose himself [itself]. This is how he [it] controls interpretation and bends it toward Eurocentrism. Thus, there is a corollary relationship between the white subject and social location. Whatever else, readers are made aware of how double consciousness operates in two different geographical locations: Du Bois emphasizes the effects of social condition within social location; Fanon emphasizes the effects of psychological conditions within social location – within the veil.[33]

Double Consciousness, the Veil and the Female Black Body

In addition to a sociopolitical symbol, the veil has a highly symbolic relation with the Algerian woman's black body. It is the veil that represents the femininity of the woman of color. It is the veil that reminds us that the woman of color is to be honored, protected and kept virtuous from wrongful impositions (whether from French or Algerian men). It is the veil that serves as the symbolical value of the female black body. In Eurocentric culture, the virtue of the human body and particularly the female body is freedom, liberalism, and nakedness. In the black world, the female body represents sacredness, piety and the regenerator of human life. The black female body in the Algerian resistance movement was the first casualty in the debate over interpretation. What is of

---

33. Ibid., 41. Fanon writes, The method of presenting the Algerian as a prey fought over with equal ferocity by Islam and France with its Western culture reveals the whole approach of the occupier, his philosophy and his policy. This expression indicates that the occupier, smarting from his failures, presents in a simplified and pejorative way the system of values by means of which the colonized person resists his innumerable offensives. What is in fact the assertion of a distinct identity, concern with keeping intact a few shreds of national existence, is attributed to religious magical, fanatical behavior.

concern however is when the female black body is not affirmed, its virtue too often is made invisible.

Fanon in *Black Skin, White Masks*, provides what only can be described as a controversial psycho -analytic profile of a black woman and her blind love for a European male. Fanon inadvertently risks stereotyping all women of color with his analysis. To his defense, a very thoughtful African American scholar, Tracey Denean Sharpley-Whiting writes, "Attempts to shame Fanon out of the category of a liberation theorist whose ideas are relevant to the lives of black women are, at best, disingenuous. Fanon's honesty in *Black Skin, White Masks* may be brutal but it is not brutalizing."[34]

The psychiatrist Fanon writes in "The Woman of Color and The White Man," about Mayotte Capecia, a black woman; who wrote a book *I am a Martinican Women,* which Fanon characterizes as "a third rate book, advocating unhealthy behavior." The following excerpt from Mayotte's book is included in *Black Skin, White Masks:*

> Some evenings, alas, he had to leave me to fulfill mundane duties. He went to Didier, the elegant section of Fort-de-France, where the "Martinican Bekes," who, perhaps, *were not pure white, but often very rich (it is accepted that one is white if one has a certain amount of money)* and the "French Bekes," for the most part officials and officers lived.
>
> Among Andre's comrades, who like him were blockaded in the Antilles by the war, some had managed to have their wives come over. I understood that Andre could not remain apart; I also accepted not being admitted to this group, since *I was a colored woman,* but I couldn't help being jealous. It was useless for him to explain to me that his private life was something that belonged to him and that his social and military another, over which he had no control. I insisted so much that one day he took me to Didier. We spent the evening in one of the villas that I had

---

34. T. Denean Sharpley-Whiting, "Engaging Fanon to Reread Capecia" in *Fanon: A Critical Reader*, 161.

admired since childhood with two officers and their wives. These women treated me with forbearance that was insupportable for me. *I felt too heavily made-up, inappropriately dressed and that I didn't do justice to Andre, perhaps simply due to the color of my skin.* Indeed, I spent such an unpleasant evening that I decided never again to ask Andre to accompany him again.[35]

I have identified Mayotte's inferiority complex in what Fanon calls, a "double process." First, I identify her inferiority complex in her economic condition. Then secondly, I identify her inferiority complex in her internalization or rather epidermalization which too signifies her perceived condition of inferiority.[36]

In short, Fanon's double process or double consciousness is a constant companion for people of color. It manifests in black – social and economic separation. It manifests in our limited privileges and opportunities to overcome Eurocentrism's forms of hegemonies. You can see the correlation between Du Bois' understanding of race, economics and politics when Mayotte writes, "it is accepted that one is white if one has a certain amount of money."[37] Though a beautiful Creole woman, as Fanon describes Mayotte, it was not enough.[38] In Fort-Du-France; she needed other credentials such as socio-economic gravitas to make her white. In any respect, however, Du Boisian preachers must recognize this evidence; this psychological manipulation of human dignity and self-respect imposed by Eurocentrism's isolation – within the veil.

Mayotte's black body is located within the veil. Her make-up, which she said was too heavy and her skin, which she felt it was

---

35. Fanon, *Black Skin, White Masks* (New York: Grove Press, 1952), 26. Also see *Mayotte Capecia, Je suis Matinquaise,* English translation by Beatrice Stith Clark: *I am a Maritinican Women,* Passeggiata, Pueblo, Colorado, 153. I have added emphasis to certain words in the excerpt.
36. Fanon, *Black Skin, White Masks,* xiv-xv.
37. See Du Bois, *Dusk of Dawn,* ix.
38. Ibid.,26. Also see W.E.B. Du Bois, *Dusk of Dawn: An Essay Toward An Autobiography of A Race Concept* (New Brunswick, NJ: Transaction Publishers, 2011), ix.

too dark for her social acceptance is an indication of psychological and social dysfunction. Her discomfort with her appearance hindered her ability to negotiate her acceptance among Andre's peers and his peer's wives. This, also, points to the woman of color's black body. What is more, Fanon draws critical attention toward pathology and how it manifest in human survivalist's instincts that Fanon associates with a black woman. For Fanon, Mayotte's account serves as a pathological profile and how pathology and double consciousness functions in social location.

According to Fanon, Mayotte's double consciousness is located in her pathological- narcissistic behavior. Fanon discusses Mayotte's narcissism by pointing to a scene that occurred in her early life where she recognizes her culturally imposed limitations: "'I took out my inkwell and threw it, showering his head.' This was her way of changing Whites into Blacks. But she realized early on how vain her efforts were. Then there are Loulouze and her mother, who told her how difficult life is for a woman of color. So, unable to blacken or negrify the world, she endeavors to whiten it in her body and mind...."[39]

What if we place Mayotte's narcissistic – survivalist's narrative alongside the biblical story of The Song of Solomon? We find that in the Song's opening episode is a story about a young beautiful maiden fighting against nihilism that threatens her social and psychological well being. I can locate this nihilistic threat in her awareness of her black body and her socioeconomic status:

> I am very dark, but lovely, O daughters of Jerusalem, like the tents of Kedar, like the curtains of Solomon. Do not gaze at me because I am dark, because the sun has looked upon me. My mother's sons were angry with me; they made me keeper of the vineyards, but my own vineyard I have not kept! Tell me, you whom my soul loves, where you pasture your flock, where you make it lie down at noon; for why should I be like one who veils herself beside the flocks of your companions? (The Song of Solomon 1: 5-7).

---

39. Ibid., 28.

In this short passage, I am able to identify this maiden's battle against her inferiority complex and how it functions in the psyche of her double consciousness. The Song is a result of Solomon recounting one of his visits to a part of his kingdom where he first sees this beautiful peasant girl. Embarrassed, the lovely girl withdraws from the King's presence. What else is plausible is that the young maiden was suspicious of Solomon's motives. I associate the young maidens' suspicions and perceptions with Renita Weems contributions to our understanding of the hermeneutic of suspicion. Weems locates the hermeneutic of suspicion in the well-traveled story of Howard Thurman's grandmother's suspicion of Eurocentric interpretations of Pauline writings.

By referring to this story, Weems brings two salient propositions to bear: "First, the experience of oppression brought African American women to understand that outlook (or worldview) plays an important role in how one reads the Bible – it became clear that it is not just a matter of whose reading is accurate, but whose reading is legitimated and enforced by the dominant culture." And "Secondly, the experience of oppression has forced the marginalized reader to retain the right, as much as possible to resist those things within the culture and the Bible that one finds obnoxious or antagonistic to one's innate sense of identity and to one's basic instincts for survival."[40] The Du Boisian preachers should compare the maiden's social location with that of Solomon's. It is plausible then to believe that she identifies him as the enforcer of the dominate culture and therefore, she resists his overtures and she deeply questions his motives.

Solomon considered as a cultural enforcer, this provides a social context for a hermeneutic of suspicion that supports Weem's claims. That is, Weems is accurate to suggest that this is a resounding characteristic and universally consistent within an African American hermeneutic process, and how it functions with prophetic and liberation leanings. That is, the prophetic in the African American tradition is resistance to dominant cultural norms. For socio-marginalized people, resistance is necessary for

40. Renita J. Weems, "Reading Her Way through the Struggle: African American Women and the Bible" in *Stony the Road We Trod: African American Biblical Interpretation* ed. Cain Hope Felder (Minneapolis: Fortress, 1991), 63.

retaining self-respect and identity over and against Eurocentrism and its claims that are aimed over and against socio-marginalized, people of color. Second, Weems is accurate to put forward that Eurocentric interpretation is always to be interrogated. In the case of Thurman's grandmother, she intuitively understood that there are alternative readings to Eurocentric doctrinal pronouncements of Apostle Paul's writings. There are other pronouncements that do not marginalize socio-marginalized people, people of color and in this instance, a woman of colors' understanding of her self-worth.

The young woman in the Song of Solomon is aware of her darker skin and that it may have her stand out among some of the other woman in Jerusalem. Her explanation for her darker skin was that it was not genetic. Instead it was because of her step -brothers who were angry with her. They made her work in their vineyards. Notice her black womanist's resistance to hegemony and oppression … "But my own vineyard I have not kept." Solomon's young bride may have associated her darker skin with cruel treatment from her step brothers but the result of her darker skin, was that she lacked economic influence; and in her case, it resulted in a lack of social mobility.

Interestingly, what made her appealing to Solomon was her physical appearance. It was her black body that empowered her and it was her black body that compelled Solomon to marry her. The biblical text indicates that she had nothing to bring to her marriage except her person and her black womanism. To Solomon's credit, he resists objectifying his new bride. I assume that Solomon understood that double consciousness is functioning in the young maiden's pyschospirituality. In order to pursue the young beauty, Solomon finds a way to respond to her double consciousness and its psychospiritual dimensions. To usurp double consciousness and her social location, Solomon chooses to disguise himself as a common shepherd. Eventually he romances her into marriage.

This passage from the Song of Solomon provides an analytical parallel to Mayotte's account. Both women are black, comely and beautiful. Both women are made aware of their black bodies, and their darker skin and their social and economic limitations. There is a difference however. Unlike Mayotte, who is not affirmed by her lover Andre, Solomon affirms her person and black beauty:

If you do not know, O most beautiful among women, follow in the tracks of the flock; and pasture your young goats beside the shepherd's tents. I compare you, my love; to a mare among Pharaoh's chariots. Your cheeks are lovely with ornaments, your neck with strings of jewels... Behold, you are beautiful, my love, behold you are beautiful; your eyes are doves... Behold you are beautiful my beloved, truly delightful... (The Song of Solomon 1: 8-10; 15-16a).

I am a rose of Sharon, a lily of the valleys. As a lily among the brambles, so is my love among the young women (The Song of Solomon 2: 1-2).

When I locate Mayotte, alongside the young woman in The Song of Solomon, and Fanon's Algerian woman, we find interesting contrasts. For example, as Fanon describes the Algerian struggle, in the early stages of the rebellion, indeed Mayotte and the Algerian woman are comparable. Initially, Andre, Mayotte's European man and the Algerian man are similar; they have taken their "woman" for granted. Perhaps this is no different than many men of all cultures. In so many ways, these stories represent many women from around the world. Mayotte and the Song of Solomon's young maiden can be located symbolically in Ralph Ellison's Invisible *Man*. On the other hand, as the Algerian revolution began to turn against the Algerian natives, what occurred parallels apocalyptic biblical revelation. While the occupiers made an attempt to divide the Algerian resistance fighters from their indigenous culture around the traditional veil; for the Algerian man an epiphany occurs.

During social upheavals, social evolution arises, and gradually an epiphany does occur. The Algerian man recognizes his epiphany in the person of the Algerian woman. Because of her loyalty and resistance to Eurocentrism, their culture could survive. Fanon's recounting of the Algerian struggle is a story about the Algerian man's recognition of the Algerian woman's equality grows. What occurs during the war of resistance, the Algerian man understands that her loyalty and love controls the outcome of the revolution. This is the revelation that is disclosed to him during the revolution and he recognizes it. His recognition of her equality grows in direct proportion with his understanding of himself, his goals, and his ultimate objective, which is Algeria be freed from Eurocentrism.

As David Theo Goldberg comments, "The native woman made a strategic choice to pursue a self-determined undertaking to discard the veil for the sake of advancing a war of position and maneuvre against colonial settlement, domination, and penetration, thereby promoting a transformation in the disposition of the unveiled – a freedom, an unconfinement, a self-possession."[41] Like Solomon who affirmed his young maiden's person and black beauty, the Algerian man wisely began to affirm the Algerian woman, her body, mind and soul. She too loved her culture and resisted Eurocentrism. She too loved her Algerian man.

The Algerian response to the Eurocentric occupier represents for us how people of color employ the Du Boisian hermeneutic of double consciousness. By this I mean the significance of Eurocentrism - psychological conditions imposed upon the Algerian people of color becomes a shared experience between the Algerian man and woman. Although I have chosen to locate the Du Boisian hermeneutic of double consciousness in the person of the Algerian woman; I notice too that the Algerian woman's self-consciousness bears witness to the Algerian man and how her self-consciousness influences him. Thus, in this way, I am able also to make comment on the psychospiritual dimensions of the Du Boisian hermeneutic of double consciousness from Fanon's perspective.

Fanon comments on the psychospiritual dimension of double consciousness and its resistance to Eurocentrism when he writes, "It was the colonialist's frenzy to unveil the Algerian woman, it was his gamble on winning the battle of the veil at whatever cost, that were to provoke the native's bristling resistance…" Here is where Du Boisian preachers recognize one of the laws of the psychology of colonization. In an initial phase, it is the action, the plans of the occupier that determine the centers of resistance around which a people's will to survive become organized."[42]

---

41. David Theo Goldberg, "In/Visibility and Super/Vision" in *Fanon: A Critical Reader*, 189.
42. Franz Fanon, *A Dying Colonialism*, 46-7.

Because of the psychological and existential realities associated with his struggle, the Algerian man recognizes a different interpretation of his living text (his experience and what he recognizes about his experience). He recognizes that in order to survive the occupier's assault, it involved his recognition of the intentional manipulation of the Algerian woman and it involved how he [the Algerian man] responded to the fourth beast's pressure on his and her self-consciousness.

Fortunately for the Algerian man, the Algerian woman possessed a deep love for her culture and people [her spirituality is something that I associate with John Coltrane's music]. Because of her deep love, she resisted the colonizer's attempt to manipulate her. In fact, because of the veil, she was able to interpret the colonizer (he could not interpret her because she could hide beneath the veil). In so many words, the Algerian woman could not, or would not, permit herself to actualize Eurocentrism as her worldview. Instead she rejects its cultural claim of superiority over her own. What is recognized here is the Algerian woman claims her black self-consciousness. Put in another way, the Algerian woman demonstrates her deep love of self and her black self-consciousness, as a negritude womanist's.

The woman of color's involvement and contributions to defining negritude changes black and white relations as Sonia Kruks remarks, "Yet, however reactive it might be, *negritude* is also necessary. For it does effect a shift in black and white relations. Not only does it offer the black sources of pride, but the white suddenly recognizes in the Negro qualities that he now experiences himself as lacking, such as closeness to nature, spontaneity, simplicity."[43] This sense of self-lack is a plausible cause for the dehumanization of people of color that I associate with the fourth beast which is Eurocentrism.

Fanon for example, suggests that universally people outside of the veil are familiar with people of color – within the veil through stories about blacks. "The black man has penetrated the culture of certain countries... In the United States, for example, the white

---

43. Sonia Kruks, "Fanon, Sartre, and Identity Politics," in *Fanon: A Critical Reader*, 130. Kruks added her own emphasis on negritude in the text.

child, even if he does not live in the South, where the Blacks are a visible presence, knows them through the stories of Uncle Remus. In France, it would be through Uncle Tom's Cabin."[44]

When referring to the fictional but symbiotic character that is Brer Rabbit, Fanon remarks, "Therefore it is relatively easy to recognize the black man in his extraordinary ironical and artful disguise as the rabbit."[45] As Fanon did, I to turn to Bernard Wolfe's interpretation of Brer Rabbit that sheds further light onto the subject of how people of color are relegated to invisibility and how the black male is castrated by Eurocentrism, and how its beastly nature assumes control over subjects and images:

> In all evidence, Brer Rabbit is animal because the black man must be an animal. The rabbit is an outsider because the black man must be branded as an outsider down to his chromosomes. Ever since slavery began, his Christian and democratic guilt as slave owner has led the Southerner to define the black man as an animal, unshakeable African whose nature is fixed in his protoplasm by "African genes [']. The black man has been assigned to human limbo not because of America but because of the constitutional inferiority of his ancestors in the jungle.[46]

Of course negritude is a forced lived black experience and this enforcement has social and psychological baggage that is associated with black life. Negritude is also another way of expressing the Du Boisian definition for double consciousness. Fanon puts it this way, "In effect what happens is this: as I begin to recognize that the Negro is the symbol of sin, I catch myself hating the Negro. But then I recognize that I am a Negro. There are two ways out of this conflict. Either I ask others to pay no attention to my skin, or else I want them to be aware of it."[47] As I have mentioned earlier, we notice negritude functioning as a dimension of double

---

44. Fanon, *Black Skin, White Masks,* 151.
45. Ibid.
46. Ibid., 152.
47. David Theo Goldberg, "In/Visibility and Super/Vision" in *Fanon: A Critical Reader,* 186. Also see Frantz Fanon, *Black Skin, White Masks,* 197.

consciousness but now I am able to locate negritude in the stories of the Algerian woman, Mayotte and the young maiden in the Song of Solomon.

This captures the essence of double consciousness. Also Fanon argues that "It is the white man who creates the Negro. But it is the Negro who creates negritude." This term negritude points to a larger literary movement, which reflects an ongoing resistance - struggle against French colonialism but it also acknowledges the psychological and emotion damages that universally, Eurocentrism causes people of color. Today negritude is a globally shared black experience which comes to the surface as a nationalist's protest against global socio-marginalization.[48]

Because of the belligerence of negritude, which is a way of saying "think of me what you will, but I know who I am," the Algerian man recognized his struggle is his and her struggle. It is a struggle that is shaped in negritude and as a result, negritude shapes people of color around this common and globally shared experience. In other words, the Algerian movement evolved into a negritude –egalitarian, resistance struggle which became recognizable in their shared experience. Without accepting the contributions, commitment and help from the Algerian woman, the occupier soundly defeats the Algerian man. "The violence of the occupier, his ferocity, his delirious attachment to the national territory, induced the leaders no longer to exclude certain forms of combat... The women's entry into the war had to be harmonized

---

48. My intention is not to overly emphasis the term Negritude but to point to its larger implications. Fanon uses the term to describe an imposed pathology upon people of color, and in this instance, Algerians. What is more, the psychological ramifications of negritude goes to the root of Algerian double consciousness which becomes a nationalist's worldview as noted in this excerpt from Fanon's *Black Skin, White Masks* (New York: Grove Press, 1952), 103. "My negritude is not a stone, its deafness hurled against the clamor of day. My negritude is not an opaque spot of dead water over the dead eye of the earth. My negritude is neither a tower or a cathedral It reaches deep down into the red flesh of the soil It reaches deep into the blazing flesh of the sky It pierces opaque prostration with its straight patience." Fanon quotes this from Cesaire, *Notebook of a Return to My Native* Land, trans. Rosello and Pritchard, 110-14.

with respect for revolutionary nature of the war. In other words, the women had to show as much spirit of sacrifice as the men."[49]

Fanon demonstrates that the Algerian struggle for freedom evolves, it moves from a male dominated struggle and transforms into an inclusive struggle that includes the woman and in this instances her affirming love and support of the Algerian man. Thus social context in the Algerian struggle serves as an example of how social contexts influence interpretation of events and I would add social context influences interpretation of texts. This is commonly accepted as a hermeneutic circle. A final note, the Du Boisian hermeneutic of double consciousness is shaped by psychosocial conditions namely; race, economics, politics, gender and male and female relations and other hermeneutic cues— *within the veil.*[50]

Hermeneutic Leap and the Du Boisian Hermeneutic Circle

A hermeneutic leap must fit squarely within a hermeneutic circle and then spring forth. Josiah Young, III, a liberation theologian, suggests that theology finds its formation in a similar way, "Theology emerges from critical theory tested in political struggle." He follows with a similar statement that I want to associate with the Du Boisian hermeneutic of double

---

49. Fanon, *A Dying Colonization* 48.
50. I argue in "Black Folk's Blues and Jazz Hermeneutic" in *Journal of Religious Thought.* Volume 60, Number 2; Volume 61, Numbers 1 and 2; Volume 63; Numbers 1 and 2 (2008-2010). 125-147 that hermeneutic cues function similarly to what David J. Randolph and Stephen Reid define as the context for hermeneutics; they call it "in light of the Bible" whereas I simply call it social context or hermeneutic cues. For people of color and namely African Americans, hermeneutic cues are in the domains of communal worlds such as psychospiritual, sociopolitical and socioeconomic worldviews and from these hermeneutic cues emerge such as spirituals, the blues, jazz and others that grow out a perspective of socio-marginalization. Also see Cleo La Rue, *The Heart of Black Preaching* (Louisville, Westminster John Knox, 2000). La Rue is influenced by David Kelsey's *The Uses of Scripture in Recent Theology* where he develops an ethos among black preachers who rely on this notion of a "master lens."

consciousness. Young writes, "Thus orthopraxis, the balancing of theory and practice, produces correct hermeneutics in opposition to the structural violence of oppressive societies."[51] Young affirms what Fanon understands about the Algerian struggle; it was a social context that made possible a different interpretation of events. The Algerian resistance struggle began as a patriarchal dominated struggle but through sociopolitical events it evolved into an egalitarian resistance movement. Also – Young rightly understands that out of social contexts and hermeneutic cues develop and as a result a hermeneutic circle emerges.[52]

In the Algerian struggle a different social context emerges for the Algerian man. He recognizes his political realities, and as a result, he begins to embrace the matriarchal contributions from the Algerian woman which shapes his sociopolitical context. It is this context where his epiphany occurs. For him, his epiphany appears through his political realities which pose questions to the Algerian man "What is the lesser of the two evils? While you resist Eurocentrism and embrace liberation and while the occupier's quest is to destroy your culture, and you, the Algerian man, in order to survive are you willing to participate in liberating the Algerian woman?" The Algerian man chose the latter and thus he embraces his new realities. Thus the Algerian man's interpretation of the Algerian resistance movement evolves; it provides for the Algerian man, an appreciation for the Algerian woman's equal commitment to their shared pursuit – which is liberation.

The Algerian resistance movement is a historical example of how the Du Boisian hermeneutic of double consciousness is shaped and how it functions. Our point of departure then is to associate with Young's contribution, specifically that a hermeneutic circle is funded by sociopolitical realities that cause our interpretations of events to progressively change as our circumstances of survival increase and decrease. Young further suggest that like theology which he claims is informed by social

51. Josiah Ulysses Young, III, *A Pan-African Theology: Providence And The Legacies of The Ancestors* (Trenton, NJ: African World Press, Inc., 1992), 83.
52. What I describe is the "hermeneutic circle," See Gustavo Gutierrez, *A Theology of Liberation: History, Politics, and Salvation,* trans. Sister Caridad Inda and John Eagleson (Maryknoll, N.Y.: Orbis, 1973), 4.

analysis, religio-cultural analysis and interpretation of Scripture, hermeneutics follows a similar circle: "These three interconnected elements mutually condition one another and shift in significance according to the realities of specific contexts."[53]

As the Algerian man's resistance movement had progressively gotten worse, his emancipation seemed to decrease from the ferocious attacks of the French colonialists. To survive the occupiers, the Algerian man begins to sense that his movement has evolved into something "otherwise." In this instance, "otherwise" is an egalitarian resistance. Young's claims parallel what the Algerian man sees [what he experiences]. In order to be successful in his struggle, he begins to see a "shift in significance according to the realities of [his] specific contexts." His reality is now interpreted and accepted as an egalitarian movement.

What else can be determined at this point? We can determine that interpretation of Scripture differs from social context to social context, which leads to different religious analysis that forms a hermeneutic circle. By employing the Algerian resistance context as an example, the Du Boisian hermeneutic of double consciousness emerges as social and psychological pathologies; double consciousness also emerges out of protest and resistance and therefore, it is associated with dialectic which funds the prophetic critique of Eurocentrism.

To address Eurocentrism and other forms of hegemonic marginalization, I posit that the Du Boisian hermeneutic begins with what I identify with Rentia Weems' contributions in the field. That is, people of color rightly have a suspicion of Eurocentrism. This is similar to the Algerian woman's suspicion of French Eurocentrism. In this instance, a much quoted passage from Justo L. Gonzalez and Catherine G. Gonzalez is helpful:

> Firstly, there is our way of experiencing reality, which leads us to ideological suspicion. Secondly, there is the application of our ideological superstructure in general and to theology in particular. Thirdly, there comes a new way of experiencing theological reality that leads us to exegetical suspicion that the prevailing interpretation of

---

53. Ibid., 85.

the Bible has not taken important pieces of data into account. Fourthly, we have our new hermeneutic that is our new way of interpreting the fountainhead) with the new elements at our disposal. [54]

The Gonzalez's ideological suspicion parallels the Algerian woman's suspicion of the French occupiers. These claims are substantiated by other common experiences shared by people of color (including Latin brothers and sisters). This is an accurate description of how hermeneutical social location functions in the Du Boisian hermeneutic of double consciousness. Also the Gonzalez's hermeneutic process is compelling and today, it is nearly normative. This is so because their hermeneutic process takes personal experience seriously such as race, gender, class, and sexual orientation.

Ideological superstructural claims, which is Eurocentrism, reinforces adherence to institutional authorities; and Eurocentrism-authoritarianism limits counter arguments whether these counter arguments are located in legal, political, scientific or theological spheres and of course this affords large advantages to Eurocentric people of non-color, privilege (i.e., biases, hegemonies). If double consciousness is important, then, it is also important to note and agree with the Gonzalez's hermeneutic contributions; which are that interpreters should be suspicious of hermeneutics informed by Eurocentrism. Secondly, it is important to see Eurocentrism as a biased institutional authority that knowingly, or unknowingly, limits possible alternative readings of texts.

The Du Boisian hermeneutic takes the Gonzalez's hermeneutic process seriously but it adds Weems' suspicions of Eurocentrism. It further embraces black womanist's claims over and against Eurocentric feminists' claims. As I earlier indicated, I cannot separate negritude and black womanist formation. It is the Algerian woman who emerges as the heroine in Fanon's "Algeria Unveiled." When she participates in the resistance movement instead of embracing a Eurocentric imposed liberalism upon her culture, she affirms an actualized identity for herself; she also affirms her

---

54. Justo L. Gonzalez and Catherine G. Gonzalez, *Liberation Preaching: the Pulpit and the Oppressed* (Nashville: Abingdon, 1980), 31.

Algerian man and his actualized identity. I turn again to Sharpley-Whiting and her defense of Fanon's interpretation in this instance of Mayotte Capecia:

> But can we speak of such a concept, past and present, of Fanonian feminism, Fanon as a feminist, or a liberatory anti-racist praxis that employs Fanon? Given the totality of Fanon's writings on Algerian women, the veil, feminist resistance to colonial exploitation his usefulness in revealing Capecia's *blackfemmephobia* and racial malaise as an attendant response to the colonial enterprise, and his continued relevance for the colonized in the United States and contemporary black feminist literary and cultural studies, one is compelled to deliver a resounding "yes."[55]

I am prepared to defend Fanon as egalitarian as does Sharpley-Whiting. I am not willing however, to identify Eurocentrism's feminism with black womanism. When Sharpley- Whiting refers to "black feminist" she does employ the term but only as an African American thoughtful scholar. I however, associate feminism with the dominating female white Eurocentric classes, or simply as another dimension of Eurocentrism. Feminism, in disguise, is Eurocentrism's false benevolence toward women of color; and when women of color refuse to support the white female's agenda; which is to replace the white male as the new white subject, this benevolence is withdrawn.

Frances Beale, points out this hypocrisy. In her essay, "Double Jeopardy: To Be Black and Female," she creates distance from feminism so that she can define black womanism. Beale correctly cites that a major difference between Eurocentric feminism and the black woman's struggle is that the latter is fighting for her very existence, "Black people are engaged in a life and death struggle

---

55. T. Denean Sharpely-Whiting, "Engaging Fanon to Reread Capecia" in *Fanon: A Critical Reader*, 161-2. Sharpley-Whiting adds emphasis to *blackfemmephobia* in the text.

and the main emphasis on Black women must be to combat the capitalist [Eurocentrism], racist exploitation of Black people:"[56]

> Another major differentiation is that the white women's liberation movement is basically middle-class. Very few of these women suffer extreme economic exploitation that most Black women are subjected to day by day. This is the factor that is most crucial for us. It is not an intellectual persecution alone; it is not an intellectual outburst for us; it is quite real. We as Black women have got to deal with the problems that the Black masses deal with, for our problems in reality are one and the same.[57]

For the female black woman, her reality cannot be compared with that of some white females who see themselves as well provided for "Desperate Housewives."

Historically white feminists have earned their voice but they too have become insiders of Eurocentrism. Like their white male counterparts, white feminist's claims are spoken from a very privileged social location of power. Their location of power is quite different from that of people of color; and specifically the woman of color. White feminists have institutional advantages that far exceed that of a woman of color whether her location is among the wealthiest in her race.[58]

Thus a reasonable case can be made that Eurocentric feminism can be a manipulator and can find ways to exploit even some of the most intelligent black women unaware of the white feminist's agenda. The feminist's agenda may parallel the Algerian woman's veil and the sociopolitical ramifications that surrounded it. As the Algerian woman did, the black womanist must place her agenda alongside that of the white feminist's for comparison. The

---

56. Frances Beale, "Double Jeopardy" To Be Black and Female" in *Black Theology" a Documentary History volume one: 1966-1979* eds. James H. Cone and Gayraud S. Wilmore (Marykoll, NY: Orbis, 1998),290.
57. Ibid., 291.
58. The Clarence Thomas and the Anita Hill incident was not solely about sexual harassment in my view. It was a Eurocentric feminist's battle over equality fought in black face.

hermeneutic of suspicion, which grows out of the Du Boisian hermeneutic of double consciousness funds for the black woman a way to analyze these two different agendas.

What is clear, the black womanist's agenda is for black liberation. In "Violent Women: Surging in Forbidden Quarters," Nada Elia, as a Fanonian, writes about emancipation of women. Elia remarks, "I seek to claim Fanon's discourse on liberation as a framework for women's liberation"[59] Though Elia does not explicitly define black womanism as a separate category from feminism, she admits that she knows best the experience of the woman of color and her journey toward emancipation for herself, her man, and her family is informed by her black womanist's experience. Elia further knows that because of her experience, Eurocentrism does not willingly displace itself as the white subject. What funds the white subject? It is Eurocentric mythologies such as the notion about the aesthetic superiority of the white male, his masculinity, and his intellect and the notion about the aesthetic superiority of the white female, her femininity and intellect are superior to all other people. This mythology reinforces the white subject which is Eurocentrism.

This helps to understand Elia's point of departure, "I also hope to explain certain actions undertaken in the name of liberation, which would be hard to describe as feminist – namely the adoption of physical or psychological violence by women."[60] She adds, "The subject of my discourse will be women of color, since I am most familiar with their circumstances, but also because I believe an analysis of their emancipation can be transferred to that of white women with much less difficulty than the other way round."[61] This is black womanism informing white feminism and it of course makes the woman of color the sociopolitical and literary subject of her own story and mythology. As a result, it changes Eurocentric interpretation to black womanist's interpretation at the very least, but it is more. It is an egalitarian interpretation because men of color are not attacked nor replaced but indeed affirmed.

---

59. Nada Elia, "Violent Women: Surging into Forbidden Quarters" in *Fanon: A Critical Reader*, 168.
60. Ibid.
61. Ibid.

A woman of color is the subject, teacher and facilitator; she is in control of her substance, story and initial interpretation. Elia is rare; she seems to separate feminism from femininity stating that the latter "cannot advance the cause of women, if femininity means submissiveness, subordination, meek acquiesces, and other such 'lovely' and delicate' attributes."[62] To make clear her thesis's argument, Elia, employs Sojourner Truth's remarks in a speech where Truth denounces "the denial of her very humanity by white men and women, the latter being, on the racial level…"[63]

Anglo females benefit from their skin privileges as do their fathers, husbands, brothers and sons. For example, I return to Fanon's "The Man of Color and the White Woman," in *Black Skin, White Masks*. In this chapter, Fanon introduces his readers to what appears to be the black male's infatuation with the white female. Fanon posits, there is a primary reason for this:

> Out of the blackest part of my soul, through the zone of hachures, surges up this desire to be white. I want to be recognized not as *Black*, but as *White*. But – and this is the form of recognition that Hegel never described – who better than the white woman to bring this about? By loving me, she proves to me that I am worthy of a white love. I am loved like a white man. I am a white man. Her love opens the illustrious path that leads to total fulfillment… I espouse white culture, white beauty, [and] white whiteness.[64]

Perhaps because Fanon is a psychiatrist, it may explain why he seems indifferent. He reminds his readers that he is merely offering analysis "By analyzing *I am a Martinican Woman* and *Nini* we have seen how the black woman behaves toward the white male. With a novel by Rene Maran – apparently an autobiography – we shall endeavor to understand the case of the black man."[65]

---

62. Ibid.
63. Ibid., 166.
64. Fanon, "The Man of Color and The White Woman" in *Black Skin and White Masks*, 45.
65. Ibid., 46. See Rene Maran's autobiography is *Un home pareil aux autres*.

Fanon's critique of Maran, suggests that he is manipulating his readers. Fanon writes of Maran's principle character, Jean Veneuse as a "magnificent example that will allow us to study in depth the attitude of the black man. Jean Veneuse is a Negro. Of Antillean origin, he has lived in Bordeaux for many years so he's European. But he is black, so he's a Negro. This is the crux of the matter. He does not understand his race, and the Whites don't understand him."[66] By understanding "the black man," Fanon means a doubling of sorts which he clearly expresses in the last quotation that I've cited where Maran funds for Fanon his analysis of double consciousness and how it functions in a black man. Fanon and Maran conclude that there is a breed of black man who is socially located and possessed psychologically within – the veil.

Fanon knows well that Maran is a radical democrat in our Americanized terms. He knows that Maran is also considered the father of negritude in literary terms. But Fanon wants to transform the literary function of negritude into a national if not an international social movement. As a movement, Negritude parallels the American Black Power movement. Both signal a kind of cultural zeitgeist where people of color began to realize that time had come for them to protest and resist further cultural hegemony and by definition is Eurocentrism.

Conclusion

Fanon uses the Algerian woman and her struggle for self-consciousness and independence from Eurocentrism to show us how the Du Boisian hermeneutic of double consciousness functions in different world regions and different historic periods. The hermeneutic is birthed out of protest and it informs rhetorical refutation. It follows then, the Du Boisian hermeneutic funds Du Boisian preachers with rhetoric of refutation against cultural hegemony which I clearly see in Eurocentrism.

I suggest that through an epiphany, the Algerian man understands, appreciates and shares human equality with the Algerian woman. I ground this in the Algerian man's revelatory recognition of her equality in his transcendent experience. It is the personification of the Du Boisian hermeneutic of double

---

66. Ibid., 46.

consciousness' deferred understanding of meaning. The Algerian man recognizes the equality of Algerian woman through her loyalty to country and culture and her commitment to his struggle to be an independent woman from French Eurocentrism. Without the Algerian woman, the Algerian man knows that their movement fails.

Like Du Bois, Fanon employs the Du Boisian hermeneutic of double consciousness but Fanon's double consciousness differs. On the first hand, Du Bois's double consciousness was primarily an analysis of human social conditions. Fanon on the other hand, his analysis seems primarily to emphasize the psychological life – within the veil. For Du Boisian preachers, Du Bois and Fanon provide critique of the American master/slave and colonizer/colonized human narratives and psychospiritual conditions that each addresses. What is now necessary is a Du Boisian eschatological language to communicate beyond Eurocentrism's manipulations and control over categories that render people of color as second class citizens of the world.

The following chapter will address this as we focus on the Du Boisian meta-Narrative. That chapter will take into consideration the two major chapters on hermeneutics and invent rhetoric to tell the people of color's story which is the Du Boisian meta-narrative.

Chapter Four: A Different Way to Tell the Story: The Du Boisian Rhetorical Strategy

❧

I have essayed in a half century three sets of thought centering around the hurts and hesitancies that hem the black man in America. The first of these, "The Souls of Black Folk," written thirty-seven years ago, was a cry at midnight thick within the veil, when none rightly knew the coming day. The second, "Darkwater," now twenty years old, was an exposition and militant challenge, defiant with dogged hope. This third book started to record dimly but consciously that subtle sense of coming day which one feels of early mornings even when mist and murk hang low.

"Apology," *Dusk of Dawn*, W. E. B. Du Bois[1]

In Chapter 1, I described W. E. B. Du Bois as a nonecclesial prophet. He was more than that; he was a secular-sacred prophet. He was a seer. I also suggested that by analyzing his writings, it provides a gate way into his worldview and thus provides a point of departure for a biblical hermeneutic, namely the Du Boisian hermeneutic. Because the world's populations are mostly marginalized and people of color, I further suggested that they share a worldview, which I characterized as people groups perceiving the world through a lens of marginalization.[2] It follows that people of color arrange, hear, and tell their stories in similar fashions.

---

1. W. E. B. Du Bois, *Dusk of Dawn: An Essay toward an Autobiography of a Race Concept* (Piscataway, NJ: Transaction Publishers, 1984), xxix.
2. See Alvin Padilla, "A New Kind of Theological Contextualized Theological Education Models" In *Africanus Journal 2, no. 2*

In this chapter, I suggest that a similar analysis be applied to Du Bois's rhetoric. His rhetoric will help preachers to develop a Du Boisian meta-narrative (I will address this later in this chapter) to proclaim biblical stories effectively. That is, by reinterpreting Du Bois's written publications and speeches as civic sermons, preachers can become rhetorpreachers; those who prepare rhetorical sermon strategies for two poles in one world: Eurocentric populations and populations of people of color.

Over the course of his public career, Du Bois boldly defined the twentieth century's largest social obstacle, the "colorline" as oppressive socioracial relations, something that Western institutions, including the church, would not and will not address. As a writer and a speaker, Du Bois paralleled the Hebrew prophets. Like many of his prophetic predecessors, Du Bois preached without ecclesial sanctions and ordinations. As did the prophets, he preached a secular-sacred gospel from a pulpit in the public sphere. Du Bois serves as the epitome of the rhetor-preacher, because he found ways to be heard. He did so by framing the debate around what he knew were systemic evils: economic structures determined along racial lines, distinctions of class, and other forms of human marginalization.

For nearly a century, Du Bois told a story about human marginalization. He crafted a rhetoric that included a folk and mythical rhetorical strategy that oftentimes is employed by Old and New Testament writers. This rhetorical strategy provides rhetorical incarnation that gives voice to his story. Like the Hebrew prophets, Du Bois's story is one about people who are marginalized, but they remain people of faith who personify heroes and heroines. In Du Bois's story, his people are courageous. They faced systemic evils, but they faced these evils with a hope that was yet unborn. In Du

---

(November 2010), 5-6. In this article Padilla writes, "Indeed the whole world has come to our doorstep. Learning to live well in the diverse culture of North America is no longer an option, but a necessity. The U. S. Census estimates that in 2050 the proportion of whites in the population will be only 53%. Our children will live and serve in a society in which their classmates, neighbors and fellow disciples of Christ will be equally divided among whites and people of color."

Bois's time (and ours), racism was public and private enemy number one.

Racism is systemic in Western (Anglo-North America and Europe) thought and culture. Du Bois understood that racism is tawdry and deeply embedded in Western spheres and that Western institutions do not acknowledge the heroic contributions that other-wise peoples have made to the Western meta-narrative. In fact, and to date, the West's rhetoric has not lent itself to removing the white subject from the center of the Western meta-narrative, nor is the West willing to share its rhetorical space with other heroic subjects. In response, this rhetorical strategy provides space for marginalized people to democratically dissent and find ways to be heard in a dominating culture that has been predetermined how the story should be told and how it should end.

I am attracted to Du Boisian rhetoric and suggest that it will have significant influence in twenty-first-century homiletic theory. For those who will employ it, the rhetoric offers a unique capacity to communicate effectively in a prophetic tradition. For preachers to fully appreciate this kind of rhetoric, they must become Du Boisian preachers, women and men who appropriate Du Bois's style. They must take note of the relationships that Du Bois created between his rhetoric and his meta-narrative. This analysis will help twenty-first-century preachers to effectively communicate biblical stories. If correctly employed, it will be similar to Du Bois's communication system that he employed to confront the twentieth century's human marginalization.

Du Boisian preachers committed to reaching marginalized people must find innovative ways of communication in order to be heard. Du Bois indeed found ways; he framed his arguments to suggest that a systemic relationship between race, politics, and economics exists to exploit non-European peoples of color. Several passages in *Darkwater* affirm and explain this relationship. In generation after generation, the relationship among racism, politics, and economics manipulates people of color through the dominant culture's hegemony over canonical spheres and institutions. These manipulations are plausible explanations for why the Du Boisian hermeneutic and rhetoric emerged in Du Bois's writings, speeches, and advocacy.

Confronting Race; Confronting Human Marginalization

Systemic human marginalization remains the central opponent for twenty-first-century citizens. Today's rhetor-preachers thus have an assignment to continue the Du Boisian assault on racism. However, racism extends into other complex forms of human marginalization, including economics and politics, which are often misunderstood, ignored, and overlooked. To correct this oversight, Du Boisian preachers must be bold seers who courageously confront these complexities, which are veiled underneath socioeconomic constructs that are at the root of human marginalization. This will bring incarnation to the words, "For the love of money is a root of all kinds of evil" (1 Tim. 6:10). Du Bois wrote in *Dusk of Dawn*, "It was not until I was long out of college and had finished the first phase of my teaching career that I began to see clearly the connection of economics and politics; the fundamental influence of man's efforts to earn a living upon all his other efforts."[3]

Du Bois published *Dusk of Dawn* with an "Apology" that chronicles American sociopolitical and economic history through his own intellectual lenses and experiences. Du Bois presents his life as a metaphoric representation of universal, human marginalization. In the chapter-opening excerpt, Du Bois begins his defense by revealing to his readers his reasons for writing *The Souls of Black Folk* (presumably by 1940, the time of the first publication of *Dusk of Dawn*, Du Bois knew that he had new readers, many of whom were more than likely unfamiliar with *Souls'* original rhetorical context and premise).

In *Souls*, Du Bois's metaphoric veil represents the marginalized sociopolitical and socioeconomic human condition; the worst of these conditions were its psychological and emotional apathy. I associate these forms of apathy with paralysis of the human will that keeps people from striving toward full human development and personality. What is more, these forms of apathy are conditions that set human boundaries and, even more disturbing, limitations inside those boundaries. It is apathy that symbolizes the epitome of the veil. In Chapter 1, I introduced psychospiritual

---

3. Du Bois, "The Nineteenth Century" in *Dusk of Dawn*, 41.

awareness as a part of the Du Boisian hermeneutic, and I believe that these forms of marginalization and apathy are its seedbed.

Du Bois's symbolic veil expresses the limited expectations that African Americans are forced to accept, along with the world that quarantines people of color. Du Bois's pole in our one world was thus, understandably, bleak and dreadful. In *Darkwater*, Du Bois explains that at the time of its writing, he was engaged in a dialectic struggle between dim faith and darker fatalism, the latter an exigency for 1960s' militancy, which I insist was necessary. This militancy signifies a forming black consciousness, a psychospiritual awakening, and a spiritual catharsis. These experiences created a new birth, an immersion that led African Americans to refute racial hegemony and other forms of apathy.

Du Bois struggled with Eurocentric assumptions that acted as deliberate reinforcements of psychological and emotional apathy among nonwhites: "This assumption that of all the hues of God whiteness alone is inherently and obviously better than brownness or tan leads to curious acts; even the sweeter souls of the dominant world as they discourse with me on weather, weal, and woe are continually playing above their actual words an obbligato of tune and tone."[4] By this, I take Du Bois to mean that many whites, whether consciously or not, assumed racial and cultural superiority.

These advantages afford whites permission to verbally marginalize other-wise people. This is noticed in obbligato tones, which I assume to mean that it does not matter whether whites feel they are right or wrong; they, in fact, are never wrong.

Du Bois suggested that he wrote *Dusk of Dawn* because he thought that democracy was nearing its twilight. Similar to his other publications, Du Bois's strategy is dialectic; it points toward a frame of reference that parallels human marginalization in contrast with the dominant culture, its classes and social advantages reinforced through manipulation of race, economics, and politics. Irene Diggs, writing in the introduction to a republication of *Dusk of Dawn*, provides a sociohistorical context for the project: "*An Essay Toward an Autobiography of a Race Concept* should be read against the background of race in the latter part of the nineteenth

---

4. W. E. B. Du Bois, *Darkwater: Voices Within the Veil* (Mineola, NY: Dover, 1999), 17-18.

and first half of the twentieth century when throughout the dominant world, race, color, or an ancestry of color was a badge of inferiority." What Diggs describes as inferiority is a recapitulation of psychological and emotional apathy.

It is important to add that race, economics, and politics are employed as manipulative demagogues that reinforce forms of apathy. It is important for Du Boisian preachers to understand that these conditions remain ever-present among many people of color. If underprivileged and underclassed economic and political conditions remain among people, any people, they will be filled with apathy and the metaphoric veil will remain intact. This phenomenon is central to understanding the psychological and emotional apathy among the sons of Israel in the book of Exodus, "I will bring you to the land which I swore to give to Abraham, Isaac, and Jacob, and I will give it to you for a possession; I am the Lord. So Moses spoke thus to the sons of Israel, but they did not listen to Moses on account of their despondency and cruel bondage" (Ex. 6:8-9).

This passage illustrates manipulation of race, economics, and politics that resulted in psychological and emotional apathy among the sons of Israel. Constant oppressive cruelty leads to this kind of despondent behavior. It forms a nihilistic cultural pathology. It forms shared cultural values influenced by apathy. These sociopsychological and socioeconomic conditions make it nearly impossible to respond to promises made by outsiders. In the Exodus passage, God too, was an outsider. Like the sons of Israel, people of color are conditioned to live existentially and cannot bear to believe in the covenant promise made to them through Abraham. In many parts of the world where twenty-first-century Du Boisian rhetor-preachers will preach, they will face this kind of pathology and despondency.

What is more, Diggs writes, "This concept of race was arbitrarily defined, bold, deep-seated, and sanctioned by science, law, religion, and public opinion. Science and distinguished scientists, with very few exceptions, supported the belief in the intellectual, cultural, and biological inferiority of all non-Whites."[5]

---

5. Irene Diggs, "Introduction" in *Dusk of Dawn*, viii. Irene Diggs wrote "Introduction To The Transaction Edition" for this 1984 edition.

In so many words, Diggs suggests that Du Bois understood that Western institutional spheres and canons are closed and used to manipulate people of color, thus reinforcing stereotypes and negative images that further relegated these other-wise people into the sociomargins.[6]

Commenting on race, class, science, and economics, and their influence on democracy, Du Bois wrote: "There persisted the mud – sill theory of society that civilization not only permitted but must have the poor. Western Europe did not and does not want democracy, never believed in it, never practiced it and never without fundamental and basic revolution will accept it." [7] Because of social advantages that racial unrests assures, they form a construct of Western hegemony. Without democratic protest, Du Bois is persuaded that Western culture will neither change, nor can it change, and he echoes reasons why Western rhetoric is benignly self-limited.

The Du Boisian Cultural Aesthetic

The limitations placed on people of color are embedded in Eurocentrism and through the beast, a permanent caste system that is better known as Western hegemony. This is evident in Western canonical formation. To counter Western culture's racial hegemony and canonical formation and its insatiable insistence for a permanent racial, economic, and political underclass, Du Bois began to construct a counter culture aesthetic to support and inform his rhetoric. In terms of canonical formation, Du Bois was a forerunner of black arts as an aesthetic and as a movement. What differs from other Western cultural assumptions is that the African American aesthetic is born of prophetic refutation; it refutes the dominant culture's claims of universal superiority.

Thus the African American aesthetic is dialectic, as is Du Bois's rhetoric; both are a part of a global advocacy movement that

---

6. I recognize and affirm Henry Louis Gates, Jr., for his contribution to addressing this "closed canon." As Du Bois understood the hegemony over the Western canon, Gates responded by writing *Loose Canons: Notes on the Culture Wars* (Oxford: Oxford University Press, 1992).

7. Du Bois, *Dusk of Dawn*, 170.

continues to evolve. The Arab Spring is a contemporary example. Arabic and African nations such as Algeria, Egypt, Libya, Syria, and Tunisia are engaged in twenty-first-century pan-African demonstrations and civil rights struggles. These demonstrations and struggles parallel African American aesthetical thought, which spiritually parallels the Black Power concept. In this way, the African American aesthetic is in the center of a radical reordering of the Western cultural aesthetic. "It proposes a separate symbolism, mythology and critique and iconology."[8]

In large measure, the Du Boisian aesthetic began a paradigm shift toward full self-affirmation and identity among people of color. Du Bois, writing to encourage and challenge black public intellectuals to further create a counterculture understanding of aesthetic beauty said:

> ... [I]t is the bounden duty of black America to begin this great work of the creation of Beauty, of the preservation of Beauty, of the realization of Beauty, and we must use in this work all methods that men have used before. And what have been the tools of the artist in times gone by? First of all, he has used the Truth – not for the sake of truth, not as a scientist seeking truth, but as one upon whom Truth eternally thrust itself as the highest handmaid of imagination, as the one great vehicle of universal understanding.[9]

Du Bois was joined by many black intellectuals in the early stages of the twentieth century to address the perceptions of aesthetic structure, taste, and polite rules of engagement in the Western cultural main. He, however, was the pioneer who understood beauty as taste, and beauty as form, and that aesthetic beauty is highly subjective. He also knew that Western cultural assumptions needed to be challenged, if not changed, to achieve full equality for people of color in the West and, I add, the world.

---

8. Houston A. Baker, Jr., "Generational Shifts" in *African American Literary Theory: A Reader*, ed. Winston Napier (New York: New York University Press, 2000), 184.

9. W.E.B. Du Bois, "Criteria of Negro Art" in *African American Literary Theory*, 22.

In general terms, aesthetics are culturally inspired perceptions of beauty articulated in language. Cornel West suggests that aesthetics is a "normative gaze, an ideal from which to order and compare observations."[10]

This ideal was drawn primarily from classical aesthetic values of beauty, proportion and human form and classical standards of moderation, self-control and harmony. The role of classical aesthetic and cultural norms in the emergence of the idea of white supremacy as an object of modern discourse cannot be underestimated.[11]

In short, West's definition of aesthetics is a "normative gaze" and a sense of order. His definition is expanded by Henry Louis Gates, Jr.: "Inadvertently, African slavery in the New World satisfied the preconditions for the emergence of a new African culture, a truly Pan-African culture fashioned as a colorful weave of linguistic, institutional, metaphysical, and formal threads. What survived this fascinating process was [were] the most useful and the most compelling of the fragments at hand." Gates defines African-American culture in this way: "Afro-American culture is an African culture with a difference as signified as the catalysts of English, Dutch, French, Portuguese, or Spanish languages and cultures, which informed the precise structures that each discrete New World Pan-African culture assumed."[12]

Gates's comments about "difference as signified as the catalysts... which informed the precise structures that each discrete New World Pan-African culture assumed" suggest that African American culture is born out protest and rhetorically expresses itself in every discipline in forms of dialectic. If this is a fair reading of what Gates asserts, his understanding supports my premise that African American culture is a constant struggle with and for self-affirmation and identity. On the other hand, black culture is a

---

10. Cornel West, *The Cornel West Reader* (New York: Civitas Books, 1999), 75.

11. Ibid.

12. Henry Louis Gates, Jr., *The Signifying Monkey* (Oxford: Oxford University Press 1988), 4.

dialectic struggle that influences all cultural thought in every way, in every discipline—including theology and homiletic theory.

For Du Boisian preachers, it is vitally important to understand and appreciate the black aesthetic in its various forms. They must understand that the aesthetic form is influenced by dialectic. This informs Du Boisian preachers to be counterculturalists and advocates for different definitions of beauty, order, and canonical formation. This is a prophetic call to collective consciousness and shared values. This cultural aesthetic provides rhetorical form and empowers intellectuals, priests, and prophets to speak truth against hegemonic power (this is another way to describe the aesthetic shape that leads to dialectic function). Amiri Baraka's enigmatic poem "SOS" is an example of art and beauty, collective consciousness and activism:

> Calling black people.
> Calling all black people, man woman child
> Wherever you are, calling you, urgent, come in
> Black people come in, wherever you are, urgent, calling
> You, calling all black people
> Calling all black people, come in, black people, come on in.[13]

The poem is a work of art and symmetrical beauty; it has a rhythm like a hypnotic sermonic drum cadence. Its rhetorical strategy is calling people to collective consciousness without actually defining the reasons they should come. Because people of color share a similar existential condition, Baraka does not need to define the call. Baraka deliberately leaves the poem's meaning hidden so that it is only discernible to those who have a pre-understanding. This is because Baraka employs double-talk. At a close reading, however, it is a call to demand justice. Because the call for justice is laden with beauty and symmetry, it is also a call for harmony.

Baraka's poem is also a call to self-affirmation and identity; it is very similar to African and African American call–and-response. The call is to black nationalism; by political implication, it is also a

---

13. Jay R. Berry "Poetic Style in Amira Baraka's Black Art," *CLA Journal,* December, 1988.

pan-African response of advocacy. By this I mean that Baraka effectively portrays black people as a group who have shared values and experiences. This provides for Baraka's rhetorical space to employ a collective folk and mythical hero/heroine rhetorical strategy. In this way, his poem is a function of the black aesthetic. Furthermore, Baraka's rhetorical strategy invents the courageous black subject. His poem parallels a biblical folk and mythical hero rhetorical strategy that I have identified in the Isaiah 52:1-3:

Awake, awake, O Zion,
Clothe yourself with strength,
Put on your garments of splendor,
O Jerusalem, the holy city.
The uncircumcised and defiled
will not enter you again.
Shake off your dust;
Rise up, sit enthroned, O Jerusalem.
Free yourself from the chains on your neck,
O captive Daughter of Zion.
For this is what the Lord says:
You were sold for nothing,
And without money you will be redeemed.

Notice the parallels between Baraka's and Isaiah's poetry that I have located as Du Boisian rhetoric. Each is a call to collective consciousness, to self-affirmation and identity and to nationalism; the response is to become an advocate for justice. Each identifies shared values and experiences; each employs a folk and mythical hero rhetorical strategy; each functions as an aesthetic. Thus the black aesthetic parallels the Hebrew prophetic tradition and is a spiritual countercultural movement; it is an incarnation by way of dialectic.

The Du Boisian Pan-African Aesthetic

Though the Hebrew prophetic tradition precedes that of Du Bois, he is nonetheless the forerunner of a pan-African aesthetic. In "Of the Dawn of Freedom," an essay that appears in *Souls*, Du Bois makes this familiar statement, "The problem of the twentieth century is the problem of the color-line—the relation of the darker to the lighter races of men in Asia and Africa, in America and the islands of the sea."[14] Du Bois calls attention to divisive racial constructs and their implications. It is also a call to people of color to acknowledge their shared consciousness and the potential it has to harness social synergy. This is the seedbed for the pan-African aesthetic that began as an intellectual paradigm shift that would fuel the twentieth century's African and African American protest movements.

To make public this social synergy, Du Bois crafts mythical heroes and heroines that are evidenced in *Souls* ("Alexander Crummell" and Josie in "The Meaning of Progress" are examples), and his rhetorical strategy is employed to paint his self-heroic portrait. He does so to break from the dominant culture's aesthetic hegemony. Du Bois cast himself as a person born within the veil, a man who could not change his birth status and nearly could not break his racial social caste; he writes, however, that he does so through heroic strength. With this strength, Du Bois fights against this bleak and dreadful condition as noticed in *Dusk of Dawn*'s, first chapter, "The Plot":

> Little indeed did I do, or could I conceivably have done, to make this problem or to loose it. Crucified on the vast wheel of time, I flew round and round with the Zeitgeist, waving my pen and lifting faint voices to explain, expound and exhort; to see, foresee and prophesy to the few who could or would listen. Thus very evidently to me and to others I did little to create my day or greatly change it; but I did exemplify it and thus for all time my life is significant for all of men.[15]

Du Bois employs metaphoric language to express the literalness of his social condition; he makes metaphoric comparisons and alludes to Golgotha ("Crucified on the vast wheel of time") and to German philosophical constructs: "I flew round and round with the Zeitgeist, waving my pen and lifting my pen and lifting faint

---

14. W. E. B. Du Bois, "Of the Dawn of Freedom" in *Souls of Black Folks* (New York Bantam Books, 1989) 16.
15. Du Bois, "The Plot" in *Dusk of Dawn*, 3-4.

voices to explain, expound and exhort," an expression that often is associated with legal and homiletic rhetorical theory. In addition, Du Bois's metaphoric language serves as an example of how he cast himself into the Hebrew prophetic tradition "to foresee and prophesy to the few who could or would listen." He transforms himself into the hero of his autobiographical narrative, a story told through the lens of the "black subject" as hero.

The rhetoric of the black subject acknowledges collective black consciousness and awareness of potential social synergy, an agent for rhetorical change in Western culture. By way of the black subject, Du Boisian preachers create people of color as the heroic characters in the biblical stories. In part, by employing this rhetorical strategy, Du Boisian preachers decentralize Eurocentric hegemony over Western mythologies. Thus, their rhetorical goal is to create an emerging social synergy to confront Western mythologies with their own emerging mythologies located in the Western socio-margins and beyond, wherever people of color are located.

Creating the black subject as hero and heroine is necessary to counter conventional and racially biased Western mythologies, which are tools used to continue human marginalization. For Du Bois, Western mythologies that exploited people through race, class, and science were an unholy trinity. It stands to reason that those Western intuitional spheres—public and private, secular and sacred—share similar myths that James Baldwin would refer to as types of American myths. Baldwin is correct to contend that African Americans and perhaps other people of color are suspicious of Western mythologies (values, traditions, beliefs, and opinions that inform thought and culture):

> The American Negro has the great advantage of having never believed that collection of myths to which white Americans cling' that their ancestors were all freedom-loving heroes, that they were born in the greatest country the world has ever seen, or that Americans are invincible in battle and wise in peace, that Americans have always dealt honorably with Mexicans and Indians and all other

neighbors or inferiors, that American men are the world's most direct and virile, that American women are pure.[16]

This is an example of how Western mythologies function. They are a part of the Western aesthetic and are self-perpetuating, informing the majority culture's Western meta-narrative. Baldwin describes this meta-narrative as a construct that naturally forces other peoples of nonwhite or non-European descent into a status of permanent inferiority.

For Du Bois, then, to continue to tell the Western story about the human family from a Eurocentric perspective, through the conventional Western aesthetic that informs the conventional meta-narrative and influences institutional spheres of power, is to subconsciously tell a Western story that subjugates African Americans, African peoples, and peoples of color into permanent inferiority. Du Bois knew that if they continued to use biased Western mythologies, Africans and African Americans and people of color could neither develop a positive self-affirmation, nor determine their identity without reinforcing an inferiority complex among the masses.

Black collective consciousness is an initial response to Western mythologies and their psychological and emotional effects on people of color. The formation of national consciousness for African Americans can be traced to nineteenth-century ideologies. As Dexter B. Gordon argues, "Early-nineteenth century black nationalist ideology was fashioned out of the shared black experience of white oppression, and especially among activist blacks, the sense of a common need to extricate themselves from that experience."[17] This, according to Gordon, was a "Group-trait and preferences shared by people of African descent were often demeaned by the larger society."

Gordon cites early trends of an emerging collective black consciousness—what I call social synergy—that is located in David

---

16. James Baldwin, *The Fire Next Time* (New York: The Modern Library, 1995), 100.

17. Dexter B. Gordon, *Black Identity: Rhetoric, Ideology, and Nineteenth-Century Black Nationalism* (Carbondale, IL: Southern Illinois University Press, 2003), 78.

Walker's "Appeal" and Robert Alexander Young's *Manifesto* and they serve as foundational points of departure:

> With their call for self-affirmation and self-development among blacks, in contrast to many earlier black appeals that petitioned whites, these two pamphlets ["Appeal" and *Manifesto*] advanced the need for black people to rely primarily on themselves in vital areas of life—economic, political, religious, and intellectual—in order to affect their liberation. These documents are therefore arguably the foundation documents of black nationalism.[18]

In fact, Walker and Young were Du Boisian preachers and timely proponents for protest and advocacy. This is apparent in Young's *Manifesto* and Walker's "Appeal," which were calls to Black Nationalism; each were inventors of the black subject as a mythology, the principal point of departure for developing a shared black consciousness. Walker was a brilliant intellectual and writer. He was well-read and capable of marshaling his defense for African American humanity. He developed what I characterize as a Jeremiad apologetic, as seen in the following passage from the "Appeal":[19]

---

18. Ibid., 79.

19. See Jonathon S. Kahn's "Rewriting the American Jeremiad: On Pluralism, Black Nationalism, and a New America" in *Divine Discontent: The Religious Imagination of W. E. B. Du Bois* (Oxford: Oxford University Press, 2009), 89. Kahn writes compellingly that Du Bois's Jeremiad differs from traditional descriptions of African American Jeremiad, that African American Jeremiad affirms Western mythologies and African American rhetors craft their speeches and essays to appeal to whites, and that blacks do not want to overthrow these mythologies. Instead, blacks want to appropriate Western values and become a part of the American mainstream. Kahn's argument suggests this is not Du Boisian Jeremiad. He writes, "In this chapter I argue that Du Bois' Jeremiadic writings—in particular *Souls* and *Darkwater*—represent just such a pluralistic alternative. Like his prophetic predecessors, Du Bois sought redemption through the Jeremiad by using language of denunciation to introduce the terms for language of affirmation." I agree with Kahn's views namely, Du

Has Mr. Jefferson declared to the world, that we are inferior to the whites, both in endowments of our bodies and our minds? It is indeed surprising, that man of such great learning, combined with such excellent parts, should speak so of a set of men in chains. I do not know what to compare it to, unless, like putting one wild deer in an iron cage, where it will be secured, and hold another by the side of the same, then let it go, and expect the one in the cage to run as fast as the one at liberty.[20]

Walker employs irony to make his defense. First he satirizes Jefferson's hypocritical claims of racial superiority, using double-talk to scold Jefferson's hypocritical behavior: "It is indeed surprising, that a man of such great learning, combined with such excellent parts, should speak so of a set of men in chains." Walker may have been referring to Jefferson's clandestine relationship with his slave and concubine, Sally Hemmings, with whom he shared children.[21]

Jefferson had said that blacks were inferior precisely because they would not rebel to their death against enslavement, while no white man, according to Jefferson, would permit himself to be

---

Bois does not employ his Jeremiad to affirm or appropriate Western cultural norms. Instead du Bois crafts an otherness Jeremiad. In addition, what consider different about Du Bois's so-called Jeremiad is that it is an apologetic. It is consistent with the classical argumentation discussed in *Aristotle's Rhetoric* and Cicero's *Of the Orator.* Also see Jacqueline Bacon's *The Humble Shall Stand Forth: Rhetoric, Empowerment and Abolition* (Columbia, SC: University of South Carolina Press, 2002). Bacon provides an in-depth and thorough treatise on Jeremiad rhetoric which was commonly employed by nineteenth century black abolitionists. I have expanded Bacon's thesis to include apologetics because African Americans are refuting claims of racial inferiority and defending their racial equality. Jeremiad apologetic is a synthesis of these two concepts.

20. David Walker, *To the Coloured Citizens of the World: But in Particular, and Very Expressingly to Those of the United States of America* (New York: Hill and Wang, 1965), 10.

21. Annette Gordon-Reed, *Thomas Jefferson & Sally Hemmings: An American Controversy* (Charlottesville: University of Virginia Press, 1997).

enslaved.[22] This too is an example of a nineteenth-century invention of Western mythology that celebrated the courageous white subject. In response, Walker again employs irony when he suggests "I do not know what to compare it to, unless, like putting one wild deer in an iron cage, where it will be secured, and hold another by the side of the same, then let it go, and expect the one in the cage to run as fast as the one at liberty."[23] In our contemporary times, Walker would be called an advocate for affirmative action, because he makes compelling arguments that are similar to those made by contemporary proponents for affirmative action policy and legislation. Of course, affirmative action is the result of prophetic protests and advocacy.

Robert Young's *Manifesto* is another example of a Jeremiad apologetic; it is clearly a model for tracing the origins of a collective black consciousness. His pamphlet is brief, but Young uses it to invent a black subject and, in this instance, a people who doggedly pursue their own humanity through their protests for liberation:

> We find we possess in ourselves an understanding; of this we are taught to know the ends of right and wrong, that depression should come upon us or any of our race, of the wrongs inflicted of us of men. We know in ourselves we possess a right to see ourselves justified there from, of the right of God; knowing but of his power that he decreed to man, that either in himself he stands, or by himself he falls.[24]

Young writes in sonorous, sermonic cascading tones, each thought giving fuller expression to the one that came before. Similar to Isaiah 52:1-3, his rhetorical strategy is to awaken enslaved blacks a self-affirmed consciousness. Young challenges

---

22. See Thomas Jefferson, *Notes on Virginia*. ED. William Peder. Introd. and notes by the ed. Chapell Hill, NC: N.P, 1989.
23. David Walker, *To the Colored Citizens*, 10.
24. Robert Alexander Young, "The Ethiopian Manifesto, Issued Defense of the Blackmans' Rights, in the scale of Universal Freedom" was published by Robert Alexander Young in New York City in February 1929 and republished in H. Aptheker, *A History of the Negro People in the United States, Vol. 1* (Secaucus, NJ: Citadel, 1973), 90-93.

bondsmen to take personal responsibility for their liberty, a liberty that defines humanity, the willingness to take one's freedom away from tyrannical hegemony. Second, because of his personal understanding of the moral nature of the Divine Actor, Young believes that God justifies African American advocacy. It is obvious that Young believes the Scriptures' descriptions of God's attributes. For Young, God gives liberty and authority to rebel against slavery.

Like Du Bois, Young grounds his call to liberation in religious language, and in this instance his language is informed by the Christian doctrine of justification: "We know in ourselves we possess a right to see ourselves justified there from, of the right of God; knowing but his power hath he decreed to man, that either in himself he stands, or by himself he falls." Notice the similarities in the Apostle Paul's writings in Romans 4:24-25; 5:1 "but also for us, to whom God will credit righteousness—for us who believe in him who raised Jesus our Lord from the dead. He was delivered over to death for our sins and was raised to life for our justification. Therefore, since we have been justified through faith, we have peace with God through our Lord Jesus Christ." It is clear that Young appropriates this biblical doctrine and applies its claims to African American liberation.

Both pamphlets employ a similar rhetorical strategy: a call to self-affirmation and self-reliance. Dexter Gordon summarizes these documents in the following way:

> The Appeal is a seventy-eight page document divided into four major articles each addressing one of Walker's four primary reasons for nineteenth-century black degradation: Article I. "Our Wretchedness in Consequence of Slavery"; Article II. "Our Wretchedness in Consequence of Slavery"; Article III. Our Wretchedness in Consequence of the Preachers of the Religion of Jesus Christ"; and Article IV. "Our Wretchedness in Consequence of the Colonizing Plan." *The Manifesto* is a brief, seven-page document that addresses black oppression and prophesies the liberation of Africans. Framed and influenced by religious themes, present confusing and "half articulate beliefs. Both, however,

exhibit something of the primordial, the suggestion of profound beginnings, intimations of the coming sovereignty of certain ideas and, as such, offer critical insights into the early development of this black ideology and the new black subject its animus.[25]

Young and Walker were born into an oppressive culture protected by Western mythologies about Eurocentric superiority that reinforced negative images of black people. For these reasons, Young and Walker planted seeds that form a collective black consciousness that certainly informed what would become the Du Boisian aesthetic and metanarrative.

Walker and Young's documents provoked rage among whites, particularly those who controlled the American institutional spheres. "Proslavery newspapers were 'thrown into paroxysms of rage.' *The Richmond Enquirer*, for example, called Walker's *Appeal* a 'monstrous slander,'" while the "Northern newspapers sympathetic to 'endangered whites' joined in the condemnation."[26] These examples demonstrate, however, that Young and Walker were successful in part; because they began to prove that "black humanity as it was posed by Anglo America's racist depiction of the black subject" was devised to sustain and therefore justify negative images of African Americans. Second, their agitation created a national, if not an international, debate over the equality of peoples of darker hues. Their prophetic intellectualism continued in the formation of Du Bois's aesthetic.

Du Boisian Aesthetic and Afrocentrism

Informed by Walker and Young's pioneering efforts in the twentieth century, the Du Boisian aesthetic evolved through the Harlem Renaissance—which is sometimes called the black arts movement—through the emerging musical art forms, the blues, and jazz, and through civil rights and Black Power movements into Afrocentrism. Afrocentrism is first informed by African American rhetoric; it is a way to persuade, refute, and redefine ideologies that label people of color as unequal to all whites. Afrocentrism seeks to

---

25. Dexter Gordon, *Black Identity*, 80.
26. Ibid., 81.

refute the claims that people of color have not made significant contributions to Western thought, culture, and civilization. It emphasizes the black subject and employs the African aesthetic as its point of departure. "African aesthetics must be employed to get the full spectrum of what African American rhetoric is."[27]

Like Africans, African Americans place high value on oral performances. These similarities suggest that African and African American aesthetics are functional, that is, an incarnation is expected and advocacy its result. Put in another way, both are products of consciousness; each takes on a life of its own. For example, "Functional in this case, refers to the object that possesses a meaning within the communicator's and audience's 'worldview, a meaning that is constructed from the social, political and religious movements in the society's history."[28] Thus the aesthetic is born of a people's preunderstanding of themselves. The African and African American shared aesthetic is a pragmatic tool that helps Du Boisian preachers find ways to support ethical motifs and ideologies as long as those motifs and ideologies support their rhetorical goal, which is the manifestation of justice.

Interestingly however, when the African aesthetic is separated from the African American aesthetic, it shares with Western aesthetics a perception of beauty. Where it differs is that the African aesthetic particularized beauty that is "articulated in language." Language in the African aesthetic is a way to express organizing principles and what defines "good" and therefore what is communally accepted to be ethical and just. According to Adisa A. Alkebulan, the African aesthetic functions as a holistic communal group dynamic:

> By African worldview I mean the guiding principles and values that determine how Africans see and respond to life and interact with the universe. Worldview is the means by which culture determines what is beautiful and

---

27. Adisa A. Alkbebulan, "The Spiritual Essence of African American Rhetoric," *Understanding African American Rhetoric: Classsical Origins to Contemporary Innovations* Eds. Ronald L.Jackson II and Elaine B. Richardson (New York: Routledge 2003), 33.
28. Ibid., 36.

what is not. In other words, aesthetics is the part of African worldview that is associated with beauty.[29]

For Alkebulan, the African aesthetic is determined by a group's communal dynamic that is a kind of collectivism; this group dynamic has an ethical emphasis on the group's shared principles and values. In any case, the group dynamic informs perceptions of beauty, which also are interpreted as a justice motif. African perceptions of beauty or justice transcend geographical boundaries and function on certain commonalities.

Similarly to the African aesthetic, Afrocentrism is a worldview that transcends geographical locations and boundaries; it shares the African aesthetic's claims and commonalities. Philosophically, Afrocentrism is concerned with the black subject-location. In his book *Africentric Christianity*, theologian J. Deotis Roberts addresses the importance of locating the subject in a text:

> Africentrists [Afrocentrism] seize the opportunity to reinterpret Europeanized writings of early Africans in Africa and the Americas. Literary interpretation is based on location, which can be manifest in psychological, cultural, economic, social and other forms. By identifying elements in a text that reveal an author's location, one is able to interpret a text in the language of Africentricity…. Thus it is possible to determine location, dislocation by observing the centeredness of a text.[30]

Africentrist scholars, then, respond to Eurocentric ideologies with dialectic. Like Du Bois and earlier black nationalists and pan-Africanists, the Africentrists attempt to decentralize the Eurocentric subject in order to free the black subject from hegemonic definitions and other forms of subjugation. Alkebulan

---

29. Ibid., 34.
30. J. Deotis Roberts, *Africentric Christianity: A Theological Appraisal for Ministry* (Valley Forge, PA: Judson, 2000), 4. Roberts provides a thorough critique of Afrocentrism's philosophical points of departure. He validates the discipline but provides for his readers several departures from its central claims when he believes those departures are warranted and necessary.

affirms this claim when he writes, "Crucial to our understanding of Afrocentricity is the idea that Africans should be viewed as subjects in their own right as acting agents in their own historical and cultural reality rather than as objects on fringes of Western scholarship and civilization."[31]

This is Du Boisian; Alkebulan reinforces Du Bois's claim that a culture (not a subculture) can and does exist within the dominating culture, thus providing evidence for a two-poles theory existing in dialectic in one world. These Afrocentric intellectuals are concerned about the black subject's presence and how it is used to critique dominant canonical texts and spheres. Without the presence of the black subject and its critique on Western canonical thought, those who employ Western canonical texts uncritically diminish other-wise peoples' contributions. As a result, Western thinkers, informed by their own canon, create for themselves psychological, cultural, economic, and social advantages.

Afrocentrism is also rhetoric; as Roberts notes, "[Molefi Kete] Asante's main academic discipline is rhetoric."[32] Molefi Kete Asante is the fountainhead for Afrocentrism, and he is an early catalyst for establishing Afrocentrism as an academic discipline. Asante has called into question "privileged discourse of the traditional rhetorical criticism."[33] The *Afrocentric Idea* can be summarized as tracing an establishment of an African and African American (I add people of color) worldview that discloses a universal pattern and writing and speaking style shared by marginalized people.[34] Gordon adds:

> This rhetorical theory pays attention to "African ownership of values, knowledge, and culture" as a way to understand the discourse of African people and that of other oppressed groups and, even more important, as the lenses through which we can understand and achieve other ways of knowing (*Afrocentric Idea*, 181). This alternative

---

31. Adisa A. Alkebulan, "The Spiritual Essence," 24.
32. J. Deotis Roberts, *Africentric Christianity: A Theological Appraisal For Ministry*, 6.
33. Ibid., 11. See Asante's *The Afrocentric Idea* (Philadelphia: Temple University Press, 1998).
34. See Asante, *Africentricity*, 173.

epistemology is necessary to give new scope and vision to literary theory in general and rhetorical theory in particular, both long held hostage and blinded by their "essentially European" epistemic with its binding commitment to the fundamental concepts of Western thought rationality, objectivity, and progress (179).[35]

Asante's Afrocentric rhetorical theory is holistic and communal, defined and informed by cultural preunderstanding, self-affirmation and self-identity. His rhetoric can be traced to commonly shared values that are universal among marginalized people. Their worldview invents a different epistemology that frees people of color from conventional Western definitions and assumptions. It further calls into question arbitrary categories such as Western rationality, which is the West's point of departure for all philosophical claims, pedagogy, and canonical aesthetics.

Asante suggests that three characteristics are embedded in twenty-first-century African American rhetoric: "It will be based on discourses on correctives, reconciliation, and challenges to the last vestiges of the doctrine of White supremacy." Asante further suggests that "The best rhetors will be those who imbue these characteristics. This is the grand rhetorical tradition."[36] In this way, Asante's rhetorical theory serves a dialectic function. It bypasses Western biases and creates a black subject. In this way, Afrocentric rhetoric continues to call into question all institutional spheres that silence other voices. In other words, Asante's Afrocentric rhetoric unveils undemocratic features of Western rhetoric.

Roberts is correct: Afrocentrism is rhetorical; it is dialectical in form and function. It gives scholars, writers, and Du Boisian preachers rhetoric that places the black subject in the center of their narrative. Asante, too, is correct. His rhetoric's characteristics are similar to those that I attribute to Du Bois's rhetoric: aesthetics, interpretation, and assumptions. Like Asante, who employs

---

35. Gordon, *Black Identity*, 12. The page numbers in Gordon's excerpt refer to the pages in *Africentricity* on which this passage is located.
36. Molefi Kete Asante, "The Future of African American Rhetoric" in *Understanding African American Rhetoric: Classic Origins to Contemporary Innovations*, ed. Ronald J. Jackson and Elaine B. Richardson (New York: Routledge, 2003), 286-87.

Afrocentric rhetoric to serve as a corrective to Western discourses and mythologies, I employ Du Boisian rhetoric in a similar way, not only to discourses and mythologies, but also to create space for literary and rhetorical form and function for people of color. In addition, Du Boisian rhetoric, consistent with the African aesthetic, is concerned with a redefinition of beauty, which is the personified incarnation of justice and harmony.

Asante's second characteristic of twenty-first-century rhetoric is reconciliation. It is akin to other-wise interpretation, the second characteristic in the Du Boisian model. Reconciliation and interpretation are similar in this way: each seeks to reconcile racial indifferences and hostilities. I focus on Du Boisian interpretation, because he understood that whoever controls interpretation, or who shares in the interpretation process will indeed facilitate reconciliation. Asante's third characteristic, "challenges to the last vestiges of the doctrine of White supremacy," is akin to Du Boisian rhetoric's call to make one's own assumptions. To be prophetic, the Du Boisian preacher must understand that her or his preaching assignment is intentional and functions as a broad apparatus. For Du Boisian preachers, making one's own assumptions is incarnation, "the Word becoming flesh." That is, assumptions informed by an affirming aesthetic and an interpretation process that mirrors people's poles in the one world are an active demonstration of personal and, at times, shared convictions along with moral and ethical belief systems that guide a rhetor-preacher's actions.

Du Bois had a lifelong commitment to eradicating institutional racism. Advocacy such as his is an active call to refute a myriad of conditions—not just racism, but also other forms of marginalization, such as undereducation, underemployment, poverty, starvation, genocide, gender, and environmental discrimination. Sermons in this context must have a biblical theme that points listeners toward active participation in solving contemporary challenges; this creates space for rhetor-preachers to critique all unjust cultural claims and behavior, whether those claims and behavior are Eurocentric or other-wise.

Cornel West, a Union Theological Seminary professor and public intellectual, and Tavis Smiley, an author and media personality, have demonstrated how advocacy functions rhetorically in the Du Boisian prophetic tradition. Recently, West and Smiley were subject to public criticism from some African Americans for taking President Barack Obama to task over issues such as urban poverty and the ever-increasing divide between rich and poor; this includes African Americans who have risen to sustainable middle-class economic status. West is on record about his current prophetic critique of black leadership. Readers need only to remember these chapters in West's groundbreaking book *Race Matters*: "Nihilism in Black America" and "The Crisis in Black Leadership."[37]

The latter is a prophetic critique of African American leadership that largely fails to create a black agenda. In fact, without progressive leadership, black America will continue to have tendencies toward nihilism; and what is more, black America will become, perhaps unable to pull itself out of nihilism's bleak and dark grip. These are among the reasons why West criticizes President Obama's neglect of black and urban poverty and pain. Mr. Obama, however, is not a product of black leadership. He became president because he functions outside of black leadership's dysfunctional sphere. Obama is an African American leader, but he does not have an allegiance to a black leadership agenda; the two should not be confused.

West and Smiley's challenge to the establishment's power serves as a challenge for Du Boisian preachers and for how they must be guided by their theological and ethical principles.[38] In this instance, West and Smiley are functioning in the Du Boisian prophetic

---

37. Cornel West, *Race Matters* (Boston: Beacon Press, 1993).
38. On an April 10, 2012, MSNBC television program, Cornel West and Reverend Al Sharpton engaged in verbal debate over President Obama's leadership. It was unusual to see African Americans publically disagree about what West saw as Obama's lack of moral courage in the fight against urban poverty. West further alleged that Sharpton was naïve about Obama's position and Sharpton was being manipulated by presidential power. Sharpton has made a public name by defending the rights of the underprivileged and a spokesman for the masses. West too speaks on behalf of marginalized people but certainly is not a mass leader; they however, are engaged in ideological juxtaposition. Also see Tavis Smiley and Cornel West, *The Rich and the Rest of Us: A Poverty Manifesto* (New York: Smiley Books, 2012).

tradition, in part because they believe that they must place their convictions and their theological and ethical belief systems above sociopolitical conveniences and racial classifications.

This further explains how the Du Boisian rhetoric is dialectic and how the dialectic is informed by universally shared values among people of color; this is consistent with Asante's Afrocentric rhetorical theory. Both Du Boisian and Afrocentric rhetoric evolved into something pan-African, a worldview that grew out from an African aesthetic. In this way, the Du Boisian and Afrocentric rhetorics are similar to the African aesthetic. Both refute dominant cultural claims of singular significance and superiority, which inherently subjugate people of color. As part of its refutation of Eurocentrism, the Du Boisian aesthetic seeks to shape perceptions of beauty (self-affirmation and identity); its intention is to create its version of just harmony and balance.

These universal African and African American attributes are personified in the Du Boisian aesthetic. What emerges is the black subject as hero and heroine and Du Boisian preachers, whether knowingly or unknowingly, employ this species of aesthetic to tell their stories. Specifically for this purpose, Du Bois invented a rhetorical strategy that gives incarnation and voice to the story tellers. "The Du Boisian Folk and Mythical Hero Rhetorical Strategy" appeared in nearly all his literary works for nearly a century. This rhetorical strategy gave Du Bois agency, and it became his most prominent propaganda tool against Eurocentrism, cultural hegemony, and homogeneity.

Du Boisian Folk and Mythical Hero Rhetorical Strategy

I have identified Du Bois's rhetorical strategy in his autobiographical narratives where he has created mythical heroes and heroines who are to be interpreted as metaphoric. In the following excerpt, there are at least two significant points that support this perspective. I associate my perspective with Edward J. Blum about Joseph Campbell's commentary on the Du Boisian rhetorical strategy:

According to Campbell, whenever folk and mythical hero narratives are interpreted as straight biography or history, the myth is killed and the hidden lessons lost. This has been the case with Du Bois's autobiographical narratives. Historians have most often looked to them for an outline of Du Bois's life, only recently have scholars approached them as metaphorical texts or presentations of self and society. Even the most astute biographers have looked to them, not in the tradition of hero narratives but as historical works to find the who, what, and where of Du Bois's life. The narratives mean so much more, however. By casting himself in the model of the hero, Du Bois revealed a spiritualized understanding of his self and also articulated a cosmic religious schema by which Du Bois hoped his readers would view him and the world.[39]

Campbell is correct to say that linear biography and history can be dry and lack imagination, which can create unmotivated listeners who will not discover hidden truths. I would add that another way to explain Du Bois's rhetorical strategy is to acknowledge that Du Bois was biblically literate, which is evident throughout his published works. It stands to reason that Du Bois appropriated his folk and mythical hero rhetorical strategies from Old and New Testament writer s' narratives. The following passages demonstrate those similarities:

Then Moses and the people of Israel sang this song to the Lord, saying
I will sing to the Lord, for he has triumphed gloriously;
The horse and his rider he has thrown them into the sea.
The Lord is my strength and my song,
And he has become my salvation; this is my God, and I will praise him, my father's God, and I will exalt him. The Lord is a man of war; the Lord is his name.
The Song of Moses
Exodus 15:1-3

Then sang Deborah and Barak the son of Abinoam on that day: That the leaders took the lead in Israel that the people offered themselves willingly, bless the Lord. Hear, O kings, give ear, O princes; to the Lord I will sing; I will

---

39. Edward J. Blum, *W.E. B. Du Bois American Prophet* (Philadelphia: University of Pennsylvania Press, 2007), 25-26.

make melody to the Lord, the God of Israel. Lord, when you went out from Seir, when you marched from the region of Edom, the earth trembled and the heavens dropped, yes, the clouds dropped water. The mountains quaked before the Lord, even Sinai before the Lord, the God of Israel.
The Song of Deborah and Barak
Judges 5:1-5

And the woman sang to one another as they celebrated, Saul had struck down his thousands, and David his ten thousands.
The Song of David
1 Samuel 18:22

My soul magnifies the Lord, and my spirit rejoices in God my Savior, for he has looked on the humble estate of his servant. For behold, from now on all generations will call me blessed; for he who is mighty has done great things for me, and holy is his name. And his mercy is for those who fear him from generation to generation. He has shown strength with his arm; he has scattered the proud in the thoughts of their hearts; he has brought down the mighty from their thrones and exalted those of humble estate; he has filled the hungry with good things, and the rich he has sent empty away. He has helped his servant Israel, in remembrance of his mercy, as he spoke to our fathers, to Abraham and to his offspring forever.
The Magnificat
Luke 1:46-55

These are but a few examples of the folk and mythical hero rhetorical strategies that Old and New Testament writers employed in shaping their narratives. Consistent with Campbell's observations, these writers employ a similar strategy to avoid straight biography and history. Instead, this kind of rhetorical strategy is imaginative and creates ways for listeners to sense "deep recesses of the human spirit and of cosmic desires," as Campbell describes the biblical writers' employment of this kind of rhetorical strategy. It provides space for listeners to discover emerging hidden truths about psychologies and spiritualities that are embedded in human personalities.

Biblical narrative serves as the point of departure for the folk and hero mythical rhetorical strategy that is located in many of Du Bois's autobiographical writings. I have included two passages from these narratives that provide us a brief comparison with the styles of the biblical writers. The first passage is an imaginary conversation that exemplifies dialectic struggles between mythologies and interpretations of culture and historical events:

> Between Me and the other world there is ever an unasked question: unasked by some through feelings of delicacy; by others through the difficulty of rightly framing it. All, nevertheless, flutter round it. They approach me in a half-hesitant sort of way, eye me curiously or compassionately, and then, instead of saying directly, How does it feel to be a problem? [T]hey say, I know an excellent colored man in my town; or, I fought at Mechanicsville: or, Do not these Southerners outrages make your blood boil? At these I smile, or am interested, or reduce the boiling to a simmer, as the occasion may require. To the real question, How does it feel to be a problem? I answer seldom a word.[40]

"Of Spiritual Strivings," the first essay in *Souls*, begins with a mystic journey to upset his readers' social predisposition and equilibrium. His readers find themselves in the middle of an ongoing commonly held conversation about race and class between Du Bois and apparently a white man. The conversation identifies Du Bois's interrogator as a symbol of demonic forces, perhaps unaware that he is a soothsayer who is reinforcing stereotypes associated with depictions of permanent social caste structures. Notice that Du Bois's introduction paragraph is intended to point out that Western use of a folk and mythical hero rhetorical strategy is informed by biased Western mythologies that hinder racial reconciliation and the pursuit of justice.

This second passage also involves an imaginary journey. It is an illustration of bleak and dreadful conditions. Du Bois, however, employs a folk and mythical hero rhetorical strategy and inserts the black subject, namely Alexander Crummell, as heroic:

---

40. Du Bois, "Of Our Spiritual Strivings" in *The Souls of Black Folk*, 1-2.

> This is the story of the human heart, the tale of a black boy who many long years ago began to struggle with life that he might know the world and know himself. Three temptations he met on those dark dunes that lay gray and dismal before the wonder-eyes of the child: the temptations of Hate, that stood out against the red dawn: the temptation of Despair, that darkened noonday; and the temptation of Doubt, that ever steals along with twilight. Above all, you must hear of the vales he crossed – the Valley of Humiliation and the Valley of the Shadow of Death.[41]

This is a brilliant introduction paragraph that begins with a summary of his essay. Du Bois begins deductively but tells his story in an inductive style. He has created what Campbell refers to as monomythical hero; in this instance, it is Alexander Crummell who is at the very heart of his mythology. Du Bois takes his readers on a journey filled with cosmic demonic inequalities and injustices. Through spiritual language—Temptations of Hate, Doubt, and Despair, and the Valleys of Humiliation and the Shadow of Death—Du Bois exposes us to the systemic evils that minorities face.

Du Bois understands that history and empirical evidence do not exhaust any truth claim. Thus, Du Bois employs a folk and mythical hero rhetorical strategy to inform his autobiographical narratives. He often includes poetry and parabolic methodologies to tell a different version of truth. That is, Du Bois wants otherwise people to be included in the larger stories of truth, so that their contributions are appreciatively known. A single written history does not cover an entire subject; it is told primarily by a chronicler and includes what she or he believes to be significant and particular to her or his interests.

What is more, historians are often informed by their cultural myths and worldviews. Though credible historians and hermeneutic interpreters strive to employ research methods that disclose objective truth, they are subject to biases because of their relationships with their cultural mythologies and worldviews. This universally influences their understandings and perceptions about

---

41. Du Bois, "Of Alexander Crummell" in *The Souls of Black Folk*, 139.

their subjects. In response to biased Western mythologies, world-views, and spheres, Du Bois begins a formation of dialectic, a countercultural alternative commonly known as the black aesthetic. The black aesthetic is prophetic, because it is a call to employ other-wise people's aesthetic and mythologies into their narratives.

The Du Boisian Metanarrative

Du Bois is a brilliant storyteller. He is masterful at developing his narrative as a representative of marginalized people. Through narrative autobiography, Du Bois presents himself as the black subject hero, displacing the conventional white, Eurocentric subject hero that dominates Western letters. In Du Bois's self-portraits located in *Souls*, *Darkwater*, and *Dusk of Dawn*, I am able to trace the African and African American shared epistemology and shared values, which I have located also in Asante's rhetoric. Du Bois's employment of the black aesthetic and rhetoric results in a universally recognized pan-African metanarrative.

Theoretically, narrative helps us to identify the central action of an experience; the action then helps us decide what a particular experience is all about. In addition, narrative helps us to connect the dots between the narrative's action, its plausibility, and how these intersect with readers' personal stories and experiences. And, narrative is designed to give us choices for whether a particular narrative is relevant to us.

All narratives include characters, settings, and plotlines. Characters serve many purposes in a narrative; for example, they facilitate reader analysis of the narratives' content and substance. Settings are sometimes referred to as major events, and they may be called kernels; they also point readers toward characters in the setting. In addition, kernels are major events that suggest critical points in the narrative that force movement in particular directions. "They cannot be left out of the narrative without destroying its coherence and meaning."[42] Narratives also have minor plot events, which often involve developing characters. They are also referred to as satellites: "they are the development or working out of the choices made at the kernels." What is more, "satellites do not have

---

42. Carlos D. Morrison "Death Narratives from the Killing Fields" in *Understanding African American Rhetoric*, 191.

to appear in the immediate proximity of the kernels to which they are linked; they may appear anywhere in the narrative."[43]

A final element of narrative is persuasion. When the narrator-storyteller is effective, it is because she or he has been persuasive in telling their story. It is the narrator-story teller's ability that gives voice to the characters. Also, it provides context for the settings and plot lines. The narrator-story teller presents a theme, controls the story's movement, and provides appropriate signals to the listeners. In this way, a narrator-story teller persuades listeners to focus closely on the kernels, and at times the satellites; this is artistry that I associate with connecting dots, creating images, and helping auditors to pay attention to necessary details. How the narrator-story teller develops these components, will determine the substance of the story and how the story's content is communicated.

The African American storyteller's narrative includes these characteristics. I have noticed these characteristics in Du Bois's essay "Of the Coming of John." Du Bois writes in detail about a folk and mythical hero he calls John Jones. Du Bois contrasts John Jones, a subtle reference to racially motivated whites calling all black men "John" regardless of their names, and his aspirations to earn an education in a northern school with another John, a boyhood playmate in the old South. By naming his parallel white character John, Du Bois employs African American signifying. Du Bois, furthermore, makes it easy for his readers to identify the narrative's kernels and satellites, settings and plotlines in this passage:

> Up at the Judge's they rather liked this refrain; for they too had a John—a fair haired, smooth-faced boy, who had played many a long summer's day to its close with his darker name sake. "Yes sir! John is at Princeton, sir," said the broad shouldered grayhaired Judge every morning as he marched down to the post office. "Showing the Yankees what a Southern gentleman can do," he added and strode home again with his letters and papers. Up at the great pillared house they lingered long over the Princeton letter,—the Judge and his frail wife, his sister

---

43. Ibid.

and growing daughters. "It'll make a man of him," said the Judge, "college is the place." And then he asked the shy little waitress, "Well Jennie, how's your John [her brother]?" and added reflectively, "Too bad, to bad your mother sent him off,—it will spoil him." And the waitress wondered.[44]

The following statements in this passage serve as a diagram for establishing Du Bois's use of kernels as settings and characters, and satellites as characters and plotlines:

1. "Up at the Judge's" is development of setting, character, and major plotline.
2. "Up at the great pillared house" is further development of the setting.
3. "Yes sir! John is at Princeton, Sir" is the development of a character (the Judge) and a satellite and character (John, the Judge's son), a minor plotline.
4. "The Judge and his frail wife, his sister and growing daughters" is both setting and satellite (minor event with minor characters) that give readers insight into whom and by whom the Judge is surrounded. "Frail wife" characterizes the Judge's overwhelming personality.
5. "And then he asked the shy little waitress, 'Well Jennie [,] how's your John [her brother]?'" This statement is both a satellite and plotline.
6. "Too bad, too bad your mother sent him [John Jones] off,— it will spoil him." This statement is both satellite (minor character) and plotline (major event).

The Judge's character is associated with developing the setting and plotline. His physical build is described in detail; his age and gait are noticeable. In the mornings, the Judge marches down to the post office to boast about his accomplishments, namely, that John, his son, is attending Princeton. On his return climb to his "great pillared home," the Judge's pace slows to "strode." Possibly Du Bois is making satire and puns that the Judge has expended his

---

44. Du Bois, "Of the Coming of John" in *Souls* with an "Introduction" by John Edgar Wideman (New York, Vintage Books, 1990), 167.

energy bragging on his son; it also suggests that the Judge is now empty of his hot air and unable to easily climb the elevation to his home. What is certain, Du Bois masterfully uses physical and geographical boundaries and architecture to help readers visualize the setting and anticipate the developing plotline.

Du Bois makes clear that the Judge is a man of Southern pride and its accompanying biases. Every morning, he proudly makes it known that his son John, the "fair-skinned" boy, is a student at Princeton. Du Bois subtly makes his readers aware that the Judge hides his envy of northern privilege, suggesting that the experience is solely for John. The Judge sent him to Princeton so that "It will make a man of him." Du Bois cajoles the Judge; pointing out that he has breached a well-worn Southern taboo: he has abdicated his personal responsibility to teach his son how to be a Southern gentleman. Instead, southerner Judge is found liable. He has relied on northern culture and education to make his spoiled son into a man. In this way, the Judge's character is important, because Du Bois uses it to reveal the racial attitudes and hegemony that exist in this southern town (Altamaha, Georgia). It also is an indication of the evolving plotline.

While the Judge sits down to eat, he speaks to John Jones's sister Jennie and asks her about the welfare of John, adding "Too bad, too bad your mother sent him off,—it will spoil him." Du Bois employs rhetorical irony that reveals the Judge's cultural biases; he believes that formal education will make a man of his son John, but the same process will spoil the John of African descent. This serves as an illustrative parallel to traits located in Asante's rhetorical theory. Du Bois's Judge is a metaphor for Western culture's aesthetics, interpretations, and assumptions. Du Bois further implies that Western culture is held "hostage and blinded by their [its] 'essentially European' epistemic with its binding commitment to the fundamental concepts of Western thought rationality, objectivity, and progress."[45] I affirm Du Bois's use of rhetoric and narrative because it shares commonalities with Asante's Afrocentric rhetoric. For Du Boisian preachers, then, it is important to learn how to develop a similar relationship between

---

45. Gordon, *Black Identity*, 12.

rhetoric and narrative that exists between Du Boisian rhetoric and his metanarrative.

In "Of the Coming of John," Du Bois skillfully places a narrative's kernel and satellites in close proximity. He poignantly uses the Judge's character to tell us that it was a nameless mother who sent John Jones to a northern school. As the Judge sent his John to Princeton, the mother sent her John to Johnstown to the Institute to be formally educated. Du Bois does not tell us the name of John's mother; it is not necessary. Her aspiration for her son is the same as the Judge's aspirations for his son.[46] This is an example of how a satellite functions in narratives. Still, I think that Du Bois focuses on formalized education in order to dramatize that blacks and whites share a similar value.

This passage, published in *Souls* in 1903, is a model of how Du Bois employs the German concept of *schadenfreude*, defined as purging and catharsis, or sometimes enjoyment of someone else's sorrows. In this way, Du Bois uses sorrow narrative to find a way to be heard. By "sorrow narrative," I mean that African American expressions have been narrowed to a cultural preoccupation with death and mourning. This narrative style, as employed by the dominant culture, is marketable and constantly noticed in film, journalism, politics, economics, and religion. Unfortunately, however, it has been used to exploit stereotypes of African Americans and people of color.

When the African American cultural narrative is defined solely as a survivalist motif, it leads to a malignant African American cultural identity. To be sure, sorrow narrative influences African American intellectualism, be it in theology, law, the liberal arts, or music. All have been conditioned to negotiate their understandings of truth through the lens of marginalization. It remains problematic, however, because the larger Western narrative, informed by its heroic mythologies, and using positive reinforcements of images in every institutional sphere, defines itself as heroic and capable of sustaining life.

I suggested that the sorrow narrative has been mainly decided for African Americans, because it has been shaped primarily by outside forces. African American visibility has been negotiated by

---

46. Du Bois employs signification with his use of Johnstown.

the dominant culture's hegemony obsessed with a racism that veils unethical economics, politics, and other spheres of influence; thus relegating African American narrative to sorrow and other forms of human marginalization. These are some of the terms and conditions of Western residency that people of color have historically endured. It makes it difficult, if not impossible, for people of color to define themselves in Western culture without inventing their own narratives.

Those who blindly employ the conventional Western metanarrative also blindly support the dominant cultural ideology. This blind support subjugates other-wise peoples and reinforces negative self-images and affirmations.[47] By implication, the Western metanarrative causes racial indifferences and hostilities and defines people of color as insignificant, worrisome, and, sometimes, as an absence. By absence, I mean that visibility and presence of African Americans and people of color often conjure negative, reinforced stereotypes of people of color as nuisance on societies at large.

Du Bois invented a counterculture metanarrative to refute Western claims of universal superiority over peoples of color. Du Bois's metanarrative is a story informed by the Du Boisian hermeneutic and told through Du Boisian rhetoric. Each is a dialectic narrative, by which I mean that it acknowledges the dominant culture and classes' contributions to the world's societies when and where it is appropriate. These contributions cannot be denied; but the Du Boisian metanarrative corrects and refutes Western Eurocentric claims of superiority over others who have made contributions to the Western story: this includes its literary, political, economic, historical, and, particularly, theological canons.

Consistent with my understanding of Du Boisian refutation, which is an important component for creating dialectic, I return to Molefi Kete Asante. As previously mentioned (but it bears repeating), Asante is considered the fountainhead for Afrocentrism and is a chief proponent for establishing Afrocentrism as a formal academic discipline; he is also a trained master rhetorician. In his

---

47. Karla F. C. Holloway, "Cultural Narratives Passed On: African American Mourning Stories" in *African American Literary Theory*, 653-59.

essay, "The Future of African American Rhetoric" I have identified similarities consistent with Du Bois's rhetoric.

Asante has written that there are three characteristics necessary for the future of an African American rhetoric that makes the art form transformative. He argues that a discourse of correctness, reconciliation, and challenges to the last vestiges of the doctrine of white supremacy are essential for persuasive African American rhetoric.[48] With these three characteristics in mind, Asante suggests that "Every speaker who will take the platform as an African American rhetor [Du Boisian preacher] and every writer of essays will have to deal with one or all of the characteristics of rhetoric of the twenty-first century in order to establish meaningful presence in the nation."[49]

I believe that African American rhetoric's key characteristics are aesthetics, interpretation, and assumptions. These lead Du Boisian preachers and thinkers to become advocates and activists. This is the result of Du Bois's and Asante's rhetoric. Asante, correct in his observations, makes a strong case for the future of twenty-first-century rhetoric as the means of communication with the world's populations. Western orators, preachers, statesmen, and politicians must employ this kind of rhetoric to communicate with a world divided along lines of race, economics, politics, at times, religion, and, increasingly, gender. Du Boisian rhetor-preachers must engage in the world through prophetic speech. That is, Du Boisian preachers on both sacred and secular platforms must craft messages that are heard as civic sermons with sermonic language that demands action from their auditors. For this to occur, Du Boisian preachers must be the theological and ethical statesmen of our time, capable of speaking prophetically to two poles in one world about Christian claims.

Conclusion

W.E.B. Du Bois was perhaps the influential figure in twentieth-century intellectual thought. His influence certainly transcends every sphere of African American culture. His largest contributions are expressed in these ways: he understood that because of

---

48. Asante, "The Future of African American Rhetoric," 286.
49. Ibid.

systemic racism, African Americans experienced inherent forms of inequality; because of systemic racism, they were denied equal political and economic opportunities; because of systemic racism, they were unrecognized as equal citizens under the law; because of systemic racism they were not considered contributors to the Western metanarrative.

As Irene Diggs said of Du Bois and what motivated his actions, "the history of the race concept, was the dominant factor in Du Bois' life: race guided, embittered, illuminated and enshrouded his life and the lives of all Blacks."[50] His passion to say something else, something different, about African Americans led him to investigate laws and customs deliberately set to keep rule over peoples of color. Du Bois understood this while he attended the University of Berlin. He understood that the race problem was not limited to the United States; instead, it was the problem of peoples of Asia and Africa and, again, at its root, the politics and economics of Europe: this was the building of colonial empires.

Du Bois understood that African American culture is born out of protest, and that it searches for democratic justice. Thus, African American culture is dialectic. Its aesthetics, interpretations, and assumptions are independent findings, separate from Eurocentric influence; Du Boisian preachers therefore become advocates and activists, the children of the dialectic. As Asante pointed out earlier, rhetoric is a by-product of cultural worldview and values. Like African American culture, African American rhetoric is dialectic, and African American dialectic influences all spheres of African American cultural thought and informs the black intellectuals' work. Du Boisian rhetoric is present broadly in African American blues and jazz, film, literature, political worldviews, and religious language. A consistent characteristic in all of these spheres is a call to self-affirmation and self-identity. Du Boisian rhetoric is a part of a communication theory that calls all African Americans to be prophetic.

---

50. Irene Diggs, "Introduction" in *Dusk of Dawn*, viii.

Afterword

ತಿ

In 1993, David Levering Lewis published the first of two books dedicated to the life of W.E.B. Du Bois. The first was entitled *W.E.B. Du Bois: Biography of a Race*. Lewis, writing in that volume's acknowledgments, remembers meeting Du Bois while standing beside his father on Wilberforce University's campus. He was twelve years old. Du Bois asked the younger Lewis about his future. Of the meeting, Lewis writes, "I cannot recall the answer I gave when the latter [Du Bois] asked what my plans were for life, but it certainly could not have anticipated what I would say to him today about the plan my life has followed for the past eight years."[1] Lewis's words are vague and mysterious, but they do give us glimpses into his worldview.

Subtly characterizing the meeting as a kind of apocalyptic symbolism, Lewis draws a comparison between his meeting of Du Bois and Du Bois's meeting with Alexander Crummell years earlier. Du Bois said of Crummell, "I bowed before the man, as one bows before the prophets of the world. Some seer he seemed that came not from the crimson Past or the gray To-come, but from the pulsing Now – .... Fourscore years had he wandered in this same world of mine, within the Veil."[2] In any case, Lewis is not sure whether his meeting Du Bois was predestination, election, or fate. In so many words, Lewis characterized the unforeseeable assignment to become a Du Boisian biographer as just an "it."

Du Bois and Time Magazine

R.Z. Sheppard published a two-part review of Lewis's *Biography of a Race* in the November 15 and 29, 1992, issues of *Time*

---

1. David Levering Lewis, "Acknowledgments" in *W. E. B. Du Bois 1869-1919: Biography of Race* (New York: Henry Holt, 1993), xi.
2. W.E.B. Du Bois, "Of Alexander Crummell" in *The Souls of Black Folk* (New York: Bantam, 2005), 160.

magazine. His title, "The Great Enunciator," was vague, unmoving, unrevealing, and explored neither the two pieces nor the enormous intellectual contributions that Du Bois made on the twentieth century. In fact, it is difficult to tell whether Sheppard grasped the exploits of W.E.B. Du Bois. In short, Sheppard's review does not lift; it does not inspire; it does not inform.

Du Bois's image does not appear on the cover of either issue of *Time*. Whose images do appear? The first was an artist's rustic sketch depicting the rugged endurance of the American myth of the Reverend Billy Graham. The second was an impressionist's rendering of a withdrawn, mysteriously modern Dr. Sigmund Freud. Writing in the November 15 issue, Nancy Gibbs and Richard N. Ostling-Montreat, co-authors of "God's Billy Pulpit," claim that "Graham's legacy will be measured not only in the lives he has changed but in the cause he has championed. If modern evangelicalism is in many ways Graham's passionate creation, it could suffer grievously once he is gone."[3] According to the writers, Graham had a singular influence over the religious psyche of twentieth-century evangelicalism. This does not explain, however, *Time*'s calculated editorial choices not to make Du Bois its cover image and story.

Over the course of the twentieth century, Freud's image appears on the *Time*'s cover four times (1923, 1939, 1956, and 1999). Freud was born on May 6, 1856, in the small Moravian town of Freiberg (now Pribor, Czechoslovakia). He died in 1939, in London, as an expatriate from Germany because of Nazi occupation. Peter Gay, a Freud biographer, says of him, "Sigmund Freud, more than any other explorer of the psyche, has shaped the mind of the 20th century."[4] Gay goes on to say, "The book that made his reputation in the profession—although it sold poorly—was *The Interpretation of Dreams* (1900), an indefinable masterpiece—part dream analysis, part autobiography, part theory of the mind, part history of contemporary Vienna."[5] Gay further writes, "Freud was intent not

3. Nancy Gibbs and Richard N. Ostling-Montreat, "God's Bully Pulpit," *Time*, November 15, 1993, accessed June 17, 2013, http://www.Timemagazine.org

4. Peter Gay, "Sigmund Freud: Psychoanalyst," *Time*, March 29, 1999, accessed June 17, 2013, http://www.Timemagazine.org

5. Ibid.

merely on originating a sweeping theory of mental functioning and malfunctioning. He also wanted to develop the rules of psychoanalytic theory and expand his picture of human nature to encompass not just the couch but the whole culture."[6] Gay, adroitly, reinforces his proposition: Western culture is Freudian. Whether it was Graham or Freud, *Time* chose not to feature Du Bois as its cover story. Instead *Time* featured two men who represented the establishment's institutionalism, culture, and ideology.

Du Bois was born February 23, 1868, in Great Barrington, Massachusetts, and he died in Accra, Ghana, on August 27, 1963, just hours before the historic civil rights march on Washington, August 28. Du Bois, like Freud, was an expatriate. Freud fled Germany because of political persecution; Du Bois left America because he no longer felt faith that his American citizenship mattered. His hope for equality had dimmed. He did the only thing that he thought he could. He chose to protest his inequality among Anglo American citizens. In his mind, this was the last democratic act he could exercise. He chose to exercise his freedom of choice in the face of bad choices.

I implied earlier, but I now plainly say that Du Bois never appeared on a *Time* magazine cover. Despite his long literary, civic-social, and intellectual career, he was relegated institutionally within the veil. He served as the secretary of the First Pan-African Conference in London in 1900. He was the founder and general secretary of the Niagara Movement that met to develop a pan-African narrative to refute the unyielding twentieth-century's Eurocentric hegemony. Du Bois was among the original founders and incorporators of the National Association for the Advancement of Colored People (NAACP), organized in 1909. He was a key figure in the organization of the Second Pan-African Congress that convened in Brussels and Paris in 1921.

By way of contrast, I noted that Freud published *The Interpretation of Dreams* in 1900; Du Bois published *The Souls of Black Folk* in 1903. As Gay noted, Freud's book was insignificant, and it is recognized not so much for its content but for its author. I

---

6. Ibid.

further note that few publications such as *Souls* still matter.[7] Fewer books have had a more significant impact on how people of color understand themselves. The very fewest of books have been translated into more languages as Edward J. Blum confirms, "First published in April 1903, reprinted numerous times since and translated into numerous languages."[8] And, as Manning Marable writes, "In 1959, a Chinese edition of *The Soul of Black Folks* was printed in Peking."[9]

The Reaction to The Souls of Black Folks

When *Souls* was published, few people knew its author. The African American public sphere made laudatory remarks about Du Bois's literary achievement: "John Daniels, the reviewer for the black Boston periodical *Alexander's Magazine*, pointed to 'the dominating spirituality of the book' and called *The Souls* 'a poem, a spiritual, not an intellectual offering.'" "William Philips Dabney...saw clearly that *The Souls* was a 'masterpiece.'"[10] W.H. Johnson, writing for *The Dial*, and John Spencer Bassett, writing for *South Atlantic Quarterly*, employed *Souls* to berate white supremacists such as novelist Thomas Dixon, Jr. and theologian Charles Carroll.[11]

There were also immediate and negative responses to *Souls*. The establishment, the keeper over Eurocentrism's institutional

---

7. Du Bois, *The Souls of Black Folks* (2005 edition). In this revised edition, Henry Louis Gates, Jr. is the author of the "Introduction" and "A Note on the Text." In the "Note" Gates writes: "Herbert Aptheker discovered that the book sold 9,595 copies between 1903 and 1908, and 4,250 copies between 1926 and 1946. (Record sales between 1908 and 1926 have not been found). But as of March 4, 1935, according to Aptheker, McClurg told Du Bois that 15,000 copies of *The Souls* had been printed, making it reasonable to presume the book's total sales between 1903 and 1946 amounted to approximately 20,000 copies" (xxvii).
8. Edward J. Blum, *W. E. B. Du Bois: American Prophet* (Philadelphia: University of Pennsylvania Press, 2007), 61.
9. Manning Marable, *W.E.B. Du Bois: Black Radical Democrat* (New York: Paradigm Publishers, 1986), 212.
10. Gates, "Introduction" *Souls*, xv.
11. Edward J. Blum, *W. E. B. Du Bois*, 61-62.

hegemony, understood its content and ramifications of its truth claims and sought to discredit them. Lewis writes "most southern white newspapers pretended not to notice *The Souls of Black Folk.* Those that did claimed, like the *Tennessee Christian Advocate,* not to know what to make of the book or the author. *The Nashville American* however, was sure of one thing: This book is indeed dangerous for the [N]egro to read."[12] Gates adds, "The reviewer for the *Louisville Courier-Journal* thought Du Bois's book 'crudely written' and characterized by incoherent statements and disconnected arguments." And "*The New York Times* saw the book as a strange admixture of 'acquired logic' with racial characteristics (i.e., the 'sentimental,' the 'political,' the picturesque') and 'racial rhetoric.'"[13] As Lewis writes, "The editors of the *New York Times* took no chances. They chose a white southerner whose anonymous review conceded that *Souls* was interesting and even deserving of praise here and there."[14]

Du Bois's writing style differs from those of Lewis and Sheppard. As Gates reminds us of Du Bois, "He was a wordsmith, a master craftsperson of the English language. But with no form was he more adept at rhetorical manipulation than with the essay. And never would his essay collection exceed the power and effect achieved in *The Souls of Black Folk.*"[15] Gates is correct to point toward Du Bois's employment and mastery of word manipulation, poetry, and prose. I point toward how boldly Du Bois proclaimed that black folks have had past impact on the world and will have a larger impact on the world to come. So why does Du Bois remain invisible in the mainstream's consciousness?

I have concluded that it is because Du Bois belongs to the prophetic tradition. Du Bois is *sui generis.* In so many words, Du Bois would not conform to Eurocentrism's institutionalism. Though the Socialist and Communist parties are Eurocentric constructs, Du Bois became a member of the former in 1934 and the latter in 1961. As a result of his joining the Socialist party, he was dismissed as the editor of the NAACP's signature propaganda arm, *The Crisis* magazine. At the invitation of President Kwame

12. David Levering Lewis, *W. E. B. Du Bois*, 293.
13. Gates, "Introduction" *Souls*, xvi.
14. David Levering Lewis, W. E. B. Du Bois, 293.
15. Gates, "Introduction" *Souls*, xiii.

Nkrumah, Du Bois relocated to Ghana and became a citizen in 1963.

Irene Diggs, Du Bois's longtime assistant, wrote in the "Introduction" to *Dusk of Dawn*: "That Du Bois was in agreement with the aims of socialism and communism there can be no doubt; [Du Bois said],'Capitalism cannot reform itself; it is doomed to self-destruction. No universal selfishness can bring social good to all,' [and] 'Communism—the effort to give all men what they need and to ask of each the best they can contribute—this is the only way of human life.'"[16] What is of import is that Du Bois was an intellectual who had the integrity to stand by his convictions. I would add, however, that whether Du Bois was a capitalist, socialist, or communist, these are all constructs of Eurocentrism. (Du Bois does admit that he was fascinated with Sigmund Freud and Karl Marx; they did influence him to reconsider psychological and economic analysis and its connections between racism and capitalism.)[17]

Unfortunately, I am not able to see that Du Bois achieved full self-identity. Ironically, despite Du Bois's commitment to pan-Africanism, he did not break fully from Eurocentrism's classifications, theories, grasp, or grip. What I think is plausible, is that Du Bois may have made an attempt to interpret economic theory through his reading of the New Testament. I have posited throughout this book that a Du Boisian lens is one of sociomarginalization. Manning Marable characterized Du Bois's religious convictions in this way: "As an artist and black Christian, radical democrat, and cultural pluralist, Du Bois viewed socialism as a humanistic enterprise. It proposed a radical reconstruction of world society on the basis of 'high, ethical ideal'"[18] I cite Acts 2:41-47 as an example. I see the early church as the manipulated, exploited, and oppressed followers of Jesus who resisted materialism but instead chose to live by the highest ethical ideals.

When exegesis and hermeneutics are applied to Acts 2:41-47, I take into consideration that historically, Eurocentrism's economic

---

16. Irene Diggs, "Introduction" to W. E. B. Du Bois, *Dusk of Dawn: An Essay Toward an Autobiography of a Race Concept* (Piscataway, NJ: Rutgers University Press, 1968), xx.

17. Blum, *W. E. B. Du Bois*, 41.

18. Marable, *W.E.B. Du Bois: Black Radical Democrat*, 91.

constructs had not been developed. It seems, however, that the early Christians of Acts 2:41-47 depended on communal sociopolitical and socioeconomic systems to survive. I also posit that the early church was not necessarily an early adopter of egalitarian ideology, but instead I suggest that the early church adopted equalitarianism ideology. It is through equalitarianism that people achieve independent self-identity, and I think this applies to early and contemporary cultures.

The exclusion of Du Bois may be anecdotal evidence, but I believe that the Western intellectual establishment and its opinion makers (and certainly *Time* magazine has been among them) have intentionally excluded the mastery and, *sui generis,* genius of Du Bois. Even Charles Darwin's image has appeared on *Time*'s cover twice, February 10 and November 24, 2009.[19] The question remains, why?

Race, Economics and Politics

Throughout this book, I have identified Du Bois among the prophets. I have also argued that Du Bois was a prophetic critic who employed democratic protest to refute Eurocentrism, Western intuitionalism, and hegemony. Clearly Du Bois understood that Eurocentrism's global dominance lies within its manipulation of race, economics, and politics:

> It was after Du Bois left Harvard, while at the University of Berlin, that he began to envision the race problem in the United States to include the problems of the peoples of Africa, Asia, the economics and politics of Europe.... He realized how the building of colonial empires "turned into the threat of armed competition for markets, cheap material and cheap labor." For him, politics were inextricably intertwined he perceived politics as dominant, but because most Blacks were workers and

---

19. Carl Zimmer, "The Ever Evolving Theories of Darwin" *Time*, February 12, 2009, accessed June 17, 2013, http://www. Timemagazine.org. See also Eben Harrell, "The Dark Side of Darwin's Legacy" *Time*, November 24, 2009, accessed June 17, 2013, http://www.Timemagazine.org

earners of wages he was fascinated by economics.[20]

In *Dusk of Dawn*, Du Bois writes, "It was not until I was long out of college and finished the first phase of my teaching career that I began to see clearly the connection of economics and politics: the fundamental influence of man's efforts to earn a living upon all his other efforts."[21] In the same context, Du Bois makes the following comments about colonialism:

> The politics which we studied in college were conventional, especially when it came to describing and elucidating the current scene in Europe. The Queen's Jubilee in June, 1887, while I was still at Fisk, set a pattern of our thinking. The little old woman of Windsor [Queen Victoria] became a magnificent symbol of Empire. Here was England with her flag draped around the world, ruling more black folk than white and leading the colored peoples of the earth to Christian baptism, civilization and eventual self-rule.[22]

> The Congo Free State was established and the Berlin Conference of 1885 was reported to be an act of civilization against the slave trade and liquor. French, English and Germans pushed on in Africa, but I did not question the interpretation which pictured this as the advance of civilization and the benevolent tutelage of barbarians.... In all of this I had not yet linked the political development of Europe with the race problem in America.[23]

What Du Bois describes can only be thought of as the very nadir of human nature. It is a description of Darwin's theory of evolution and Freud's proposition that the so-called culturally advanced civilized people have learned to repress their debased instincts for their personal mutual survival. What Du Bois may have criticized of Western intellectual classes' obsession, Darwin's

---

20. Ibid., ix-x.
21. Du Bois, *Dusk of Dawn*, 41.
22. Ibid.
23. Ibid., 42.

"Struggle for Existence" was their belief that Africans, African Americans, and people of color are not considered as co-laborers in that struggle for existence.[24] It further describes Europe's deliberate global strategy of excluding people of color. The strategy is located in Eurocentric socioracial, socioeconomic and sociopolitical constructs.

A Direct Challenge to Eurocentrism's Interpretation

European racial, economic, and political hegemony, then, breeds double consciousness among Africans, African Americans, and people of color. That is, there is a direct correlation between colonialism, its exploitation of these people, and double consciousness. The constant pressure to conform to a social order only to be cast as second- and third-class citizens is a contradiction to human nature. This forced conformity causes a duality to form in the human personality. Gates adds, "Du Bois's most important gift to the black literary tradition is, without question, the concept of duality of the African-American expressed metaphorically in his related metaphors of 'double consciousness,' and 'the veil.'"[25]

As a response to colonialism and the rise of Eurocentrism, I am able to trace Du Bois's evolution into a pan-African thinker. He saw Europe's insurgence into Africa as a strategy to consolidate European economic power that facilitated organized political hegemony. Because of these events, Du Bois came to understand that European hegemony was directly related to the race problem in America. When Du Bois made this statement, "I did not question the interpretation which pictured this as the advance of civilization and the benevolent tutelage of barbarians," this serves as a point of departure for why Du Bois became suspicious of Eurocentric interpretation of events and texts.

Throughout his career Du Bois attempted to shape a "grand" pan-African narrative. When I closely read and analyze his narrative, I notice that it is grounded in the arts of refutation. I further notice that there is a relationship between refutation and double consciousness. Double consciousness causes a paradigm

---

24. Charles Darwin, "Struggle for Existence" in *The Origin of Species* (New York: Barnes and Noble, 2004), 72-92.
25. Gate, "Introduction" in *The Souls of Black Folk*, xix.

shift in hermeneutic interpretation. Double consciousness is both psychological and spiritual twoness. If double consciousness is only psychological, then it solely belongs to nihilism. If double consciousness is only spiritual, then it belongs solely to escapism. If double consciousness is both psychological and spiritual, then it belongs to rational and irrational claims. Another way to think of double consciousness is that it holds faith and reason in balance.

Du Bois's marginalization by the establishment is precisely because it did understand his motivation and strategy. Du Bois understood, critiqued and added to the Western intellectual tradition. He understood that nomenclature definitions and classifications that are used to assign power and status permanently remand people of color to remain inside the veil. Whether Du Bois appropriated the term double consciousness from his former professor, William James, is not relevant. I am aware, however, of James's influence with Du Bois:

> Du Bois probably heard James expound on the neurological and epiphenomenal nature of the mind; certainly he would have read his favorite professor's groundbreaking book soon after publication, in which suggestive terms such as "alternating selves and primary and secondary consciousness appeared.... That said...the irreducible fact that Du Bois's existence, like that of other black men and women of African descent in America, amounted to a lifetime of being "an outcast and a stranger in mine own house," as he would write, was a psychic purgatory fully capable by itself of nurturing a concept of divided consciousness, whatever the Jamesian influences.[26]

Du Bois's double consciousness is nonetheless an informant of hermeneutics. The Du Boisian hermeneutic of double consciousness provides the lens for a critique of Western letters and texts. It further provides a social location to refute hegemon interpretation that originates from places of unchallenged privilege. There is no agreement between Billy Graham, Charles Darwin, Karl Marx, and Sigmund Freud except that they are insider members of the house

---

26. Lewis, *W.E.B. Du Bois*, 96.

of Eurocentrism. For this reason, which is because of their Eurocentric racial classifications, they are considered qualified to interpret.

Whether by sacred or secular claims, it did not matter; Graham's and Freud's interpretation of the world reinforced Western hegemony. What matters is that each has played a significant role; a role that proclaims the Eurocentric psyche is superior to all other psyches. This explains *Time Magazine*'s and other intellectual establishment s' motives. What differs, of course, is that Du Bois understood precisely the role of those who reinforce Eurocentrism's superiority and authoritarian interpretation over the world and its texts. This is precisely why his role is to lift the veil over the psyche and soul of Eurocentrism, which is to refute myths of superiority. Du Bois's double consciousness means that I see you through the veil.

Bibliography

Alkebulan, Adisa A. "The Spiritual Essence of African American Rhetoric," in *Understanding African American Rhetoric: Classical Origins to Contemporary Innovations*. Eds. Ronald J. Jackson and Elaine B. Richardson. New York: Routledge, 2003.

Aristole. *The Rhetoric of Aristotle*. ed. Lane Cooper. Englewood Cliffs, New Jersey: Prentice-Hall, Inc., 1932.

Asante, Molefi Kete. *The Painful Demise of Eurocentrism*. Trenton, New Jersey: Africa World Press, 1999.

_____. "The Future of African American Rhetoric" in *Understanding African American Rhetoric: Classic Origins to Contemporary Innovations*. Eds. Ronald J. Jackson and Elaine B. Richardson. New York: Routledge, 2003.

Alexander, Michelle. *The New Jim Crow: Mass Incarceration in the Age of Colorblindness*. New York: New Press, 2010.

Bacon, Jacqueline. *The Humble Shall Stand Forth: Rhetoric, Empowerment and Abolition*. Columbia, South Carolina: University of South Carolina Press, 2002.

Baker, Houston A., Jr. "Generational Shifts" in *African American Literary Theory*. Ed. William Napier: New York: New York University Press, 2000.

_____. *Turning South Again: Re-Thinking Modernism / Rethinking Booker T*. Durham: Duke University Press, 2001.

Baldwin, James. *The Fire Next Time*. New York: The Modern Library, 1995.

Beale, Francis. "Double Jeopardy: To Be Black and Female" in *Black Theology: a Documentary History Volume One: 1967-1979*. Eds. James H. Cone and Gayraud S. Wilmore. Marykoll, New York: Orbis, 1998.

Bernasconi, Robert. "Casting the Slough; Fanon's New Humanism for a New Humantiy" in *Fanon: A Critical Reader*. eds Lewis

R. Gordon, T. Denean Sharpley-Whiting and Renee T. White. Oxford: Blackwell Publishers, 1996.

Blair, Hugh. Lectures on Rhetoric and Belle Lettres. Eds. Linda Ferreia-Buckley and S. Michael Halloran. Carbondale, Illinois: Southern Illinois University, 2005.

Blum, Edward. *W.E.B. Du Bois: American Prophet.* Philadelphia: University of Pennsylvania, 2007.

Briggs, Charles. The Christian Ministry: An Inquiry Into The Causes Of Its Inefficency; With an Especial Reference To the Minstry of the Establishment. London: L.Seely, Burnside and Seely, 1744.

Cone, James. *The Spirituals and the Blues.* New York: Orbis, 1972.

_____. *The Cross and the Lynching Tree.* Marykoll, New York: Orbis, 2012.

Costen, Melva Wilson. *African American Christian Worship.* Nashville: Abingdon, 2007.

Crable, Bryan. "Race and Rhetorical Moves: Kenneth Burkes' Dialogue with Ralph Ellison" in *Rhetoric Society Quarterly* vol. 33 nu 3 (summer, 2003).

Crawford, Evans E and Troeger, Thomas. *The Hum: Call and Response in African American Preaching.* Nashville: Abingdon Press, 1995.

Du Bois, William Edward Burghardt. *The Souls of Black Folk: Essays and Sketches.* Chicago: A.C. McClurg, 1903.

_____. *The Souls of Black Folk.* New York: Bantam Dell, 1989.

_____. *The Souls of Black Folk.* Introduction by John Wideman. New York: Vintage Books, 1990.

_____. The Souls of Black Folk. New York: Bantam, 2005.

_____. *Darkwater: Voices Within The Veil.* Minneola, New York: Dover, 1999.

_____. *Dusk of Dawn: An Essay Toward An Autobiography of a Race Concept.* New Brunswick, New Jersey: Transaction Publishers, 2011.

Derrida. Jacque. Of Grammatology. Baltimore and London: Johns Hopkins University Press, 1976.

_____. *The Gift of Black Folk.* Garden City Park, New York: Square One Publishers, 2009.

Dyson, Michael Eric. *Holler If You Hear Me: Searching for Tupac Shakur.* New York: Basic Books, 2001.

Eagleton, Terry. *After Theory*. New York: Basic Books, 2003.

Elia, Nada, "Violent Women: Surging into Forbidden Quarters" in *Fanon: A Critical Reader*. . Eds. Lewis R. Gordon, T. Denean Sharpley-Whiting and Renee T. White. Oxford: Blackwell Publishers, 1996.

Evans, Joseph N. "The Black Folks Blues and Jazz Hermeneutic" in *The Journal of Religious Thought* Vol. 60 nu2, Vol. 61 nu. 1-2, Vol.62 nu.1-2; Vol. 63 nu.1-2, 2008-2010.

Fanon, Franz. *Dying Colonialism*. New York: Grove Press, 1959.

_____. *Black Skin, White Masks*. New York: Grove Press, 1967.

_____. *Fanon: A Critical Reader*. Eds. Lewis R. Gordon, T. Denean Sharpley-Whiting and Renee T. White. Oxford: Blackwell Publishers, 1996.

Freud, Sigmund. *The Basic Writings of Sigmund Freud*. trans and ed. A. A. Brill. New York: The Modern Library, 1995.

Gailett, Lynn Lewis, ed. *Scottish Rhetoric and Its Influences*. Mahwah: New Jersey. Hermagoras, 1998

Gates, Henry Louis, Jr. *The Signifying Monkey: A Theory of African-American Literary Criticism*. Oxford: Oxford University, 1988.

_____. *Loose Canons: Notes on the Culture Wars*. Oxford: Oxford University Press, 1992.

Giddens, Garry and DeVeaux, Scott. *Jazz*. New York: Norton, 2009.

Glaude, Eddie, Jr. *In a Shade of Blue: Pragmatism and the Politics of Black America* (Chicago: University of Chicago, 2007.

Goldberg, David Theo. "In/Visibility and Super/Vision" in Fanon: A Critical Reader. Eds. Lewis R. Gordon, T. Denean Sharpley-Whiting and Renee White. Oxford: Blackwell Publishers, 1996.

Gonzalez, Justo L., and Gonzalez Catherine G. *Liberation Preaching: the Pulpit of the Oppressed*. Nashville: Abingdon Press, 1980.

Gordon, Annette Reed. *Thomas Jefferson & Sally Hemmings: An American Controversy*. Charlottesville, Virginia: University of Virginia Press, 1997.

Gordon, Lewis R. "The Black and Body Politic: Fanon's Existential Phenomenological Critique of Psychoanalysis" in *Fanon: A Critical Reader*. Eds. Lewis R. Gordon, T. Denean Sharpley-

Whiting and Renee T. White. Oxford: Blackwell Publishers, 1996.

Gordon, Dexter B. *Black Identity: Rhetoric, Ideology, and Nineteenth – Century Black Nationalism.* Carbondale, Illinois: Southern Illinois University Press, 2003.

Gordon, Lewis R., Sharpley-Whiting and White, Renee T. "Introduction: Five Stages" in *Fanon: A Critical Reader.* Oxford: Blackwell Publishers, 1996.

Gutierrez, Gustavo. *A Theology of Liberation: History, Politics, and Salvation.* Trans. Sister Caridad Inda and John Eagleson. Maryknoll, New York: Orbis, 1973.

Habermas, Jurgen. *Habermas and the Public Square.* Ed. Craig Calhoun. Cambridge: MIT University Press, 1999.

Hayes, Floyd W., III. "Fanon, Oppression, and Resentment: The Black Experience in the United States," in *Fanon: A Critical Reader.* Eds. Lewis R. Gordon, T. Denean Sharpley-Whiting and Renee T. White. Oxford: Blackwell Publishers, 1996.

Holloway, Karla F.C. "Cultural Narratives Passed On: African Mourning Stories" in African American Literary Theory. ed. Winston Napier. New York: New York University Press, 2000.

Kahn, Jonathon. *Divine Discontent: The Religious Imagination of W. E. B. Du Bois.* Oxford: Oxford University Press, 2009.

Kruks, Sonia, "Fanon, Sartre, and Identity Politics," in *Fanon: A Critical Reader.* Oxford: Blackwell Publishers, 1996.

LaRue, Cleo J. *The Heart of Black Preaching.* Louisville: Westminster John Knox, 2000.

Lemert, Charles. "Cultural Politics in the Negro Soul" in *The Souls of W. E. B. Du Bois.* London: Paradigm, 2004.

Lewis, David Levering ed. *W.E.B. Du Bois: A Reader.* New York: Henry Holt and Company, 1995.

_____. *W.E.B. Du Bois: Biography of Race.* New York: Henry Holt and Company, 1993.

Marable, Manning. *W.E.B. Du Bois: Black Radical Democrat.* Boulder Colorado: Paradigm, 1986.

Margolick, David. *Strange Fruit: Billie Holiday, Café Society, and an Early Cry for Civil Rights.* Philadelphia: Running Press, 2000.

Marsalis, Wynton. Congo Square: Marsalis, a Grammy award trumpeter, pays tribute to his birth place, New Orleans with this recording. Shanachie, March 4, 2008.

McClure, John. *otherwise preaching: a postmodern ethic for preaching.* Saint Louis, Missouri: Chalice Press, 2001.

McFague, Sallie. *Speaking in Parables: A Study in Metaphor and Theology.* Minneapolis: Fortress Press, 2007.

Mitchell, Henry H. *Black Preaching: The Recovery of a Powerful Art.* Nashville: Abington Press, 1990.

Morrison, Carlos D. "Death Narratives From the Killing Fields" in Understanding African American Rhetoric. Eds. Ronald J. Jackson and Elaine B. Richardson. New York: Routledge, 2003.

Padillia, Alvin. "A New Kind of Theological School: Contextualized Theological Education Models" in Africanus Journal vol. 2., nu. 2., (November 2010).

Perleman, Chaim and Tyteca, Olbrechts, L. The New Rhetoric: a Treatise on Argument. Notre Dame, Indiana: University of Notre Dame, 1969

Randolph, David J. and Robert Stephen Reid. *The Renewal of Preaching in the Twenty-First Century:* The Next Homiletics. Eugene, Oregon: Cascade, 2009.

Ricouer, Paul. *The Rule of Metaphor: Multi-Disciplinary Studies of the Creation of Meaning in Language.* Toronto: University of Toronto Press, 1975.

_____. Memory, History and Forgetting. Trans. Kathleen Blamey and David Pellauer. Chicago: University of Chicago Press, 2006.

_____. "The Metaphoric Process as Cognition, Imagination, and Feeling" in *Critical Inquiry* vol. 5, nu. 1. (Autumn, 1978). See also JSTOR vol. 5 no. 1.

Roberts, Deotis. *Africentric Christianity: A Theological Appraisal for Ministry.* Valley Forge, Pennsylvania: Judson, 2000.

Shakur,Tupac. "Black Jesus" 2PAC+OUTLAWZ, *Still I Rise*, 1999, Interscope Records, 4904132.

Thurman, Howard. *Jesus and the Disinherited.* Boston, Massachusetts. Beacon Press, 1976.

Walker, David. *David Walker's Appeal.* New York: Hill and Wang, 1965.

Walker, Wyatt Tee. *Somebody is Calling My Name: Black Sacred Music and Social Change*. Valley Forge, Pennsylvania: Judson Press, 1979.

Weems, Renita. "Reading Her Way Through the Struggle: African American Women and the Bible" ed. Cain Hope Felder, *Stony the Road We Trod: African American Biblical Interpretation*. Minneapolis: Fortress, 1991.

West Cornel. *Race Matters*. Boston, Massachusetts. Beacon Press, 1993.

_____. *The Cornel West Reader*. New York: Basic Civitas Books, 1999.

_____. *Democracy Matters: Winning the Fight Against Imperialism*. New York: Penguin Press, 2004.

_____. "Dr. King Weeps from His Grave" in *The New York Times*, August 26, 2011.

Willimon, William H. and Lischer, Richard eds. *Concise Encyclopedia of Preaching*. Louisville: Westminster John Knox, 1995.

Whiting-Sharpley, Denean T. "Engaging Fanon to Reread Capecia" in Fanon: A Critical Reader. Eds. Lewis R. Gordon, T. Denean Sharpley-Whiting and Renee White. Oxford: Blackwell Publishers, 1996.

Young, Josiah Ulysses, III. *Dogged Strength Within the Veil: Africana Spirituality and the Mysterious Love of God*. New York: Trinity Press, 2003.

_____. *A Pan-African Theology: Providence And The Legacies of the Ancestors*. Trenton, New Jersey: Africa World Press, 1992.

Young, Robert Alexander, "The Ethiopian Manifesto Issued Defense of the Blackmans' Rights in the Scale of Universal Freedom" in *A History of the Negro People in the United States* Vol. 1(Secaucus, New Jersey: Citadel, 1973.

Index